Tyler McNamara

# THE MOTHER OF DARK SPACE

Earwig Publishing

# THE MOTHER OF DARKSPACE

## BOOK ONE

Tyler McNamara

**The Mother of Dark Space**

by **Tyler McNamara**

**ISBN-10:** 1981141502

**ISBN-13:** 978 -1981141500

First Edition

Library of Congress Control Number: 2017918617

**Cover Art by:** Will Sweeny

# *Acknowledgements*

The Lone Hero trope is a farce...

And to continue without acknowledging all the people who helped me finish this book would be a disservice to anyone who has ever tried to do something momentous.

To all of you who read an earlier draft and gave me your honest feedback...

To my beautiful wife for being my biggest fan, and for supporting us while I wrote the final draft...

To Peter for helping me craft my Patreon video...

To Marissa for helping me with story development...

To Will for the beautiful cover...

To Satya for drawing the Earwig logo...

To all of you who ever asked, "How's the book coming?"...

And to all of my followers on Patreon...

...Thank you so much. Your support gave me strength to continue pulling, tearing, and wrenching this story out, and patience when it came time to polish until it was good enough for me, and then continue polishing until it was good enough for you.

# The Storm

## Rae

*"Mom, Mom! Guess what? I got accepted to the doctorate program at the University of Mars! They're even giving me a travel scholarship!"*

*Deborah's face puckered as she tried to wrap her mind around the sourness of what Rae had said... or what she'd just heard, which could have been anything. Rae felt her chest ache and collapse inward, as if she had just presented some useless piece of paper and Deborah was crinkling it up to throw it away.*

*"Mars?" Deborah said. "I thought you wanted to work with animals." She was referring to Rae's first and long-abandoned interest in animal behavior. "Do they even have animals on Mars?"*

*"They do. Mostly livestock, but that's not—"*

*"I don't understand why you don't want to stay here and work with livestock. The feedlots in Tennessee could really use someone with your talents."*

If I wait a minute, she'll change the subject, *Rae thought.*

*"You won't make a big deal about coming home for Christmas, will you? You're my only family left."*

*"Deborah," Rae said, still pissed from her initial reaction and now fuming as her mother wedged a crowbar of guilt between them, "it's a three-month trip during opposition — the point when Mars is closest to us — and that only occurs every two years. Once I'm there, I'm staying there."*

*"What about when you finish school?"*

*Rae imagined herself eventually working for Kander and Jansen Laboratories, but even if they wouldn't take her, there were more research and development companies moving to Mars every opposition.*

*"Rachael Michelle Dahlia, are you telling me this is goodbye forever? You're planing to go die on Mars and get buried in some little green sarcophagus?"*

*"No. Of course I'll come back. I'm just not sure when."* Or what would ever entice me to.

*Deborah was quiet for a long time, during which the grimace never left her face.*

*"Well, I hardly think 'goodbye' is even appropriate. More like, 'see you soon,' because I'm sure I'll see you in a few months after you've been there and realize how much you hate it."*

That had been over two years ago. Rae wasn't sure who had stopped calling whom, but between Deborah's constant disapproval and the minutes of lag due to the sheer distance of the two planets, they hadn't spoken for some time.

*Dear Deborah,* Rae thought, writing a text in her mind she was sure she'd never send. *You were wrong about Mars. I love it here, in fact I can't wait to return to Nili Fossae and the big city under the dome. I got that job at Kander and Jansen Labs I was telling you about. Nothing big, just as a research assistant, but it means I get to travel outside the terradome to an ancillary lab at the South Pole. I'm one of two microbiologists on the team, so I'm pretty important. Though the work is mostly looking through a microscope at frozen $CO2$ samples, the idea of maybe finding a Martian organism keeps things pretty exciting. It's pretty tight quarters down here, but not as bad on as on the shuttle to Mars, and every three weeks they send me back to Nili Terradome for a week off.*

Rae sat on the edge of her bed in her small white bunkroom and thought, *God, wouldn't it be nice to have a normal fucking conversation like that? Something real dry and bor-*

*ing where I'd get to lie about how shitty this job is, and then she'd tell me about what the neighbors are up to, and never even mention how lonely she is or how nice it must be to be breathing fresh air all the time.*

A text chimed and drew her attention.

> **A.Manfield:** Report to the rover room, there's another blizzard approaching and we need your help monitoring it while we finish the mission.

> **R.Dahlia:** On my way.

\* \* \* \* \* \*

*What a bunch of tech jocks,* Rae thought, shaking her head at the scientists gathered around the rover control station. Their eyes were glued to the screens as if they were watching some championship game, but the screens were boring: each displayed a different angle of a hollow drill slowly descending into frozen $CO_2$. The real performance was watching Rockwell, the rover technician, who had just as much, if not more, experience in ballet as in robotics. His delicate body motions were watched by full-spectrum motion-capture cameras and communicated to the rover approximately two hundred meters away, and the rover fed back hundreds of data points of information to his elbow-length haptic gloves. Rockwell described the gloves as feeling like it was his actual hands plunging through the ice. When the drill felt pressure, he swore he could feel it in the bones of his arms.

Dr. Manfield, the principal researcher at Kander and Jansen Laboratories, and Rae's boss, turned his head and caught her watching Rockwell. He walked over to her and loudly whispered, "Ms. Dahlia, you have been given the very simple yet very important task of monitoring that radar screen. We need to get the rover to safety before that blizzard hits or we risk damaging or destroying a very sensitive and very expensive piece of Dr. Kander's property. Do you understand?"

"My name is *Dr.* Dahlia."

"Excuse me? Never mind, just watch the radar."

*Pig.*

Once the storm hit the mouth of their canyon, Chasma Australe, the katabatic force would increase the wind speeds by hundreds of kilometers per hour and drop the temperature to somewhere around minus 80 degrees Celsius. The driving force of frozen carbon-dioxide flakes would entomb the rover, and the pressure drop would likely cause the sensitive ice core samples to explode.

"The storm is entering the Prometheus Basin," she warned. "ETA ten minutes."

Rockwell, barely moving his lips, said, "I only need five to get back to the hanger. I can't rush this — the drill is under a lot of strain, but I can almost guarantee this is going to be a premium sample."

The promise that it would be a good sample affected her as well. *Maybe this will be the one. Maybe I'll be the first person to discover life on Mars. Or more accurately, an intact chromosome from Martian haloarchaea.* Rae's mind started to swim with the possibilities that would open up for her with that kind of fame. Kander would certainly make her principal researcher, and she'd have the freedom to drive research in whatever direction she chose. Then she realized that running her own department would come with the added responsibility of managing a team, and the thought soured. *I like the idea of assigning someone to run menial experiments, but having to manage their personalities and moods sounds terrible. And what if they don't trust me?*

"It's not worth the risk," Manfield declared. "Pull out."

"Doctor, I'm almost there. Just one more minute," Rockwell begged.

The geologist chimed in, "Manfield, think of the revenue this sample could generate for K&J Labs." He looked at the radar screen in front of Rae. "Look at that. The storm is still a ways away. By my estimate, we've got half an hour at least!"

Rae shook her head. "You're underestimating the katabatic force. Trust me, I've been watching—"

"Last I checked, you weren't a meteorologist."

Manfield placed his hand on Rae's back, as if trying to shield her. The gesture made her feel vulnerable and unclean. With his other hand he made a dismissive gesture at the geologist, and to the technician he said, "Terminate the dig. Abandon the mission. Return to the hangar."

Rockwell sighed. "Yes, of course, Dr. Manfield. Sorry." And he began slowly — yet much faster than before — lifting his hands and the drill from the cold Martian ice. Once it had been fully extracted and tucked away in its travel position, the technician curled his hands as if around invisible joysticks, and to the movements of his wrists the rover responded by turning in place and trundling back toward the hangar.

Manfield pointed at the geologist and another scientist whom Rae had yet to be introduced to. "You two are the welcoming committee. Suit up and get to the hangar."

Check the drill," Rockwell called after them. "If we're lucky, a piece of that sample broke off in the bit."

Two minutes later the weather buoy in Prometheus Basin sent a red alert that popped up on Rae's radar station. The blizzard was moving much faster than anticipated and was bearing down on Chasma Australe.

"It's coming! Arrival in maybe three, maybe four minutes," she called out, but Dr. Manfield had already left for the hangar, leaving her alone with Rockwell. Rae texted Manfield the alert and walked over to the screens. Two of the monitors showed the rover's front-facing view. After it had traveled about a hundred meters, the first tiny flakes of frozen $CO_2$ started to blow past the rover, creating the illusion that it had started to move backward. The third monitor watched the long canyon behind the rover vanish in a wave of white. Rockwell was visibly sweating, and his eyes were locked on the screens. "Don't say it," he said.

"Say what?"

"Don't say 'drive faster.'"

"I wasn't—" Rae began.

"Around this corner is a tight squeeze between two ice formations, and I can't thread the needle at this speed." Almost as soon had he finished the sentence, Rockwell drove the rover into a branch off the main canyon; the hangar came into view and so did the two pillars of ice. The geologist stood between them, hacking away with a hatchet, but his visor and suit were quickly being covered by $CO_2$ frost.

"Drive faster," Rae commanded as she dialed Dr. Manfield.

"I can't—"

Rae interrupted him. "I heard, but if you slow down the Rover's fucked 100 percent of the time; this way at least there's a chance."

"Miss Dahlia, unless this is—"

"Call your men back, the storm is here!" In the background she heard Manfield shouting through the geologist's comm channel. On the screen she saw him stop chopping, turn and run in great leaping bounds. The doors to the hanger started to disappear behind the swirling curtain of snow that blew past the rover.

"Drive faster, damn it."

"It's too narrow," the technician whined.

"Use the snowdrift on the left to tip it diagonally."

"This is a scientific instrument, not a stunt car," said Rockwell, but he had already made the decision to try.

"DAHLIA!" Manfield screamed through her forgotten receiver. "TELL ROCKWELL NOT TO BE A HERO."

"Did you catch that?" Rae asked the technician.

"The gist, but something just occurred to me: the insurance. User error is covered. Negligence is not."

The rover sped toward the choke point at thirteen meters per second until a proximity alert flashed, followed by an "unsafe speed" warning, which triggered an internal fail-safe that took control of the throttle, slowing the craft. The rover trudged up the frozen drift at a wholly unsatisfying pace and stalled as its front wheel slipped on the ice. Again the rover's safety measures took control by giving priority to the back wheels, and the rover made it through despite its painfully slow speed. $CO_2$ flurries were falling harder now, and it became impossible to see the terrain. Rockwell's only guidance was the light of the hangar. He punched the throttle back up to full, but sixty meters later they were met with another obstacle: the hangar door.

Dr. Manfield stormed into the room. "Well, Mr. Rockwell, how badly have you managed to entangle my rover? Next time answer me when I call you."

Rockwell released himself from gestural control and pushed his OmniView augmented-reality glasses up onto his forehead, "Sorry, Doctor," he said, not sounding sorry at all. "I was focusing on getting the rover — and your precious ice core samples — to safety! Why'd you close the hangar doors?"

Manfield crossed his arms. "When it was clear that you wouldn't fit, I recalled the team and sealed the hangar. Now answer *my* question."

"Zero. Zero percent entangled. The rover is just outside the hangar door."

Manfield looked shocked. "But... there's no way... we need to—"

Suddenly Rae felt the pressure increase, and in a synchronistic choreography everyone on the team yawned to pop their ears. The rover popped up an alert: "Sample

Storage Compartment compromised!"

Manfield shook his head in disappointment. "The ice core samples just shattered.

"This mission is over. Everyone is on personal time until further notice."

Somewhere nearby a frost geyser shook the lab like a small earthquake, as if the storm, or Mars itself, was laughing at them.

# Hearts

### Rae

The vitamin D lights in her cramped bunkroom were supposed to help with depression.

They weren't working.

Another frost geyser shook the entire laboratory, and she could hear her team's loud, jovial reaction from the rec room at the end of the hall. The geysers had been unnerving at first, but Rae was so bored she almost wished the next one would breach the walls and instantly freeze everyone solid. She had tried spending time with the other scientists, but it was during these periods of *personal time* that Dr. Manfield made his most obvious attempts to hit on her. It wasn't so bad as harassment went, certainly not worth starting a scandal about. She couldn't even imagine how poorly it might affect her climb up the corporate ladder. Or worse, that it might give her an advantage over others, and that people might think it was all just social manipulation.

With no window to gaze longingly out of, she simply stared at the ceiling and wondered what a $CO_2$ blizzard looked like. The digital sensors on the rover, before being sealed in a tomb of frost, claimed winds over three hundred kilometers per hour, and temperatures around minus 90 degrees Celsius. It had been fifty-one hours since the storm hit, and there was nothing for her to work on.

She'd even gone so far as to retest the previous batch of ice core samples, but the task didn't outlast her boredom.

*"You always had to have some project you were working on."*

*She was a week into summer break and so bored that she had started texting her mother again. "Like what sort of projects?"*

*"When it wasn't ruining your bedroom walls with finger paints, it was taking apart small appliances to try to 'fix' them. I wish, at least once, helping your dear old mom could've been enough to occupy you."*

*And there it was, the icy chill of guilt that had kept her from texting in the past.*

*I do have my Hakaru project.* Rae rolled onto her side and picked up her Omni, tracing the edges of the index-card-sized device and remembering the days leading up to her departure from Earth, and how she'd watched them print the Omni for her at the store. How each layer of micro-circuitry added up to an obsidian window incased in a pearlescent blue shell no thicker than a credit card. She had imagined this would be her connection to home, but she could count on her fingers the number of times she'd used it to talk to anyone she'd left behind. Mostly she used it for school, work or Hakaru, her favorite puzzle game. The simple app took real bioengineering research and put it in the hands of tens of millions of eager players. A tetrahedron of colored DNA strands appeared on the screen representing a synthetic microorganism, which had taken Rae three hours to design. It was complete, save for one missing strand. She flicked her finger as if she were turning the page of a book, and the tetrahedron responded by rotating on its x-axis. In Rae's opinion, the best thing about these Hakaru puzzles was that they weren't created with a solution in mind. There were puzzles that were three years old just gathering victory points for every day they went unsolved, but Rae was not ashamed to admit that being the first to solve the weekly puzzle was more exciting than going after the older unsolved puzzles.

Rae spun the organism around for five minutes getting nowhere. The fact that this puzzle was only eight hours old yet two other players had already found solutions infuriated her and clogged all hope of creativity. *Given an infinite number of monkeys...* she thought. After spinning the organism around a few more times, she decided she needed a bigger screen. She pulled herself out of bed and awakened the nearby workstation. Before her Omni could pair with the desk's ergonomically curved screen, it displayed a large, glorious image of the new Evermore Industries building. A moment later the desk asked her which screen she wanted to work on. She selected the building.

A button in the lower right corner read, "Take the tour!" and was followed by the E.I. logo, a black *E* and white *I*, stylized to look like brackets enclosing a gray Möbius strip twisted into a diagonal, asymmetrical figure eight. The aesthetic was clean and tight and seemed to pose a question, but Rae wasn't sure what it was. She had taken already "taken the tour" four or five times. The video touted the recently completed facility built by a Martian architect of Swedish origin. The twelve-story dome-scraper had a neo-organic style; the building itself seemed to be growing phototropically from the downtown district. To Rae, the building's design proved that Everett Evermore was still able to push the leading edge of scientific innovation.

Kander and Jansen was still the biggest research and development company in the dome, but from the presentation it was clear that Evermore was looking to challenge that, and Rae wondered how long it would be before K&J joined the pissing contest with an even bigger erection. The presentation faded to a gray screen captioned by four words: "Making a Future Possible," and the E.I. Möbius strip. The first time she had taken the tour, it had concluded by presenting her with an application for a very competitive position as principal researcher. Rae had filled it out on a whim assuming it was either an accident or devised to drum up controversy as part of a multi-layered buzz campaign.

Yet time and again she found herself returning to the image of the Evermore Industries building. *Get real, Rae. You're barely three months into your first paid position as a research associate; there's a zero percent chance Evermore Industries would want you, or even think you're ready to run your own lab.*

Rae gave up on it and went back to Hakaru try one of the unsolved puzzles, but her focus kept drifting back to Evermore Industries. She switched windows, selected the E.I. presentation, and deleted it with a crumpling gesture. *The application was an accident. Dr. Evermore does not even remember you.*

She closed the app and instinctively grabbed her Omni off the workstation and slid it into her pocket before taking a short trip around the oppressively small room.

*"You always had to have some project you were working on."*

After graduating from the University of San Diego with a master's in microbiology, Rae realized that although she had achieved something quite difficult, it wasn't enough. The next day she applied for Yale's synthetic bioengineering program. Three years through her PhD, her adviser told her about a grant for women interested in studying on Mars. Six months later, after being accepted to the University of Mars, she held a one-way ticket to the Red Planet, where she finished her PhD and was offered a position at Kander and Jansen Labs.

Rae looked around and realized that her world was only getting smaller. From the entirety of Southern California to a cloistered Connecticut campus to a terradome to this... She looked around her tiny bunkroom. *This isn't the end of the road. This is the right way to do things. I've got the grades and scores, and now I need the training and experience. This time at Chasma Australe is the requirement every good scientist has to put in. This room is the possibility that things will all come together, the promise that someday I'll have the freedom and the funding to create something meaningful.*

She paced the perimeter of the four white walls, the single bed with white sheets crammed up against a white workstation, all drenched in full-spectrum white light. There was enough room to stretch her arms out and not much else.

"Fuck the possibilities. I need to get out of this fucking coffin!" she yelled as quietly as she could, self-conscious of the revelers down the hall. *God, when did I become such a mope?* She thought back to the last time she was happy. But that doesn't really count.

*"In the future, don't buy stims from anyone but me"; it may have been the only time the Chemist made eye contact for a brief moment before looking back down at his Omni. "The stims and the CrashPads work as a team. The white pill brings you up, and the red pill slows your fall."*

*Rae nodded. "I just need the reds."*

*"Not just yet. Swallow the pill whole." The Chemist emphasized the last word. "Do not take it if it's cracked or broken. The time-release layers are working for you; otherwise you'll just spike and crash even harder. If you want to get fucked up—" he reached a hand into another pocket.*

*"I don't," she told him. "Is it traceable? I start working at Kander and Jansen at the end of summer."*

*"I'm selling chemistry, not magic; of course it's traceable. And if we happen to cross paths at K&J, we've never met. In fact, this is the last time we ever talk in person. From now on, texts only."*

*The Chemist slipped her a crinkly square of foil, which presumably contained the two CrashPads. She'd gotten the stims from a classmate and had swallowed them without a second thought. She had already worked out the morality of it the first time she used them at the University of San Diego, and had come to the conclusion that it wasn't cheating. The stims hadn't magically given her the answers, they merely kept her focused for longer than normal. Was the ability to focus for hours on end part of the aptitudes the university was testing? No. Had she scored higher than her smarter peers because she'd gotten chemical help? Debatable. But this time she felt guilty about something. Why now? What was different about these illegal drugs?*

*She knew that without them the next few days would be miserable as the stims took their toll on her body. And without the crash there was nothing bad about drugs anymore. So why guilty? Was it the privilege that afforded her enhancement without drawback? No. It was part of her drugs-are-bad upbringing; it was her conditioning telling her that she was getting away with something. Rae made a conscious decision to leave it back on Earth with everything else and swallowed the first one the moment she was alone. The guilt was replaced by shame, but only until the sugar layer dissolved and the CrashPads started to work their magic... or their chemistry.*

*The CrashPads were more than just time-release energy, they allowed her to experience a brightness like a subtle warmth which filled her days. She had made more friends during graduation than she had during all her years at UMars combined, and she might have kept in touch if they hadn't become unbearably boring as she became sober.*

Rae massaged her temples. *God, that makes it sound like I don't have friends. After Deborah and I moved to the new place it only took me a few days to make friends at the new school. I wasn't popular by any means, but I wasn't a loner.*

*See, that's not even true. I fucking hated that we had moved away. I hated Deborah for it and I wanted to rub my dour teenage angst in her face, but I mean, I could've made friends. People were interested in me.* As she thought it, Rae realized that those people, who had eventually become her closest friends, were now 34.6 million miles away. Maybe it's time to make some new friends.

Through the past, Deborah reminded her, *"No one's going to want to meet you if you're such a sourpuss all the time."*

Thinking back to finals week and graduation was like watching someone else's memories. *What about before then? When was the last time I was really happy?*

"The art class at USD," she answered. Rae had always loved painting, but she had never given it her full attention. Deborah had never implicitly said it was a waste of time, but the papers decorating the refrigerator were report cards with *A*s, not the photo-realistic self-portrait she painted in eighth grade. The last drawing to grace the fridge was of their stick-figure family holding hands, labeled "Mom, Dad, Rachael, and Angelina" in thick brown crayon. Their old house sat off in the background on a bucolic purple hill. She had been happy in those days, though "blissfully unaware" was more categorically accurate. Back when they called them "Rach" and "Lina"; but remembering those days only made her feel hollow.

*Well, so what if I'm not glowingly happy about my current life situation. Not everyone is happy all the time.*

An explosion of laughter from the rec room echoed down the corridor. Rae's frustrated pacing brought her to the corner of her bunkroom, left her staring down at her single piece of crumbled luggage. She knelt beside it and rifled through forgotten pockets until she found a tiny square of foil. When she unfolded it, a single red pill looked up at her. She had swallowed her last stim over four months ago during finals week, and the one Crash-Pad had been enough to bring her back to baseline. *Why did I buy two?* she wondered and immediately knew: she always needed a contingency plan. I don't have a plan now. That's why I feel so trapped.

The Chemist had told her that the stims and the Crash-Pads worked as a team. *I don't need a pad; I need a little memory of what it feels like to relax and have fun.*

Rae slowly folded the pill back into its foil and set it on the floor beside the leg of her bed. She lifted the bed and slammed it down on the foil, crushing the pill. Laying her Omni on the floor, she unfolded the foil, examined the white powder with flecks of red, and carefully poured some of it onto the screen. "How much does this weigh in milligrams?" she asked it.

The screen displayed the number 17, and she continued pouring until it read 21.42, about one-seventh of the 150-milligram pill. Rae folded the remaining dust back in the foil, licked her finger and dabbed at the powder on her Omni until it was all stuck to her finger, then rubbed it on her gums. It tasted awful, but the unpleasantness somehow helped her feel better about it. She imagined the foul taste seeping into her blood and dripping down fleshy stalactites in that hollow place deep inside her. The assurance that something would change  brightened her mood even before the chemicals hit her bloodstream.

She slid her Omni back into her pocket and walked off down the corridor.


"Goddamn it, Rockwell, Manfield is trying to shoot the moon; you've got to stop him," said the geologist.

"I can't do shit about it," Rockwell said, throwing an off-suit card in the center of the table. "...it's up to you," he said looking to the player on his left.

"I got it," said the new scientist. But he noticed Rae approaching before he laid down the card. "Hello. I don't believe we were introduced earlier, what with the storm rolling in." He stood and stuck out his hand. "I'm Dr. Peter Dorian."

"Jesus, Dorian!" Manfield complained. "The suspense is killing me; take your turn, for God's sake."

Rae shook his hand and found her grip to be twice what he was offering. *I know that limp handshake; that's the "I'm trying to be fuckable, feel how sensitive I am." It's as if there's only one person up here, and everyone else is just a clone of the same asshole.* She barely committed to the smile she gave as she said, "Dr. Rae Dahlia. What are you playing? Hearts?"

"It's only a four-player game, but I'll happily sit out the next round." Rae watched the geologist and the rover technician share a bemused glance as the new guy used the same old tricks they had tried to pique her interest.

"You'll sit out the rest of *this* round if you don't take your turn," Manfield grumbled.

"That's kind of you," Rae said, dragging a folding-chair over to sit beside him. The other scientists seemed surprised at her choice. *I'm here to make friends and have some fun. I can tell him off later.*

Dorian laid a jack of hearts face up on the table. "Big man on the table," he said coolly. The two other men shook their heads.

Manfield started to laugh, tossed the queen on top, and said, "That's a common misconception among young men such as yourself; thinking you're in charge when it's the queen with all the power."

The volume of the room increased well above the roar of another frost geyser. Someone shouted, "How did you not know he had the queen?" Dorian lifted his voice over them to make excuses about being distracted. A delicious burble of laughter floated up above the noise, and Rae was as surprised as anyone to discover that she was its source, and that a smile was stretched wide across her face.

"And what do you mean, 'young men'? We can't be more than three years apart!" Dorian pouted.

"Not every barrel produces the same vintage." Manfield smiled and took a sip of dark liquid from the paper cup beside him. The group rose into laughter again, but it was cut in half by someone's Omni ringing.

It was Rae's, but it took her a while to realize it. She hadn't had a call in long enough that she had forgotten the sound of it. She pulled out her Omni and looked at the screen.

Rockwell had been looking over her shoulder and exclaimed. "Evermore Industries! Why is Evermore Industries calling you?"

*Why is Evermore Industries calling me? It's got to be about the application, right? I should answer right now and tell them I filled out the application as a joke. Unless they're calling to apologize for accidentally sending it to me. But they wouldn't bother to do that. Would they?*

Dr. Manfield stood and leaned over on the table. "That's a good question. Dahlia, why *is* our competition calling you?"

"I... I don't know," Rae answered, somewhat truthfully. Somewhere was the feeling that she should be scared, but it felt like someone else's concern.

"Does Dr. Kander know about this?" Manfield asked, but Rae was too slow to answer, and he continued by threatening, "Well, he will soon enough."

"Who's Evermore?" Dorian whispered. It had been almost a decade since anyone had heard anything about Everett Evermore.

"God, you really did just arrive," said Rockwell. He turned to the geologist and said, "Does he really think that he can pull himself back into the spotlight by throwing billions of dollars into the new building on Mars?"

"Oh shit! *That's* Evermore?"

"He certainly will not, as long as the employees of Kander and Jansen remain loyal." Manfield gave Rae a look that should have moved her finger to disconnect the call. *But what if he can offer me freedom years ahead of schedule? What if they're calling to save me from this god-awful place?* Rae became aware of a heavy pounding in her chest, but the sense of whether she was excited or afraid was somewhere far away.

"I better see what they want," she said.

# CHAPTER TWO

# Reagents

### Rae

As she walked briskly down the corridor to her room, Rae extended her Omni and tapped the screen with her thumb. The home screen was replaced by the caller's video. It wasn't Evermore.

The young man looking out had green eyes and mousy brown hair that fell into them as soon as he began to speak. He looked a few years younger than she and wore an Evermore Industries ID tag that said "Ashley Rephaireal."

"Hello?" she said.

"Dr. Rachael Dahlia?"

She entered her bunkroom and closed the door behind her. "Yes. What can I do for you, Mr. Rephaireal?"

He cleared his throat. "Ashley's fine. I'm calling on behalf of Evermore Industries. We've reviewed your application, and you've made it to the first round of interviews. Is there a time when you would be available for a workforce compatibility survey?"

Her heart was thumping uncomfortably hard in her chest. *I'm high*, she thought. This is a bad time to be tested. Yet her voice said, "Ashley, I'm at the Martian South Pole in Chasma Australe waiting for a storm to break. There's nothing to do, and it's likely to continue like this for days. You've called at the perfect time."

Something she said caught him off guard. "Oh, you want to take it now? I... I can't promise it will be entertaining."

*You can reschedule this call for any time you want.* Rae recognized the thought as her own, but it sounded more like her nagging mother. She almost told it off, but when she focused on it, its logic flooded her awareness. This wasn't part of the plan. Kander and Jansen Labs was her home; they had taken her in when she was a wet newborn. They had invested in her and believed in her, and Evermore was a has-been. He had hit his big idea, made his billions, and fallen away like dead skin shed by the society he had saved. The nagging voice told her she should be concerned, that her career was on the line, that saying yes to Evermore would be the career equivalent of dousing herself in gasoline and taking up smoking.

Ashley cocked his head and raised an eyebrow. "Is everything alright?"

"No, nothing at all. I mean...  sorry, I thought you asked if there was anything wrong. Yes, everything's alright." *Except that I'm almost tearing out my own hair in boredom, my boss is a condescending pig, and my coworkers look at me like a sex toy.*

"You're sure?" Ashley's brow furrowed as he scrutinized her.

"I'm just nervous, is all. You've caught me off guard," Rae said, but as soon as she did, she realized that the look on Ashley's face wasn't scrutiny, it was empathy. And she wasn't nervous, she was excited! And she couldn't even remember why she was supposed to be concerned when the only thing she could smell was the intoxicating scent of freedom and the opportunity to create something meaningful and beautiful.

"Well, don't be. I'm sure you'll do fine," he said.

They sat there for a moment, both waiting for the other, until Ashley said, "Let's begin, then." His eyes looked off-screen to what she assumed was his script. "According to the International Employee Database, this would be the first time you've held a position with this kind of responsibility."

"That's true," she nodded.

He clearly expected her to say more, but when she didn't he looked off-screen again and read, "Your experience is *one* of the factors we compare against other applicants. However, the Doc—" He stopped himself. "I—I mean, Evermore Industries recognizes that all of its employees are individuals, and character and personality factor strongly into the hiring process. This first section is a personality evaluation so I can gauge if we would be a good fit for each other."

"I'm sure we'd be a good fit," she said. She had intended to flatten her tone to keep it ambiguous as to which "we" she was talking about, but she was out of practice. This was the first time she'd allowed herself to get flirtatious since she'd arrived on Mars.

Ashley did his best to ignore the comment and turned bright red in the process. "Dr. Evermore tries to avoid drama in his labs by organizing teams with complementing character traits. Would you classify yourself as more routinized, or whimsical?"

The questions and answers continued back and forth for several minutes. Ashley read directly from his script, oblivious to Rae's wandering attention. She did her best to behave herself, but with a script between them she felt disconnected from Ashley. Her interest started to drift. In the back of her mind the part of her that didn't think she looked good on paper tried to convince a more conventional part that they needed to go off-script. *He called Evermore "Doc"; they're close. Get Ashley and you'll get the job.*

This question seemed familiar to Ashley and he looked up from the sheet. "When you finish a job—"

Their eyes connected. Rae interrupted him. "How

many of these questions are there?"

"Seventy-two — are you more likely to: move on to new things, or tie up loose ends?"

Rae said, "When I finish a job, there *aren't* loose ends — but couldn't I fill this out online? That way we could talk now, I could fill out the form after, and you can ogle my colorful spreadsheet on your own time."

Ashley pretended to cough and hid a boyish grin behind his fist. "Dr. Dahlia, this video session is being recorded."

Rae felt incredibly foolish and sat up straighter. "Ah. I see. The test *is* a test. Continue."

He seemed relieved at her willingness to cooperate. "Who do you look up to, and—"

"Wait a minute, you *never* told me this call was being recorded. That's illegal!"

"No it's not, it's a courtesy, and I did tell you. It's the first thing I'm supposed to say," he looked over his notes off-screen, and suddenly his eyes widened.

"I'm right! You didn't tell me. You can't use any of this."

Ashley seemed totally derailed. She let him flounder there for a moment before saying, "Ashley, I'm just messing with you." He smiled, and Rae felt a warmth of attraction melt and run down her body.

He composed himself. "Just for good measure, we should start back at the beginning... Dr. Rachael Dahlia, this call is being recorded for storage and review purposes. According to the International Employee Database, this would be the first time—"

She interrupted him again. "Is this you teasing me now? You'll have to be less obtuse if you want to catch me off guard."

"Obtuse? You're the one who just turned the conversation one-eighty."

She gave him a courteous smile. "Just for the record,

I was only asking about doing it online to save you some time. I like that *you're* reading the test to me.

"The question: Who do I look up to? Um... Victoria Crellinger."

"I—" He started, but she kept going.

"When I was a little girl, I knew I wanted to be a scientist the moment I realized that Dr. Crellinger's was on the cover of every magazine. Obviously, the tech and science publications wanted to tell her story, but political magazines and Hollywood gossip rags wanted a piece of her as well. I remember one that called her 'the smartest person alive.' My ninth birthday was coming up, so I shopped around online for the best beginner science kit, but when I showed it to Deborah — my mom — and told her I wanted to be a scientist... I don't remember her exact words, but basically she said I wasn't smart enough."

Ashley sat there with his mouth open. Not with the surprised oh-face, but as if he were forming a word and had paused. He looked back and forth between the screen and questionnaire. He seemed to choose human connection over doing his job, and the word was allowed to fully form: "Ouch."

*Too easy*, she thought. "Yeah, well, that's Deborah for you. After that I really started tearing through books and magazines on anything science I could get my hands on. All my girlfriends at the time were talking about the latest teen romance, but all I could think about was Émilie Du Châtelet."

"Who?"

"She was an eighteenth-century French mathematician and physicist. She was talking about infrared light before William Hershel — its *supposed* discoverer — was even born. I had a picture of her as the background of my Omni for the longest time."

Ashley lit up, and two dimples sunk into his face. "My Omni backgrounds were a series of classic movie posters from before the turn. Ever heard of *Back to the Future?*"

"No," she smiled, and restrained herself from calling him a nerd. "I don't really go to movie parlors."

"You're missing out; there's nothing better than that moment you awaken out of a 4D movie and you, your friends, and the whole parlor just explodes with everybody talking about their different versions."

Rae considered something. "Actually, I take it back. Victoria Crellinger and Andrea Stancin are both tied for first as my most influential heroine."

"Oh. I thought you were taking back the... never mind. Why Andrea Stancin?"

"She was the first woman to set foot on Mars. On top of that she's smart and beautiful and globally respected."

"Thanks for bringing it back; I guess we got a little off track there. Not that this hasn't been... useful."

"...for Evermore Industries," she added, grinning.

"Right." He blushed again and busied himself with something on his workstation she couldn't see. "Dr. Dahlia, this call is no longer being recorded."

"But... what about the compatibility test?"

"I'm more concerned about what my boss will think of me for letting you get so far off topic. But I want to hear more about what you want to share. Tell you what, you tell me anything you like, and I'll just plug in the answers as if I asked you the questions."

Rae said, "You think I just want to blab on about myself? I'm bored, not shallow."

He winced. "I didn't mean it like that. Do you have any hobbies?"

"Besides my addiction to Hakaru?"

"Hakaru? You're not just saying that because the Doc... tor Evermore had a hand in its creation?"

"Absolutely not! Check my scoreboard: I actually received the 'most efficient design' achievement, twice."

Ashley said, "Sorry, I didn't mean to... whatever."

"Hakaru is hardly a hobby, though. I'm also a painter. Although I haven't painted in years."

"Really, an artist *and* a scientist? Which came first?"

"Both? I'm actually a terrible painter. I was far more interested in the psychology of observation. Say you've got a bunch of colors spread across a two-dimensional field: In certain shape/color combinations it means nothing to some people, but to others, even if they're still non-recognizable shapes, something entirely abstract can evoke meaning. Even my painting was scientific; each piece was a hypothesis."

"Hmm," Ashley nodded as if considering something he'd heard before. "Victoria Crellinger was a painter, too."

Rae had almost entirely forgotten Ashley was there, and when he spoke up she realized that she had been talking to her reflection in the smaller window in the lower right of her workstation. It had been years since she'd thought of any of this. *I've been so focused on the future, I've forgotten why I chose to be a scientist in the first place. I knew it had something to do with Crellinger, but it was her art, her freedom of expression that attracted me, not her fame.*

Rae shrugged. "All artists are scientists."

"How so?"

"Artists must learn the science behind their medium. A potter is also a crystallographer and knows the exact temperature at which their clay will harden, and an architect is also a physicist with a complex knowledge of loads, mechanics, strength of materials..." She abandoned the thought. "Art needs science, and conversely, science needs the artistic eye to discover things beyond logic and measurement. As humankind reaches deeper into the unknown, we find that it has less to do with empirical cause and effect and more to do with probabilities which artistic intuition is far more adept at dealing with." She looked back down at her vid reflection and directly told herself, "I chose to study synthetic bioengineering because it will be the medium of the next artistic renaissance."

Ashley was silent for a moment, then shook his head and said, "Come on! As soon as I turn off the recording you drop the perfect soundbite. Dr. Dahlia, if the Doc had heard you say that he would have hired you on the spot."

"Call me Rae, and most of it was stolen from my UMars application essay."

"Rae it is." He smiled. "I've heard UMars has a great synth-bio department."

"It's amazing. What did you major in?"

"I haven't been able to narrow it down to one thing; recently I've been interested in gene therapy during embryogenesis. Unfortunately, my high school grades weren't high enough for the University of Mars."

Rae sighed, remembering the day she'd been accepted into the synthetic bioengineering program at UMars. It was one of her proudest moments, to have an outside presence affirm that she was good enough, and smart enough, to be accepted at one of the most competitive colleges on either Mars or Earth. *Take that, Deborah.*

"So you're pretty close with 'the Doc,' then?"

Ashley frowned. "You're not supposed to know that."

"No?"

"He said I could be easily compromised."

"Ouch," she said, returning his sympathy.

Ashley shrugged. "Well, it's true, isn't it? He told me to stick to the script. I didn't. He told me to record the conversation, but I didn't do that either."

"If he knew you were so easy to influence, why didn't he call me himself? I say this is his fault." She could tell he appreciated the comfort, but he didn't respond. She continued, "Tell me, what is he like in person?"

Ashley raised an eyebrow. "I thought you had met him before. At the trial?"

"Oh God. I was hoping he wouldn't realize I was *that*

Dahlia." During her junior year at the University of San Diego, Evermore had been accused of biosynthesizing a human in the state of California. While synthetic transplants were perfectly legal, human cloning had been banned at the turn of the century. Evermore claimed that the ethical line had already been crossed with the countless species of bacteria, viruses, algae and fungi that now called the planet home, and the only difference between having a lab filled with synthetic human tissue and an entire synthetic human was the proximity of the organs. If people thought that synthetic organisms were abominations, then no organism should be synthesized. The legal battle stretched on for months. The question that needed answering was not whether it was ethical to construct a human being: both the religious and scientific communities agreed that it was not. But where was the line? At which point in the creation process did Evermore break the law?

Rae had written an editorial piece for the student newspaper, the *Daily Aztec*, in which she criticized Evermore's abuse of the moratorium on embryonic gene editing. It had been opinionated and scathing and gained her quite a bit of attention around campus (both positive and negative). Somehow the prosecution got a hold of it, saw an angle, and brought her in to testify against Evermore.

"Of course he remembers you," Ashley said. "Why do you think he sent you the application brochure?"

"I... I kind of assumed it went out to everyone on Mars."

He shook his head. "Nope. It went out to thirty people, all of whom Evermore has had some connection with. We were looking at the applications together, and he chuckled when he saw yours."

Rae frowned.

"No, not in a bad way. There was a fondness to it; he told me the story about when you came into the courthouse and spoke on behalf of the up-and-coming generation of scientists. He knew the case would evoke clearer laws and prohibitions against biosystems engineering on humans, but that humankind still wasn't sure what it was ethically and socially comfortable with. The Doc said he was using the court system as a soapbox and attempting to guide the line as close to cloning as he could. Until you showed up. He says you helped him realize that he had a responsibility to something much larger than the law."

"So that's why he suddenly switched his plea to guilty." Rae thought back to the statement that ended the trial but realized that Ashley hadn't answered her question. "But what's Evermore like in person?"

"You'll see for yourself when you meet him."

Her heart skipped. "Really? You can do that?"

Ashley made a show of examining some piece of paper. "It's just that your evaluation looks so well-rounded." He checked to see if she was smiling. She was. "I need to do a few more things here before my workday ends."

"What are my next steps?"

"Given that all record of our conversation was somehow corrupted — wink wink — I'll need to build a case for you and present it to Evermore. All that's left is his okay."

"So. We'll talk soon?" she asked.

"You can call back anytime you like," he said. "Good afternoon, Rae."

She disconnected the video call, leaned back, and smiled. Closing her eyes, she imagined Ashley's dimples and his soft green eyes. Then his face was replaced by the memory of Evermore's trial.

Rae made a *C* shape with her hand and quickly circled it twice around her face; the gesture opened the Cloud9 search engine, and she said, "Evermore's closing statement at the Synthetic Man Trial."

A list of possibilities appeared, and Rae recognized

and selected the top choice.

With gyrocopter mics swarming around Evermore's face like flies around shit, he said, "Humankind has been modifying evolution for thousands of years through agriculture, animal husbandry, and genetic modification. Human biosystems engineering is no different."

This was not the "Person of the Century" from the magazine covers; this was a different man, a tired, defeated man who already knew he had lost. As Rae listened to him she ran a search for that "Person of the Century" image.

"There are global problems that need solving *now*," Evermore said. "The expansive growth of the human race is speeding toward a brick wall, and we can't afford to let our prejudice of the unknown cut our brakes. Earth's systems are trying correct the imbalance, but we are that imbalance. We have already broken nature's laws with our technology, but it's too late to say that tech isn't okay. If we want to escape the total annihilation that awaits us, we need to break a few more of our mother's rules."

Rae found a photo from back in the twenties labeled "The kings of synthetic bioengineering." Dr. Everett Evermore and his partner and best friend, Dr. Clyde Kander, were standing with their arms over each other's shoulders in front of the first genome printer ever built. Rae had used the latest version at UMars to build micro-organisms from raw elements.

Evermore's speech continued. "I concede, growing a living being is unethical, but we're running out of space down here, and there's plenty of room in space. The only problem is that we're not built for zero-G. This new man *is.*"

There it was: "Person of the Century," above an article about a bioengineered class of lichen that feed on the
common pollutants monoxide and sulfur dioxide and ex-
hale oxygen. She remembered the Skyscraper Lichen being spray-planted all around the city when she was young.
She had always wanted to see the sprayers but somehow
never did. Suddenly the back of the billboard by the su-
permarket was gray-green. Or one day the inside of the
traffic tunnel under the canal was coated and smelled of
summer rain.

From the magazine cover she imagined Evermore
as an inspirational renegade, unbound by norms, conventional thought, or scientific responsibility. It was the
freedom that made him powerful and exciting. Evermore
made the leap from bioengineering lichen to human organs. Within a few years Evermore Biomedical Systems
had labs across the globe supplying hospitals and individuals with PerfectDonor™ synthetic organs engineered
from the recipient's own cells.

Evermore looked straight into the cameras. "I believe
there is no cost too high that I would not pay it to save
humanity."

A chill ran through her. She was afraid to work for
that stop-at-nothing Evermore. But that man had been
stopped by a jury of his peers. He lost his corporate spon-
sorship, he was fired by the board of Evermore Biomedical Systems, all his research bonds were cashed in, and
he was forced to sell his second home in California. She
wondered how the fall had affected him. For the last eight
years the media had forgotten (or avoided) him, until...

Rae ran another search and was rewarded with the
vid of a sparsely attended press conference outside Ev-

ermore's bungalow in Naperville, Illinois, where he announced the creation of a new company, Evermore Industries. Rae watched this third Evermore with suspicion and curiosity. He was softer than the other two, but still passionate and still free. She watched the vid again, searching for the man for whom "no cost was too high," but her mind drifted off to daydreams of running her own lab, and the vid ended before she'd started paying attention. Frustrated but also mildly amused, she tried again with the same result. There she sat, watching a freeze frame that asked "Replay?" while the clouds cleared from her eyes.

*This must be fun*, some distant part of her mind thought, *because I'm grinning like an idiot*. She did it again, and the sheer joy of smiling escalated into waterfalls of shimmering bliss that cascaded down her neocortex. Her bunkroom seemed too small to contain her heart, which leapt against her chest like a bird trapped on a screen porch. But she maintained enough control over her freedom-starved bones that she didn't leave her bunkroom, especially once her body felt as if it were broadcasting on all frequencies on the visible-light spectrum, and her thoughts became tachyons moving backward through time.

After being awake most of the night, she slept for twelve hours straight. When she awoke that trapped bird sat docile at her feet, too exhausted to fly. Rae felt like a fool for acting so loose with Ashley, and ashamed for manipulating his male weakness. He seemed so sweet and charming, and she had taken advantage of him. *Maybe I'm wrong, though; who knows what kind of asshole he's become now that I'm sober. Maybe he deserved it.*

# CHAPTER THREE

# Red Rover

### Rae

The more Rae thought about it, the more she realized she'd made a goddamn fool of herself in front of Ashley, and ruined any attempt at getting the job. She had distracted him and hadn't completed the interview. She'd even convinced him to stop recording her, which was clearly part of the test.

Her Omni chimed with a text and awakened her from her loathing.

> **A.Manfield:** All staff, suit up and report to the hangar. The storm has passed and I want everyone's help digging out the rover.

> **R.Dahlia:** On my way.

*Ugh. I feel like shit.*

Rae had the women's locker room to herself, not for the first time. *I guess there are some perks to being the only woman at the South Pole.* Once she was inside the EVA suit, her sluggish movements could be blamed on the lack of mobility, and her heavy eyelids hidden behind the reflective glass. In the hangar, Dr. Manfield handed them each a sublimating tool that Rae half expected to shoot fire, but it turned out to be a glorified leaf blower. As she thought about it, she realized that flames (or even blowing hot air) would vaporize some of the CO2 but some of it would liquefy and leak deeper into the rover.

Around the forty-minute mark, as the ice-sample storage compartment was almost freed from the frost, Rae's Omni rang. The heads-up display projected a notice directly onto her face shield: "Call from Kander and Jansen Labs."

"I keep hearing a clicking; is someone getting a phone call?" Dr. Manfield complained in her ear.

"Yes. From K&J. I thought it was you, actually."

"Well, Dahlia, take a break and see who it is," Manfield demanded.

Stepping away from the hangar out into the predawn light, which lasted all day this time of year, Rae couldn't help but admire the frozen landscape of Chasma Australe. "Hello?" she answered, looking up past the walls of ice that protected their tiny lab. The alien constellations that made up the Martian night sky were replaced by the round pink face of Dr. Clyde Kander projected on her helmet glass. He carried heavy bags under his eyes, and his brown hair was starting to blond as it grayed.

"Dr. Dahlia," he said, "I hear that you've been talking to Evermore Industries."

Rae couldn't believe it was really him. "Dr. Kander, I'm so sorry," she began.

He cut her off. "Don't be sorry. I know all about Evermore and his antics. He and I were once friends, and he still finds it amusing to meddle with Jansen and me. That twelve-story lab, for example."

Rae tried to listen to him ramble on about the many times Evermore had put roadblocks in his way, but her mind soon drifted to how she was going to keep her job. At the first break in his monologue she said, "Dr. Kander, I meant no disloyalty. I assumed they sent me the application by mistake. I only filled it out to pass the time and indulge some childish fantasy. I'm sorry."

Kander nodded, not entirely satisfied by her apology. "I can't pretend that my pride isn't hurt that K&J isn't your dream job, but I understand the temptation: You've been working for years to end up at our worlds-renowned synthetic bioengineering lab, and just when you think you got it, you find yourself down at the South Pole doing lab work an intern could handle. Then some has-been doctor comes along and offers you an exit."

The endless sky above her no longer beckoned with a siren song of freedom. Instead it reminded her how small and insignificant she was. *I fucking hate this feeling.* Her fists clenched, but she forced herself to remain civil. "I was just indulging a fantasy. I didn't accept the job."

"So he *did* offer you a job?" There was a hint of worry in his voice that gave Rae a rush of confidence.

"Yes, they offered me my own lab."

"And you turned them down." He seemed relieved. "That is a smart choice, Dr. Dahlia; Evermore Industries is a new business built on old ideas. That's a bad combination and a risky investment, don't you think? I've heard Mars is a *terrible* place to end up homeless."

Rae's first reaction was to assume he was threatening her livelihood, but his features and his tone suggested he was making a casual observation. *Casual. Wait, why is Clyde Kander, the head of K&J labs, making this call? Why am I worth his time?* She asked him as much.

Kander suddenly looked guilty, then embarrassed. "I guess I'm still playing my part in that old rivalry. Our HR department could lay out the extent of your contract, they could tell you the exact amount K&J has invested in you thus far, and let you know how much you'd owe us for the trip back to Nili Terradome—"

Dr. Hideaki never shut up about the space elevator fees. Once he had noticed she was wearing eyeliner and scolded her for bringing too much unnecessary weight.

"But," Kander continued, "my HR department would be unable to warn you about Evermore. They don't know what kind of man he is, or that..." Rae could see there was something he didn't want to say but would. She waited. "...he's been watching you since the Synthetic Man Trial. He saw something in you then. Even though you were against him, he was impressed."

"Evermore told you this?"

"I'm sure you are aware that we used to be partners. During the trial he would sometimes forget that I was the one who blew the whistle on him, and act like he did back when we were friends. Or maybe he didn't forget and was trying to manipulate me to side with him. He is a man constantly looking for opportunities to leverage the situation. Also, HR wouldn't have been able to warn you that there's a good chance he's interested in more than just your synthetic bioengineering skills."

Rae shivered with disgust. "What is *that* supposed to mean?"

Kander shook his head. "No no, nothing like that. After you think of what Victoria Crellinger achieved, what's the next name that comes to mind?"

Automatically, Rae said, "NMC Labs."

Kander nodded. "Exactly. They go together like Aldrin and NASA."

"What does that have to do with me?"

Kander's features softened. "Correct me if I'm wrong, but you're the kind of person who likes recognition based on their merits. Well, I wouldn't be surprised if Evermore will try to use you as the new face of Evermore Industries, not because you're a talented scientist, but just because you're a woman.

"How about we put this Evermore nonsense behind us and talk about shortening your time down there?"

A text popped up in the corner of her display:

**A.Rephaireal:** Dr. Dahlia, I spoke with Evermore. Please forgive my lack of professionalism during the interview, but I wanted to let you know that the job is yours if you want it.

*What the fuck is going on?* Rae was silent for a while, spinning the puzzle around in all dimensions.

She turned back toward the hangar. The geologist was pointing in her direction and arguing with Dr. Manfield about something.

"Dr. Dahlia? What are you looking at? What's the matter?" Kander asked.

"I think they need my help with the rover."

Kander's blond-gray eyebrows knit together. "I'm sure they'll manage without you. What's really on your mind?"

"You put words in my mouth before, and now I feel as if I've been untruthful: I never said that I turned Evermore down, just that I didn't give him an answer."

He looked surprised. Maybe even betrayed. "But... your contract with us?"

"I understand," she nodded, nearly knocking her forehead on the helmet glass. "And I don't want to break our agreement, but if you'll provide me some flexibility on your end, perhaps we can bend it."

"Dr. Dahlia, I'm not—"

"Please, Dr. Kander, set me up with a K&J lab room back at Nili, and I'll continue my core sample analysis on nights and weekends until I've paid you back for your investment in me."

He shook his head. *Is that disappointment or remorse?* she wondered.

"I would have done the same thing," Kander scoffed, and shook his head again. His eyes were looking elsewhere, some place far away, "I *did* the same thing. I did backflips for that man. But that's his gift." Kander returned to the present. "Take some time to think about your next move. I believe you're due for a week here at the terradome; please make your decision before that week is up, and please consider the things I've told you. Be careful, Dr. Dahlia, Everett is the kind of man who has a reason behind every action."

"Thank you, Dr. Kander, and I'm sorry for all of this."

Kander accepted her apology with a tired nod, and hung up.

Finally the day arrived when her savior descended from the heavens on a ribbon of incredible strength. It took the form of a teardrop-shaped freight elevator ten meters in diameter. One end of the elevator's ribbon was anchored deep in the crust of the Red Planet, and the other end led upward and out past Mars' gravitational pull and connected to a thrust-assisted counterweight station. From there a small cargo shuttle would take her and their ice samples to Phobos, and then they would return to the surface of Mars via the Skylon D4 space plane.

Rae had cleaned her room and packed her things the night before. Out of the twelve kilograms of stuff she had brought out here, she was only bringing back her Omni and the clothes she was wearing. Everything else was tossed into the garbage chute and vaporized into its base elements. Including a small, carefully folded piece of aluminum foil. Rae had stared at it for a long time before throwing it away. She wanted so badly to experience the joy she should be feeling, but she had lost it somewhere between the fear, doubt, and myriad forking possibilities. She had unwrapped one fold, but then she thought of Ashley. *I want to meet him when I get back to the dome, but this time I really want to meet him.*

Rae felt her heartbeat quicken as the moving walkway carried her to street level. The breath of the terradome rolled down the passage and brushed the loose hairs from her face. Nili Terradome smelled just as it had the first time she arrived. The primary scent was part doctor's office and part pottery studio, followed by a bouquet of jungle, photosynthesis, and spring rain. Stepping off the end of the walkway, she waded through a crowd of University of Mars students listening to their professor. "—reliant on local materials, the buildings in Nili are built from compressed bricks of Martian clay. Here, near the edge of the dome, is one of the only places in the city where the dark-red rammed-earth and clay wall is visible."

The students followed their professor's extended finger to the top of the three-story high wall that encircled the city and provided the foundation for the dome. The city of Nili had been a mere seven years old when Rae first arrived. Some of the buildings had yet to be plastered, and the new parts of the city had looked very much like a seventeenth-century mill town until midway through her senior year.

The professor continued, "It is here that the clash of old and new technology is most apparent. Nili Terradome was built with 98 percent local materials, which were provided by clay deposits on the floor of the trench. Even the very dust was used, heated to great degrees in ferrite furnaces and pultruded into white-hot webs of a strong, light, and thin material called poly-carbon. A misnomer, as it contains neither polymers nor carbon but is more akin to a ceramic graphene."

The poly-carbon he was talking about composed the hexagonal armature that gave the multi-million-screen simulated environment its structure. As one looked out across the city, the virtual environment made the terra-dome appear as if it were situated beneath a crisp blue sky somewhere in the Alps. Rae had hated the simulation at first, or maybe she had just hated that it had confused her for a moment the first time she emerged from this corridor. But here and now, after three months at the Martian

South Pole, living in a room barely larger than a coffin, returning to the simulated blue skies of the terradome felt like coming home.

A student's hand raised hesitantly, and when called on he asked, "What about the other 2 percent?"

Rae slowed her pace through the crowd to hear the answer, though she already knew it. She had been ten years old when humans first landed on Mars. There were so many nights she had spent lying awake trying to imagine what it would be like to land on a planet knowing you would never leave, and what it would feel like to have your life and the lives of your team depend on how well your resources were managed. The entire mission was broadcast live on the internet, and Rae watched it so fervently that she started measuring her conservation of energy. If Andrea Stancin, the first woman on Mars, could spend 1,500 calories digging a well for six hours, Rae could conserve her energy by walking everywhere very slowly. It got so that she was confining herself to the same 1,500-calorie diet and spending calories like a frugal child spends their allowance. This didn't make her any friends, and once her teachers noticed her "obsession with dieting" the school psychologist begged her to quit.

The professor said, "This question is really the core concept of this class: everything you see that isn't from here, was brought here. The 2 percent exotic materials found in the dome were recycled from the one-way colony ship commissioned by the United Nations Space Administration and built cooperatively by its member nations. While the dome couldn't have been constructed without materials from the colony ship, namely the honeycomb of stratosphere plates, the mission and subsequent construction wouldn't have been possible without the missions that preceded it. The underground bunkers hand-dug by the Mars One crew, and the Chinese National Space Administration's centrifuge station on Phobos."

The professor was just getting started, but Rae had no desire to audit the class and continued on her way through the crowd. She waded her way through the traffic jam of automated rickshaws the UMars students had left piled beside the charging station, climbed into one of the few that weren't gridlocked and said, "Home."

"You will reach your home in three minutes," it told her.

As the rickshaw turned down the main road, the light of the sun hit her face from just above the edge of the Pennine Alps and seemed to welcome her home. Even though in reality, the sun was an average of 230 million kilometers away and was nearly half the size when it set in a subdued bluish-gray behind the wall of the Nili Fossae trough.

The rickshaw turned down Long Street in the direction of her apartment, and Rae realized there was nothing for her to do there. It was early in the evening, and she had enough water credits built up from her time at Chasma Australe that she could actually fill the bath. But at the same time she felt so anxious about the decision between Evermore and Kander that she didn't want to be alone inside her tiny, empty apartment. *No. Nothing empty.*

It was Friday night, and even though most of the scientists worked seven days a week, she knew the bars would be crowded, as would the theaters, cabarets, and casinos. People went to the casinos to meet people, but she wanted to be alone in a crowd. The bar closest to her apartment, the Relativity Lounge, often had good music, and the VR atmosphere was always entertaining. She looked down and realized she was still wearing her lab coat. *Bath, then bar,* she decided, but then thought of Ashley.

# CHAPTER FOUR

# Endings and Beginnings

**Ashley**

Hoping this was the place she meant, Ashley waited outside the Relativity Lounge, nervously pondering his body odor to cologne ratio. He tried to imagine himself as one of the dead movie stars from before the turn coolly hanging out on a street corner enjoying a cigarette, but smoking wasn't allowed inside the terradome, and it wasn't particularly unique or cool to stand around looking at one's Omni.

Finally, one of the automated rickshaws approaching the club was carrying Rae.

"Rae," he said, going over to her as she docked the bike. As far as he could tell, the only makeup she was wearing was thinly applied eyeliner beneath her stunning hazel eyes.

"Ashley," she said.

The moment stretched on too long, and to fill it, Ashley initiated a handshake. "Welcome back to the dome."

Rae was kind and didn't draw attention to the clumsy gesture, and as he held the door open for her, the music assaulted him on one side, and the smell of her, like some flowering jungle tree, brushed his cheek as she walked past. The inside of the Relativity Lounge looked like pulp sci-fi night at the Space Needle. The translucent tables and chairs each had a single leg with a wide round base like a wineglass, and their edges glowed with neon fiber optics. The walls were all virtual reality screens that inflated the square room beyond its walls and bent it into a round observation deck. Beyond the "windows," the club appeared to be teetering on the edge of a black hole. At the top of every hour they would be hit by a "gravitational event," and part of the club would sustain some damage, or appear to be ripped away and sucked into the nearby singularity.

The room was not as crowded as Ashley had expected, but it was still early in the evening. Rae made a beeline to the table farthest from the music.

"Do you ever listen to freedom jazz?" he asked.

She seemed to be listening for a moment. The base line and melody went down smooth, while the improvisational tangents created a mood of intelligent contemplation with a high refresh rate. "This is entirely undanceable."

"The point isn't to dance do it," he said. He put his Omni on the payment square and asked, "What're you drinking?"

Rae laid hers alongside his, signaling the table to charge them separately. "I'll have a tequila old-fashioned,"

Ashley combed through the tabletop menu, but all the drinks had been renamed to fit the "unified theory" theme.

He looked up. "I can't find it."

Rae looked at the menu. "Sorry, I forgot, they call it a 'Proton Decay' here."

"Ah," he said, ordering one for her and selecting a "Weak Interaction" for himself. It was a whiskey and water, neat.

"So... tomorrow's your first day at E.I. Are you still feeling nervous?"

He watched her imagine it and saw a look cross her face, like that momentary darkening when Phobos transits the sun.

"No. Should I be?" She smiled. "I'm excited to see the building, and I guess a little anxious to meet Evermore."

"He's a normal guy, don't let the stories get to you."

"What stories?"

"Well, if you haven't heard any, it'd be better not to mention them."

"Come on," she grinned.

He smiled back and for a moment everything was a wonderfully normal, classically predictable, modern fairytale cliché. He submitted, "Well, there was that time when Dr. Jansen thought Evermore wanted to blow up the world." And the moment was gone.

"Oh God, right." Rae said. A year into his house arrest, Evermore had called James Jansen looking for help, and Jansen had gone to the national news telling them about Evermore's plans to build a bomb that could destroy an entire planet. Evermore's house and lab were raided, and his computers and hard drives were seized, but they never found any evidence of such a bomb.

Rae smiled and returned with a story of her own. "There was the time he gave that huge grant to those ghost hunters, and his stock tanked and his board almost rioted."

Ashley shrugged, and in the silence their drinks were delivered. He took a quick drink, coughed a little, and said, "It's like what you were talking about the first time we spoke; he's an artist looking for a new medium."

"Easy for you to say, you're his personal assistant, you get see him at his most vulnerable. All we see are all the mistakes and victories the media shows us."

"I *was* his personal assistant," he corrected her, but he must have looked miserable, because she cocked her head in question. "I was... relocated yesterday," he said and watched the spark between them fizzle out.

"Fired?" She looked really concerned. "It wasn't because of our interview, was it?"

Ashley thought back to the note attached to the short stack of personnel folders on his workstation.

> Ashley, if you want to keep learning from me, you need to shadow someone else for these next few years. Interview these three people and decide which one you find the most interesting to work with. Be warned, there is a woman in this list. Do not let her charm you. ~E

*It basically was, but I can't say that; she'll feel like she owes me.* "No. Evermore said it was time for me to learn from someone else, but I didn't realize it was coming so soon. My replacement just arrived on the shuttle from Earth."

She made a consoling pouty face, reached across the table, and put her hand on his. It was not a romantic gesture; it wasn't even a pity-fuck gesture. This was the worst possible gesture: the sympathetic nurturer. His forced the lump from his throat, hardened his face, and drained the rest of his drink. "It's fine. Really it's Evermore's way of looking out for me, and I'm sure this will open up new *opportunities*." He tried to make the last line an insinuation. *Idiot, she doesn't know yet.*

"How can you believe that? Do you know what you'll be doing instead?"

He hesitated, looked down at her hand, and put his other hand on top of hers. It was cold and clammy. *Maybe from the cold glass table?*

"Actually... I'll be working for you."

"As... department liaison?" she guessed, but she seemed worried.

"No. As your personal assistant."

She slid her hand from in between his and took a big sip of her drink, draining the glass.

"This," he motioned at the connection he was desperately trying to forge, "doesn't have to be weird."

"No," she nodded.

He frowned. "Fuck. It's already weird."

She shook it off. "I'm sorry, Ashley, it's just... I've been traveling all day, and the time difference, maybe the alcohol is catching up to me." She stood.

"Rae, wait. Don't be distracted by the title. I can be really helpful if you let me. I may not have much traditional education, but I've been working beside Evermore for almost eleven years." He could feel tears forcing themselves from his burning eyes.

Rae looked like she might panic and run at any moment, and he didn't blame her. "Eleven years? I assumed you started working for Evermore *after* he was released from house arrest."

"No. For the first fifteen years of my life I never knew who owned the house next door until the day after the trial ended and Evermore started living there full time. I saw him mowing the lawn and recognized him from the magazine covers." He let his tears flow unabashedly. Rae didn't sit back down, but at least she stayed to listen. "My mom told me to stay away from him, but I offered to mow his lawn if he would help me with homework, and the next thing I knew, he had me running errands and learning to code."

Rae looked as if she was puzzling through everything he'd just said. He'd seen that look on Evermore's face when he was sorting through data. She looked him over once more, seemingly assessing his usefulness to her. "That I invited you out tonight feels inappropriate given that you are my personal assistant. I apologize for being so unprofessional during our last interaction, and I'm looking forward to working with you on Monday."

Before he could respond, she had paid the full tab and slipped away from the table.

*Why couldn't I lie? Just once, just to kill the loneliness for a night?* He opened up the menu on the table and was about to order another drink when he thought, Rae was right, this music sucks.

## Rae

The following morning the rickshaw docked itself outside the Evermore Industries building. Rae looked up, admiring the newest and tallest building in the terradome for a moment before approaching the double-wide, tinted glass doors of Evermore Industries. She took notice of her reflection before the doors automatically parted. Her fresh lab coat and dark-blue suit were crisp and professional. Her light-brown hair was perfectly in place, and her makeup was carefully applied to thicken and lower her eyebrows, straighten her lashes, thin her lips, and enhance her look of resolve. The ensemble was carefully stylized to reflect her professionalism: smart, serious, collected, and in command. But she saw something else in that reflection too: the same fierce, determined look she had seen so many times on her mother's face. *Deborah, you were convinced that Mars would be awful and that I'd hate it. Do you ever wonder if you were right?* She imagined her mother's reply: *"Do you ever wonder if I was right?"*

The doors opened, slicing her reflection in half to reveal an expansive lobby of poly-carbon and stone. The compressed clay floor was so well polished that it could have been mistaken for a dark-red granite. Glossy graphite panels covered the walls and gave the space a cold, earthy twinkle like a wintry starscape, or a silver mine. Across the room was a receptionist's desk occupied by a blond man in his twenties. On either side of the entry there were two waiting areas defined by black suede chairs surrounding low coffee tables made of the same tinted glass as the front doors. On her left, a group of young men were lounging and quietly joking among themselves. Ashley stood from the group and briskly walked to her.

Afraid that he would ruin her carefully crafted demeanor with some mention of last night, she crushed him with her eyes as he briefly made contact, and watched the look of recognition wilt as his gaze fell to the floor. "Good morning, Dr. Dahlia. Welcome to Evermore Industries. I'll be your. . ." He fumbled. "My name is Ashley, and I'll be your personal assistant. Follow me; we've got a busy day ahead of us."

*Why is he pronouncing each syllable like that? It sounds like he's reading from a script. Oh, it's satire. He's become an unwitting actor in a role he never applied for.*

She wouldn't begrudge him this small protest... until it got annoying. "What exactly do we have ahead of us today?"

His bargain store dress shoes squeaked ever so slightly on the polished floor as he walked across the lobby. He obviously wanted to get in the elevator before answering, but Rae wasn't playing along. Walking back to her so he could answer without shouting, he said, "For starters, we need to go to HR so you can sign a contract and get an ID badge. Then you've got a meeting with Evermore and the other lab heads at eleven in the... recreation facility, which I've not been invited to. Then, after a short break for lunch, we can start reviewing applications and setting up interviews. If we're quick, you'll get to do some shopping in the Kander and Jansen Scientific Instruments International. So, whenever you're ready..." He waited for her to start walking this time.

"Ashley, if you don't mind me asking, why is it that I get to pick all of my staff, yet you seemed to come with the lab?"

His eyes shifted to the other assistants, who were making faces at him behind her back. "Dr. Evermore wanted there to be someone to aid you the moment you stepped inside; however, if you are dissatisfied with me," he couldn't hide the underlying pain in his voice, "I can easily be replaced."

"I didn't mean it like that," she whispered.

"It's going to be an exciting first week," he smiled, but it didn't fool her.

As they walked into the elevator, Rae asked, "Before you were relocated, were you in charge of all the interviews, or...?"

Ashley met her eyes for the briefest of moments. "You were a special case."

She came face to face with her reflection again, but this time it was interrupted by the E.I. logo etched across the elevator doors. Rumor had it that Evermore had imagined the E.I. Mobius strip in a dream, but if half the rumors were true, Evermore wouldn't have gotten so much as a building permit. *I hope to God he's not crazy, or if he is, I hope this is worth it. Please don't let this be the end of my career. If this thing degrades, I'll never be respected as a bioengineer.*

In the elevator, as she took off her lab coat and handed it to Ashley to hold while she took off her lab-suit jacket, she said, "I'm used to the lab at Chasma Australe being cold."

"You can count on it being an even seventy-three degrees every day. The whole climate-controlled dome thing tends to make the weather pretty predictable. Expect rain the first Wednesday of every month from 11 p.m. until one."

"Thank you for the weather report," she said, putting her lab coat back on, "but it's only been three weeks since I was last here on leave from Chasma Australe. I just forgot how warm they keep it."

He directed her attention to the elevator's twelve round, feather-touch buttons. "I assume you're familiar with the Omni Workforce?"

"Yeah, the buttons read my fingerprint, and accounting uses it to track my hours."

"It's proximal recognition, so your ID card and your Omni need to be on your person.

"Your lab is on the seventh floor," he continued, pointing to the seven. "But we're going down, to human resources. B2 is the cafeteria. B3 is the recreational facility: sauna, showers, game room, gym, and multi-sport courts—"

"You have a sauna?"

He smiled and said coolly, "We have a saltwater pool."

*How could he afford all that water?* she thought, frowning. Her reaction obviously disappointed him.

"Wait, did you say my meeting with Evermore was at the pool?"

Ashley sputtered, "I didn't. Did I? No, I said in the recreation facility." Oddly, he seemed to be trying to convince himself as much as her.

He pressed the button for HR, and they descended in silence.

*Dr. Kander gave me a week to decide where I'm going to work. I wonder if there's any way I can defer signing this contract until later?*

## Ashley

Ashley lounged in one of the black suede chairs in the lobby with four other personal assistants, waiting for their new bosses to finish up in HR so they could guide them into the elevator and push the button for them. Evermore had been very specific about this step.

Behind the receptionist's desk was a man around Ashley's age who was fair-featured and blond, the kind of blond he'd imagine seeing down in the entertainment district dealing blackjack, the kind of blond who knew exactly how good-looking he was. But this one was looking up a corporate ladder only those with brains and degrees could climb. What he was doing here Ashley couldn't guess, other than the obvious: counting ceiling tiles in boredom. Suddenly his gaze dropped and he caught Ashley staring at him.

"How many are there?" Ashley asked, then remembered his name. *Julius... something.*

Julius leaned forward and, ignoring Ashley's question, asked one of his own. "You're friends with Dr. Evermore's new assistant, that Samuel kid, yah?"

"No," Ashley said, not bothering to hide the disdain in his voice.

Julius looked unsure if he should continue or not. "Is he... some kind of child prodigy or something?"

"No," Ashley said again, trying to tone down the jealousy. "A, he's in his forties, and B, he's not even that smart."

In one of those loud whispers that seem to be reserved for gossip, one of the other assistants said, "His forties? He doesn't look any older than my cousin, and he's only eleven."

"Samuel's got some kind of dwarfism," Ashley said. "A few years after the Synthetic Man Trial he came to Evermore looking for help. The Doc's been trying to develop some kind of retroactive gene therapy for him."

Julius said, "Guess it isn't working. I'm sorry, that was rude."

Ashley shrugged. "I don't give a shit; he creeps me the hell out. But Evermore's therapy *is* working: the first time I met Samuel I would have guessed he was six."

Julius leaned back in his chair. "In any case, Dr. Evermore seems to like him. They always enter and leave together."

Ashley got defensive, almost violently so. "What are you implying?"

Julius put up his hands. "You never know..."

Ashley stood. "I *know*. He used to hit on my mom for Christ sake! He's not... like that."

"Like what? Gay? Listen Ashley, things are different up here. The population is 80-something percent male, but 100 percent of us still need satisfaction." He smiled.

Ashley took a step back.

"I'm with you," one of the assistants said, gesturing at Ashley, "I'm content to grease my own pole."

Julius put his feet up on his desk. "All I'm saying is: Why limit your options? I knew a guy in college that liked to use warm fruit."

The other assistants laughed. "I knew a guy who liked to sit on his hands until they lost sensation."

"Ah, the familiar stranger!" Julius laughed.

Ashley walked to the elevator and waited until the doors opened before saying, "Samuel isn't warm fruit."

He pressed B4 and backed against the wall in the blind spot beneath the security camera. "What's wrong with *me*?" he asked the empty room, and realized that the camera could still see him in the reflection off the doors. He shook it off and stuffed it away for the nth time since he found out he'd been replaced. *He didn't even have the nerve to tell me to my face.*

The humid warmth hit his face as the doors opened on the pool facility. Ashley walked around to the woman's changing room on the far side of the pool and closed the door. Rae was the only woman in the E.I. building, and it was a good bet that she wouldn't be doing any swimming today.

Ashley slumped down on a bench and tried to clear his head, but in the silence he could hear his own words echoing through his head, *What's wrong with me?*

He clenched his fists and squeezed his eyes shut. *Your timing was fucking terrible, Doc! I wish I could show you the way Rae looked when she found out I wasn't working for you anymore.*

*"Don't take it personally," you said, but what a hell of a way to show someone you care about them. Fuck you, Doc!* He wanted to scream it, but he knew that at any moment Samuel and

Evermore would be arriving in the pool area. *Ten fucking years, and you replace me with some freak!* Ashley clenched his teeth to fight back the tears. *Do I deserve this? Is this what I get for being so fucking weird?* Grief shivered through his body, though he fought, grunting with exertion, to hold it back. He balled up his shirt around his face and screamed into it.

*I'm not good enough for any of them.* He thought of Evermore, Rae, Sarah his first love, and his faceless father — a shape without form or feature that was the shadow of a memory of a man. No, not a man, a coward.

*Fuck you, you self-righteous prick! If you want to take everything from me, then I'm going to take something from you. You think you fucking fooled me with that "retroactive gene therapy" bullshit? You built another synthetic human, didn't you? I'm going to find where you're hiding the proof and take it.*

# CHAPTER FIVE

# Evermore

### Rae

Rae sat in a small waiting room outside a labyrinth of cubicle partitions that defined the boundaries of the human resources department. She watched in her best not-interested posture as the three HR personnel went through the contract-for-ID-badge exchange and knew she wouldn't be getting anywhere without a badge, and she wouldn't get a badge without signing a contract. *But who's to stop me from going to listen to Evermore? Everyone's new here, and the only one watching is the elevator. Ashley said it's detecting my Omni, so theoretically I'll be invisible. I just won't be able to control the elevator.*

A vaguely-familiar-looking black man in his early twenties finished with his rep, stood and walked toward the elevator. He wore heavy steel rings in each ear, a pair of thick-rimmed glasses, and a hooded designer lab coat. There were still people who chose glasses over corrective surgery, but she hadn't seen any on Mars. She wondered if they could be designer-augmented-reality lenses, but when he got closer she could see that they lacked the tell-tale glow. She turned off her Omni, and, when he passed her, she followed him in. He clearly noticed her, but he was more focused on affixing his ID badge, and whatever thoughts he had about meeting Evermore, than accusing her of... what? *I'm not even doing anything wrong. This is just an experiment.*

They returned to the lobby in silence, but while he met his assistant who led him down to B3, Ashley was nowhere to be found. After watching two other assistants guide their principal researchers into the elevator and send them down to B3, she got fed up and followed the third set to the elevator. As she passed the blond receptionist, she said, "If Ashley ever shows up, tell him I've already gone."

On B3 there was a semicircle of ten folding chairs set up at one end of the "multi-sport court," which just looked like a big room with faux wood flooring. All of the lab heads were dressed to impress in their unique de-signer lab suits. Rae scanned the faces for Evermore. He wasn't there, but she did discover that many of the lab heads were remarkably younger than she had expected. She guessed the mean age to be late thirties, early forties, and noticed that the length of their facial hair correlat-ed to their age. Those in their early thirties had a small hairy patch under their chin or extra-long sideburns. At forty it was worn shaggy around the mouth, and by fifty it had covered the whole face and was starting to have some length to it. Rae wasn't the only one without facial hair, but she was the only woman. As she approached the group of eight men chattering away and exchanging contact info, they quieted slightly, and she could hear her name within the murmur. She ignored them and coolly walked past to sit in a cold poly-carbon chair at the far end of the semicircle.

As she waited, Rae wondered if the others were as skeptical as she felt, but she couldn't decide if Evermore's odd choice of venue made her more curious or doubtful. Five minutes before eleven the elevator doors parted; ev-eryone in the room seemed to hold their breath at once and release it when they saw that the person who rolled into the room was not Evermore. He was a Norwegian built like a cheese sample: a white cube of cheddar on a toothpick. He had a high forehead that ended in a thinning, medium-length cut of platinum-blond hair, and a chiseled jaw, outlined by a chinstrap beard. "Good morning," he said with only a slight accent as he rolled across the room in a skeletal-assist chair. Bands of cushioned armature ran down each of his legs, connecting him to a self-balancing two-wheeled apparatus that held him in a standing position. He crossed the room to the chair-free gap beside Rae and "sat down." The apparatus bent his knees and lowered his ankles to the ground while positioning the wheels behind him, forming a tripod.

A full-bearded man sitting on Rae's left leaned around her and asked, "You're Asbjorn Breivik?"

"That's right," said the Norwegian.

"I'm Dr. Theodore Giordano. It's such a pleasure to meet you. I was at your solar station last year; what a wonderful piece of design." He offered his hand, and when Asbjorn shook it, the old Italian's arm brushed across Rae's chest.

Rae scooted her chair back and said, "Excuse me," in a tone that started to accuse him but finished with courtesy. Before the encounter could escalate, it was interrupted by a chorus of vibrating electronic cicadas, followed by the fluttering wing beats of lab coats being flipped open. Rae pretended to check her Omni's dark screen as she read over Giordano's shoulder:

> **E.Evermore:** Change of location. Meet me on B4. Poolside. No need for swimming apparel.

She remembered Ashley's strange reaction when she asked if the meeting was by the pool. *He knew Evermore was going to switch locations,* Rae thought. *I wonder what else he knows?* A few of the scientists shot each other annoyed looks, but they stood nonetheless. One murmured, "Non-sense. We're all here, couldn't he just come to us?"

"He wants to show off his wealth," one of them surmised.

A shorter man whom Rae recognized from the flight to Nili Fossae said, "Evermore's just *trying* to be different."

While they each reacted individually, they moved toward the elevator as a group. Rae forced herself to be objective and became amused by the whole thing. *So what if we have to change locations. He's the one paying us, so what if he decides to waste our time. He has already proven he can afford the best facility and the best scientists; he probably just wants us to all arrive at the same time.* Rae imagined the awkward wait and the rolling lines of small talk as each person arrived separately, but then she decided that all that could be avoided by being the last to show up.

Stepping into the crowded elevator, Rae noticed a small plaque that read, "Max Load 15 Persons." On a normal day six would have felt like a crowd, but no one wanted to be left behind. All eyes were on her as she entered, and after she turned her back she could still feel them scrutinizing her, and worse. She was the only woman, again. And again her options were to ignore the scent of testosterone that filled the elevator like the rotten-egg stink of a gas leak, or fight them all.

*I can't castrate the population of Mars, but I could cut off my left breast. Then at least they would recognize me as an Amazon.*

Someone behind her touched her shoulder lightly and said, "Hi, I'm Hugo Voss."

Rae turned her head and made a flash judgment: he wasn't networking, he was hitting on her. She turned back to face the doors. In the reflection she watched his smile fall from his face. "I don't believe we've met—" he tried again. The doors opened, and a humid breath poured into the cramped elevator.

"Dr. Rachael Dahlia," Evermore said as if he were happy to see her. He reached out his hand, and their eyes locked. "So glad you could make it in time for opening day. I trust you had a pleasant journey from Chasma Australe?"

His green eyes, which seemed intent on piercing the mystery of the infinite unknown, gazed out from beneath bushy black eyebrows. Her body relaxed as she stepped toward him. He shook her hand warmly, and she felt a spark, a tiny electric shock. She was star-struck for sure, but there was more; Evermore wasn't just regurgitating some phony introduction, he had asked an honest question, recognized her, and knew her.

"It was fine, thanks." She forced herself not to say how honored she felt.

He gestured toward the narrow patio between the wall and the edge of the pool, where an eleven- or twelve-year-old boy stood waiting, and turned to greet the next doctor. "Dr. Voss. . ."

*It's a threshold*, Rae realized. *Being first allowed him to welcome us into the space. But holding it here. . .* She still didn't know what that was supposed to achieve.

There were two rectangles drawn in crayon on the pink tile wall as big as the OmniWatch "chalkboards" her professors had used at UMars. As she neared the rectangles, the young boy looked at her, wrote something on his Omni, and looked back up to the approaching Dr. Voss. She remembered the boy from the boarding area at the centrifuge station on Phobos during her last flight back from the South Pole, but she had assumed he was traveling with the older couple she had labeled as tourists. His ID badge said "Samuel Reznick." *I'll give you the benefit of the doubt, Evermore, but you must know how bad this looks.* Samuel caught her staring and gave her a curt of nod in greeting. *His skin is perfect*, she thought. *You wait, Samuel, puberty is just around the corner.* In her peripheral vision she saw Hugo

Voss approaching her again.

"I'm sorry. I shouldn't have touched you in the elevator. Honestly, I just wanted to introduce myself, I never—"

"It's fine," she said. In the past she used to explain that being on Mars felt like being surrounded by hungry predators all the time. During her freshman year at UMars she had tired of being prey and decided to train them. Within a week she had a retinue of men jumping through hoops at the chance of a date, but the problem they presented was too easily solved, and she became bored after half a semester.

"Friends?" Hugo Voss extended his hand.

For a moment she considered training him, but she could tell he was a five-minute mystery at best.

She ignored his hand and said, "Please stand somewhere else."

After Evermore had welcomed the final doctor into the pool area, he approached the crudely drawn whiteboards, and the doctors formed a tight semicircle around him. For the first time Rae realized what Evermore was wearing under his old, off-white lab coat: Mismatched tube socks sprouted from worn sheepskin slippers and snuck under the elastic ankle bands of a pair of gray sweatpants. There was a mustard stain on his left thigh, and tucked into the waistband was a white (honestly, it was gray) T-shirt with hints of yellowish sweat stains around the neck. The worn lab coat had mysterious bulges in each of the pockets, but the only visible item was an eight-pack of crayons in his breast pocket.

Rae forgot all of the reasons she had risked her career to come here and decided to go back to Kander and Jansen. *Frankly, Doc, I'm disappointed,* she imagined telling him. *I came here expecting a genius with his shit together, and what I see is a rich jackass in the accoutrements of a midlife-crisis cliché.* In her imagination he turned his piercing green eyes on her and answered, *"Do you imagine I had the attention and funds to create the biggest building in Nili Terradome but somehow forgot about appearances when I got dressed this morning? Do you think I can't afford nicer clothes, or that I don't care how I look? Did you even notice my new haircut?"*

She had.

*Then what are you trying to communicate?*

Without so much as a sign from Evermore the quiet side conversations died down until there was complete silence. Samuel unfolded the only chair, which Evermore sat in and crossed his legs. The semicircle of eleven scientists standing around him shifted from foot to foot awkwardly. Evermore allowed the tension to build, but the look on his face seemed just as expectant as those waiting for him.

*Is this some kind of role reversal? You sit while we all stand over you, dressed in our expensive suits while you're in the outfit of a retired bachelor? Maybe you don't want us to see a genius; you don't want the pedestal we've put you on.* She looked at him and for the first time saw beyond the stories, beyond the headlines, beyond her own expectations, and looked at a man. Just a man in his late fifties with dark-green eyes, a fresh haircut, and a second chance to do something meaningful. She imagined that knowing hint-of-a-smile to be saying, "Forget it all. Forget who you expect me to be and imagine, for a moment, the weight of what you expect me to achieve. It's all too high, and we can't start there."

Rae looked down at Evermore, so calm and collected sitting there. *You're a rocket about to launch, how can you possibly be so calm? Are you really that confident?*

Evermore ran a hand through his short salt-and-pepper hair and said, "Why are we here?"

Rae had to force herself not to raise her hand and shout out the answer: *Because this is the lowest floor of the building, and we, as a team, have to start at the bottom!*

When no one risked an answer, Evermore followed it

with another question, "Why does Evermore Industries exist?"

The black man she had followed into the elevator spoke up without raising a hand. "According to the mission, E.I. is 'dedicated to the future of humanity.'"

"While you are accurate as always, Ariel, those are just words."

Rae realized why he looked so familiar; Ariel was the lead programmer and designer behind the Hakaru app.

"Just words," Evermore repeated. "What has Evermore Industries actually done? What has it built, or designed, or discovered?"

The Norwegian raised his hand, but Evermore cut him off. "Not yet, Asbjorn."

He opened a pocket and took out an old TV remote from the twenties. He pressed the largest circular button in the center of the remote, and their Omnis, all at once, beeped a loss of signal alert. It was a chilling noise that made Rae feel stranded and alone every time she heard it. The sound was followed by each doctor pulling out his Omni and staring at the "no signal" icon in disbelief. Rae resisted the urge, as she knew her Omni was still off.

"You are all old enough to remember what this is," Evermore said, holding up the remote. "It's so strange that we ever made a device that only had one function: to control a TV. Even more bizarre is that that function only worked on one device. Obviously, it's not a TV remote any longer; a clever young man named Ashley took out its guts and replaced them with an Omni jammer.

"I appreciate your willingness to meet me in this unorthodox setting, and in answer to the question, Why are we here? — truth be told, this is the only location in the building where I could jam your Omnis to prevent them from sending or receiving data."

*Dr. Evermore, you are a puzzle more interesting than any Hakaru I will ever play.*

Evermore stuffed the jammer into one pocket and took a box of crayons out of another.

"This is also the only level where the Martian porcelain walls were left exposed," he said, dumping two crayons into his hand before closing the box and putting it away.

The rectangles and crayons finally made sense. *Of course,* Rae thought. *The jammer would break a OmniWatch whiteboard.*

Evermore held a red crayon in his left hand and a blue in his right, stood and approached the pink tile wall. "I have come to believe that when my mind is solely accommodated in one hemisphere, I invite unoriginality into the other," he said.

"Just as electricity arcs between two poles," Evermore's right and left hands simultaneously, awkwardly, drew plus and minus symbols, "when your cerebral hemispheres are alternately utilized, an arc of creativity flashes across the gap." His hands got in each other's way as he drew opposite arcs of wax between the symbols. "Please, utilize this facility in whatever method you choose, so that you remain dynamic and creative. The endeavor that we attempt requires only those two things: vibrancy and creativity. I'll repeat myself: Be aware of existing within a singular mindset. Take risks, balance your extremes, and together we will arc across the void between speculation and actualization."

The diatribe received blank stares, and the unanswered question, *What does E.I. do? What are we doing here?* still clung to the group like a wet bathing suit.

"Evermore Industries is a sole proprietorship owned and funded by me and through the support of anonymous investors. What you don't know is that our goal is to create a vessel capable of transgalactic travel at faster-than-light speeds."

There were grimaces and skeptical looks between the doctors, but nothing close to what Rae would have expected from a group of highly educated scientists. She wanted to bark a belligerent "What?" but the fear of standing out and looking foolish held her back. The moment passed, and Evermore continued, "As you are well aware, this is a feat that physically cannot be done. Even if we were to find exotic materials that could be accelerated to the speed of light, the stray hydrogen atoms in the void of space would have the relative energy and effect of running headlong into large hadron collider.

"And yet... here we are. Maybe you're waiting for some explanation or demonstration to change your mind, some magic show revealing how I plan to bend the laws of the known universe to allow a vessel to access distant star systems in a matter of days rather than centuries. Maybe you even assume that to convince our investors I must have given them some shred of evidence, and indeed I must have." Evermore carefully examined the crowd, his eyes conveying an innuendo to no one in particular. The group had begun to look suspicious and impatient. "But perhaps... perhaps there is something, some yet-to-be-discovered mystery of the universe that will allow us to succeed. Isn't that assumption the same force that has driven innovation for thousands of years?" No one answered him.

Evermore continued, "In spite of the fact that I wholeheartedly agree with you that FTL —faster-than-light — travel is merely speculation on a scale of supreme naïveté, I expect us to, one day, reach some Goldilocks planet in some distant star system. Not our children or our grandchildren. Us. We will reach that planet.

"To answer my own question, the reason we are here today is to begin that search. Whether you believe it to be possible or not is irrelevant. I believe that anything can be achieved with either unlimited time or unlimited funds. In spite of the fact that we have neither, I still expect the impossible from each of you."

An older man whom Rae recognized from the cover of *Speculative Science* spoke up: "So if it's impossible, why don't we focus our efforts on something possible?"

Evermore held out his crayon. "Building a car from a crayon is impossible. FTL is only impossible in that we cannot create it with the tools and truths we currently possess. Therefore it remains speculation until it can be *proven* impossible."

The man snapped, "There is plenty of proof, and the question still stands: What are we all doing here?"

"I'll show you." With his left hand, Evermore wrote "Tools" on the wall in red crayon, and a shoulder's width to the right with the other hand he wrote "Truths" in blue. He then, with both hands at once, drew two circles around the words. When he had finished, the two circles had a gap in between them the width of his hand. Evermore pulled out a third crayon and wrote "FTL" between the circles in violet.

"This is a map, a diagram of our current world. These two circles, Tools and Truths, are approximate representations of everything humans have created, built, or designed, and every idea or concept we have observed, felt, measured, or somehow unanimously agreed belongs in reality. You'll note that neither of the circles are big enough to encompass FTL.

"Some of you will be focusing your efforts to extend what we know, or the current truth of our reality." He drew a series of lines stemming from the blue Truths circle like spider legs, and labeled them with numbers. "... and the rest of you will be focusing on designing tools to both measure and manipulate our new truths." He drew more red lines and numbered them. "When each of us has taken our specific project to its fullest capacity, we will have extended the circles of possibility to encompass our vision." He connected the dots at each of the tips of the spider legs, drawing a bigger circle around both the

Tools and Truths circles, and now both circles were large enough that they encompassed "FTL." As he was numbering the departments in the Tools or Truths circles, Rae noticed that Lab Seven was listed in both.

Evermore continued to speak for what could have been half an hour or two and a half hours. He talked about various aspects of his vision. How, down the road, each of them could be running their own branch of Evermore Industries. He addressed the fact that, on the whole, they were a younger crowd than would usually be hired to run a lab. He called Kander and Jansen the kings of scientific growth and said that their subjects would never risk presenting an idea beyond the kings' comprehension. "I will challenge your ideas," he told them, "but I will not behead you. I recognize that you are my heirs and invite you to usurp me with your idealism, your curiosity, and your insight."

Raising his voice above the applause, Evermore said, "Your aides are waiting in the lobby with your first assignment. If you have any questions or comments, feel free to send them to me directly." He pushed the crayons back into his pockets and fumbled with the remote until all of their Omnis chirped the soothing string of notes that celebrated their reconnection with Cloud9. Everyone reflexively looked down at their screen, and by the time they looked up Evermore and Samuel had walked to the elevator. A few of the doctors tried to follow him in, but Samuel held out his hand in a gesture that was disproportionately threatening for his size.

The crowd that formed around the elevator was interested in introductions and networking, but Rae waited anxiously for the doors to open.

*I'm a synthetic bioengineer, what benefit could I possibly lend to transgalactic travel?* she wondered. *Was Dr. Kander right, is Evermore just using me to build his brand?*

*But the way he talked about the new generation...* A shiver of

excitement ran through her. I feel as if he sees our potential in a way Kander never will.

*Too bad I already decided to go back to Kander*, she thought,
deriding herself for flip-flopping so quickly.

She jammed her finger into the call button a third time
and realized why it wasn't working. *Time to make a friend.*

In the lobby a group of young assistants looked expectantly in her direction, but Ashley was not among them.

Hugo Voss said, "It was a pleasure, Dr. Dahlia," as he
walked away toward his assistant.

*I guess I'm waiting here if I ever want to see my lab.*

# CHAPTER SIX

# Inertia

## Ashley

From Ashley's vantage point on the far side of the pool behind the door to the women's changing room, he could see everything. The plan for the assistants was to wait in the lobby, but he had been helping the Doc research the lab heads' ideals, styles, motives, and beliefs for the last two weeks: there was no way he would miss this.

The first phase had gone as planned. The Doc had instructed the team to gather in one location, and just as they got comfortable, he upset their homeostasis with a change of plans.

When Ashley asked why, Evermore had said, "A mind off balance is more amenable to new ideas."

After Evermore welcomed them into the new situation, he made the big reveal, then carefully started teasing a thread from each of their personal dreams and goals, interlacing them into his own. Ashley's only criticism was that the presentation was based more in poetry than reality, but that didn't seem to bother anyone, judging from the volume of their applause.

Evermore called over them, "Your aides are waiting in the lobby with your first assignment. If you have any questions or comments, feel free to send them to me directly." He pushed the crayons back into his pockets and turned off the Cloud jammer.

After Evermore left, Rae was the first to push her finger repeatedly into the elevator button. "Shit," he cursed under his breath. "Ashley, you are so fucking dumb." He tried willing one of the other doctors to go over and join her, and to his surprise she left the elevator for a moment and quickly made friends with a doctor named Hugo Voss, and the two went into the elevator together. He would have to risk being seen. When the light above the lift rested on the "G," Ashley emerged from the women's changing room. Faking that *I-belong-here* confidence, he walked across the pool area and called the elevator. He imagined himself in a spy movie making the ballsy move to escape the scene, but it worked too well. Even when two doctors who accompanied him to the ground floor looked at him, their gaze just slid off; they didn't recognize him as a person. When they stepped out he could see Rae waiting for him. She looked angry, but no less beautiful. I wish I had thought to bring her assignment with me, he thought, lightly touching the 7.

As the lift rose, he messaged her:

> **A.Rephaireal:** I'm going to be late.

When the doors opened, Ashley dashed across the empty lab to the only piece of furniture, a lonely workstation. As he snatched the assignment folder from its top drawer he heard the elevator doors sliding closed. Turning, he sprinted back, but it was clear he wouldn't get there in time. Thinking only of the blockage sensors, he threw the folder at what remained of the crack between the doors. The folder flew through the air like a giant throwing star, deftly slipping through the crack with millimeters to spare, but it failed to trip sensors, and the doors finished closing. Ashley hung his head in defeat as the elevator descended with Lab Seven's secret assignment. His Omni chirped with a text.

**R.Dahlia:** You're already late. Where are you?

**A.Rephaireal:** I'm sorry, Rae, I'll be there soon.

**R.Dahlia:** Let's get out of that habit right now. My name is Dr. Dahlia.

**A.Rephaireal:** Sorry, Dr. Dahlia, my timing was off. I'll be there soon.

A picture is worth a thousand words, but her silence was worth a thousand pictures, and he had time to imagine each one as the elevator made a second trip to the pool before climbing all the way back to the seventh floor. Ashley held his breath as the doors opened, then released it in a sigh of relief as he saw the manila folder labeled "CLASSIFIED! EYES ONLY! DSc. Rachael Dahlia" on the floor at the back of the elevator.

Inside he avoided looking at himself in the reflective doors. Then, ashamed even of his low self-esteem, he forced himself to turn and face the reflection and stare at his too-round head that made him look simple, and into his eyes so close together it made him appear cross-eyed even though he wasn't. Brushing aside his light-brown hair, he stood up straight and faced himself. "Bring it on," he said. His green eyes burned for just a moment, but as the doors parted he slouched with embarrassment at almost being caught talking to himself. Then he caught himself slouching and stood up straight again.

Aside from the receptionist, Dr. Dahlia waited alone in the wide open lobby. As he walked toward her she looked as if she had something to say, but instead she glared at him in silence. When he was a boy, Ashley had had a book of ancient Greek myths. The artist had drawn the gorgon Medusa with wide, exaggerated eyes. Beneath the illustration was a caption explaining that Medusa's gaze could turn men to stone. Rae had those same eyes. They unnerved him, and though he didn't want to stare he found he couldn't look away.

"I'm sorry for the wait, Doctor," he said, trying to release the tension. "So, you've met the man, you heard his vision, do you regret choosing Evermore Industries?"

The question shifted something in her hard stare, and he thought he saw a hint of fear beneath the anger. *She's afraid?* The realization surprised and, actually, comforted him. *Your skin isn't so thick after all. Maybe eventually I'll get to see the woman I met during our interview.*

Rae almost said something, glanced at the receptionist who was absent in the glow of his Omni, and continued, "Do you have any idea how humiliating it was to have each of the other lab heads see me waiting here? I almost walked out. Can you imagine how your conversation with 'the Doc' would have gone?"

*If she keeps frowning like that, she's going to run out of face.* Ashley tried not to smile at his own thought.

"You wouldn't leave before seeing whatever is in this secret document, would you?" He waggled it at her.

She held her hand out for it.

"Not yet. You took so long in HR I didn't get to give you the tour of the other facilities, and after that lecture you must be hungry," he said. This time she followed him obediently into the elevator. Once inside, Ashley said, "Though it may not appear impressive by our earthly standards, the E.I. building stands twelve stories above street level. Two taller than Kander and Jansen Laboratories, and six higher than your alma mater, the University of Mars. You've already seen the rec facility and the pool—" Ashley reached out for the B2 button, which had the fork and knife beside it, but Rae intercepted his hand, grabbed his finger, and mashed it into the 7. The elevator immediately rose.

"I'm not hungry," she said, holding her hand out for the folder again.

He gave it to her as the doors opened on Laboratory Seven.

## Rae

In spite of the huge rec facility and pool, Rae's experience set her up to expect a traditional Martian laboratory: a low-ceilinged, labyrinthine series of hallways and thin room dividers. Resources in the terradome were rare and therefore more valuable than back on Earth, and space would only get more limited year after year. At least Mars had the option of expanding into another terradome; back on Earth the only options were building higher and digging deeper. The doors parted, and before them was a room the size of the building's footprint. It was big enough to house two hundred workstations, and nothing interrupted the windows to the east, south, and west. And not even K&J Labs was tall enough to obstruct the view of the terradome's simulated landscape.

"There aren't any room dividers; how much of this..." And then she realized, *My lab isn't on the seventh floor, it is the seventh floor.* Rae stepped into the room and felt that same rush of freedom she got looking up at the stars at Chasma Australe. "Is it real?" She walked across the room to the far wall, searching the floor for the telltale edge of a VR screen.

Ashley didn't answer; instead, he waited for her to reach the western wall unhindered.

*All this for me?* she thought, but even as her imagination starting filling the space with equipment and projects, another part overtook it and wondered what Evermore wanted in exchange. All the freedom she had felt melted into paranoia as she wondered where the confines of this new arrangement began. *Just because I can't see the walls doesn't mean they aren't there. This might be just another cage.* The hollow inside her expanded to fill the room, and she felt impossibly small in its immensity. *This doesn't feel right. I'm not supposed to be here. What will Evermore do to me when he figures out I'm not as special as he thinks I am?*

Ashley said, "I imagine you'll want to work through lunch. I'd be happy to pop down to the cafeteria to grab you something while you take a look at your assignment."

As she turned back to him he asked, "Where's your ID badge?" A look of realization crossed his face and he said, "During our date at the Relativity Lounge when we started joking about some of Evermore's eccentricities, I thought you took it a little too far. Actually, you were pretty disrespectful. I wanted to say something then, but our conversation..." he paused, and she cut him off.

"It wasn't a date."

He was not sidetracked. "It made me think that you might be undecided about working here; is that still the case?"

*That's not a question; it's an accusation,* Rae thought. "Where do you think Evermore will place you if my answer is no?"

Ashley was taken aback.

"I've caught you in a lie, Mr. Rephaireal: you said I 'took sooo long in HR,' but I was only there a few minutes; where were you?" She crossed her arms and waited for him to answer.

Ashley spread his hands in a gesture of defeat. "What are you doing, Rae? I thought you wanted this job. Look at this fucking room, how are you not interested?"

Rae smiled, took a flippant tone and said, "Relax, Ashley, I just wanted to be sure E.I. was a good fit. This is the last test," she held up the folder.

He seemed to take her advice and coolly took out his Omni. "I may have lied, but you're trespassing on E.I.

property and about to commit corporate subterfuge."

Rae looked down at the folder and wondered if he'd really make the call, then noticed the instructions on the back. It had a three-tiered decryption key: The first unlocked based on its proximity to her Omni, but the second two required an Evermore Industries ID badge and a DNA sample, which she had yet to give them.

*I couldn't unlock this if I wanted to.*

She crossed the room to the single workstation and tossed the folder on it. "If you're so dedicated to doing everything by the book, then why don't you escort me down to HR so I can be fully assimilated."

Their ride back down the elevator was silent, and Ashley seemed embarrassed for escalating the situation so quickly. *Perfect*, she thought.

When the doors opened, Ashley said quietly, "I'm starving. While you're here I'm going down to the caf. Can I get you anything?"

"Nothing fried, and I'm not in the mood for hexapro."

He frowned. "E.I. doesn't serve any real meat, but I wouldn't worry about the hex; they get it from a vendor who guarantees that it's mostly grasshopper and cricket."

"Personally, I don't care if it's all mealworm; I'm just not in the mood."

He nodded. "I'll be back shortly."

"Bring me a coffee."

The HR department was surprised to see her, but her representative had gotten the process down to a science, and she was done within a few minutes and returned to Lab Seven as soon as she was able. When the elevator doors closed, Rae was alone but for a workstation, an ergonomic chair, and a short wire-mesh trash bin. The feeling that she didn't belong there still worried her, but she summoned a hardness, pushed everything from her mind, and focused on putting one foot in front of the other.

Crossing the lab, she placed her Omni on the workstation's surface. The Hakaru she had been working on appeared, and the ergonomic chair automatically adjusted to her. As the workstation completed the info-sync, a pop-up appeared: "Error. The ePaper file you are attempting to drag-and-drop is protected."

She raised the folder to her lips and lapped the corner of the file like a cat sampling bad milk. As she licked the roof of her mouth, trying to wipe the taste of the DNA sampler off her tongue, the manila cover changed and a short letter appeared.

From the desk of Everett Evermore DSc.
CEO Evermore Industries | Floor 12 | ext #112
Date: October 12th, 2049
To: Rachael Dahlia DSc.
Lab Seven Principal Researcher | ext. #107
Subject: Lab 7 Research Assignment No. 1

I would, in the same instant, like to extend both gratitude and salutations at your agreement to join the team at Evermore Industries.

Being a synthetic bioengineer, I supposed you may be wondering what you are doing here purportedly working on faster-than-light travel. No doubt you are aware of the field's important advancement, Crellinger's light. Victoria Crellinger's work has given rise to many applications for both the scientific and civilian worlds, all of which rely on that same basic principal of organic cells communicating along beams of light. Along those lines, your first assignment at Evermore Industries is to take her work a step further by discovering, manufacturing, and producing a trans-biological exchange of information beyond the electromagnetic spectrum.

Rae felt the floor drop out from beneath her. She had assumed so much of Evermore's speech was poetic hyperbole, but everything he had said about expecting the impossible from them became suddenly concrete. *He told us to usurp him, but I never expected my first assignment would be to knock my hero off her pedestal. No, it's worse than being knocked off. If Crellinger's groundbreaking discovery was lapped so soon after it was made, I wouldn't be showing her up, I'd be erasing her name from history.*

I expect a progress report every two weeks. Please save your reports in the E.I. Cloud Net folder on your desk, and if you don't hear from me assume that you're doing a great job. In addition, during our first week I will be conducting face-to-face interviews with each of the principal researchers. Yours is scheduled for next Monday. You may arrive at the 12th floor no later than 10 a.m. I have long looked forward to us meeting as peers.

I hope you find our facilities both comfortable and sufficient. If you should need anything, be it personal or professional, do not hesitate to have Ashley order it for you.

While we're on the subject of Ashley, I request that you take good care of him. He is very dear to me. When we first met I immediately recognized his intellect and took him under my wing, but I could not shelter him from his less than nourishing upbringing.

Later in life I tried to use my clout to get him into the University of Mars, but they did not accept him. This remains a point of shame for him, and I urge you to avoid the topic. All this is to say that I have spent a great deal of time teaching him and request that, on top of your other responsibilities, you continue mentoring him where I left off. Doting aside, Ashley is a font of talent and understands the language of technology far better than I ever will; it would be a waste to use him as a mere secretary. Thank you in advance.

~*Dr. Everett Evermore*

Postscript: I apologize that this may come too late and if it's unwarranted, but do not directly lick the DNA sampler; it could have been tampered with or poisoned.

# CHAPTER SEVEN

# Regression

## Rae

Rae put her assignment in the bottom drawer of her desk slowly, as if her limbs were weighted down by the heaviness of the task before her. She tried to force the idea that anything was impossible from her mind as soon as she felt it corrupt her attitude, but it was too late. *Evermore, what does a "trans-biological exchange of information beyond the electromagnetic spectrum" have to do with faster-than-light travel?*

*The "beyond" implies no particle or wave, leaving only strong interactions on the quantum level, or gravitational. I have a hard time believing that any living thing can feel or sense anything on the quantum level, but while we can feel gravitational force, it's already proven to be limited to the speed of light.*

*He didn't say it needed to be faster than light, just beyond the EM spectrum. Okay, so, let's assume we do this thing: my new team creates a multicellular organism that communicates using gravitons (and we also discover the graviton particle). Evermore's ultimate goal is faster-than-light travel, but even if we send our little organisms out into space and apply infinite energy to get them up to light speed, they still wouldn't be able to communicate with each other because of the time barrier.*

Rae had reached the limit of her knowledge of physics and her patience for pointless tasks. *Does Evermore really want to use me for publicity like Kander suggested, or is this some kind of revenge for the house arrest purgatory that I helped send him to?* But even as she said it she remembered the warmth of his greeting. The way he said her name was as old friends meeting after years apart. Is he so evolved as to find some gratitude in his misfortune?

Moving of their own accord, her hands picked up her Omni and started scrolling through her contacts. They jumped to the *T*s and tapped a name: The Chemist.

*I can't do this alone,* she thought. *I can't do it at all if I feel like this. I just need a boost for one week. Then I'll be back to normal.*

She held down the text-to-speech button, said, "I'm hungry. I'd like to place an order," and hit "send."

"You've got to be kidding me!" Ashley said as he emerged from the elevator with a cafeteria tray covered in food.

"Er... Never mind," she told her Omni, pretending someone was on the other line. "He's finally back."

"I'm sorry, the caf was crowded! Literally everyone but Evermore is down there, talking about his presentation," Ashley said, setting a coffee and a salad on the edge of her workstation.

She pried off the lid. "How did you know I drink my coffee black?"

"Because of your bitter outlook." He smiled.

*Don't smile,* she thought, *staring at his dimples. Please. Don't complicate this.*

Her Omni chimed with a text.

> **T.Chemist:** "Meet me at our usual spot in three days."

She stabbed the disposable bamboo fork into her salad. "What's next?"

"Hiring your team. But what are we working on? What did Evermore say?" he asked, forking some "chicken" strips into his mouth.

"Evermore asked me to build a sentient organism capable of living at speeds faster than light," she said, carefully watching his face for his first reaction. It was plain to see he believed her, which told her he didn't know what their assignment really was. But his face was all screwed up and confused.

"That doesn't—" He looked at her and realized she was testing him. "What do you think is going on here?"

She swiveled her chair to face him and crossed her arms. "You tell me."

They both stared at each other for a moment, but Ashley put it together, "You think Evermore is up to something, and you're so egotistical you think you're at the center of it."

"It's not ego, it's data. According to you, Evermore changed his plea to guilty because of me. Years later I receive a personal invitation to apply for a position I have no experience with. Next I'm interviewed by Evermore's student, who is then given to me, and I'm asked to take him under my wing." *Funny, that last part should have surprised him, but he just looks angry.* "I'm at the center of something, Ashley."

Ashley threw his hands up in frustration. "Where's the conspiracy? You impressed him, he offered you a job, and—" His words cut out.

She was going to wait him out, but the way his lips clamped shut changed her mind. "Ashley, this arrangement," she gestured at them both, "isn't going to work unless we are 100 percent honest with each other. Starting now."

"Truth? Okay. Evermore didn't make the choice to hire you, I did. He told me it was time to start apprenticing with someone else and gave me three options. You were the one I chose. Or, if we're being 100 percent honest, whoever I spoke to at the Martian South Pole was the one I chose; she and I could work together."

*Who is this kid? One minute he's a nothing, the next he's...* She felt her guard slipping and held on tighter. She forced herself to look into his eyes and lie. "If we're being honest, I was playing you. There is nothing between us. There will never be anything between us. I'm—" Don't say "sorry." "—willing to continue working with you, but I require formality. The jokes, the tardy delivery of my assignment, the casualness has to stop." With the verbal knife lodged firmly in his heart, she waited for him to hate her, but instead he grinned like an idiot. He wasn't hiding behind it; he felt this joy with his whole body, and it felt like a slap in the face to her authority. That smile made her feel like a weak, inconsequential child. She felt herself spiraling out of control, trapped in a dome sixty-something-million kilometers from home, balanced on the edge of success and defeat, alone outside and empty inside. She lashed out for stability by slapping Ashley across the face.

## Ashley

He threw his hands up in frustration. "Where's the conspiracy? You impressed him, he offered you a job and—" His words cut out. *But I hired you.*

"Ashley, this arrangement," she gestured at them both, "isn't going to work unless we are 100 percent honest with each other. Starting now."

*She needs to be in control. If she finds out I had the power to hire her, it's over. Too bad I'm an awful liar.* "Truth? Okay. Evermore didn't make the choice to hire you, I did. He told me it was time to start apprenticing with someone else and gave me three options. You were the one I chose. Or, if we're being 100 percent honest, whoever I spoke to at the Martian South Pole was the one I chose; she and I could work together."

Her face hardened, and the Medusa eyes were back. "If we're being honest, I was playing you. There is nothing between us. There will never be anything between us. I'm... willing to continue working with you, but I require formality. The jokes, the tardy delivery of my assignment, the casualness has to stop."

He could see that she wanted to believe it, but there was a loneliness so enormous that it towered over the walls surrounding her. *She wants to control me so she can control herself. She's lying.* He flipped everything she said and played in back in his mind: *There's something between us. There will always be something between us.* He couldn't help but smile at the thought that one day, at the very least, she would let him in close enough to smell the scent of her hair.

That's when she hit him.

* * * * * *

*His eyes were closed, but he could smell the wine on her breath. He held half a sob deep in his chest, but a silent procession of tears escaped before he was able to control them. The sting of her hand on his face didn't recede; it increased and melted out from the point of impact until his entire head was pounding with waves of pressure and pain. He tried to hide his face so she wouldn't see him cry. She hated that. He told her what she wanted to hear: "I'm sorry, Momma." He could hear the old linoleum crackle beneath her wobbling weight.*

*"Sorry for WHAT?" she challenged. It wasn't a question of what he had done: he was a bad child. A forgetful, ungrateful boy. He was the reason his father left.*

*He tried to remember what it was that he had done: Don't wet the bed, don't talk back, don't slam the door, don't make a mess, don't leave the lights on. Why'd you hit me?*

* * * * * *

"Asshole," Rae said, hastily gathering her work papers. She walked to the elevator, slammed her hand into the button, and waited. Four long seconds passed. She avoided looking anywhere but straight ahead at the E.I. logo engraved on the doors.

Ashley stood. *Say something. Anything, or she's gone forever.* The elevator doors opened... and closed. As she disappeared from sight, Ashley's cheek throbbed, but the only pain he experienced was in his chest. He sat down on the floor. *I'm so goddamn stupid.*

Evermore had often told him that someday he would need to get his balls back. It had always embarrassed him, and it pissed him off to be called something less than a man, but he was less than a man. He replayed the scene in his head. *Fuck that. I stood my ground! I stood there facing her fury and her fire. I knew she was lying, and I chose not to eat her bullshit.*

His heart began to beat faster, and he started to sweat. *That was Rae. That was the real Rae. Raw and real and hot.* He thought of that loneliness behind her wall of fire and thought, *I had a crush on you before, but now I think I'm in love.*


## Rae


Rae was enormously dissatisfied at how peacefully the elevator doors slid shut. On the ground floor she held up her professional air as she walked across the lobby, nodded politely to the pretentious blond receptionist, and exited the E.I. building. It was just past one in the afternoon, and the digitally enhanced sun shone in her eyes. At the corner she turned west down Maple Avenue. A private courier zipped past on a souped-up scooter, making her feel slow, but it felt good; everything else in her life was moving too fast.

After a distance, she settled into the anonymity only a city can provide, her shoulders relaxed, and she allowed herself to feel the event for the first time, but the emotions came all at once. The memory of Ashley's vacant, terrified eyes, which seemed to be looking somewhere else completely. The feeling of power and control that she had stolen through violence now turned into compassion and shame. The sound of the slap almost brought tears to her eyes, but then she remembered that sleazy, overconfident smile.

*It's amazing how clueless men are. Put yourself in my shoes, Ashley Rephaireal. You're part of a minority, and everyone you work for looks at you with X-ray eyes. Do you have any idea how many fantasies I'm probably in? Do you even have a concept of what would happen if I indulged in a single one of them? From where I stand I'm one of them, but once I cross that line I become a different animal and I can never go back.*

But she was the one who had lost control and shown him that animal. *I baited him with my flirting. I led him into an emotional ambush, and I punished him for it. I should resign. Ugh, I would have hit me! I would have at least expected him to get angry, but it never crossed his mind. I wish I could know what he was thinking.*

In spite of herself she smiled as she remembered his grin. She thought back to their phone conversation, back before he was Evermore's protégé, before he was so young, before he was even remotely connected to her career, when he could be the object of her fantasy.

A heavily bearded man in a lab coat walking the opposite direction down the street gave her a friendly nod as they passed. It was quick, but she saw him glance at her chest.

Rae gagged dramatically. *Ugh, why can't I just be a scientist?* A hollow opened in her heart and brought with it a loneliness, which she tried to crush under all the work she had ahead of her. Ashley was probably right. Evermore doesn't want anything from me but excellence.

She noticed Deimos, the smaller of Mars' moons,

speeding toward the western horizon. She watched it for a moment, wondering if it had passed in front of the sun, as it should, or behind the sun, since it was actually just an image created by the simulated environment. But then she realized that so was this large version of the sun, and she found that she no longer cared.

*I live on a world named after the god of war, orbited by his sons, Phobos and Deimos: fear and dread. This is no place for women who are anything less than Amazons.* She smiled. *Ashley certainly met my Amazon today.* But he had never actually tried to show her up. *He was just trying to hold his own, which is even more important now that he doesn't have anything to back it up. His relationship to Evermore was the only credentials he had. Maybe that's what Evermore was talking about when he asked me to take care of him.*

Rae looked around and realized she'd been aimlessly walking and didn't know where she'd ended up. She checked the map on her Omni. She was close to Kander and Jansen Laboratories. She had told Kander that she would make her decision by the end of the week. *I don't need that long; maybe I should tell him in person,* she thought, and oriented herself in the right direction.

After half a block she realized that her hand had been searching for something in her pocket, that she was looking for the square of folded aluminum foil. Her hand retracted, empty. *Three days.*

Rae arrived at the lonely, Sycamore-lined courtyard in front of Kander and Jansen Laboratories. The receptionist seemed to recognize and be surprised to see her. "Dr. Dahlia," he said. "You're not due at work until Friday."

"I'm aware. I was hoping to see Dr. Kander. If he's not available now, I'll make an appointment."

"Please, have a seat." He gestured at the chairs sprinkled around the courtyard. They were the same model as the ones at E.I.

She took out her Omni and opened the contacts list; the entry for the Chemist was still there. "Three days," it reminded her again. She closed it and selected "Ashley."

"Call or text?" asked a pop-up.

"Neither," she said, and put it away.

# CHAPTER EIGHT

# Daisies

**Ashley**

The doors to Lab Seven slid open, and the big fake yellow sun shone bright in Ashley's eyes as it crested the Alps to the east, as if the terradome were nestled somewhere in Liechtenstein where the mountain range was exactly the same height as the eastern wall of the Nili Fossae.

It was clear that although Rae had left early the day before, she hadn't finished working. The lab had been morphed by the early morning K&J delivery, which had outfitted Seven with big machines designed for little tasks; and work-space designers, who had moved through and subdivided the room into eight private workstations, with a common station in the middle. Though Rae's desk hadn't been touched, Ashley couldn't help but notice that she had included a workstation for him that faced the elevator doors. It was the only station with no view of the outside world.

When he saw that no one was there, he released the breath he had been holding and hastily placed a small bouquet of flowers on Rae's desk, hoping that they would convey the exact amount of "I'm sorry" without straying across the line into "Dear Rae, I'm desperately in love with you and even your perpetual loathing will suffice." It was a fine line, shaved finer given the rarity of flowers on Mars. In addition to saying "I'm sorry for your loss,"

Martian flowers modified the sentiment with "my love." "Get well soon, my love," or "Congratulations, my love!" He reasoned that any romantic connotation was removed by the fact that that they hadn't cost him a cent. Ashley happened to know an electro-botanist with a penchant for daisies. Besides, he had been raised a traditionalist, and even if grandmas don't get flowers on Mars, people still deserve something nice when you've been a jerk.

Ashley would have liked to write his entire thought process on the note, but he decided it was better to keep it short.

> Sorry for being an asshole. I hope we can start over.
>
> ~Ashley Raphairael

The moment the pen left the paper, it reformatted his handwriting into a boring, all-business sans-serif font.

## Rae

Rae arrived at Lab Seven later than she had intended to. She barely arrived before her first interview of the day, but even though she was in a rush, as the doors opened Rae was stopped in her tracks, overwhelmed by the glorious sight of her new science toys. In the midst of releasing a sigh, she choked on it as she stepped from the elevator and noticed a bouquet of daisies on the edge of her workstation. *Maybe they're from Evermore,* she hoped. Then she read the card. "Start over!" she scoffed. "Every man's dream: the restart button." She threw the bouquet in the trash, where the daisies looked up at her like the faces of hungry Unicef children. She carefully pulled them out and whispered an apology.

*Accepting the flowers is to accept his apology, but it wasn't entirely his fault, was it?* She took half of the bouquet and half the water and put both into a coffee cup from the trash and put it on Ashley's workstation. Now we're even.

Moments later, when Ashley stepped out of the elevator, he wasn't alone. Accompanying him was a man maybe fifteen years her senior. He was of average height, and his dark skin had a deep golden glow like antique furniture. He had dark hair, but none on his face. On his left ring finger was a wedding band.

"Good morning, Dr. Dahlia," Ashley said with a slight bow of his head. "This is your first appointment, Doct—"

"Dr. Cyrus Ma'at, welcome," she said, shaking his hand and leading him toward her workstation, which the designers had outfitted with two white poly-carbon chairs. "Please, join me."

She sat in the chair beside him instead of at her own on the other side of the workstation. She recited his résumé: "Dr. Ma'at, you have a master's degree in physics from the American University at Cairo, and a science doctorate in crystallography and material engineering from Oxford University. Why crystallography?"

"Well, my original interest was in solid-state physics, and then I fell in love with resonating frequencies, the fact that matter can be excited by sound and light. From this I began to wonder if there was another frequency beyond the electromagnetic spectrum that could affect matter."

That was the exact phrase in one of his hypotheses she'd read last night. The feeling of synchronicity had swept over her, and she knew that if she didn't hire him someone else at Evermore Industries would.

Ma'at continued, "I am not the only Muslim scientist, nor am I the only one interested in discovering the connection between the observable world and the truth of the Qur'an. But after publishing a hypothesis on how spiritual energy affects living matter, I was publicly humiliated and debased by many scientists. I realize now what a gift it was that Copernicus died before his life's work was deemed heretical. I have spent six years in limbo, but it was the speculative scientists who welcomed me into their community. With their help I was able to find an absence of evidence to support my theory, and I mean that as a good thing."

Rae stared at him. None of the other questions on her interview mattered anymore. She smiled and reached out to shake his hand. "You got the job."

He looked confused and on the edge of tears. "Why? What do you see?"

"I know how you feel. Evermore built this building as an opportunity to do something beyond science. I read your résumé, and I've skimmed your hypothesis on spiritual energy, and I see you as a man able and unafraid to look beyond. We need you in Lab Seven."

"I'm so glad you're able to see the sense of it," said the man on the other side of her workstation. His thick, unkempt brown hair didn't match his graying reddish eyebrows or sideburns. His eyes were sunken and dark, and his skin had the color and glossy sheen of wet paste. Rae subtly checked the time. Four-thirty. Rae nodded and took the interview in another direction. "How is it that you arrived on Mars?"

"I was hired to design a quantum vacuum zero-point engine."

"Like on the *Magellan*," Rae said. Not understanding her reference, he shook his head. "Arthur C. Clark...? Never mind, it's a made-up starship from a classic science-fiction novel."

He seemed offended. "I assure you, Dr. Dahlia, that this is not science fiction."

"I didn't mean to imply..." Rae stood and reached over the desk to offer him her hand. "Mr. Xepher, we'll be in touch."

"Excellent!" he said, standing and grasping her hand in both of his.

Once the elevator had closed and carried Xepher away, Ashley said, "You're good. When you said you'd be in touch, I *believed* you."

Rae looked back down to her desk. "We will be in touch with Andros Xepher."

"Really? Are you going to call him up and tell him to get some psychiatric help?" He smiled.

"No. We're going to hire him... unless someone better comes along."

Ashley flapped his jaw in disbelief before crying out, "He thinks the Canadians have a three-hundred-year-old secret facility in the Arctic!"

Rae looked up from her desk. "By better, I mean less obvious."

Ashley didn't seem to know how to respond, and she went back to sorting personnel folders into two categories, one labeled "Team Seven," and the other, "Recycle Bin." Rae looked at Xepher's file. Written at the top of his International Employee Database record was: "Fired from Kander and Jansen Labs for an inability to deliver results." In spite of herself, she felt he'd just been dealt a bad hand, and she wanted to live in a world where one could recover from that. *Maybe he's not the scapegoat I'm looking for,* she thought. *I need someone who I can destroy without feeling terrible about it afterward. She looked through the remaining folders. None of these will do. I need someone lower on the social ladder than Ashley.* She looked back to Xepher's file. *Right now he's unemployed, probably late on his rent and days from becoming homeless. If I hire him it just prolongs the inevitable.*

"Well, Mr. Xepher was your last interview..." Ashley was fishing for permission to leave.

"Okay," Rae said, waving him off while skimming the E.I. employee contract.

"Great, see you tomorrow."

"Mmm," She said without looking up. She spoke a text to Evermore, "One of the guys I want to hire is playing hard-to-get. I'd like to give him some assurances. Can I add into his contract a clause that says we'll fly him back to Earth if he's ever fired?

Evermore's terse answer came almost instantly.

> **E.Evermore:** We can make an exception if you really need them.

"I didn't hear that request. Who's that for?" asked Ashley as he waited for the elevator to arrive.

"Mr. Xepher."

"What? Why?"

"Primum non nocere."

"Oh." Ashley said as if he understood, but as the elevator doors closed she heard him repeating the phrase to his Omni.

"First, do no harm," it told him.

# CHAPTER NINE

# Gaining Speed

### Rae

Thursday morning, Ashley stepped from the elevator with a group of seven men of various heights, races and ages close on his heels. They were smiling as if the laughter of a joke had just died down. Ashley met her eyes and must have determined her mood before she'd had a chance to realize she was nervous. "Good morning, Doctor," he said in a tone that was both professional and reassuring.

*Just imagine you're back in university and this is one of the many group projects you'll have to carry.*

Rae steeled herself against all possibility of failure, cleared her throat, and said, "Gentlemen, welcome to Lab Seven."

After she had given each of their hands a hearty shake, a semicircle formed naturally around her, and she said, "I have handpicked each of you for your expertise, your creativity, and your willingness to take the risks required in making history." She led the group around the lab, teasing them with shiny new machines. "I left the workstations basic with the expectation that each of you would want to customize your own apps to your preferences and fields. If you feel you should need a particular piece of machinery, I want you to justify it in a formal proposal."

Rae led the group to the conference table in the center

of the room and gestured for them to sit. "We'll all be working in this lab together, so I trust that we will all adhere to a unified commitment to remain professional, to co-create diplomatic relationships, and to keep our work areas safe and clean."

She said the word "professional" directly at Ashley, but his mind seemed elsewhere. "Before I get too far into why we're here, let's go around and introduce ourselves." Her eyes fell to Dr. Ma'at on her left.

As the introductions passed from doctor to doctor clockwise around the table, each seemed more pompous than the next. Rae imagined them circling around each other like feral dogs, hackles raised and ears back. As she rolled her eyes she noticed Ashley, who had been excluded from the table but was standing on call. Instead of looking like an outcast he stood confidently in his own space. It was as if being excluded from the pissing contest had freed him from any need to compete, but then she realized that the look on his face was awe. He was basking in the light of their combined knowledge and experience. *Watching this team work might be as close as he gets to a working in a lab.* She could see that he was hungry to learn from someone other than Evermore, but what he didn't realize was that these men weren't Dr. Evermore and that, in their world, Ashley was as important as a bug and as transparent as a ghost.

She silently envied him as it approached her turn to introduce herself, which she had reserved for last, mostly so she would have the last word. She didn't love her speech and ended up wishing she'd gone first so they had time to forget it. After summarizing her educational background, recapitulating her spiel about where science and art meet, and sprinkling in bits from Evermore's talk about creative electricity, she said, "And that brings us to the big reveal: What are we building? Evermore Industries has dedicated itself to the research and creation of a vessel capable of trans-galactic travel at speeds faster than light." Rae had planned to pause for dramatic effect, but in her nervousness she plowed right through it. "As this has long been a thing of science fiction, your ability to invent fiction is just as important as your ability to create science.

"The first task that Dr. Evermore has assigned to Lab Seven is to observe and create a trans-biological exchange of information beyond the electromagnetic spectrum," Rae finished.

Reflecting back, she wished she had had the creativity to give a big inspiring presentation like Evermore's, but she was exhausted from working at K&J Labs until late in the night. Dr. Kander had wanted recompense for her breach of contract, so they had worked out a deal that didn't involve a commute to the South Pole.

"Does he mean for us to use Hawking radiation?" The interruption had come from Dr. Benjamin Washington, the molecular physicist.

"I understand your line of reasoning," said Joseph Allan with an air of annoyance, "You're probably thinking that if it is able to escape a black hole *then* it must be moving faster than light. Being the only astrophysicist here, please allow me to correct you. Hawking radiation is a form of thermal electromagnetic radiation emitted by all matter above zero kelvin. It's produced not in the center of the hole but at the event horizon."

Rae cut in before the conversation could devolve. "I'm sorry to put you on the spot, Dr. Ma'at, but I believe your theory of spiritual resonance is the most promising place to start. You have the next three hours to prepare a presentation of your research and analysis. I especially want to see the degree to which you have ruled out stimulus on the electromagnetic spectrum. The rest of you suspend your skepticism until Ma'at has made his case. I believe that if we can find out what's vibrating Dr. Ma'at's crystals, we'll be able to complete Evermore's assignment."

Ma'at nodded. He seemed both excited and overwhelmed. "Dr. Dahlia, I shall do my best."

"I expect genius."

He looked into her eyes, searching for some hint of levity, but she gave him only cold seriousness. "Yes, Doctor," he said.

Rae stood from the table but stopped before walking away. "I have a correction. I want the rest of you to spend these next three hours getting comfortable, situated, and reading Dr. Ma'at's paper."

Rae returned to her own workstation feeling the exhaustion taking its toll. She watched the seven doctors as they wandered among the identical workstations. Some chose carefully, as with Dr. Raymond Hubert, the transitional metaphysicist, who looked as if he were divining the best one, while others plopped themselves down at the first station they reached. Andros Xepher headed straight to the corner of the northwestern wall, the station farthest from Rae's desk. The first action each of them took was identical to hers; they placed their Omnis on the workstations, and like candles winking out, their eyes glazed over as they were pulled into Cloud9. Yet again Andros Xepher stood out; he was staring at his workstation looking lost.

"Ashley, would you mind helping Mr. Xepher sign in?" Without waiting for a reply she returned to her workstation, but a few moments later she looked up and noticed Ashley was still at his desk counting ceiling tiles.


## Ashley


Ashley was lost in a maze of memories. He was thinking back to Evermore's poolside meeting and trying to see the faces of everyone who stepped from the elevator. He was certain each person was someone Evermore had worked with before. Ariel, and Asbjorn Breivik, were easily the most recognizable, but who was that guy who followed Rae from the elevator? Where had he seen him before? All he had was the hint of a memory of that man and Evermore shaking hands. *Of course*, Ashley thought. *The answer is right in front of me*. He awakened his workstation and started combing through the file system of the E.I. cloud net. Searching for a list of principal researchers, within seconds he found the name that jogged the memory. Hugo Voss. Voss was the parapsychologist who had won a million dollar grant from Evermore Biomedical Systems, sending both the board and the majority of shareholders into a rage. The memory of Evermore shaking Voss's hand wasn't a memory of an event but rather the memory of an image he'd seen on a news blog he liked to read in his teens.

A thought was forming, waiting to emerge from the connections between Crellinger's light, Lab Seven's assignment, and Voss as the head of Lab Five. *Why would Evermore hire a ghost hunter?* he thought, feeling the solution calling to him like a plant reaching for the sun.

"Hellooo? Ashley?"

"Yes, Dr. Dahlia?"

"Would you mind helping Mr. Xepher sign in to his workstation?" She sounded annoyed.

"What's wrong with it?" he asked, but as her eyebrows rose he realized he was asking the wrong person.

Ashley walked across the lab and looked over Xepher's shoulder at the workstation's login screen, "Alright, so your Omni should have asked if you wanted to sync with the desk, —wait, where's your Omni?"

"I didn't see anything like that." Xepher's tone blamed Ashley for being incompetent.

Keeping his voice low, Ashley said "Okay, well, can I

take a look at your Omni to make sure it's connected to the cloud?"

"Isn't that why you're over here?" Xepher said, turning around in his chair. The two stared at each other, waiting, Xepher for an explanation, and Ashley for him to produce an Omni. Finally Ashley said, "Well? Where is it?"

Xepher seemed to realize that he was the source of the misunderstanding. "Isn't this my Omni?" he said, touching the desk.

It took all of Ashley's will to remember his place, and to afford himself a moment to cool down, he went to his station and grabbed his Omni. He handed the ePlastic card to Xepher, the so-called expert of reverse-engineering alien technology. "This is an Omni, see how it's telling me to put it on the workstation to allow it to sync?"

"I see," Xepher said. "I thought Omni was short for Omnify, the company that manufactures these workstations. I don't have one of those."

"That's fine, it'll work with your iCard or your Android HUD."

"Can I do it with my laptop?" Xepher said, and produced a computer that was at least thirty years old. Xepher carefully unfolded the screen, and the ancient creature awakened with a whine of processor fans. Xepher's desktop screen was filthy with shortcut icons, many of them labeled with strange characters. He expertly found his way to the network settings menu and said, "This is what I get for trying to upgrade. Should I connect to the network named 'Evermore' or 'Dahlia'?"

"Mr. Xepher, it's time to stop carrying a processor and keyboard around and upgrade to an Omni. It's all you need to be able to access all the projects you work on from anywhere."

"That's the problem," Xepher said, as if it were an explanation. "With a laptop, the only place my secret information exists is here. Not off in some holographic server farm. Which network do I connect to?"

"But if you lose your information — never mind. There should only be one network option." Yet, looking over Xepher's shoulder, he saw hundreds of them. "What program are you using?"

Xepher leaned closer to the screen. "It says 'Network Con...' I assume it means connections."

Ashley noticed his own name among the list. "Can I try something?" he asked.

"Sure," said Xepher, offering him the computer.

Ashley connected to the "Rephaireal" network and found that he could access his entire Omni from this ancient computer, and through his Omni he could access all of his private files in the cloud that should only be accessible through his Omni. It wasn't unheard of to access that information through another desk, but it required the Omni's encrypted registration number, and Ashley's personal password. "Sure, I can connect your workstation and your laptop, but it's going to take me a second. Do you mind if I take this to my station to work? In the meantime, just use your E.I. ID badge to connect to the desk."

"I just saw you connect to your account. Can't you just sign in to mine?"

Ashley broke eye contact and pretended to look stymied by Xepher's screen, "I did, but I have an Omni... " It wasn't a lie per se.

"Sure," Xepher conceded. "What do I do?"

"Just swipe your ID badge over that symbol that tells the desk — there! Now sign in with the password you created at Human Resources." After he'd done that, Ashley said, "Good. Now open your email there. And there's Ma'at's paper that Dr. Dahlia sent to you. Good. Happy reading; I'll be right back with this."

Ashley set the laptop on his desk, went back to the

Network Con program and selected "About." A window popped up with the version number, the year it was released (two years prior), and the designer: <Euclid> </Euclid>.

*What the hell?! how did this guy get his hands on a Darknet program?*

Xepher had been correct: connecting his laptop to his workstation would just be a matter of selecting the right network, but Ashley had seen an opportunity. On Xepher's laptop, Ashley selected Evermore's network and found that he had access to all of Evermore's files in Cloud9. Ashley pulled up a search program and, with his heart racing, typed "Samuel Reznick" and hit "enter." The laptop was slow. Three seconds elapsed and Ashley assumed it had frozen, but a moment later two files were revealed. The first was a .pdf of Samuel Reznick's birth certificate, and the second was an .mp3, an audio file. Ashley stared at the files for a full minute before selecting them. Before doing anything with them, he changed his mind and closed the window. He was about to return the laptop to Xepher when he changed his mind again. Reopening the search window, he found the files and selected them, but before he could hit "copy," he stopped. *This is suspiciously easy.* This was the perfect opportunity, and any trace of the theft would lead back to Xepher. Ashley tried to tap into his anger to fuel the resolution to take something precious from Evermore, but thinking and doing were two separate things. If this were one of Evermore's tests, he'd have to get Xepher in on it and find and install a Darknet program, and all of those things were out of Evermore's wheelhouse. *The only reason I can think of not to take it is that it's too easy.* He set Xepher's network connection so it would connect with his workstation and returned the laptop.

## Rae

For the next three hours, Lab Seven was almost silent as her team read Dr. Ma'at's paper, and she counted the minutes before noon. Ashley was the first to blink his screen-weary eyes, stretch, and ask, "Is anyone else ready for lunch? I could continue our tour of the Evermore Industries building."

Rae wanted to jump up and ride the elevator down with them, but she waited patiently for them all to leave. As the elevator doors closed, she allowed herself to rise. She took her Omni but left her lab coat. She called the elevator, but as she waited she realized she wasn't alone. Cyrus Ma'at was still at his desk, typing hurriedly and looking concerned. That was the passion she was hungry for.


Although she was waiting in a corner diner, menu in hand, Rae wasn't hungry in the traditional sense. She had spent three and a half days working at Evermore Industries and half her nights at Kander and Jansen; she had a craving for sleep, but more than that, the hollow had opened back up, and she could feel it slowly devouring her like a hungry cancer. One does not fight with improper weapons, and she wanted this thing dead. It hadn't been this bad since she month she waited for UMars to accept her. In the darkness, the unknown created an amalgam of the worst horrors she could imagine.

Then and now she experienced the hollow as a dull sensation that consumed pieces of her. It grew over hours and days, threatening to consume her entirely. She felt that if it ever reached her head she might jump off of something very high and try to land on it. She had tried throwing food and alcohol into it; food only made her feel worse about herself, and alcohol acted like the Higgs mechanism, imparting mass on the hollow, which in turn gave it gravity. Once, before coming to Mars, she had tried feeding it mushrooms. Never again. It had given the hole a voice, and without warning she had two mothers telling her how meaningless her life was.

"Having trouble navigating the menu?" asked the fry cook/waiter/owner. She looked up from the ePaper menu expecting sarcasm, but met kind eyes under thick, dark eyebrows.

"No, I'm just waiting for somebody."

"Your boyfriend?" he asked, moving along the bar, clearing plates and silverware as he went. "No," he decided before she could answer. "You are too pretty to be kept waiting this long." Before he could guess any more, another customer walked through the open door. He was lanky but not much taller than she, pale, with a round face on the end of a long neck. Resting on ears big enough to flap in the wind (if there had been any beneath the dome) sat a pair of OmniView glasses. The Chemist had that glazed, internal look that let people around him know that they were merely obstacles to be avoided while the rest of his attention was in Cloud9.

Without making eye contact, he took a seat at the bar beside her and said, "Coffee. Two eggs. Wheat toast, butter. Toast and coffee both black."

The cook said, "You got it, buddy. How would you like your eggs?"

The Chemist looked up with dark-hazel eyes that were wet and pink from overuse. "Over hard," he said.

"You want jelly with your toast?"

"Do you have pluot jam?"

The cook chuckled. "Take off your glasses and take look at this place. You've got two choices—"

Without touching his glasses, the Chemist said, "Silverberry and 'grape,' though we both know that the main ingredient is apple." It wasn't a hard guess; the list of fruit available on Mars could be counted on one's fingers.

Forcing a smile, the cook nodded. "So, which'll it be?"

The Chemist tapped his fingers on the dinner counter like a keyboard, as indeed, in his augmented world, it was. The flickering light of the OmniView in front of his eyes winked off. "There. My glasses are off. You know what I see?" He didn't wait for an answer. "I see a greasy spoon on the same street as four others, all with the exact same menu..." Rae's Omni buzzed with a text. She dropped out of the conversation to read it.

> **T.Chemist**: I couldn't produce enough for a week. I'll charge you for five and you'll get two free the next time you're hungry.

> **R.Dahlia**: And what if I don't get hungry again?

"—per pound?" the cook said, disbelieving. "That'll cook down to little more than a cup of jam!"

The Chemist raised his eyebrows. "Let's do the math: There's forty-eight teaspoons in a cup. If you charge the same amount for a serving of "raspberry jewel" pluot jam as you do for cream cheese, that's a 180 percent profit margin, *and* you begin to distinguish yourself from the rest of the mediocrity on this street."

"Until you go to them with the same deal."

The Chemist shook his head. "This is private stock. I only get one pound a month, and if you buy that pound then I don't have anything to sell."

The cook seemed excited at the prospect but turned to Rae. "You sure I can't get you anything, hon?" She shook her head.

The Chemist tapped on the counter again, and her Omni buzzed.

**T.Chemist**: Then you only get charged for five. BTW, I hear you got a job at E.I. The price just went up by 10 percent.

**R.Dahlia:** What? Why? Because you think I'm making more money?

**T.Chemist:** No. Because you're a turncoat.

It felt ridiculous messaging with the person sitting next to her, but this was the game, and games have rules.

**R.Dahlia**: Whatever. Fine.

The cook turned his back to them, opened a refrigerator drawer beneath the grill, took out two eggs and cracked them into a sizzling puddle of butter. Having both created and waited for this opportunity, the Chemist, without looking up, reached into his pocket and slipped an envelope of aluminum foil under her napkin. He then placed his Omni on the counter right at the invisible border between the countries of their personal spaces.

The cook took a pinkish mug the color of Martian ceramics from beneath the counter, filled it with thick, dark coffee, and set it in front of the Chemist. "You got a deal. I'll take the pound, and if I can move it in a month I'll take another," he said, and turned back to the griddle.

Rae opened her wallet app, typed in the number and gently tapped her Omni onto the Chemist's, transferring the money.

"I don't think my friend's going to show," she told the cook, using the wallet app again, this time to leave him a small tip. "Sorry for just sitting here. Here's a few bucks for the seat."

"You sure I can't get you anything? How about a Reuben? I got fresh kraut in this morning; got a crunch like you wouldn't believe."

"No, thank you," she said, standing and stuffing the napkin, foil and all, into her pocket.

"See you around."

The Chemist looked up as if he had just become aware that someone else was there, took a sip of his coffee, and decided not to participate in the world outside his Om-niView. His eyes glazed over.

> **T.Chemist**: Pleasure as always. I'll be in touch.

A few blocks down, Rae ducked into a blind alley and unwrapped the foil. Five pills. Stimulants. Stims. "Chalk" if you were in high school, "greenies" in sports, and "speed" to an older generation that still remembered the amphetamine uppers of yesteryear. This product, which the Chemist told her to order as "Queen Anne's Lace," was not a big batch product. In the terradome at least, rules were too strict and freedoms too scarce to supply a customer base of addicts, and Queen Anne's Lace was not a slang term for stims; it was Rae's stim, built from her hacked medical files and bio-samples taken directly by the Chemist. It was a near perfect key to the lock of *her* neurotransmitter receptors.

As the pill scraped its way down her throat without water, she could feel everything change. While the Crash-Pads she had taken at Chasma Australe brightened her perception of reality, Queen Anne's Lace took the turbu-lent, chaotic world and nailed it down in a logical matrix. The steps required to reach the rickshaw docking station were of even number, and there was no need for a half step. Even the whine of the electric engine started low and climbed a musical scale in an even, orderly way as she accelerated to top speed. The glass doors of the E.I. building slid open for her seamlessly, and the elevator was held by a balding doctor traveling to the ninth floor. From the moment the rickshaw docked until she stepped into the elevator, her stride remained unbroken. For a moment she found herself on the edge of tears, overwhelmed with relief that everything was finally sliding into place.

# CHAPTER TEN

# Strange Energy

## Rae

After Ma'at's three hours were up, Rae walked casually across the lab. As she passed Dr. Joseph Allan, she noticed that the astrophysicist was slouched over his workstation, which was a mess with graphs and formulas; one of them compared wavelengths, conductivity, and thickness. *He's attempting to build a container that could block a wide swath of the electromagnetic spectrum.* She leaned over and whispered, "Keep at it, Dr. Allan, I can't imagine what this 'living crystal' would do to science."

He turned and frowned at her. "I know you are betting everything you have on this Ma'at fellow. Do not waste your energy stroking my ego."

*Misread that one, she thought. But if we're going to solve Evermore's puzzle and communicate beyond the electromagnetic spectrum, this might be the most useful Dr. Allan will ever feel.*

Finally, she made her way to Ma'at's workstation and asked, "Are you ready?"

He nodded nervously, finished typing some final sentence and met her gaze. *His eyes,* she thought. *He doesn't just have the presentation jitters.* Part of her was ashamed she had spent the morning worrying about her Queen Anne's Lace instead of paying attention to the shape of Ma'at as a puzzle piece. *It was all too recently that he'd shared this idea with the scientific community and been metaphorically chased out of the village with torches and pitchforks.* She felt bad for not realizing what she was putting him through, but not bad enough to let him off the hook.

"Out of all of these doctors," she whispered to him, "your hypothesis is the closest we've got to solving this. There's no need to be—" *Don't say "afraid"; he wants to think it's hidden.* "—nervous."

Dr. Ma'at tried to play it off, but when she held him in her gaze, he nodded, let out a sigh, and pushed himself up from his desk.

The team gathered at the large table in the center of the room without Rae having to say a word.

She nodded, and Ma'at began. A gray electron microscope image covered the surface of the conference table. It looked like an aerial photograph of some ancient stone temple built from impossibly small bricks; among the angled bricks, a soft-looking mortar seemed to hold it all together.

"What we're looking at is a bacteria with the very clever name S30:60—" the room chuckled, and Ma'at relaxed and continued, "which was originally discovered growing within the crystalline structure of a Rochelle salt in a hydrothermal vent community in the Cayman Trough in the Pacific Ocean. Notice how they are attached to these bricks of potassium-sodium-tartrate crystal?"

"Is it mining the salt for nutrients?" asked Dr. Kaspar Mora, a chemist.

Ma'at shook his head. "That's what I thought it was at first, but after a few days of observation I found more salt, not less. It's actually constructing the salt around itself. What you're looking at is not a bacteria inhabiting its environment; this is not the original S30:60; this one was built from scratch and kept alive in a solution, and from its naked structure this is what it has produced."

Andros Xepher raised his hand like a schoolboy and asked, "That's why you call it a living crystal?"

"No, I'm calling it a living crystal because it's vibrating at a frequency many factors faster than the human brain. The bacteria cannot be the source, and the crystal alone would require an electrical charge to vibrate on its own."

Joseph Allan raised a finger in question, and when Ma'at looked at him he said, "It seems to me that you've just disproved your own theory, if neither the crystal nor the bacteria are the source."

"My gut tells me otherwise, and my funding disappeared before I was able to truly discover the source."

Dr. Allan persisted, "So you're not even clear if this crystal is detecting or producing the vibrations?"

Rae was getting annoyed at the number of interruptions. "Let's let Dr. Ma'at finish his presentation."

"Thank you, Dr. Dalia, but Dr. Allan is correct. The only reason I was able to notice the vibrations at all is because of the piezoelectric nature of the Rochelle salt."

Xepher raised his hand again. "Will you remind me what that means?"

Ashley spoke up, surprising everyone present. "It means that when the crystal is mechanically compressed, it generates a small electric charge. And conversely, when an electric charge is applied, it deforms."

Xepher's hand stayed down, but he raised his voice instead. "That's the second time you have spoken to me disrespectfully. I will not tolerate a third."

Rae watched the threat crash upon the rocks of Ashley's resentment. She tried to impose herself between the two, but it didn't stop Ashley from saying, "I've done some reverse engineering myself, when I was ten. The big red button on the barbecue grill taught me all about piezoelectricity. But maybe the alien technology you encountered didn't use electronics?"

"Excuse me gentlemen," Ma'at spoke up. "Let's keep things professional."

Xepher ran a hand up his forehead, lifting his long

bangs and revealing a round burn scar on each temple. "See these? They're electroshock burns, a result of someone wanting to 'help' me forget. Doing this work, being here on Mars, it helps me remember. I know I sound like a nut, but I'm willing to take that risk until I can prove what I was forced to forget."

Rae raised her voice and cut off Ashley's retort. "Mr. Xepher, Ashley is my employee; if you have an issue with him, please take it up with me. I will not have these who-knows-more-than-whom arguments in my lab. That goes for everybody. We are all from very different scientific backgrounds and disciplines, and this must become a safe, open, and creative space if we are going to even approach solving Evermore's assignment."

Dr. Luther Brando put a hand on Xepher's shoulder. "I didn't know what piezoelectricity was either. Let it go, let's get back to work."

Rae thought it apropos that one pseudo-scientist would comfort another, but Brando wouldn't be out on the street if Lab Seven was crushed under its own weight. He had been poached from the Martian governing council, where he used his own branch of science, called "archaememeology," to help design new laws. The way he described it, he was an anthropologist who focused on the cultural trends that arise after technological advances.

Andros Xepher looked to Rae one more time before correctly reading the fire in her eyes as absolute inflexibility. As he backed down, Rae saw his eyes glaze over. *This has happened to him before,* she thought. *This isn't the first time he's tried to stand up for himself and been crushed under the heels of disbelievers.*

Hesitantly, Ma'at continued, "If you look at the cubist structures of the salt, they continue all the way down to the molecular level. In the instances where I let the S30:60 starve to death, I found that it stopped vibrating. Additionally, I was able to confirm the Rochelle salt's piezoelectricity.

"If you're interested, I would like to grow more S30:60 crystals in our lab and continue testing for the origin of the vibration."

Dr. Benjamin Washington asked, "Do you have either a sample with you or a genome printer file?"

"I have both," Ma'at said. "But S30:60 is quite fragile outside of its natural environment. I would suggest we also try to build something new that exhibits the same characteristics. Namely, a bacteria that builds itself into a living crystal with its excess materials. If it also produces the mysterious vibrations, I believe that is more proof than simply recreating the same S30:60."

"And what if it doesn't vibrate?" The question was asked by Dr. Mora, the chemist. His hair and face were generally unkempt, and his blue button-down shirt was wrinkled and looked as if it had spent the night in the dryer.

He answered his own question before anyone else had the chance to. "We won't know whether we simply weren't able to produce the right kind of crystal or whether Ma'at made a mistake. No offense, doctor. We all make mistakes, and that's why the scientific method exists, to save our time in the long run by being thorough in the short. So I think for the sake of all our time, let's reproduce Dr. Ma'at's experiment to the best of our abilities."

On any other day Rae might have had an internal freak-out, but today she was in total control. *He's right, of course. But he said it as if he were making the decision for the entire lab. If I agree with him, I reinforce that behavior.*

Mora was in the midst of collecting nods of agreement like alms when Rae interrupted his moment by saying, "Gentlemen, I'm guessing that you aren't here because you're attracted to the mundane. I'm guessing you aren't here because you love the systematic research involved in destroying your own hypotheses. We have taken the path of the scientific method before — *many* have taken that path before — and many have found that the journey from our physical universe to a unified theory to the discovery of the graviton to faster-than-light travel is all dead ends. Does it make sense to continue walking the worn cart path we all know is a dead end? I, for one, am hoping that Evermore gets what he set out to achieve. He is reaching high, higher perhaps that anyone else ever has. He's created a different kind of facility; this is not the Kander and Jansen model of taking tiny, bite-size portions of the unknown and studying how it fits into our universe; Evermore Industries is a research and development facility. Of what use is a scientific discovery that has no application?

"Evermore will be watching us closely these first few weeks, and we need to show him that we can reach high. So—" Rae fixed her gaze on Kaspar Mora, "I'm not looking for suggestions on *what* we should do; I want ideas of what kind of organism we are going to build that might produce a crystal around itself."

There was a long silence. The energy in the room crackled with potential, but Rae had to wait to see which way it would be directed. Finally, Dr. Ma'at said, "What if we continued using the S30:60 but developed a bacteriophage that increased its performance and reliability?"

"Good. Other ideas?" Rae barked, and gestured at the conference table. She touched the tips of her index and thumb together and dragged them across her opposite palm three times; a camera somewhere in the conference table saw her, and an empty checklist appeared along with a message box: "List type memo selected. Each entry will appear on a new line. Select a title."

Rae touched the corner of her mouth and said, "Organisms brainstorm." The words appeared half a meter long in the center of the table.

She gestured to Ma'at, who touched the corner of his

mouth and said, "Bacteriophage." The word formed beneath the title in teal blue based on Ma'at's voice signature.

"Blue-green algae," said Dr. Brando, adding the suggestion to the list in a deep yellow font.

Ashley walked over from his workstation, touched the corner of this mouth and said, "Fungi." Rae scowled at him. "What? Fungi can break down minerals."

"Anyone else?" she asked. The room was silent.

"What about an amino acid that converts certain molecules into Rochelle salt?" suggested Xepher, forgetting, or not knowing how, to gesture.

"Nope," Rae said.

Xepher shook his head. "I'm confused. I thought you were looking for ideas. During my interview, you said you valued the fact that I'm creative."

"Creative, yes, creative is great. The issue is with abstract ideas that use up the group's time."

"What was wrong with my suggestion?" Xepher whined.

"Xepher... everyone, actually, listen up. I acknowledge that we're still in our first week together, and maybe we've been going a little fast. Maybe we should clear away all these workstations, get out our meditation pillows, set up a sharing circle, and really get to know each other. Or maybe we could skip all that bullshit and get to work? Make friends on your own time. Here, I expect a group of seven professionals to bring their best selves every hour of every day until each of us have unequivocally witnessed what each other is capable of, and we all know how to rely on each other like the parts of an engine. I don't want to hear what you think you're capable of, I want to experience it empirically."

"And where's our evidence?" Xepher snapped back. "You expect us to trust you until we can rely on each other, but I want to 'unequivocally' witness why we should trust someone whose lips are barely wet with the taste of her first internship. What gives you the right to treat us this way when everyone here has more experience than you?"

Rae stood there as her worst fears were thrown back in her face, but because they came from this eccentric character instead of someone like Ma'at or Allan, it left her unfazed. *Xepher, you really are perfect for the role I hired you for*, she thought. After he had finished his diatribe, Rae lazily took out her Omni and typed something while she said, "Dr. Washington, will you please explain to Mr. Xepher what was wrong with his amino acid suggestion."

Clearly uncomfortable with the position she'd put him in, Washington ran a hand over the bald patch at the top of his scalp and scratched at the short gray hairs growing at the back. "Well, one of the stipulations Dr. Ma'at specified was that the crystal needs to be made by a living organism. Otherwise they won't be interwoven at the molecular level. An amino acid isn't technically alive. But I think we all need to take things down a notch; this is our first week here, and there's bound to be a few hiccups."

Xepher shook his head, "That's not true. Amino acids are alive. Down at the molecular level, you will observe the molecules moving with their own orgonomic energy."

"That's... not an energy type I'm familiar with," Rae said, hoping no one would notice that she was fanning the flames.

"That's because it was suppressed! Wilhelm Reich discovered it, and his peers in the scientific field discredited it and went so far as to attempt to drive him from the country. Reich even went to Einstein for help, but he ended up using his influence to publish a paper directly contradicting Reich."

The story was all too familiar; Rae could see the team stealing glances at Ma'at, looking for a reaction, but no one wanted to say anything to support either side. Before the silence became uncomfortable, the elevator doors parted and two huge security guards stepped out, assessed the room, and crossed it to stand behind Rae.

Xepher eyed them nervously. "For Christ's sake! Aren't we *all* here to prove Einstein wrong? Rachael, I'm only doing what you hired me to do."

Rae visibly winced as Xepher used her first name. "It's not a matter of you doing your job or not. It's how you've conducted yourself. I do value the ability to suspend preconceived beliefs about our universe, but you're not just challenging preconceptions, you're challenging me and through me, Evermore. You asked what gave me the right. It's not a right, it's my job, and you empowered me to do it the moment you signed the employment contract."

"Don't you see what's happening? Ma'at, you are in the same position as Reich—"

"I am nothing like Reich." Ma'at slammed his open palm on the table. "Reich was a bad psychologist playing with a science he had no formal training in. What Reich tried to do was bend his observation of Brownian motion to prove his crackpot theories."

"Mr. Xepher, please collect your belongings and remove yourself from the building." She turned to the rest of the team. "I apologize, everyone. I was the one who hired Mr. Xepher. The one thing he got right is how new I am, and I should have seen how unstable he is."

"Are you nuts?" Xepher said, eying the guards with increasing panic as they stepped between him and Rae.

The team looked startled, but they said nothing as they watched Xepher scoop up his giant laptop and be hurried into the elevator by the guards. When the doors closed, Rae erased everything from the list on the conference table. Using the draw feature, she said, "I'm taking all of your suggestions and combining them." With her finger, she drew a three-layered something that could have been a cross-section of skin, or layers of the Earth, or... "Lichen," she said. "It's like a sandwich of fungus, sometimes algae, sometimes bacteria, and it grows in the harshest environments. We can even start with your bacteria and build it into a symbiotic partnership with an appropriate fungus. Ultimately, we need a resilient substance, and lichen has a secret ability. It's cryptobiotic: when severely desiccated, lichen enters a metabolic stasis rather than dying. What do you think, Ma'at?"

It was obvious he hadn't really heard her. He looked at the table and repeated one word. "Lichen." He nodded. "It fits."

## Ashley

Later that evening, Ashley sucked a Weak Interaction through a thin red straw. Every time someone walked through the door who even remotely looked like Rae, his heart jumped, but mostly he just sat and wondered was on the Samuel_Reznick.mp3 on Evermore's computer.

After two-thirds of the Relativity Lounge had been ripped away and crushed in the black hole, the freedom jazz trio took a break, and someone familiar walked through the door. Ashley had the sense it was someone who worked at E.I., but before he could figure it out he was caught staring. The young man waved, and, when Ashley returned the gesture, he stopped waiting for a table and walked over. He pushed his round glasses back up his nose with a ring finger and with the same hand reached out to shake Ashley's. "Ashley, how are you? You're not... with anyone, are you?" asked the nameless assistant.

"No no, please." Ashley gestured to the seat opposite him.

"Great." He brushed Ashley's Omni off the payment square and replaced it with his own. He ordered a Strange Spin and hit Ashley's refill button.

Ashley cocked his head as if he had a kink in his neck and read the man's name off the payment screen.

"Oh thanks, Leon, you didn't have to do that."

"You here for the jazz?"

"Not really. I'm avoiding my apartment."

"Why, what's wrong with it?" Leon looked worried, like he'd accidentally signed up for something he didn't want.

"It's empty."

He relaxed and smiled. "Yeah, mine's got the same problem."

Ashley said, "So you work for Voss, huh? What's he like?"

The question was thrown back at him, "You work for Dr. Dahlia, right? I thought I saw you two in here last week."

Ashley hoped the blue neon glow from the table was concealing his rouge of embarrassment. "Yeah. That was just a work meeting."

Leon seemed to buy it. "Oh. Yeah, she seems cool like that, but also really — I don't want to say uptight — highstrung?" Ashley smiled. "Voss is much more relaxed. So much so that he drives the natural scientists crazy, especially when he forgets to call them 'doctor' so-and-so, or when I accidentally call Voss 'doctor.'"

"He's not a doctor?"

"He not, but he could be; he's been studying the paranormal for over twenty years."

"Can I ask what you've been working on? No offense, but I can't imagine what the paranormal has to do with faster-than-light." *Or with fucking anything Evermore would be interested in,* he thought.

"Sorry, I can't tell you what we're working on, but our assignment is to discover a cross-biological information exchange beyond electromagnets."

A waiter arrived with a tray burdened with cocktails. In one motion he set down their drinks and picked up Ashley's empty glass before hustling off to the next table.

"Thanks," Leon said to the waiter.

Trying to hide his look of shock, Ashley said, "Thanks again," raised his glass, and took a big swallow, which was more whiskey than water. The fumes made him choke, and he nearly spit it all over Leon in the process.

"You alright?" Leon asked.

"Yeah," Ashley wheezed. "Went down the wrong side. So you're big into the freedom jazz, huh?"

"I wouldn't say 'big.' I enjoy it, but I know enough about it to know that the people who really like it don't actually listen to it."

Ashley chuckled.

"I'm serious," Leon said. "At first I thought it was some hipster bullshit, going to live performances to just ignore the performers, but F-jazz is ambiance music, like a soundtrack. A good soundtrack should affect the scene without being noticed. So true freedomists come to be affected, not to be entertained."

Ashley took another gulp; he wasn't listening. *If Voss is working on the same project... that means Evermore is setting up an elimination challenge. I wonder when he was planning on telling the research heads? He kept it from me, so probably never.*

The trio stepped back on stage, and the conversations in the room fell silent.

# CHAPTER ELEVEN

# Hidden Behind Doors

## Ashley

Ashley had spent the weekend wondering whether or not he should call Rae and tell her that Voss's team was working on the same assignment as Lab Seven.

The problem came when he imagined her reply: *"If Lab Four is working on the same assignment, how many others do you think Evermore's got working against each other?"*

The only way to find out was to break into Evermore's office or hack into the E.I. cloud net and get into his workstation files. There was a third option, but it required talking to Evermore, and he couldn't imagine a way to bring it up without Evermore guessing that he knew, which would ultimately lead to Leon getting fired. Then he remembered a fourth. *If I had Xepher's laptop, I could use the Network Con program to connect to the E.I. cloud net.* The chances were high that Xepher's computer was the only place that program was available on Mars. Omni wouldn't allow any unapproved apps on Cloud9, and he couldn't imagine Yún, the highly censored Chinese National Space Program's internet, would either.

*Is it worth tracking down Xepher and—* The thought was interrupted by his Omni buzzing with a message.

> **E.Evermore:** I want to meet with you Monday at 9:30 a.m.

*He knows. Voss's assistant must have realized that he'd leaked sensitive information and told Evermore.*

> **E.Evermore:** Nothing to worry about; I want to hear how things are going with Dr. Dahlia.

The follow-up message made him angry. That Evermore knew him enough to know that Ashley's first reaction would be to assume he was in trouble reminded him of everything they shared and the emotional wall Evermore had raised between them.

＊ ＊ ＊ ＊ ＊ ＊

Ashley sat in one of the two poly-carbon chairs that faced Evermore's workstation, which had its screen flattened down so that it also functioned as a table, and looked across it. Evermore's leather executive chair stood empty and inviting, and his Omni rested on the corner of the workstation, tempting Ashley.

*Maybe I've got time?* he thought as he rose, wandered deeper into the expansive office, and pretended to examine the fake books lining the shelves of Evermore's library, searching for a hidden camera in case Evermore was paranoid enough to monitor himself. The library was decorated by a worn, woven rug that looked like it had come from a street market in Mexico somewhere. In the center of the rug was a simple, glass-surfaced table riddled with coffee rings. Facing the table were two leather parlor chairs edged with brass tacks that Evermore had stolen from the last century. The chairs were angled forty-five degrees off the square of the room so as not to block the spectacular view of Evermore's rooftop garden and the view of the city from twelve stories. Ashley scanned the garden for places Evermore could be hiding. Not that the Doc would be playing games, just overlooked while bent over weeding. When neither Evermore nor cameras revealed themselves, Ashley settled into his mentor's big leather chair. His hands hovered over the virtual desktop and slowly lowered past the point of no return. The desk awakened, and Ashley was about to run a search for "Samuel" when he noticed that the birth certificate and the .mp3 were right there on the desktop. He heard a sound from somewhere outside and chickened out. Thinking fast, he opened a game of solitaire and was actually able to play a few turns before Evermore's voice boomed from within the room, startling Ashley.

"On time as always, my boy."

Ashely had assumed Evermore had come from somewhere on the rooftop garden, but when he turned he saw the man entering from behind the shelves of books on the northern wall. Ashley's mouth hung open. "Is that a secret door behind a shelf of books?"

Evermore smiled. "Yes. What began as a necessity to meet fire codes became shaped by a childhood fantasy and clever carpenters. Once I'd tucked my head into the rabbit hole I found I couldn't stop. Suffice it to say that I have installed passages all throughout the building."

As he and Evermore switched chairs, Ashley shook his head and laughed at himself. *That would have been nice to know about on the first day. I could've gotten the assignment folder to Rae on time.*

Reading Ashley's face, Evermore said, "Already thinking of potential uses?"

"No... Sort of. I was hiding in the poolside bathroom so I could listen to the speech you gave the department heads."

One corner of Evermore's mouth twitched into a smile, and he said, "You're normally so punctual; when I saw Dr. Dahlia waiting there in the lobby, I wondered what had happened. So did you tell her why you were late?"

Ashley relaxed as the version of Evermore who was his friend and mentor reappeared for the first time since he had been reassigned. "You know I'm a bad liar."

"You told her the truth?!"

"Well... I told her that I'd been in the bathroom and let her fill in the details."

The Doc barked out a single laugh and changed the subject. "In a matter of minutes, Dr. Dahlia will arrive for her first progress review, but I'm afraid her accounts will be skewed by her fear of me, or what I represent. You're my man on the inside, so I wanted to get your opinion first. How is the Lab Seven team doing?"

"Your man on the inside? Is that why you—" the anger that bubbled up inside him was so intense it startled him, and in pushing it down one more time he felt a lump forming in his throat as it tightened to resist. "Is that why you made me her personal assistant? When you asked me to choose someone to work *with*, I thought I'd be doing just that, not working *for* her."

"If you were led to believe that, it wasn't by me. How would that make sense, my boy? Don't take this the wrong way, but anyone I hired to run a lab would feel insulted to be paired with an undergrad co-researcher."

*If you think I'm going to help you, you can go fuck yourself!* Ashley thought, yet found himself saying, "The first few days were pretty chaotic." *Do I help Evermore, or Rae? It's not as if I'm about to tell Evermore anything Rae wouldn't want him to know.* But he realized there were things he didn't want Evermore to know about, like their fight on the first day. Things hadn't changed much since then; Rae only spoke to him to give him orders, and she had never even thanked him for the flowers.

*Maybe if I feed him pith, he won't notice.* "The first assignment didn't give her much of a starting point. She has a tough job since Seven is in charge of both research and development, which spreads—"

"I prefer 'tools and truths,' my boy; 'research and development' fails to convey the depth of our undertaking. It's a pet peeve. I'm sorry, please continue."

"She's spread her resources thin trying to cover all of the sciences, and then there was the incident with Xepher."

Evermore leaned forward, smiling. "I still can't believe she hired Xepher."

"He was on the list *you* gave her, but he's a conspiracy theory nut, and he's unstable."

Clearly amused by something, Evermore confessed, "I know. Kander told me just about the same thing when I asked him why he had fired Xepher."

Ashley wasn't smiling. "I don't see what's so funny about it."

"My boy, you were desensitized to the humor of the situation because you and he are so alike."

"Like hell we are!"

Evermore looked at him for a moment with amusement twinkling in his eyes. "It's true that you have yet to accuse me of brainwashing you, but you both have "Mr." in front of your names, and you both have a bad habit of saying the first thing that pops into your mind."

Ashley tried very hard to say nothing. The act was not lost on Evermore, and he smiled with adoration.

*How can you look at me like that yet treat me so badly?*

Finally, Evermore said, "And how is your relationship with Dr. Dahlia?"

"Fine, good!" Ashley blurted out. *Does he know? He could have used any word, yet he chose "relationship."* Evermore waited for a real answer. Ashley swallowed and said, "I trust and respect her like the rest of them, and she isn't overworking me."

"That's not what I meant, but I think you know that."

There was a pause as Ashley searched for something to say. *And he'll call bullshit on that, too; I'm only making it harder on myself. Just tell him.* "I may have said something that upset her on the first day, and now I don't think she likes me very much."

Evermore sighed. "Ashley, oftentimes when I listen to others, I find myself filtering out their subjective modifiers, such as 'may have' and 'very much.' Don't minimize, my boy; embody whatever it is you are feeling and embrace whatever it is you have done. And if you cannot embrace it, than make amends and move on."

Ashley had been lectured on this before, and his obvious irritation made Evermore's loving smile even bigger. He thought for a moment and tried again. "Basically," he winced. *Stop minimizing.* "I made a series of inappropriate comments and..." *She hit me for some reason.*

Evermore raised his eyebrows and said, "I have received no reports of sexual harassment."

"No no, nothing like that. I've gotten used to how casual we used to be," he said, gesturing between them. "But Rae read my blasé attitude as disrespect."

"This caution reaches you much too late, but I suspect she's not a flowers-and-chocolates kind of woman."

Ashley turned bright red. "How'd you know about the flowers?"

A voice from his virtual desk cut into their conversation. "Dr. Evermore, Dr. Dahlia is here to see you."

Evermore rose, quickly crossed the room, and opened the secret door he himself had arrived through. He playfully repeated a complaint that outlined their relationship: "Why must you ask me *every* question that pops into your head? Are you too lazy to discover your own answers once in a while?"

The look Ashley shot him made Evermore chuckle. "Julius, at the front desk, told me."

"Good, I had begun to assume that you've been spying on me," Ashley said, climbing through the door.

"Good chatting with you, my boy." Evermore started

to close the door, but stopped. "Ashley? Do you love her?"

Ashley's heart leapt up his throat and he said, "No! She's cold and opinionated and controlling."

Evermore smiled, not believing a word of it, said, "That's all the answer I needed," and closed the door.

## Rae

As she waited outside Dr. Evermore's office, her gaze shifted from the dancing lights of the virtual syndications on the coffee table in front of her to the water cooler in the corner and anywhere at all to avoid staring at Evermore's man-child receptionist, Samuel Reznick. He had already caught her staring once when she first approached his desk and told him she had a ten-o'clock appointment.

"Have a seat," Samuel had said, and had gone back to typing behind his workstation. The desk made him look like a boy in a man's suit. Though, if the stories were true, Samuel *was* a man, in his forties.

*His eyes do seem older than I remember, darker and almost sunken. Actually, he looks a little ill, maybe just tired.* Samuel looked up, and she bent over and pretended to peruse the magazine readers. One of the articles caught her eye. "Is There Life on Mars?" it asked, but after reading one paragraph she realized that it was about the pros and cons (mostly the cons) of moving your business to Mars. Rae was about to set it down when she noticed the words "Evermore Industries." The article was using E.I. as an example of a successful move to Mars. It cited the rising equity and a multi-million-dollar figure invested by crowd-funders alone. Rae felt her attention drift from the magazine. *Is Samuel sick? Or is he just really tired?* She recalled the past weekend, the fourteen-hour days she had spent at Kander and Jansen Labs, and the layers of concealer she'd used this morning to hide the dark rings beneath her eyes. He glanced up and looked right into her eyes.

"You came quite a way to work for Evermore," she said.

"Yes, I did." His voice was high and squeaky, but his tone was entirely mature. He eyed her curiously, and a shiver went through her. "We all have our goals in life. I'll be the first to admit that traveling to Mars to work as a personal assistant was not how I'd envisioned spending my midlife crisis, but if Evermore is on Mars, so must I be if I want to beat my ISS."

Rae did not ask what ISS stood for, assuming it was the name of his condition. "What do you think of the terradome?"

The look on his face answered the question before he did. "What Vegas is to bachelors, Nili is to nerds; a self-indulgent fantasy world for one hyper-specific subculture."

She scowled, but Dr. Evermore's voice from the workstation stunted the growth of her budding reaction. "Samuel, please send in Dr. Dahlia."

Rae lightly tossed the magazine on the table and walked to the door. Touching the handle, she turned back to Samuel. "—"

"The Doctor will see you now," he interrupted.

"You must be so lonely," she said.

"Dr. Dahlia, this dome is full of people who have vivisected Life, brutally sawed through its chest, spread its ribs apart and examined the heart of Life down to its genetic code, but even as that corpse rots away beneath their scalpels and scopes, no one here knows what it is. Loneliness is living with you walking dead. You want to know how I like the dome? This is purgatory with color." Uninterested to her reaction or reply, he looked back to his desk.

Samuel's words bypassed whatever armor she thought she had, awakened her from the illusion she had been believing in. Though it was a dark version of reality, Samuel confirmed a thought that had been lurking in the back of her mind ever since she'd arrived and seen the shiny clean city, the perfect infrastructure, the homogenization of creeds and cultures, and the stark polarization of classes and sexes. It was a fantasy world, and it was unbearably lonely. Rae could feel the logical matrix of her world start to unravel into uncontrollable chaos. What she wanted in life could only be achieved on Mars, but on Mars she was forced to take part in the lie that this was a utopia. Even before the thought had finished forming, she had unwrapped one Queen Anne's Lace from its foil and hidden it in her hand. In the moment that her back was to Samuel and the door still blocked her from Evermore, she popped the little white tablet discreetly into her mouth. She swallowed, feeling it scratch a long red mark down the inside of her throat.

# CHAPTER TWELVE

# Inner View

### Ashley

On the other side of the hidden door, Ashley found a small peephole like on a hotel door. Peering through, he watched Evermore stretch, run a hand through his hair, and despondently watch a scattering of dandruff settle to the desk.

"Samuel, send Dr. Dahlia in," he said.

When the door opened, he said, "Please come in, Dr. Dahlia, I have many reviews to analyze, and should the first appointment break the ranks of the advanced guard that is my schedule, I am sure that the rest of my day will be overrun."

Evermore half-stood and reached a hand across his desk. Rae shook it, sat down, and started examining the office.

"Tell me, how was your first week at Lab Seven?"

Rae cleared her throat. "Honestly, I wish I had more to show for it, but much of our time has been spent helping the team normalize. I have a theory that when you hire a doctor, you're actually hiring two personalities: one who is interested in being useful to their employer and another who is only looking to further their career. Obviously, only one can show up at any given time, and part of my job in the first few days is convincing the two personalities that they have the same goal in common. I assume you read my note about Andros Xepher?"

"Yes, and frankly I'm surprised you hired him in the first place." Though Ashley could only see the back of the Doc's head, he heard him smiling.

"Yes, well, there's something I didn't mention in the note: I hired him so that I could fire him."

"That's—"

"Before you say anything, I know it looks like I wasted company time and resources, but I guarantee you that my team will be more productive sooner than any other lab, which will be a savings to Evermore Industries in the long run."

"No one can guarantee the future," Evermore pointed out.

Ashley had seen or overheard Evermore in many heated conversations, and more often than not they sounded like a game of verbal Ping-Pong. It was rare to see the Doc swat the ball out of the air like that, and then only when he wanted to put Kander on the defensive. Ashley watched to see if Rae would return the volley.

"Well, of course there's always free will, but, when training an animal, you have to guide it toward the condition you want by rewarding the good actions and punishing the bad. Human minds can make great leaps in reason such that you only need to punish one of them. The English monarchs in the fifteenth century would raise a common boy alongside their prince; the boys would learn everything together and often became friends."

"I'm familiar with the history and use of a whipping boy, but its efficacy was discovered by necessity. The royal blood was divine, and only the king was allowed to touch the prince. But I hadn't imagined your experience at the San Diego Zoo would apply to managing your team." Evermore's tone implied respect.

The first image Ashley imagined was Rae feeding the lions, rendering them docile with the intensity of her eyes, but then he remembered she had interned there as a behavioral biologist.

"*Homo sapiens sapiens* belong to the animal kingdom, after all; we think our self-awareness sets us apart, but it's the youngest part of our brain, whereas the limbic system—"

"I'm also familiar with the evolution of the brain, Dr. Dahlia. What I would like to know more about is what you observed after firing Xepher."

"Of course. I'm getting carried away. I'm sure you realize what a challenge it is to be responsible for extending both the tools and truths boundaries. You really put me and my team in quite a situation. Dr. Cyrus Ma'at has an untested hypothesis that is rather unorthodox, and I was afraid exploring it would tear our lab in half. But when I fired Xepher, I made sure to underline the behaviors I didn't want, namely his air of self-importance and his bad habit of challenging me. The team almost instantly got over their intellectual pissing contest and started accepting their differences of field and opinion, which was my primary goal for the first week."

"Congratulations," Evermore said, without sounding very heartfelt. "Tell me about Ma'at. Is he the 'good dog' you're rewarding? Aren't you afraid he'll overshadow you?"

Rae puzzled over his question before answering. "Boys will wrestle over a dirt mound, playing king of the hill, while men wrestle over ideas, replacing brute force with superior logic. I find this method of scientific one-upmanship to be exhausting, so after establishing myself as matriarch by figuratively killing Xepher, I removed myself from the hill and named Ma'at as my champion. Were this a physical game the winner would have to be at the top of the hill, but because I'm the judge of who wins the battle of hypotheses, I can keep picking Ma'at, establishing him as the gate through which all the other doctors have to pass to gain my favor."

"Hm," Evermore said, but without seeing his face Ashley couldn't tell if he was impressed or skeptical.

After a moment Rae decided to continue. "Before Ma'at took the job, he was experimenting with a strain of deep-sea bacteria that excretes Rochelle salt, building a piezoelectric crystal around itself, but he found that these bacteria crystals were producing a small electrical charge independent of external stimulus."

"My dear," Evermore cut her off, "I am familiar with Ma'at's previous work. There's no need to repeat your report. I'm not your professor, there is no test to pass. Just upload your reports to the cloud like the rest of the lab heads and assume you're doing a good job. My true reason for scheduling this meeting was to..." he trailed off, and then said, "Piezoelectric," to no one.

*Here comes the watch,* Ashley thought, shaking his head.

"My dear, before the whole synthetic man nonsense, the most common question I was asked was: How was I able to read the market and create something just right to fit the need? What I told them is that I was lucky, but the truth is that I check everything against my watch."

Rae raised an eyebrow. "You still use a—" She stopped herself.

Evermore took something out of his desk drawer that Ashley couldn't see but knew was a gold Casio wristwatch. "When I was ten, I wanted to discover how clocks measure time. So I sneaked into my father's room and took this watch from his bedside table."

Evermore expertly popped off the back. "Do you see that small metal cylinder?"

Rae leaned closer. "Yes. Is it dented?"

"Among all the gears, it was that small cylinder which caught my eye. I tried to pry it out with my mother's eyebrow tweezers, but as soon as I dented the cylinder, the watch stopped."

Ashley lip-synced as Evermore said, "That was the moment I became a scientist." He missed working with Evermore; he missed the late nights in Evermore's garage lab when it was just the two of them. He remembered the first time the Doc had shown him his father's Casio, and how he'd told the story so many times Ashley knew by heart how many times quartz vibrates in one second: 32,768. It wasn't the only number Evermore had forced him to memorize, either. Pi to eleven digits, the golden ratio, and the half-life of uranium 238, the Doc's favorite isotope.

"You might say this old watch is a dowsing rod of sorts. The tarnish that has built up over the years gave me the idea for the skyscraper lichen, and do you know what is so special about that tiny cylinder?"

Rae sat in stoic silence, unsure of what to say next.

"There is a small quartz crystal in that cylinder. Quartz is piezoelectric." Ashley could hear sadness in his voice and realized that the move to Mars had taken Evermore out of the labs. *He misses the work.*

Suddenly, in a loud voice, Evermore said, "In one week you have assembled a cohesive team, forged a unified vision, and discovered an unknown energy source. I asked you to give 100 percent, and you have delivered. Well done, my dear." Ashley felt a pang of jealously.

Evermore continued, "My true reason for scheduling this meeting was to talk about Ashley."

Rae looked concerned for the briefest instant, but then she shook it off, and a blasé veneer covered her face. "Go on."

"On Tuesday, Ashley Rephaireal came to me with a... concern, but I've been waiting to see how things would play out. How are you two?"

Ashley clenched his teeth. *What are you doing, old man?*

She shook her head dismissively. "You asked me to treat Ashley—"

"Yes, I know what I asked."

*I fucking hate it when you do that*, Ashley thought. *Why ask a question and then get impatient when the answer isn't immediate?*

Rae didn't let it phase her. "I acted too friendly with him, and it gave him the wrong impression. He became unprofessional, overstepped my boundaries, and I..." she trailed off, but Evermore didn't seem to be listening. His eyes scanned the ceiling as if in thought.

Finally he said, "In the future, if you would record such events it would allow me to track causes. Lucky for you, because of my relationship with him, I was able to tell that he was lying."

Rae looked worried. "Lying about what?"

"He told me that you have been putting in eight-hour days here and overtime at K&J, yet you seem abnormally energetic."

"I never said that," Ashley defended himself under his breath.

"That's all true," she said.

Evermore continued, "But that's not what I'm concerned about. He also said you had complained of headaches and stomachaches, that you'd been twitchy and often looked sweaty."

"Sweaty? I'll admit I may have skipped a shower in favor of sleeping in, but I don't understand why he would concern you with that."

Evermore made a dismissive gesture. "Ashley can be overly casual, but he didn't mention your confrontation. Initially I thought his 'concern' sounded too much like a list of side-effects, but now I see that he was trying to stir up trouble."

"Trouble?"

Evermore sighed. "Without coming right out and saying it, I think he wanted me to test you for stimulants."

"EXCUSE ME?!" Rae stood, almost knocking over her chair.

"Dr. Dahlia, please sit down."

Evermore put out his hands in a calming gesture. "You and I both know that these are empty accusations. It's been near a week and you haven't been subjected to any drug tests, have you?"

"No. But he's clearly trying to get me fired. I'm sorry, Doctor, but I want him out of my lab." She dropped back into her seat.

*What is he doing?* Ashley wanted to punch the wall, but he forced himself to hold still. *Rae, I never said any of that.*

Evermore said, "I very much doubt he was trying to get you fired. His aim was more likely to make us enemies of each other by painting me as the paranoid, micromanaging boss, and you as the victim of my power tripping. He desperately needs you on his side right now."

Rae said nothing and sat there as if Evermore's words had left a bad taste in her mouth.

"So you understand him better, Ashley's had a hard life; he thinks like a survivor. It took him years to trust me, and asking him to work for you has felt like a betrayal, I'm sure. I sorry it had to be that way. On top of that I imagine he's having a hard time trusting you. Especially since you are such a strong woman and have power over him."

There was a moment of silence. Rae's fierce gaze never changed. "Is it true he made the decision to hire me?"

"He chose to work with you, but I made the ultimate decision to take his advice. I suppose you'll want to take away his doggy bone, but I don't believe that will address the root of the problem, which is that he won't truly be on your team until he trusts you."

Rae shook her head. "There is no reason to reprimand him. This behavior is my fault; I didn't know he would react so strongly."

"My dear, you realize that you don't have control over people's reactions, right?"

"Of course," she said, scowling. "But I could have

been more sensitive."

*So now she thinks I can't handle her, that I'm a weakling.* Ashley's fingers coiled into his fists. *You fucking manipulative asshole.*

Evermore said, "Would it make your job easier if he were located elsewhere?"

"No!" Rae said immediately, "Ashley has been a valuable member of the team; he's even made a few good suggestions."

*Careful, Rae,* Ashley grumbled. *That's almost a compliment.*

Rae continued, "Part of the reason I was so surprised by that accusation is that I thought our working relationship has been improving since that incident."

"Maybe it has, I don't know, that was last Tuesday, but please let me know if things between you change in either direction."

"Yes, of course."

"Good. Well, I'm excited to see where this piezoelectric crystal takes us."

She stood and reached across his workstation to shake hands, "Thank you, Dr. Evermore, I am too."


Evermore opened the secret door to find Ashley slumped against one wall. He looked up at his mentor and choked out, "Why would you do that?"

Evermore smiled. "It's all just a game, my boy. The whole goddamned thing is just a game. You, me, Rae; we're all just pieces moving each other around."

"It's my fucking life. You told her I think like a survivor. She's going to wonder, a survivor of what?"

"So? What's the risk in telling her?"

Ashley thought for a moment, then admitted, "I don't know."

"Come on, what's the risk?"

"I don't know," Ashley repeated, then said, "It's like giving away pieces of myself."

Evermore took off his shirt, revealing a long scar across his stomach. "You have to remove the bad parts to make room for healthy bits. Blow your nose, my boy." He tossed the shirt in Ashley's lap. "Are you telling me you wouldn't give away that part of you if you could?"

"No. It's part of who I am."

"As I've told you before: it's the part of you keeping you small and getting in the way of your greatness."

Ashley couldn't meet his eyes.

"Look at Dr. Dahlia. You and she share such a similar past, yet the same thing that cripples you, empowers her. Why do you think that is?"

"Because she self-medicates?"

"Oh come on, I made all that up about the stimulants. Is that the solution you think I'm guiding you toward?"

"Screw you and your 'guiding' and your moving all the game pieces around!"

Evermore looked at him lovingly, which made Ashley all the more angry that his blows hadn't landed. He blew his nose in the middle of Evermore's shirt.

"Why did you tell her I tried to get her in trouble?"

"Every student at UMars is subjected to a drug test, and while she had been clean for a while, they received a history of stimulant abuse in Rae's hair. I'm concerned she'll reach for the support of an old friend when the stress of E.I. starts to get to her." Evermore reached out to Ashley and helped him to his feet.

"So it's just a trick to prevent her from starting. If this whole thing is a game, what do you get when you win?" Ashley asked, following him out into his office.

Evermore took a badly wrinkled shirt from a drawer in his workstation, put it on, and started buttoning it up. "What do you want more than anything else in the world?"

"I meant you. What do *you* get?" he pointed a finger at Evermore.

"I know what you meant. Answer me first."

The image that popped into Ashley's head made him ashamed, and he tried to hide it behind ignorance. "I don't know."

"My boy, I know you do, and I already know what it is."

"Then why bother fucking asking me?"

Evermore smiled. "I want you to hear yourself say it. There's a power in saying it, a power in claiming it."

"I want to be a world-famous scientist."

Evermore opened his arms as if to hug and celebrate him. "The way you get that is to diversify your teachers. If you only learn from me you'll only be as great a man as I am. That's why we hired her, remember?"

"How am I supposed to learn anything as a personal aide? All the doctors treat me like a moron."

"Well... do you sharpen your ideas? Or do you grab the closest concept and stab at it like a moron?" Ashley made a face, and Evermore changed the subject. "A real man claims his dreams and doesn't allow anything to shake him or get in his way. You must, in every moment, imagine yourself taking one step closer to becoming that world-famous scientist you've always wanted to be."

Unconsciously, Ashley was standing a little straighter.

"Good. Very good." Evermore's tone changed. "But let's not get carried away. Remember you are working for me, and this is not the place for you to surpass me."

When Ashley's features slouched, Evermore gave him a playful shove. "Look how easily you can be pushed off your path. Do you want to be a great man or a cowering plebeian who distinguishes himself through his willing-ness to abandon his own path and serve another's?"

Ashley threw the snotty shirt back in Evermore's face and left his office.

# CHAPTER THIRTEEN

# Confrontation

### Rae

As the elevator carried Rae down from the twelfth floor, she thought, *It's just a coincidence that Ashley chose stims. He made up those side effects days before I took the first pill.* She looked at her reflection in the steel doors. *Or... Ashley somehow hacked the results of my UMars entrance physical.*

The doors parted, and Ashley's empty receptionist desk greeted her. Rae looked at it and imagined for an instant that it would be empty from now on, and she was surprised to realize she would miss him if that happened. *Would Ashley really go so far out of his way to get me flowers, just to cover up his backstab? His note said he was sorry and wanted to start over. I had assumed he meant go back to before the incident, but fuck, maybe he meant back to our phone conversation?*

She walked across the lab, casually looking for him among the other stations.

*Maybe he is far more sneaky than I gave him credit for, and the whole mousy thing is an act. I have seen him hold his own, but I've also seen him try to lie. Ashley is not a manipulative person; that's Evermore. I think it's true he feels betrayed by Evermore, but if he truly did it to turn me against Evermore, I feel like there's a hundred other ways he could have tried that didn't bring up my chemical history.*

Rae realized that her hand was fondling the folded square of aluminum foil and the final pill in her pocket.

*Seriously? I just took one.* She withdrew her hand.

"Where's Ashley?" Rae called across the lab. The researchers looked the direction of Ashley's desk and realized for the first time that he wasn't there. No one answered.

She remembered what Evermore had said about Ashley being a survivor, and thought back to the moment she had struck him. *Ashley...* Rae shook her head to jostle the thought out of her mind. She hadn't thought it. It didn't belong there, and now it was gone.

She found Dr. Joseph Allan hunched over his workstation. "Dr. Allan," she said quietly as she approached, "I was hoping you could help me understand the implications of the vibrating crystal."

Allan looked up from a nauseating grid of numbers he was examining, visibly reorganized his thoughts, and said, "Well, it's important that we don't get ahead of ourselves. Dr. Ma'at's statement that two crystals were vibrating at the same time miles apart isn't as convincing a statement as he'd have you think. It really just means that whatever is causing the crystals to vibrate is affecting both locations. If we put two solar panels on opposite sides of the Earth, they're both going to be affected by the sun. Now if we..."

*That wasn't Ashley,* she decided, *that was Evermore using Ashley because he's afraid of being one of those micromanaging bosses. That was Evermore's way of accusing me without threatening. He was giving me a chance to change.*

Allan was still regaling her with his wealth of knowledge. "...still most likely a wave, probably from his Omni connecting to Cloud9. The possibility of something beyond the electromagnetic spectrum is like saying there's a room in your house you've never been in."

*If I quit cold turkey, I'll be a mess; I won't be able to do one job, so that's not even an option until after I finish my hours at Kander and Jansen. But if anyone has any suspicions and mentions them to Evermore, I'll lose my job. Fuck me, either way I'm going to get fired and no one on Mars will ever hire me again, and then I'll be stuck on the streets of Mars.*

"There's room between the walls," Dr. Raymond Hubert said as he approached Allan's desk. The rest of the team was still out of sight behind their workstation screens.

"The analogy was that there's an entire room you don't know about," Allan repeated.

Hubert nodded, "I understand, but you're comparing the known universe, a dimension filled with 95 percent mystery, to the place you live and have arranged and organized yourself."

"Again, it's an analogy; they're meant to be oversimplified." Allan was getting frustrated.

"No no, I'm not arguing against it, it's actually a perfect analogy, but what it represents is how our team is limited to seeing the house through our preconceived ideas of 'house.' The plumber sees a much different house than the carpenter or the electrician."

Rae tried to imagine how she would survive on the streets of Nili, but the image was pushed from her mind by a much stronger one: her face headlining the top stories in *Scientific American*, *Wired*, and *Time*.

*These are my dreams, and nothing will stand in my way.*

As she returned to the present she saw Allan squaring off against Hubert, except that Hubert was so engaged in his conversation he didn't realize it was only stimulating to him. Rae said, "Which are you, Dr. Hubert? Do you see the house like a scientist?"

"Goodness, no: I'm a philosopher. The universe *I* live in is multitudes bigger! For all we know, our scientific inquiry permeates the universe like a beam of light, filling each room of the known like a light turning on, but surrounding that room in an insulating layer of unknown that keeps us confounded until someone starts thinking like an X-ray. But even then only the next layer of unknown becomes visible. I can only imagine it's layer after layer like that all the way out."

"Or maybe we're like rats in a maze, and it's designed to test and teach us," Rae said, interrupting Allan's inevitable retort. Hubert grinned, and Rae changed the subject. "How's the search? Have you found a species of lichen that could be a biological match for Ma'at's S30:60?"

Hubert shook his head. "No, not yet, Dr. Dahlia."

The elevator doors opened, and Ashley stepped out. He surveyed the room. He and Rae locked eyes for a moment. *Fuck, maybe I'm entirely wrong. He's trying to read me, and he looks nervous.*

She broke eye contact. "Thank you for your help, Dr. Allan," Rae said as she left his workstation and returned to her own. Forcing herself not to look at Ashley, she wrote:

> **R.Dahlia:** I never apologized about the other day.

> I'm so sorry about what happened.

> I can't believe I lost control like that.

> **A.Rephaireal:** Why'd you do it?

> **R.Dahlia:** I think I felt trapped. I thought you were threatening me with that smile.

> **A.Rephaireal:** It's okay, you're under a lot of pressure.

> **R.Dahlia:** I never thanked you for the flowers either.

> **A.Rephaireal:** Don't mention it. You deserved them.

**R.Dahlia:** They couldn't have been easy to get.

**A.Rephaireal:** I've got a friend.

**R.Dahlia:** Only one?

**A.Rephaireal:** Just about.

**R.Dahlia:** Now YOU deserve flowers.

**A.Rephaireal:** It's true. I don't get a lot of opportunities to meet friends.

That sounds pathetic, but I'm basically caught between the service class and scientist class.

**R.Dahlia:** There aren't many people up here looking to make friends.

**A.Rephaireal:** True. Half the people are only here to fulfill their ambitions, and the other half just want to get away from Earth.

**R.Dahlia:** I can't say I've got much waiting for me back on Earth.

**A.Rephaireal:** Is that why you're so keen to invent FTL and go somewhere else?

Rae looked across the lab to gauge his expression: He hadn't meant them to, but that didn't stop his words from cutting her to the bone. Before Rae left for Mars, Deborah had insinuated the same thing. *Why does everyone think I'm running from something?* She changed the subject.

> **R.Dahlia:** What are you doing over the weekend?

Rae waited, fully aware that she was baiting him again.

> **A.Rephaireal:** Nothing exciting. You?

Her heart sank. Had she successfully trained another one, or was he no longer interested?

> **R.Dahlia:** Working at K&J

> **A.Rephaireal:** You're going to burn out if you don't take some time for yourself.

Rae wrote: "Maybe I need you to show me how." Then she deleted it.

> **R.Dahlia:** I'll keep that in mind.

Ashley's words stayed with her for the rest of the day. They clung to her hair like a bad smell. *"You're going to burn out if you don't take some time for yourself."*

*Will he notice when I don't take time and don't burn out? I made it through four years of university without taking time for myself. This is how I operate. Deborah always said I had to be working on some project. Besides, there isn't enough time, anyway. Even cheating sleep I'm still years away from where I wanted to be years ago. I'll sleep when I've arrived.*

### Ashley

Ashley waited until everyone had gone home for the day. It seemed as if Rae was doing the same thing, because ten minutes after the last team member had left, she shut down her workstation. As she waited for the elevator doors to close, their eyes met. There was softness at first, but after a moment her face hardened, and she left him with a snide remark: "You're going to burn out if you don't take time for yourself."

He nodded acknowledgment stoically, but as soon as she left, he jumped up from his desk and combed the northern wall for the secret panel he knew was there. It wasn't hard to find. The door was a shaped panel perfectly flush with the wall. Pressing it pushed the door inward. He closed it behind him and leapt up the stairs. At the top, Ashley waited behind the wall of Evermore's office until he caught his breath. He pressed his eye to the peephole before venturing to open the hidden door. Even though no one was around to hear him, he tiptoed across Evermore's office and quietly settled into the high-backed leather executive's chair. He wiggled his finger on Evermore's workstation and it awoke, showing a mess of files. Ashley minimized each file so he could reach Samuel's birth certificate. It said that Samuel Reznick was born in Grand Island, Nebraska, in 2003. It said Samuel was forty-five.

Ashley laid his Omni on the workstation and a pop-up appeared to ask him for a password to enable the network link. Without pausing to second-guess himself, he carefully typed in: $238U4.468X10^9Y$, Evermore's favorite isotope of uranium followed by its half-life. The password was accepted and the connection established. After drag-and-dropping the audio file labeled "Samuel_Reznick" onto his Omni, he executed a little program he'd written, which would penetrate Evermore's workstation log files and delete any trace of his electronic presence. It was then that Ashley realized what had stopped him from stealing the files when he had first discovered them: It was too easy. It was a crime of opportunity. Now the risk of getting caught and the ingenuity required to get away with it allowed him to earn his prize. But even now he was still left with an uncomfortable sensation: the unaccustomed feeling of doing something for himself. *Fuck that*, he thought as he put the workstation back into sleep mode.

As he left through the passage in the wall, Ashley found himself holding his Omni close to his chest, cherishing the revenge he'd stolen for himself.

Ashley hurried from the stairwell back to Lab Seven feeling like a boy with a brand-new bike; all he wanted to do was ride. He hurried to his station and opened the Samuel_Reznick.mp3.

White noise and some soft rustling of bed sheets or fabric preceded the voice, which said "October 31st, 2024." It was Evermore, four days before Ashley's first birthday, long before he lived next door and twelve years before the Synthetic Man Trial. "I may still be dreaming, but I have been awakened by a ghost."

Ashley imagined him in a nightgown and cap like Scrooge in the *Christmas Carol*. He smiled and strained his ears at the long silence that followed. Someone was talking softly, but all he could hear were the staccato notes of the *S*s and *D*s. He turned up the volume.

"—to do that is to die—" Ashley pulled the progress bar almost back to the beginning.

"—I have been awakened by a ghost," Evermore repeated.

He cranked the volume to maximum. "I am not a ghost," said a voice in a weak whisper. "I am an energetic being that refuses to relinquish my consciousness. To do that is to die, and I was promised eternal life." It was also Evermore's voice, but he was speaking while inhaling and whispering from the back of his throat.

In his speaking voice, Evermore asked, "Well, then, if you are not a ghost, what are you?"

His own raspy whisper answered, "You may call me Samuel."

Ashley had been holding his breath so as to make out every word, but at the mention of Samuel's name, the breath exploded out of his chest in a burst of laughter. "No!" he chuckled, "A ghost? Really?"

"What can I do for you, Samuel?" asked Evermore.

Ashley shook his head in disbelief. *He knew I'd want revenge, so he gave me something juicy to steal.*

"Your one mistake," Ashley told the recording, "was putting the files right out in the open on your desktop." He thought of the birth certificate. *But why put the contradictory evidence right next to it? To keep me guessing? To pull me further into your prank?* Ashley knew the Doc would have a contingency plan for either outcome.

In the .mp3, Evermore asked, "Would an empty body work? Perhaps a coma victim?"

"No, the container must match the contents," the whisper said.

"Building a body will ruin my reputation."

Ashley paused the recording. *He's preying on my suspicions. He's known I suspected he was building another synthetic human, and yet he never explained why he wanted me to program the genome printer to build all those mitochondria cells. Obviously, he's testing my trustworthiness; he knew I'd come looking for proof someday. And if he could also squeeze in a lesson about gullibility, he would.*

Ashley was about to hit play again, but his finger stopped, hovering over the button. *If Evermore wanted to trick me into believing that Samuel is a ghost possessing a synthetic body we built together, then he wouldn't have set it in '24. Samuel looks twelve, not twenty. The timing is off.*

"Okay," he told the recording, "Let's assume for a moment that you're authentic. Why would Evermore leave you where I would find you?"

Ashley started the recording again. The passage of time between recording sessions wasn't noted, so Ashley had no way of knowing how many days, months, or years were in between each session, but if there was any similarity between them, it was that Samuel would discuss philosophy and Evermore would do his best to explain science, of which Samuel was severely ignorant. For instance, the concept of gravity as a force amazed him.

Ashley thought back to his own late-night science tutorials back in Evermore's garage. *"Are we building another synthetic human?"* wasn't the only question the Doc had never answered. Ashley had asked him why he had risked everything to build something as boring as a human. Without fail, Evermore would get a faraway look of regret, then his eyes would twinkle and he'd say, *"Someday, you'll understand."*

"Is today someday?" Ashley asked the recording, and three and a half hours later he found his answer. The recording hissed with the start of a new session, and the first voice to break the white noise had the timbre and cadence of an infant, but the tone and message seemed older than humankind itself. It said, "All life aspirates the breath of God."

Evermore sighed and said, "I don't believe in God."

Again the unripe voice spoke: "This is not some bearded white guy living in a gated community of clouds and pearls; it does not need you to believe. It only needs you to live. Life is God's chest rising and falling. As we breathe in life, light, and new energy, we convert the light to shadow. After the in-breath peaks, it is followed by an out-breath. But do not picture this out-breath moving out, away from you; it does not. It, too, moves through all life, carrying with it a shadow. And at the bottom of the out-breath the shadow is transformed into light."

Ashley stopped the recording and pushed his Omni away. It wasn't far enough; he stood and walked away from it, but turned back around as the hairs on his neck stood on end. "What the fuck, Doc? Hoax or not, something is seriously wrong with you."

# Rae

The Lab Seven team, clad in mint-green clean-room suits, were standing around a crystal incubation chamber E.I.'s contractors had built in the center of the lab over the weekend. The sealed chamber was filled with hundreds of glass dishes the size of an American quarter. Each dish contained a tiny crystal the size and appearance of a single grain of coarse sugar. Rae was pushing the team to come up with ways to accelerate the growth process when she was interrupted by her ringing Omni. She tapped her Omni twice through all her layers to silence the call. It continued to ring, and, as she patted her thigh, she realized the square of foil wrapped around the stims in her pocket was getting in the way. She pressed her hand over it to mute the noise, but a moment later it rang again. She rushed to exit the clean room, stripped off the light-green bodysuit, and gave the Omni an irritated look, but when she saw it was Dr. Evermore, her affect shifted to concern.

"Dr. Evermore," she said. "This is unexpected." *He can't be expecting results already; why is he calling?* Her fingers unconsciously slid into her pocket and curled around the square of foil.

"No need to worry, my dear. I have been reading your reports and finding myself excited to discover what was affecting Ma'at's crystal."

"The S30:60. No. We've shielding it from all forms of sound, light and radiation, but nothing has stopped it from vibrating."

"Have you tried exposing it to different spectrums to increase its vibrations?" he asked.

"No. The organism in the Rochelle salt is unique and fragile, and Ma'at is reluctant to let us test it beyond shielding and occasionally prodding it with an oscilloscope."

"My dear, there is a point in every science when external observation reaches its limit. It's time to follow in the footsteps of Henry Gray and dig a little deeper."

"That's the *Gray's Anatomy* guy?" She grimaced, remembering Samuel's tirade about vivisecting life. "I agree... I think. But I promised Ma'at that before we sacrifice his only living sample to science, we would build an analog to test on. So we've begun building our own crystal-forming organism." She swiped through her Omni gallery and sent Evermore an image of the sugar crystals. "Dr. Evermore, meet *Lepraria ptilisaccharon*. It has the mycobiont from your Skyscraper Lichen and a photobiont cyanobacterium derived from the S30:60. What you're seeing is a sucrose crystal the ptilisaccharon, or PS, has built after a week of high exposure to light, carbon dioxide, and water." Rae's lips danced into a smile as she said, "The lichen has bonded so closely within the molecular lattice of the sugar crystal that the PS has become, in effect, a living stone."

"Standing on its own this is quite the feat, my dear. But why build a new lichen when you could have replicated the S30:60 bacteria?"

Rae felt that he was accusing her of wasting time. "Dr. Evermore, not only are we trying to discover the cause of the vibration, we are looking ahead to possible applications. We chose lichen for its cryptobiotic ability; the lichen, when severely desiccated, enters a metabolic stasis rather than dying."

"There is no need to be defensive; it was not my intention to threaten. Does this lichen exhibit the same mysterious vibrations as the bacteria?"

"I wasn't threatened," she said, before answering him, "Inconclusive; we used a very precise soldering vice to hold a grain of sugar against the oscilloscope probe, but we couldn't get a clean signal. In the meantime, we're attempting to accelerate their growth, and we've got an appointment to use the UMars X-ray synchrotron tomorrow."

"Then let's talk again this Friday at 3 p.m."

Rae remembered back to her last talk with Evermore. *Yeah, I'll bet he wants to check up on my progress. Ten to one he's checking to see if I've taken him up on that chance to sober up.*

Rae started to repeat the meticulous process of getting back into her clean-room gear, but this time she made sure the foil wouldn't block her Omni.

*It's time to come down.*

*Fuck.*

Later that evening, as she rode the automated rickshaw to K&J Labs for another four hours, she texted the Chemist.

> **R.Dahlia:** I'd like to place an order.

> **T.Chemist:** You're earlier than I'd expected. I guess the rumors about you burning the midnight oil at K&J are true.

> **R.Dahlia:** Who's spreading these rumors?

> **T.Chemist:** The analysts in your lab. They're pissed. You're only scheduled to come in on weekends, but your productivity is better than 50 percent of theirs.

> **R.Dahlia:** I'm about to knock another four off my thirty-six-hour goal for the week, but I think my work ethic is about to take a nosedive.

Rae waited to see if he'd understand her hint.

> **T.Chemist:** I'm sorry, but you've got to let me know BEFORE you run out.

> Unless... You're interested in something else?

> **R.Dahlia:** I am.

> **T.Chemist:** Give me a two days to prepare your order.

Rae mentally counted the remaining pills in her pocket. *That should be perfect. I may not be able to be sober for this meeting with Evermore, but I'll get there soon.*

Even though she had been to K&J Labs over twenty times, she still needed a map to navigate the twisting corridors to her lab. As she was scanned and let in, she was surprised to see she wasn't alone. One of the other analysts, a woman whom Rae had never met, was still there, and by the samples covering her desk Rae guessed the woman wouldn't be leaving any time soon.

"Good evening, Dr. Dahlia." She looked nervous.

*Is she awestruck? I have to admit I'm a little flattered.* "I don't believe we've met before."

"Dr. Rita Jampana."

Rae cocked her head at her as she realized that the samples she was testing were already labeled. And as she stepped closer and stuck out her hand, she recognized her own handwriting on the vials.

Rae turned away from Jampana and crossed the room to the cooler in the center of the lab. "How's my work compare to your standards?" she called over her shoulder.

"I mean no offense, Doctor, but this lab works as a team. We have before you showed up and will after you leave. If we produce substandard measurements, all of our research suffers and our entire team looks bad."

"How have I been making you look so far?"

Jampana said, "Good. With one exception—"

Rae's heart immediately started pounding. She held her chest to muffle the sound, as if the analyst could have possibly heard.

"—the last sample was mislabeled. What is *Lepraria ptilisaccharon?*"

*It's what I spend all night thinking about.* Rae let her embarrassment through her cool veneer. "It's what I named the mitochondria I'm trying to build in Hakaru."

Jampana's features and voice softened as she said, "I know what that is like. I am still working on one from last month. I had to set it down because I had become obsessed. What is the latest puzzle like?"

*God, I wish I had that kind of free time,* Rae thought, but she also knew that another part of her loved the rush of being overworked. "You don't want to know."

The analyst sighed. "No, I suppose not."

As Rae carried an untested batch of samples from the cooler to her work area, she noticed that Jampana hadn't stopped double-checking her work.

"So, what is it like working for *the* Dr. Evermore? Is it true that he only talks in riddles?"

Rae scrunched up her brow. "No. That would be ridiculous." But on the other hand, she had to admit it was partially true. "It's just like working here, but because E.I. is a young business, no one's really sure if the whole thing will just supernova and burn itself out of existence. You should be grateful. K&J is stable, secure."

Jampana packed up the finished samples and returned them to the cooler. "How did you even *get* that job?"

*Is that jealousy?* "Are you asking what did I have to do?"

"I'm just curious. That was a big jump from intern to head your own lab..."

*I don't want to pick a fight with this lady.* "Dr. Evermore reached out to me. I got lucky, I guess."

"I would guess you get a lot of things just handed to you."

Rae turned to face her, though Jampana was seated at her workstation with her back to Rae. "I don't know what your problem is, but I don't want to get into it. I've already put in a full day of work; I'm tired; I just want to get through this and go home."

"So now you understand why I am double-checking your work."

"Aren't you lonely up here?" Rae asked.

Jampana didn't respond, and Rae did her best to ignore her and focus on her own work. After Rae processed a full tray of samples, she returned them to the freezer and said, "There's another one ready for you."

The analyst left five minutes later.

# CHAPTER FOURTEEN

# Breakthrough

## Rae

The elevator doors opened a few minutes before three on Friday, and Rae sat herself in one of the leather chairs after a curt nod at Samuel. *Samuel looks worse*, she thought. *Surely Evermore would give him a day off if it was just a lingering cold.* Samuel looked up from his workstation, and she averted her gaze to the live-feed magazines on the waiting-room coffee table and noticed that one had recently updated its cover story: "10 New Omni Gestures you Need to Know."

*He called it ISS*. She wondered if it was fatal, and she took out her Omni. Making a C with her hand, she circled it around her face twice, and the Omni's search function opened. The article on the table refreshed, and the number of gestures jumped to twenty. Curious, Rae forgot about whatever ISS was and began counting the command gestures she knew. She reached thirty before Samuel cleared his throat and said, "Evermore will see you now."

As Rae entered the room, her eyes went first to where she expected to see the poly-carbon chairs on the other side of Evermore's workstation. They weren't there.

"Dr. Dahlia," Evermore called from the sliding glass doors beyond the library. "Come, join me."

Walking through the doors and out onto Evermore's rooftop garden, she saw two chairs beside each other, just past a small bed of culinary herbs.

Evermore walked ahead of her and sat in one of the chairs that faced out toward the view of Nili Terradome. Before she could speak or sit, he asked, "Do you know why you're here?"

Her first thought was, *He knows,* and her heart thumped so hard it felt like a punch to the chest. Her hand unconsciously rubbed her thigh, feeling the square of foil with its one remaining tablet through her clothes.

He continued, "Tech magazines say I'm here capitalizing on the gray areas of space law that struggle to keep up with scientific discovery."

"*Is* that why you're here?"

"You know me, Dr. Dahlia; I've always operated beyond the law. Look at this place, it's almost unbelievable! How could I be anywhere else?" She sat in the chair beside him. He turned to look at her and waited for her answer.

Still recovering from the misplaced shock of being discovered, Rae said the first thing that entered her mind.

"To do something great."

"For whom?"

It sounded stupid in her head, but she'd kind of talked herself into a corner and said it anyway: "The world."

"The Earth? Or the human race? Ignore that question. Tell me about the *Lepraria ptilisaccharon.*"

"I want to do something great for the Earth," she told him, but they both knew she was just saying it. She took a small glass vial half as long as her pinky from her breast pocket and handed it to Evermore. He held it in the light and peered down his nose at the single grain of greenish sugar.

"So this is the PS crystal?"

"What do you want to know that you couldn't read in my report?" Rae asked.

"Is it strange that I regard this as living? Even though

it does not move or sing or bite, I can imagine a spark of life somewhere in there." Evermore seemed taken somewhere else for a moment. He handed the vial back to her and answered her question. "When last we met, you mentioned a date at the synchrotron, and I am interested in hearing how it went."

"It went... complicated." *Not unlike most other dates I've been on.* "To create a proper analog to Ma'at's S30:60, we specified three criteria: one, it had to be living within the molecular structure of a crystal; two, it had to be an orthorhombic crystal system; and three, the crystal had to be piezoelectric, which in turn meant it had to have formed a pure monoclinic structure." Evermore had slightly rotated in his chair to face her. There was something going on in his mind that he seemed to find amusing. "The diffractometer measured a pattern consistent with a normal orthorhombic sugar crystal, but there was something else." There was a quiet creak of cloth on poly-carbon as Evermore shifted ever so slightly in her direction. "It also produced a blurry band around the outside of the diffraction pattern, meaning that the crystal was vibrating at such a high frequency that it was scattering the X-rays."

"I know your background is in biology, but even you must know that's impossible." Evermore shook his head in disappointment. "Clearly your instrument malfunctioned."

Rae poked a finger in her cheek and said, "Well, gee wiz, Doc, I guess it *was* my first time using a synchowhozit diffracto-what's-a-majigger." She scowled at him. "Which is why I had a *doctor of crystallography* run, recalibrate, and rerun the test."

"My concern is not that you're stupid," Evermore explained. "But you are preconditioned to see the results you want to see, and you've trained your team to never challenge your opinion."

Rae said, "Actually, most of the team assumed a calibration issue. After recalibration, we got a clean pattern match for a normal sugar crystal, and another normal pattern when we retested the first *Lepraria ptilisaccharon* crystal. It was actually Dr. Hubert who went against popular opinion and speculated that the X-rays had killed the lichen and we had tested a dead crystal. So we tested a fresh living one and received the same blurred band."

Evermore shook his head. "I don't care how many times you tested it, the truth remains that the phonons within the crystal can only vibrate at the X-ray's—"

Rae raised her voice over his. "That used to be true." Evermore gave her a look of consternation and she didn't bother suppressing her smirk. "You've never been on this end of it before, so I'll explain it to you: What you're feeling is the growing pains of the known universe expanding."

Evermore frowned.

"We alternated between a living *Lepraria ptilisaccharon* crystal and a plain sugar crystal. Every time we have tested a living PS, we have seen that blurred band."

"This is all interesting in its own right, but nothing you've said so far suggests anything beyond the electromagnetic spectrum."

Rae smiled. "Last night everyone went home, leaving me with the mystery of the blurred band. I'd need a delta ray to measure it accurately, and the line for UMars' is months long."

Evermore flexed his clout. "I've given a pretty sizable donation to UMars in the past, and they may let me cut in line."

"No need. K&J Labs has a delta-ray diffractometer, which they use for testing nanotube defects in high-priority material."

"You didn't!"

"I spoke to Dr. Kander and offered him another week of labor in exchange for a time slot; lucky for me Lockheed Martin had the graveyard shift booked but they never show up."

"You spoke with Kander?" Evermore seemed disappointed

"Obviously I didn't break your precious nondisclosure agreement, if that's what you're worried about. I told Kander: 'It's for a side project I'm afraid Dr. Evermore will steal.'"

"That was a rumor propagated by the media; I never stole Kander's idea!" He cut himself off and crossed his arms. "Dr. Dahlia, I am a busy man, please get to the point."

"Were you tending your garden while I was in your waiting room?" Rae knew she was poking a hornet's nest, but she couldn't help it.

He couldn't deny it with dirt on his lab coat. "Do you think this is a game? My time is extremely valuable."

"So is mine. So the next time you're interested in checking up on me, please save us both the time and just read my weekly fucking report." Evermore stared out across the city for a long moment. Rae took a breath and collected herself. "I'm sorry—"

"No. You're right. Let's start over. Dr. Dahlia, why did you come to Mars?"

"To do something great."

"So you've said, but that answer is as sugar-coated as your *ptilisaccharon*. All you're saying is: 'I don't know,' and—" She tried to interject but he spoke over her. "—and that's okay. You're young; you don't need to know. I know you're brilliant, and you're persistent as all hell, but you're inexperienced. I'm giving you the chance to shine, and that makes it my responsibility to polish you into a reflective surface."

*Fuck! I knew he'd want something in exchange. At least I wasn't tricked by the illusion of freedom.* Rae couldn't meet his eyes. "I wish I'd known about this arrangement ahead of time."

"You're most welcome, my dear. Now, tell me, when are you scheduled to use K&J's delta ray?"

*Is he baiting me? No, I'm not going to gain anything by standing up to this megalomaniac.* She forced a smile and said, "I told you, the graveyard shift was available, so I called my team back in."

"I'm sure they were excited about the extra hours," Evermore grumbled, still holding the grudge that she'd gotten help from Dr. Kander.

"I didn't hear any complaints. Mind if I continue?"

Evermore said nothing.

"The blurred band we observed when the PS lichen died is created by the crystal vibrating at 6,828 yottahertz."

"Yottahertz?"

"Yes. Twenty-four zeroes. Yottahertz."

"I understand yottahertz. What I don't is why you're talking about frequency when you were measuring the crystal structure."

She nodded. "While the delta-ray technician was running the test at K&J, the team at Lab Seven was comparing the random oscillations of the S30:60 and the PS crystals."

"There were only a few occurrences that the two crystals agreed to, but at twelve after two today, both the S30:60 and the PS vibrated at 6,828 yottahertz. It was in that moment that the PS was killed by the delta ray. Our current truth of the universe tells us that a beam of light traveling in a vacuum would take 837 microseconds — $10^{-6}$ — to travel the four and a half miles between the K&J detector and the E.I. building. But this was entirely unaffected by distance. It happened in the same moment down to the picosecond — $10^{-12}$."

Evermore said nothing. His face screwed up as he tried to troubleshoot all of the things that could have gone wrong. "That's... That's very unusual. Does the delta-ray technician know about this? And what about the blurred band?"

"Leading up to the instant the PS is killed, the band becomes a perfect unbroken circle. The only thing the technician knows is that we have an orthorhombic crystal that appears to be perfectly round for an instant. But I think you're forgetting about the fact that what I just said is impossible! Distance and time are interconnected."

"Everything science has recorded thus far has agreed with you. So either your argument is that distance and time aren't interconnected, or that data and logic aren't."

"This isn't funny, Dr. Evermore; it has to be some enormous coincidence."

"Please, calm down, my dear." Evermore waited until she sat before asking, "Isn't there some genetic relationship between the two crystals?"

Rae said, "Yes, the *Lepraria ptilisaccharon* is a modification of the S30:60 bacterium. Why?"

"Just curious. What conclusion have you drawn from this data?"

She shook her head. "You were supposed to point out the thing I missed."

"Did you miss something?" he asked.

"I've had Lab Seven picking through it with a fine-tooth comb and we've found nothing so far, but I was hoping that you would think of something we haven't."

"Nothing comes to mind. So what's your conclusion?"

Rae rubbed her temples. "Either there was an incredible coincidence, or the lichen are communicating via a medium parallel to the electromagnetic spectrum."

Evermore smiled. "You may have discovered a fifth fundamental interaction. Who's experiencing universal growing pains now?"

Rae declined the compliment. "It's too early to even joke about that."

"Newton stretched the color spectrum from six obvious colors into seven simply because he liked the number. At the time there were seven observable planets, seven notes on the musical scale, seven deadly sins, and seven heavenly virtues. Humankind has fallen into such a numeral rut with the four fundamental interactions: Electromagnetism, gravitation, the strong and weak nuclear forces. It's so balanced. No one *wants* to find a fifth. Ugh, five. It's so odd!" Evermore's eyes twinkled as he teased her. "My dear, discovery of a fifth interaction could overturn the scientific community. It could render you legendary, yet you seem to loathe the idea?"

"What if I'm wrong? Believing in a phantom fifth interaction is Andros Xepher's wheelhouse. No scientist in their right mind should so quickly believe such a crazy idea."

Evermore said, "True, and no scientist in their right mind would ever entertain the possibility of faster-than-light without an exotic tachyon particle, a missing law of physics, or an extra dimension. And yet here we are."

She grimaced, "Jesus Christ, why I am risking my career to build a transgalactic phone?"

Evermore laughed. "That's not what I had in mind. Though if you stumbled across that application, all of Mars would benefit from communications with Earth that weren't delayed by... what is it these days, about four minutes?"

"Four and growing," Rae grumbled, and stood as if to leave.

"Before you go..." Evermore rose and returned to his office. Rae followed and watched him pull a piece of thick ePaper from a drawer in his workstation and write something on it. After he sealed it, the ePaper shifted color so that it looked like a plain manila folder, like the one she had received on the first day. He handed it to her and said, "Lab Seven has a new assignment."

"Is the DNA lock really necessary?" she asked, taking

the folder from him.

"It's standard protocol to put all of our assignments on non-copy paper locked with DNA security."

As soon as he handed it to her she licked the DNA sample and read the short letter while licking the roof of her mouth to wipe the foul taste off her tongue. Evermore chuckled. Rae looked up, raised an eyebrow, and realized her mistake. "I licked it again — sorry."

"Don't be sorry. I'm sure you are well aware that mammals are creatures of habit."

When Rae finished reading, she shook her head. "Sustain the 6,828 frequency? What do you have in mind?"

"What we have is something that constantly reacts to an unknown signal and a 6,828 yottahertz signal: a receiver. What we need is something that produces a signal, and if you figure out how to sustain the frequency, you'll probably discover how to produce new frequencies."

"But what are we moving toward? What do you expect E.I. to build? It's not the answer to free energy. The crystal doesn't distort enough to generate a significant charge."

He smiled at her, but his underlying frustration dulled the twinkle in his eyes. "I could have sworn that I saw you at the poolside inspirational meeting with the rest of the lab heads, but I'll recap just in case. We building a vessel capable of—"

"Doctor, there's no need for sarcasm. You can't tell me that you've got ten labs all working on a faster-than-light engine."

Evermore seemed to be hiding something, and for a brief moment she thought he was considering whether to tell her about it.

Rae said, "Both of us want to see this thing take off; for that to happen we've got to trust each other." It wasn't quite the right bait; he looked as if he were about to decline. She said, "My whole future is riding on this!"

"More than you even know," he blurted out.

*Now he* has *to tell me,* Rae thought, forcing herself to suppress her victorious grin.

"Between paying off your debt to K&J and accepting the new position as lab head, the last thing you need is additional stress..."

She waited.

"But you're right: I don't have ten labs working on FTL. I've got three: Labs Seven, Eight and Nine, and once one of you solves the puzzle, the other two will become superfluous. So as not to carry the weight of the vestigial labs, the losers will be liquidated."

Rae's psyche seemed to start backsliding into the hollow in her chest.

"You wanted to know, and so I told you. And you should also know that no other lab head has been receiving the attention and mentoring that I am giving you." And there it was, the look that said, *I'm helping you, therefore you have to help me.* Rae had seen this social trap before. From anything as benign as holding the door for the person who happened to have just held it for you, to the expectation that accepting a drink was the same as consenting to sleep with the man. *What does Evermore expect of me?* she wondered. Then she decided it didn't matter. *I have to turn down the drink.*

"Dr. Evermore, I'm choosing not to assume you're helping me because I'm a woman. Instead I'll believe you're giving some pointers to a rookie, and now that I've caught up, you can go back to reading my weekly reports at your leisure. Thank you for the additional support, but it's no longer needed."

Evermore watched her curiously, unaffected by her theatrics. When she finished, he said, "As you wish, but I remind you that in the contract you signed, I'm well within my rights to influence, redirect, override, or cancel any experiment at my discretion."

"Understood." Rae turned to leave.

Evermore smiled. "You really are doing a fantastic job."

"Thank you."

As she closed Evermore's office door behind her, she noticed an white cane leaning against the wall behind Samuel's chair.

When Rae stepped from the elevator into Lab Seven, Ashley looked up at her and waited to see if she needed anything. She felt excited, and for a moment she wished she could share it with him without making things weird. He raised a questioning eyebrow at her, but she broke eye contact and called across the lab, "Attention Lab Seven. Evermore wanted me to congratulate all of you on such a great job with the first part of our assignment. Evermore is particularly interested in the 6,828 signal. Thank you all again for putting in the extra hours last night. Please feel free to take the weekend early. But on Monday morning, I want each of you prepared to offer ideas on how we can sustain the 6,828 Y-hertz signal. Also, Dr. Mora, will you work with me to create some genetic variance in our PS? I want to test communication between lichen crystals that are not genetically identical."

Ashley chimed in, "The new lichen's variance should be within the mitochondria."

"Thank you, Ashley, but Dr. Mora and I will handle that." She watched as he deflated back into his worksta-tion. *Fuck. I'm sorry, Ashley, I said that without thinking. Well, no, actually what I was thinking was, "Don't steal my moment."*

Rae pivoted. "Ma'at, I want you to start the growth process on a new batch of PS crystals. I want twice as many." She turned back to Ashley's desk. "Ashley... What are you working on?"

"Code." He didn't look up.

"I didn't realize you wrote code. Where'd you learn how to do that?"

"Actually, Dr. Kander taught me how to write C/C++." Reading the look on her face, he explained, "Which... is an old computer-programming language that runs in all K&J machines, including the genome printer."

"So you probably know real story behind Evermore and Kander's relationship?"

He stopped typing but still didn't look up. "They were friends and research partners since long before I ever knew who Evermore was."

Rae lowered her voice. "The story I heard was that Kander and Evermore built the first genome printer together, but Evermore left Kander's name off the patent documentation."

Bored with old gossip, Ashley said, "Everyone knows they invented it together, and to this day they make the same percentage on sales. Evermore only did it because he wanted to move quickly."

"But was it spite that drove Kander to whistle-blow Evermore for building the synthetic man."

Ashley turned his head and looked at her. "No. It was moral obligation. If Kander had backstabbed the Doc like that, there's no way he would *ever* work with Kander again. Why are you digging up dirt behind the rivalry?"

"Evermore got pretty upset that we used K&J's delta ray last night."

Ashley stared blankly into her eyes. "He's manipulating you. The rivalry was a publicity stunt to keep Evermore's name in the media so his house arrest didn't put him on the extinct species list."

Rae thought of Dr. Crellinger and wondered what she would do to stay off that list, if anything. Rae shrugged. "Too bad it didn't work. I had forgotten all about him until I heard he was starting a new R&D company in Nili Terradome."

"The Doc says it did. Just not how he'd expected it to. Every corporation that has moved to Mars has been a media bullet point, but when the Doc made the announcement, the media ran it as a David and Goliath story."

Rae remembered it differently. Evermore's press conference had been attended by underground science-news vloggers with hits-per-day counts in the mid-thousands. "Hey. You're calling him 'the Doc' again."

Ashley's brow furrowed as he tried to refocus on the code.

"Did you two decide to start over?" she teased.

Ashley sighed, clearly annoyed with her. "No. I guess I feel like we're even now."

Rae was taken aback. *If you are playing with me right now, Ashley, you are so... winning.* "Even? Why? What'd he do?" Ashley hid a devilish grin poorly, and she revised her question. "What did *you* do?"

"It's personal," he said, and as she started to protest he cut her off. "From what I've been told, our relationship is strictly professional. Which this," he gestured at their interaction, "is not."

She took a step away from his workstation, and fumbled for something to say. "You're... right. You're right." Rae walked away and from her desk called across the lab, "Ashley, I'm famished. Will you run down to the caf and pick me up some cricket nuggets?"

He cursed her with his eyes and stood. "Anyone else forget to eat today and need a snack?"

As Rae exited the Evermore Industries building at the end of the day, her Omni buzzed with a message:

> **T.Chemist:** Your order's ready. Meet at the usual spot.

# CHAPTER FIFTEEN

# Breakdown

### Rae

The Chemist recommended that Rae take the red pill no sooner than sixteen and a half hours since her last Queen Anne's Lace, which meant waking up around four in the morning on Saturday. Though short, it was the best session of sleep she'd had since her return from Chasma Australe. It was deep and dreamless. But as the alarm roused her, she could feel the toll the stims had taken on her body. She swallowed her one and only red pill and fell back asleep.

A second alarm roused her three hours later. Rae could feel her mind taking longer to wake up; she felt unnaturally anxious about going to K&J; and there was an ache in her jaw that felt like she'd been punched.

As Rae prepared for the day, she found herself in the shower holding a bottle of conditioner and couldn't remember if she'd used it, or was just about to. *Rinse and repeat?*

During the automated rickshaw drive she was awakened by a pleasant voice telling her, "You've arrived at your destination," for the nth time. *Why the fuck am I so tired?*

She could hear her mother's voice answer, *"Could it be because you've been pounding stims for the last few weeks?"*

*Don't be so judgmental, Deborah. The CrashPad I took last*

*night should be canceling the withdrawal symptoms.*

"I need a coffee," she told the rickshaw and it rerouted her to the nearest café and guided her through preordering the drink.

Feeling slightly better with hot black coffee coursing through her, she sat down at her workstation at K&J Labs. Her plan was to work there for ten hours, but after three she was startled by a sharp, loud noise like a door slamming shut. Her heart thundered away in her chest as she examined the room for the source, and a moment later her head started pounding. Using her Omni like a mirror, she looked at her forehead and found a bright red mark. The sound had been her head hitting her workstation as she fell asleep sitting up. That's when she noticed her hands were sparkling with sweat and shaking.

## Ashley

*Today's my birthday,* Ashley thought as he entered the Evermore Industries building. It was also the first Monday of November. Whenever his birthday fell on a Monday, he would get comments like, "Too bad you have to work on your birthday." But in all honesty, Ashley would rather be at work. He was on Mars for the sole purpose of working at Evermore Industries. It was a sentiment he shared with the rest of the Martian scientific community. Come Saturday, most would have preferred to work straight on through to Monday, but Western cultural convention directed them to hang out with their peers. Ashley had no peers. The post-grad assistant/secretary class was the closest match, but they were all too predictable, like manufactured snowflakes cut from the same mold and packed into the life-size Nili Terradome snow globe. It wasn't as if he weren't smart enough to fraternize with the doctors and scientists, he just knew he would feel like the little brother tagging along. If he could, he wouldn't waste a birthday wish on making it a weekend; he'd wish that no one ever looked at him the way Rae did when she found out he was her assistant.

*Rae.* The last few weeks with her had been different. Ever since her meeting with Evermore, Ashley felt Rae's power over him vanish. Her petrifying gaze looked more flinty, and her attempts to provoke and make an example out of him seemed more accidental than calculated. And there were more and more moments of her being nice to him. He thought back to last Friday, when she'd publicly shot him down for his intelligent suggestion to alter the PS's mitochondria. *"Thank you, Ashley, but Dr. Mora and I will handle that."*

He heard Evermore's voice reminding him, *"Do you stab at an idea like a moron, or do you present honed thoughts?"*

*At least she said "thank you."*

Ashley had no idea what would happen to him if Lab Seven were liquidated. The Doc preferred the hard-knocks teaching style and would probably let Ashley fend for himself. *I have to figure out how to steer Lab Seven toward the solution.*

*How do I hone the idea that ghosts are real and that what we are trying to discover is spiritual energy?* he thought. *Evermore wants us to sustain the 6,828 Y-hertz frequency: the moment of death. Or, as the voice in the recording called it, "the point of crossover."*

The elevator doors opened, and Ashley was momentarily blinded by the rising sun. He raised his hand to shield his eyes, and when his sight returned he realized he was the first to arrive. *There's no one I can ask for help on this one. But where to start?*

*"Do you stab at an idea like a moron?"* Evermore asked again.

*No. I have to follow the scientific process.*

While he waited for Rae and the rest of the doctors to arrive, he decided to take a few stabs at a question so he could begin to make an educated guess at how to produce

the frequency. He cued up the section of the recording
where Samuel spoke for the first time. The eerie infantile
voice made his skin crawl, but he wanted to hear Samuel
talk about the breath of God again. He inserted a pair
of worn earbuds that had lasted him the whole trip from
Earth and pressed "play."

"It doesn't need you to believe. It only needs you to
live. Life is God's chest rising and falling. As we breathe in
life, light, and new energy, we convert the light to shadow.
After the in-breath peaks, it is followed by an out-breath.
But do not picture this out-breath moving out, away from
you; it does not. It, too, moves through all life, carrying
with it a shadow. And at the bottom of the out-breath the
shadow is transformed into light."

"Are you saying we're the source of these two energies?" Evermore asked.

"No, and there are not two energies. It is one energy
with two qualities. The breath can be light, and it can
be shadow. As soon as you create two, those that were
one become opposites, enemies bent on annihilating the
other."

"So even if we separated them, they would just destroy
each other?"

"There is nothing to separate. If you stand outside on
a sunny day you will cast a shadow. Can you think of a
way to separate yourself from your shadow?"

"No," Evermore confessed.

"Can I move on? Do you understand?"

There was a long pause before Evermore spoke. "No."

"You are such a man of science, but I know nothing
about the world that I cannot see: electricity, cells, viruses.
So it is hard for me to find an analogy you will understand.
Imagine this: There are two men, both goldsmiths, both
work for the same noble for the same amount of pay, everything about them is the same, except one man's job is

to take raw gold and smith it into something new, while the other man's job is to take beautiful golden trinkets, dismantle them, and melt the form back into raw material."

The smithing metaphor made sense to Ashley; it explained how there could be two versions of the same thing that were not opposite but still diametrically positioned. When he imagined this breath moving through him, he imagined every living cell in his body lighting up with two different colors, then the next moment each would switch to the other.

The lichen, he remembered, was not actually one organism but two living in symbiosis: a cyanobacterium surrounded by fungus. He wondered if there could be a network of cells small enough to create a wall that the light couldn't escape. He started typing:

> When the crystal is irradiated, the outside fungi dies, closing the holes in their "screen."' Therefore, the chaos of the energies echoes inside the cyanobacterium and distorts the crystal, which produces the frequency. If Lab Seven can create a spiritual energy trap, and force energy into that space, then maybe we can produce an artificial point of crossover.

Ashley refined his statement as Cyrus Ma'at and Joseph Allan arrived. As Luther Brando and Raymond Hubert stepped out of the elevator, carrying a playful argument with them, Ashley was researching Helmholtz resonance, the phenomenon explaining the sound produced when blowing across the mouth of a bottle. He was trying to imagine a device built entirely of crystal that might produce a similar effect when Kaspar Mora and Benjamin Washington emerged from the elevator.

Everyone was there, except Rae.

Ashley sighed and called her from his desk. It rang five times before her Omnibox offered to send her his message as a text. Ashley hung up, sent her a concerned text, then called again. Five minutes later, when she still hadn't returned the call, he opened MeetUp, a friend-tracking app. It returned an address he didn't recognize, but after a quick search it turned out to be an apartment complex.

By nine forty-five the Lab Seven team had passed impatient. Dr. Joseph Allan said, "I spent a fair portion of my weekend preparing for this brainstorming session."

"Me too," said Dr. Hubert. "And I enjoyed it."

Dr. Mora, the chemist, said, "We had plans to design another species of *Lepraria ptilisaccharon* on Sunday, but Dr. Dahlia never showed."

Ashley was about to text Evermore but then imagined the Doc would chide him for not even trying to solve it himself before asking for help.

Dr. Cyrus Ma'at stood. "I, for one, think Dr. Dahlia is testing us. She gave us tasks to perform today; we have prepared for them; let's continue with our work."

Allan spoke up again. "Why does she get to take a vacation day while we sit here watching crystals grow?"

"That's not fair," Ashley said. "For the last month Dr. Dahlia has been putting in nights and weekends at K&J Labs to pay for the breach of contract necessary to take this job."

"Why should we have to pay for that?" said Allan.

Ashley said, "Is doing your job—"

Ma'at raised his voice over Ashley's and said, "Asher's right. She used her connection there to get us time at the synchrotron. She paid for that in her own hours. Without that breakthrough we'd have given up on lichen crystals and spiritual resonance."

Allan rolled his eyes. "Is anyone else surprised that the man whose research is being done for him is the biggest proponent of our continuing to work?"

Ma'at shook his head. "My previous work may have inspired this, but this line of inquiry stopped belonging to me the moment we, as a team, built the first PS crystal."

Dr. Benjamin Washington came to Ma'at's defense. "Allan, what would we even be doing if not for Ma'at's previous work?"

Ashley shouted above the mounting chaos, "You're not going to be working on anything if Lab Eight gets to it first!" Everyone stopped and turned to look at him. *I shouldn't have said that.* "You think the interviews stopped when you were hired? He's vetting us, all of us, including me, for some project yet to be discovered or unveiled."

"You been watching us from the beginning," Allan said. "I heard you used to work as Evermore's assistant, but you never stopped, did you?"

Ashley threw his hands up in defense. "I discovered that by accident. Lab Eight's assistant has a big mouth."

Brando said, "Allan, even if he is still watching us, calling him out on it doesn't change that we're being tested."

"How far along is Eight?" Washington asked.

"I don't—" Ashley began, but Ma'at cut him off.

"It doesn't matter. The best thing we can do is continue to work on our own project and hope that we can prove to Evermore we're the team worth keeping around." He glared at Allan.

"I just don't know what we're going to do without the new PS," said Kaspar Mora.

"Well," Ma'at walked over to the conference table, now on the southern wall, where it had landed after being displaced when the clean room was built in the center of the lab. "It sounds like we've spent some time preparing ideas for how to sustain the frequency. Let's get to work."

Ashley had been angry at Ma'at for interrupting him, twice, but as he watched the man staying perfectly logical and neutral, balancing one side of each idea and weighing the other, he realized why Ma'at had been on Evermore's top three list for principal researcher of Lab Seven.

Ma'at said, "Mora, are you able to begin design work on your own?"

Mora shook his head. "Yes, until it comes to programming and using the genome printer."

Ashley stood up from his desk and shot his hand high in the air. "I've been writing code since—" He stopped.

Mora was facing Dr. Washington, who said, "Yeah, the interface is the same for all K&J products. Genome printer or molecular manipulator, it makes no difference."

Ashley walked back to his workstation determined to finish the day with some way to guide Lab Seven toward the creation of a crystal Helmholtz resonating chamber.

After work, Ashley grabbed a steak-and-cheese sandwich and a chicken soup to go and headed toward the apartment he'd found on MeetUp, which he really hoped was Rae's. On the way he called her again, but there was still no response. Outside her apartment complex he found her suite number and called her door code over and over. Eventually a security guard came out, but before Ashley could explain himself, the guard said, "You making a delivery? Which room?"

He almost said yes, but then he realized that the guard wouldn't be able to help him. "No, I'm trying to bring my girlfriend some chicken soup. She's been really sick, but I think she fell asleep and turned her Omni off."

The guard's eyes found the Evermore Industries ID badge and he said, "Oh, I'm sorry, sir. I thought—" He cut himself off. As he opened the door for Ashley, he raised his eyebrows. "You and Miss Dahlia, huh?"

The pressure of lying to a security guard paralyzed his tongue, but then he realized that the guard was treating him differently because he assumed Ashley was a scientist. Maybe things were exactly as classist as he imagined them. "It's *Dr.* Dahlia," he said.

"Of course, I'm sorry, sir. Have a good evening, and I hope she feels better soon." The guard returned to his station, and Ashley did his best to walk confidently toward a suite he didn't know the location of. Once he was out of sight down the hall, he starting counting suite numbers and extrapolating the direction of Rae's from the number on the door buzzer. Approaching her door, Ashley suddenly realized that he wouldn't know what to do if it were locked. He raised his fist to knock, but if the buzzer hadn't roused her, knocking certainly wouldn't. Ashley turned the handle and let himself in.

Rae's suite was dark and smelled of sour body odor. One of the windows was covered with large bath towels pinned to the wall, but the thumbtacks had fallen out of the second, and the room was illuminated by the terra-dome's sunset screen show. As Ashley's eyes adjusted to the dimness, he saw that the room was the exact replica of his own, a one-room suite with a kitchenette at one end and a dining/living room that spilled into a bedroom at the other. Rae had separated her bedroom from the living room with Asian-style folding dividers made of faux wood and rice paper. Ashley wasn't even sure if anyone was there until he heard her snoring, but the sound wasn't coming from the bedroom. He found her curled up on her side on the large couch that faced a fifty-inch Omni-Watch smart TV. She was wearing a pair of black underpants and a large T-shirt that was tangled up around her armpits. Her hands were tucked beneath her head, and her breasts were covered by her elbows. The yellow blanket that once had covered her lay in a pile on the floor, and something beneath the blanket was glowing.

Ashley's first reaction was to turn away and protect her modesty, but it was like trying not to stare at a car wreck. Between the smell of the apartment, the loud snore that was the triumphant cry of lungs fighting for each breath, and the bush of unkempt hair that escaped from her panties, there was nothing modest about her. In the end, the way he draped the blanket over her was less like a mother tucking a child into bed and more like a mortician covering a cadaver from view.

*What the hell am I even doing here? What did I expect to find? If I wake her she'll be furious. Maybe if I make it clear that I'm only here to help?*

The glow from beneath the blanket was her Omni. Twelve missed calls from Ashley Rephaireal. The battery was almost dead. He scooped it off the floor and set it on the charging mat on the kitchen island. Next he moved on to the sink, only to find just one dirty mug and a few pieces of silverware. The dishwasher was empty, but based on the rest of the apartment Ashley thought it unlikely that she had kept up with the dishes. Opening the fridge confirmed his suspicions: it was empty but for a jar of chunky peanut butter and a half-eaten package of celery. *It's not uncommon for professionals to subsist on takeout,* he thought, checking the trash can, but there he was only half right. The bin stank of rotting Chinese food that must have been weeks old and was curiously dotted with tiny balls of aluminum foil. He tied up the bag, carried it out into the hall, and dropped it down the garbage chute, where the organic material would be sorted out and composted and the rest would be vaporized into its base elements.

Next he went around picking up her clothes and tossing them in the unused laundry hamper, being sure to check her pockets for loose papers. Instead he kept finding tiny balls of aluminum foil. *Gum wrappers?* he thought. When he got to the pair of pants she had most recently discarded, he found a square of aluminum foil folded around something hard and round. Unfolding the square, he found an unmarked white tablet. Ashley had never seen anything like it before.

*What am I doing here?*

"What the fuck are you doing here?" Rae shouted, pulling the yellow blanket tighter around herself for protection. From beneath her tangled hair sticking out at all angles, her eyeliner-smudged Medusa gaze burned with gamma radiation. Ashley's reality blurred. One moment he was facing Rae, the next it was his mother. He startled and the tablet fell to the floor with a tiny click. Rae growled at the lowest volume she could, "What the fuck are you doing in my apartment?"

*I'm cleaning up so you won't blame me for the mess,* he realized. Letting his anger overwhelm his terror, he threw her pants to the floor and watched her face twitch with the slightest hint of fear. "It's okay," he said. He had meant it to be reassuring, but it sounded disappointed.

# CHAPTER SIXTEEN

# Chicken Soup

**Ashley**

Rae sat up and used her legs to push herself along the couch away from Ashley. "What do you mean, 'It's okay'? Ashley, what are you doing here?"

"I've been calling your Omni all day. I thought you were sick."

"So you broke in?"

He smiled weakly and gestured toward the bag of take-out by the door. "No, I brought you some chicken soup, and the door was unlocked."

"So you thought you'd let—" Rae had raised her tone, but it was too loud, and she returned to her quiet growling. "So you thought you'd let yourself in and have a peek around?"

Ashley was feeling enormously guilty for intruding on her privacy, but then he realized she hadn't asked him to leave. "I didn't mean to wake you; I was just tidying up a bit. I took your trash away, and I was going to run a load of laundry for you and leave you some clean clothes and hot soup, but you're not sick, you're..." He couldn't say it.

"I am sick," she said, "but that doesn't give you the right to go snooping around. This is my private space. It's like—"

"Like I've stolen something from you?" Rae gave him a curious look that let him know he was right. "Was it something beautiful, or something terrible you never wanted to see the light of day?"

Rae's grip on the blanket loosened, and she looked down at the floor. "Something... the second one," she said, but barely.

Ashley sat on the other end of the couch and faced the TV.

"What? Are you disappointed in me?"

He ignored the question. "I was raised an only child in a single-parent household. For as long as I can remember, I would get myself ready for school, cook breakfast for the both of us while she slept. After school I'd clean the house as best I could and do homework while cooking dinner until she got home in the evening."

Rae shook her head. "Ashley, this isn't what I want, you don't have to try to make us even."

"She was an alcoholic. She'd come home tipsy and drink herself mean."

"Ashley, stop." Rae crawled across the couch and put a hand on his shoulder.

"I used to do everything in my power to protect that secret. It didn't matter how hard she hit me: She was my mom. I loved her, and I didn't want her taken away. Part of me still wants to protect my dark secret. I feel like in giving it away I give away part of what makes me who I am." Ashley finally drew up the courage to turn and face her. The blanket was hanging off her shoulders, and tears were running down her cheeks. She nodded understanding and agreement.

"Wouldn't you give away some part of you if you could?" Ashley prompted her.

Rae took her hand back and leaned into the couch. "I'd claw it out with my bare hands if I could find it. But I don't have some terrible memory to tell; I have a dead place inside me, and I've tried everything to fill it up or make it go away. When I was a little girl, reading would help me forget, but then fiction didn't work anymore, and I had to be reading things that required all my attention. Scientific journals and studying became the best way to avoid it. At UMars I would bury myself under homework, but nothing I do ever makes me feel whole and... alive for long. I can't drink it away; alcohol only makes it louder, so working myself to death is the best way to escape."

"What about painting? When we first spoke you talked about art in such a beautiful way..."

Rae scoffed, "Yeah, I used to love drawing with crayons."

He didn't say anything, and finally she admitted, "Yes, when I was doing it, painting made me happy. But I can't make a career out of it." She seemed to remember something and said, "Not yet, anyway, but I have a theory that synthetic bioengineering will be the medium of the next artistic renaissance.

"Anyway, for now I have to work hard until my eventual burnout."

"Is that what the white pill does? Keeps you going?" He tried to ask it as a question, but was ashamed at the holier-than-thou tone in his voice.

"Yes, but Evermore has gotten suspicious, and I had to quit. Now I'm on a little red one that's supposed to cushion this agony of withdrawal."

"Is it... working?"

She made a noise somewhere between a laugh and a sob and shook her head, "You know, I don't think it's working. But it's still too early to tell; once I wake up Monday morning I'm sure I'll be fine."

*She doesn't know it's Monday.* "How long have you been asleep?" he asked, and immediately realized that it was a stupid question to ask someone who has been asleep.

Rae looked out the corner of window not hidden by the towel. The ambient orange glow of night in the terradome let her know it was sometime after dark. "I fell asleep around 11 a.m., so maybe six or seven hours. What time is it?"

"Just after six." Ashley didn't think the whole truth would help her in any way, so he said, "I know what it's like. Not the withdrawal — I mean I have a hollow nothing can fill."

She looked about to cry again, but she pinched it off, her brows furrowed, and she said, "I'm still pissed at you for breaking in, but I'm also really fucking hungry. If you bring me that soup I guess we can call it even."

Ashley left the couch and put the soup in a bowl in the microwave, then pulled the steak-and-cheese out of the bag and unwrapped it. Rae walked over to the kitchen island still wrapped in the yellow blanket. "What's that?"

"It's a cold steak-and-cheese sandwich."

Without taking her eyes off the sandwich, she asked, "Can I have a bite?"

"I got you soup." The look she gave him seemed to be a reminder of the thin ice he currently walked on. "Sure, help yourself."

She eyed him suspiciously. "This isn't some bullshit hexapro beef, is it?"

"Of course it is; you think I can afford real steak?" The microwave beeped, and in the space of time it took to collect the bowl of steaming soup and place it in front of her, she had taken three enormous bites from the sandwich. "Where are your spoons?" he asked, pulling open drawers.

With her mouth full she gestured toward the drawer by the refrigerator. By the time he laid the spoon beside the bowl, half of the sandwich was gone. "Come on," Ashley complained, "I'm hungry too."

"'ave 'ome 'oup," she suggested.

He blew across a hot spoonful of broth, and his stomach growled at him. *I know, buddy, I know.*

When the sandwich and the soup were gone, Rae

looked up from the empty bowl and said, "God, I could eat another two, at least."

Ashley took out his Omni and placed an order for grocery delivery. "I could eat another... oh wait, I didn't even get a bite of my own sandwich."

"Well, why the fuck did you order soup in the first place?"

"I got it for you when I thought you were sick!" he said, before realizing Rae was teasing him.

She smiled. "What are you getting now, pizza? That's your go-to, right? No wait, you're a little different, you probably go for take-out Ethiopian. Get me some of that spicy beef stuff. Ooh, no; get a chicken bucket."

"I'm getting groceries."

Rae made a face. "But I'm hungry now."

"*I'm* hungry now, and what I'm going to cook is worth waiting for."

She was taken aback. "Why are you doing this when I've been such a bitch to you?"

"Lab Seven needs you, and it's my job to make sure your attention is on them."

"Sure, that explains the soup. But cooking me dinner? That gets me nervous that you want something."

"Sure I want something! Did you know that I hate weekends? I hate going back to my empty apartment and watching old movies from before the turn. I've seen them all anyway. I wait for Monday to roll around like it's my birthday and everyone will be there. So maybe the soup does cover the minor "get well soon" sentiment, but I really need you to come back to work."

"Ashley, Lab Seven is going to be fine. I specifically set aside today to recover. Tomorrow I've got a meeting with Kaspar Mora to start designing a new PS, and then we've got our brainstorming session early Monday morning. Lab Seven may need me, but they didn't bring me soup." Rae waited for him to answer her implied question: *Why are you really here?*

He couldn't bring himself to tell her it was Monday night. *What, are you afraid she'll start yelling again? Yes, but she's going to yell at me either way.* "It true, I did have another reason for coming: I wanted to tell you I ran into Hugo Voss's assistant, Leon, at the Relativity Lounge about two weeks ago. He told me that Lab Eight is working on a communication system beyond the electromagnetic spectrum." He waited for her to start yelling at him for not telling her sooner, but Rae just looked disappointed.

"They're in direct competition with us!" Ashley was nearly shouting.

Rae winced at his volume and worked her aching jaw a few times. "I already know about that, but they're losing, so it doesn't matter."

*Why does she seem so disappointed?*

"You really are here just to protect your job, aren't you?"

"Not just me; I'm trying to help you."

She was unimpressed. "Uh huh, but everybody wants something."

He frowned. "It's true. I'm shopping for groceries so I can make you dinner, because *I* want to eat."

"I just thought you were after something else," she mumbled.

*Is she implying I'm here for sex?* he thought. *Not even my fantasies are that wild. I've been around you long enough to know that you're just a terrible flirt.* "Like what?"

"Me. I mean... using me as evidence to bring back to Evermore."

"Why would I do that? Evermore already suspects you're using. He wouldn't fire you unless it served a purpose."

Rae narrowed her eyes at him. "I wonder who could have aroused that suspicion. Maybe someone *told* him I was acting 'sweaty and twitchy'?"

Ashley rolled his eyes. "He was trying to scare you straight. I didn't suspect anything until this morning, when you never showed up for work." His eyes widened.

She was confused for a moment. "Omni? What day is it?" she called out to her missing Omni.

From its charging pad, her Omni said, "Rae, it's Monday, the fourth of November."

"It's fucking Monday night?" She looked angry, but moreover she looked terrified. "Evermore's going to fire me! It's Monday night. I've been asleep for like fifty hours!"

Ashley attempted to comfort her by relating what had happened at work, but as he neared the end of the story she started laughing.

"Even Dr. Allan thinks you're Evermore's spy."

"Why would I spy for Evermore?"

"To get his approval and hope that he hires you back."

"Evermore is always four steps ahead. If I tried anything like that he'd see it coming a mile away and reprimand me for it. It's clear he has no plans to hire me back, especially after—" he cut himself off and turned away from her before she could notice him turning red. "Shit, I forgot to get salt. Do you have any?"

"After what?" she asked, but Ashley had left the kitchen island and was opening cabinets one by one.

"Of course I have salt," Rae said. She stood up from the island and cornered him in far end of the kitchen. "After what? After you got even? What did you do?" She grinned.

"Rae, I don't know where to start."

Her eyes widened in anticipation.

He sighed and said, "The other day when I made that suggestion about altering the PS's mitochondria, you didn't take me seriously. You didn't even *begin* to take me seriously!"

There was the disappointed look again. "You're not

getting off by distracting me with more work shit!"

He pushed her lamely, and she took a step back. "That night at the Relativity Lounge, the moment you found out that I was your assistant and that I was a little younger than you, you wrote me off. You have no idea what it's like for me up here. I've been mentored for over half of my life by a genius who has trained me to use my talents to produce brilliant things. But now I find myself in a position where nothing I say or do is taken seriously because I don't have fucking letters after my name!" He was shouting into her face.

Rae took another step away from him. She looked as if she was going to say something but instead broke down and started to cry.

Ashley hung his head. "I'm sorry Rae, I didn't mean to—"

Through the tears she said, "No, *I'm* sorry. You would have been justified in hitting me back, but here you are apologizing again. I don't deserve an apology because—"

"Rae—"

"No! I don't deserve it because I fucking know better. I know what it's like to be instantly written off at a glance, but instead of bumping up against a couple hundred years of educational tradition, I'm pushing against a million years of sexism. I know exactly what it's like to have to prove myself in every first impression. I've altered the way I look, changed my personality and suppressed who I am just to get the respect I deserve. So I'm sorry." She took a step toward him. "I'm so sorry for hitting you." She took another step. "It fucking tears me apart that I'm doing the same thing to you. And I'm sorry that tomorrow I'm probably going to do it again. I'm sorry that I can protect you from them, but not from me. I'm so sorry that I can't show you in front of the other doctors, but I do respect you as a person." She was so close to him.

*Funny how a bad apology ends up being about the person apolo-*

*gizing*. Now he felt like he owed her something. "Thank you for saying that. I know you have to keep up appearances. I just wish I didn't make you feel weak."

She seemed to be waiting for something else. Ashley had imagined this situation a hundred different ways, but they all ended in Rae being close enough to him where he could grab her in his arms and kiss her. In exactly zero of those scenarios had he imagined her breath stinking of meat and onions, her hair tangled into a rat's nest, or that she would be high on speed. *What do you want me to say?* He thought back to the previous conversation. They had been talking about what he took from Evermore when he had changed the subject to table salt.

"I hacked into Evermore's desk and stole an .mp3 file."

The look she gave him was uninterested and disappointed. "I think he'll forgive you for borrowing a song or two."

"It's not music," he sneered. "It's a recording. Rae, I know how we can sustain the frequency."

She rubbed her temples and turned away from him. "I don't want to talk about work. I've been asleep since Saturday afternoon, and I feel like shit. I think I developed a tolerance to the CrashPad, or else my dealer is fucking with me." She returned to the kitchen island, crashed her ass onto the stool, and laid her head on the cold Martian clay-top counter.

"You don't smell that great either," Ashley added, walking into the bathroom. He tried his best to ignore her personal clutter around the sink, plugged the drain in the tub and turned on the water. Before he left he lowered the toilet lid, put her comb (whose teeth were clogged with wads of hair) into the drawer, returned the toothbrush (which had been resting on the wads of hair) to its spit-stained glass on the edge of the sink, and launched a fruitless search for the cap to the tube of toothpaste.

"The food should be here soon," he called. "Why don't

you take a bath while I cook? It'll help you feel better."

She shrugged and didn't move. He walked over, grabbed her hand, and pulled her to her feet. *We're really doing this?* her eyes seemed to ask.

"Come on," he said, leading the way. Once the tendrils of hot steam reached her, she started moving of her own volition, and as she entered the steamy bathroom he closed the door behind her.

Sometime later the bathroom door opened and a breath of humid air, smelling like some flowering jungle tree in full bloom, spilled out. Ashley, cooking on every pan in the house, took his eyes momentarily off the simmering white sauce and said, "Feeling any better?"

Rae was wearing nothing but a pair of towels. Ashley turned back to the stove and felt his face redden. "*Relax,*" he told himself, but then Rae walked up behind him and said, "Yes," into his ear. He could feel his body tighten and his heartbeat quicken.

"What's in the bowl in the microwave?" she asked.

"I couldn't find a pot big enough, so I'm boiling the linguini in small batches in those bowls. I hope you're hungry; everything should be ready as soon as you're dressed."

Rae didn't move. "Where'd you learn to cook like this?"

"The internet. When I got sick of PB&Js and cereal, I learned to make it myself."

Rae was silent, and when Ashley turned around her face was sad.

"Don't feel bad for me."

She shook her head. "I wasn't. I was trying to remember if I'd ever seen my father cook before..." Rae floundered for a moment; she clearly didn't want to talk about her father but couldn't think of a way to change the subject. Between her vulnerability and the smell of freshly shampooed hair, Ashley was overwhelmed, but as he leaned in to kiss her she pulled away.

When Ashley was eight or nine, a kid in school had pulled a chair out from under him as he was about to sit down. Ashley had wanted to knock that kid's teeth out, but when Rae pulled away, the only person Ashley wanted to beat up was himself.

## Rae

As Rae pulled on her clothes to the sound of the microwave door, water pouring down the drain, and slicing on the cutting board, she thought, *I can't complicate things. He's being such a fucking gentleman, and if he's trying to get something in exchange it's only because he can feel me begging him to fuck me.* She sighed. *He won't try to kiss me again. Not after I pulled away like that.* But she couldn't decide if that was actually what she wanted.

The Alfredo was delicious even though she wolfed down her portion before she'd really tasted it. There was a moment as she cleared the dishes when she wasn't sure what would come next. With no other plans keeping him there, he could just leave at any time. *I don't want to be alone,* she thought, holding back unbidden tears, but it was too hard to think of the future. Tomorrow was a concept she couldn't imagine in her current state. *UMars,* she thought. *We can talk about UMars.* But then she remembered he hadn't gotten in, and something occurred to her. "Ashley, how is it possible that you didn't get into the University of Mars with Dr. Evermore helping you?"

Ashley sighed. "I guess I just wasn't smart enough, or they didn't think I had anything to offer."

Rae returned to the kitchen island and sat beside him. "You can't just base your intelligence on what some department of admissions tells you. I just don't know why, with all of Evermore's clout and connections, you didn't get in... unless Evermore didn't want you to get in."

Ashley looked at her skeptically. "You really want to go digging this up now? It's too late for me to go to UMars. That ship has sailed."

"What do you mean, 'too late'? You're the same age I was when I got in."

"There are things about Evermore, about the project that I found out about on the .mp3... but you don't want to talk about work stuff," he said, obviously baiting her.

*It's true.* Whenever she thought about work she remembered that she had missed an appointment with Mora and blown off her whole team during the most important meeting they'd had.

"Let's watch some videos!" Her OmniWatch awakened even before she jumped up and started gesturing.

"I should—" he started, and it seemed as if he was trying to extract himself from her apartment, but at the last minute he changed his mind. "I mean... I should have known you'd want to watch something, and gotten some popcorn."

"If you'd done that, I would've questioned your motives again."

"I have no motives," he said defensively.

"Don't get me started." She smiled, and he smiled back. It was like watching the sun peak through the clouds after days of snow. It melted her. "I feel like watching *Bali Fu*," she said, trying to judge his reaction. Technically, it wasn't a movie but an episodic series of hour long videos.

Ashley laughed. "I can't imagine you'd actually watch that."

"Why not? Because there's fighting in it and I'm a woman?"

"Firstly, if that's fighting, then tango is a martial art, and secondly, 70 percent of its viewers are women."

"Then why?"

"Because it's ridiculous and fun, and you're—"

She frowned. "And I'm not fun?" She hit him playfully, but his instinctive flinch was violent.

Acting as if he hadn't been startled, he said, "I was going to say 'serious.'"

"Not all the time," she said, rolling over the back of the couch to land on the seats. "Come on, sit." The first episode started to play. Ashley walked around the couch and sat beside her, leaving a safe buffer between them, an unclaimed territory that, once crossed, would decide the outcome of the night.

## Ashley

Halfway through the first act she got cold and pulled the yellow blanket across them. The territory shrank. As the hero began his gratuitously colorful kick-fighting dance number, she slumped sideways and leaned heavily on him. He went rigid, but her relaxed body was diverted like a river of honey slowly creeping toward his lap. By the time the villain with the giant mustache... beard... thing stood victorious over the fallen hero, she had fallen asleep.

Ashley waited for a long time, pinned beneath her, trying to decide what to do, and as the credits ran their course and Rae slept on, he still hadn't decided. Part of him considered leaving, but he knew that wasn't what she wanted. After imagining what it would be like to awaken alone, and emboldened by the energy of the show, he decided to carry her to bed heroically. Ashley surprised himself at how easily he lifted her into his arms, before remembering that everything weighed less on Mars. Tucking her under the covers, he crawled in beside her in all of his clothes. Even though he was exhausted, the smell of her hair fueled his fantasies and kept him awake for what felt like hours.

Sometime during the night he awoke to find Rae pulling down his pants. It took all of his will not to freeze up entirely. *Maybe she's just helping me get more comfortable.* But even he didn't believe that. Though he had imagined it a hundred different ways, no part of him ever thought she would want it, too. *I was wrong. I've been wrong the whole time. That spark we felt over the phone is real, and she's finally open enough to let herself feel it.*

She took him in her mouth and slowly used her tongue until he got hard. He forced himself to remember the final showdown in the *Bali Fu*, where the hero kick-danced the crap out of the mustached nemesis. He thought about Helmholtz resonance, *Frequency equals volume over two pi times...* but distracting himself wasn't working. Just as he was about to explode, he arched his back, and she stopped. She crushed his cock in her hand and growled, "I'm not done with you yet."

The dark silhouette that knelt over him was completely naked. He reached out for her soft round breast, but just then she slapped the head of his cock, and a sharp pain exploded throughout his body, banishing the tendrils of pleasure that had bound him to the brink of ecstasy.

"...the fuck?" he complained.

She pushed and pulled his shirt up over his head and laid on top of him, smearing her breasts against his bare chest. She lay there for a moment, paralyzing him with the fragrance of her hair and gently kissing his neck. Overcoming his fear of doing the wrong thing, he grabbed her face and pressed his lips into hers. She sucked on his lips thirstily before pushing herself up so she was straddling him, and with one hand on his chest and the other on his cock she guided him inside her and leaned back.

"Oh—fuuuck! Wait! What about protection?"

She bent forward and whispered in his ear, "I'm on the pill."

He pushed himself into her in a slow, circular motion. Their tongues slipped in and out, exploring each other's mouths, and Rae took frequent sharp nibbles on his lips.

But a question was bothering him. *Goddamnit, if I don't ask I'll be distracted for the rest of the night.* He took a deep breath as if coming up for air. "Hey, Rae? Why are you on birth control? I mean, my impression of you is that you don't usually let anyone close enough... or with any sort of... regularity."

She pulled away sharply, but by the ambient light coming in through the windows he could see she was smiling. "God, you are so awkward. It's true I haven't had a good fuck since that rower at Yale. Actually, I take it for period control. It makes my hormones, cramps, and flow less intense. Plus, I don't like surprises. No no no no, don't you dare go limp on me!" Her insides starting constricting around him rhythmically, and she forced her tongue into his mouth.

Grateful that the moment of awkwardness was behind him, he tried to forget about it and began thrusting himself deep inside her, lifting her off the bed. Her wetness ran down the inside of her legs and he imagined he could feel it dripping off his balls. Giving in to the wave of pleasure, he called out her name and immediately felt her tighten around him. He came in pornographic proportions and tried to stay inside her, fucking her for as long as she would let him, but the sensitivity became unbearable and he rolled her off. She playfully slapped his chest.

"Fuck you and your first time, Ashley,"

"*My* first time? I pretty sure you made up that story about the crew jock. You kiss like a little kid at an underpowered drinking fountain." She started to get angry, but he ignored her and pushed her onto her back, guided her legs apart and brought her to climax with his mouth. Even though he was sore he was still hard, and he thrust himself into her a second time and fucked her until he was worried her cries would draw the police.

The silence that followed their second, throbbing orgasm pressed in on them heavily. After the remaining shudders coursed through his body, he rolled off of her. An hour or a moment later he heard the sound of her gentle breathing. Immediately he felt something in his body relax, which was odd because he thought he had been relaxed. But now he was as soft as the sheets and one with the bed. Something about her falling asleep relieved him of... and then he realized the extent of the façade he had built up to face her. As his own eyelids drooped shut, he wanted so badly to be given advice. *Doc, who am I supposed to be in the morning?*

Rolling onto his side, he whispered, "I feel the urge to give you everything I've got, but I don't think you want that. I want to shout out and tell all of my friends, but being with me makes you weak. How about this: you just let me know when we can be together again, and I'll wait for you."

# CHAPTER SEVENTEEN

# Unstable Isotopes

## Ashley

An alarm from the opposite side of the apartment pulled Ashley from the depths of sleep sometime early in the morning. It was his alarm. It was time to get ready for work. It took him a second to remember where he was, and another to make sure he wasn't still dreaming. Rae was still asleep beside him. The alarm blared on. He got up, walked naked across the apartment and turned it off. Returning to the bedroom, he shook her softly. "Rae, it's Tuesday. Are you planning on coming to work?" She didn't hear him the first time, and he repeated it.

"No."

"Your team is going to mutiny if you don't give them something to do."

She buried her face in the bed and pushed him forcefully away with her other hand. *Come on, work with me here.* "If you're not going to give them an assignment, I am."

The response came immediately, though it was muted by the mattress. "Fine."

"Do you realize the choice you're making right now?"

Without moving in the slightest or opening her eyes, she whimpered, "Ashley." There was a long pause as she gathered her strength to speak. "It's worse today."

He thought of the little white tablet falling to the floor when she startled him. "What if we break up the white one and just give you half?"

She didn't respond.

*Whatever; I wasn't going to do that anyway. I don't know why I suggested it.*

Ashley took a quick shower, put his dirty clothes back on, and left without eating. He had to be the first one to arrive.

As he left the apartment a thought occurred to him, and he went back and grabbed Rae's suit coat. Outside, the digitally altered sun shone bright in Ashley's eyes as it crested the Alps to the east. Though the Alps were a VR illusion superimposed over the eastern wall of the Nili Fossae trough, Ashley wished he were actually there. Not for the sights or the sounds, but for the smell of the fresh mountain air. Right now everything still smelled like the minty toothpaste he'd rubbed across his teeth with his finger. *Better than coming to work with pussy breath.* He grinned.

As he walked through the doors of Evermore Industries, Julius greeted him pleasantly. "Morning, Ashley."

"Morning." He smiled back. *I had sex with Dr. Dahlia.*

Per usual, he was the first to arrive in Lab Seven. Without a second thought, he crossed the room to the conference table and circled five of the many brainstorm ideas the team had come up with yesterday and wrote on the conference table beside it:

These five seem the most promising. Before we move forward with any of these, we'll need a Helmholtz resonator built from our PS crystals. Thanks for going ahead without me yesterday. I've gotten into the habit of working late. Was here all last night. I expect to reset my sleep schedule this weekend. Please do your best to give 100% without me. ~Dr. Dahlia.

As he made the hand gesture for "enter," the VR board transformed his handwriting into a generic sans-serif font. He reread it and decided to delete the "please." He walked to Rae's workstation, moved a few things around, and draped her coat over the back of the chair. He then remembered that she had missed her appointment with Kaspar Mora on Sunday. After quickly reviewing Mora's species design, Ashley, in Rae's words, directed him to focus more on the mitochondria of the mycobiont, then apologized for missing him on Sunday.

With his teeth still crunchy from toothpaste, Ashley decided to return after he'd gotten some breakfast from the cafeteria downstairs.

Ashley returned half an hour later, feeling slightly more prepared for the day after eating a pair of soft, warm scones and nursing a cup of scalding hot coffee. He was physically exhausted but mentally energized as the memories from the previous night replayed in his mind. Because it had all taken place in near darkness, his recollections were not images but fibers of sensation that tangled together one moment with the next until each moment was filled with the smell of her hair, the sweet taste of her pussy, the softness of her skin brushing and gliding against his.

As the doors parted, the six doctors turned and looked expectantly at him. He smiled. *I had sex with Rae Dahlia!* he told them all in his mind. They were unanimously disappointed and returned to puzzling over the message on the conference table.

Dr. Allan said, "The frequency produced in a Helmholtz resonator is related to air pressure; it has nothing to do with electromagnetic waves."

"I think it's brilliant," said Raymond Hubert. "At its root, the resonator's purpose is to trap matter."

Cyrus Ma'at saw what Ashley had intended and said excitedly, "If we can create something that blocks the frequency, we can trap it, pressurize it, and increase the frequency."

Allan scoffed, "How do you propose we block a wave

that doesn't seem to be affected by space-time?"

Before Ashley could stop himself, he shouted across the lab, "Have we experimented with forcing the PS into cryptobiosis?" The team turned to face Ashley. *Shit, I need to get them to think it's their idea.* He added quickly, "Sorry for yelling. What are you all talking about, anyway?"

Ma'at tilted his head in thought. "That's an interesting idea, Asher. Last week when we deprived our PS of all water and sunlight, it did indeed stop vibrating."

"It would need to be big enough to fit all of our equipment inside," Allan returned disparagingly. "Growing that much PS could take—"

"Three weeks," Ma'at interrupted.

"Preposterous," Allan shot back. "The crystal itself grows at a rate of one cubic millimeter per week."

Ma'at said, "I understand our limitations; however, in twenty minutes we could print a pound of PS, then use the lichen spray technology that Evermore developed to cover a form in whatever shape we want; I'm thinking a dome. In three weeks our entire dome will be covered with a layer of crystal three millimeters thick."

Ashley returned to his work with the lab buzzing and revitalized. He couldn't help but smile as he heard the team co-create a list of experiments that Ashley knew would reveal some of the qualities of the other dimension Samuel had described in the recording. Raymond Hubert, who was also a self-proclaimed master of feng shui, had assigned himself the task of rearranging the clean-room equipment to accommodate the PS form, while Ma'at, Mora and Allan started designing the chamber. By the end of the day, Ashley had two work orders in front of him, one for a pair of wooden forms in the shape of a dome and saucer, and another for a series of metal pieces that they planned to build around the crystal, enclosing it in a thin, vacuum-sealed wall.

Once Ashley had received the work orders, he turned

them in to the contractors and started to leave.

"Calling it early?" Dr. Washington teased.

Ashley froze.

"Leave Asher alone, Washington, he probably needs some rest before Dr. Dahlia shows up." Ma'at said.

Washington looked confused, and Ashley thought he was going to have to make something up about what time Rae came in. To his relief, Washington said, "I thought your name was Ashley."

Ma'at looked embarrassed. "Oh shoot, you're right. I'm sorry, have I been calling you 'Asher' this whole time?" Ma'at walked over, shook Ashley's hand and introduced himself. "Cyrus Ma'at."

"Ashley Rephaireal."

Feeling like he had just been welcomed onto the Lab Seven team, Ashley gathered up his Omni and hit the button for the elevator. In the reflection of the doors he looked about as tired and happy as he felt. Inside the elevator waited a sickly looking Samuel. His hair was noticeably thinner. His skin was so pale it was becoming translucent. Thin blue veins ran across his temples and down the backs of his hands. Clutching the rail on the side of the elevator to support himself, Samuel didn't smile as Ashley entered and attempted a friendly nod.

"How are things progressing in Lab Seven?" Samuel asked as the doors decided it was safe to close.

"Good," Ashley said, trying his hardest to act natural. *Could this guy really be a ghost in human flesh?* "I don't know how much the Doc tells you, but they may have discovered a fifth fundamental interaction."

"Yes, he mentioned that. For whatever reason, Everett has put a lot of faith in Lab Seven, but time is running out."

"Is Hugo Voss getting close?" Ashley smirked.

Here Samuel cracked a smile that seemed to pain him.

"Out of all the labs working on that same assignment, Dr. Voss was the man I put my faith in, but the buffoon has been wasting his time studying orbs in old flash photography. Everett even tried to convince him that orbs have nothing to do with spirits and everything to do with backscatter off dust particles."

"How can Everett be so sure?" Ashley baited. It felt strange to call the Doc by his first name, but he wouldn't be one-upped by this freak.

"You have known him for almost as long as I; how does he ever seem to know the unknowable answer?" The elevator doors parted.

*He cheats,* Ashley thought. "I've been trying to figure that out for years," he said, grinning.

Unblinking, Samuel said, "You're a terrible liar, Ashley Rephaireal."

*Fuck you, Samuel.* "Have a good evening," Ashley said, and walked away.

Rae was on Ashley's mind all the way home. He tried to decide if he should call her, and wondered if there wasn't some two-day rule he was supposed to follow so as not to appear desperate. *She's probably still asleep. I'm sure she'll call if she needs something.*

Back in his apartment, he thought of Rae as he showered for the second time that day and put on new clothes. He thought of her as he made dinner, as he packed up the leftovers for tomorrow's lunch, as he sat on his bed/couch to watch TV on his tiny Omni screen, as the program was interrupted when she called. He accepted the call with video.

"Hey," he said smiling.

"Hi," Rae returned. She looked terrible: her hair looked like she'd slept on it all day, and her face had pillow lines pressed into it. "I feel like shit."

"Do you need some soup?" he asked.

"Fuck you and your soup! I need steak." She smiled.

He was smiling so much he felt like an idiot. "Alright, I'll be right over. Don't fall asleep this time; I'm not sure I can talk my way past the security guard twice."

"Hey, yeah, what's up with that guy letting a creep like you into my suite?"

Before running from his apartment he ordered dinner and breakfast groceries, and packed some clothes, anticipating another sleepover.

Rae swallowed and set down her fork. "You know, I don't think I can remember what real steak actually tastes like. Next time I eat some, this is the flavor I'm going to expect. Hey, you barely touched yours," she said.

"Yeah, I just wanted a taste. I had already eaten when you called, and I thought you might want to eat mine once you'd finished yours."

"Asshole... Thanks for coming over, Ashley."

"You seem much better."

"Yeah. I've got a headache that could split atoms, but I'm almost feeling back to normal. Thanks for holding down the lab. How was it today?"

"Much better. I've been working on synthesizing our research with the information I got off the .mp3." She screwed up her face, and he realized that she might not remember what he was talking about. "Yesterday I was telling you about an .mp3 I stole from Evermore's workstation. It's a recording of the Doc talking with Samuel. Well, at first the Doc is speaking for the both of them, but you can hear Samuel's voice later in the recording."

"I thought you said it was a solution to preserving the 6,828 frequency."

"It is, but you're not going to believe it. Here, hand me your Omni." She did, and as he drag-and-dropped the Samuel_Reznick.mp3 file, he explained, "At first I thought the Doc was trying to prank me, but then I decided not to think about it. I figured that either the Doc is dreaming the solution to a long-pondered problem or he's being visited by a being from another dimension."

Rae was mid-sip from a bottle of a hoppy Martian beer; she swallowed and said, "Seriously? Wow, I think maybe you should lay off the old sci-fi movies."

Ashley forced a smile. "Not a chance, but the Doc isn't one to start pursuing crazy ideas—"

"No?" she interrupted. "Didn't he plead guilty to building a synthetic human being?"

"It's true," he said, "but that's aberrant behavior for him; he's not one to take risks."

She shook her head in disagreement. "Last I checked he wanted to build a faster-than-light engine."

"You don't understand; that's not a risk for him. If he's working on that, it's because he's got a plan, just... the goal might be different than what you might think.

"If you listen to the recording, it's Samuel who's behind the synthetic human. In exchange for a new body, Samuel tells Evermore about how the energy of life works. Rae, I think it's the same force that is making the crystals vibrate."

She glared at him. "You're serious?"

"Yes! Toward the beginning of the recording Evermore says the year is 2024. That would give him enough time to have started building a synthetic body before Kander blew the whistle on him."

"But the prototype body was confiscated after the Synthetic Man Trial."

"Confiscated and destroyed! But I think he built another in 2038 while he was under house arrest, which would place Samuel's body's age at around eleven or twelve. It also accounts for Evermore's hiatus extending years beyond his sentence. He was waiting for Samuel to grow up."

Rae rubbed her eyes. "Wait, wait. Go back to the beginning. You think Dr. Evermore's personal assistant is an

extra-dimensional being living in an artificially constructed body, which Evermore built in his garage?"

Ashley nodded, relieved that she finally understood.
"It all makes sense if you listen to the recording. And that
was just at the beginning. Once Samuel's body developed
a voice box, their conversations continued deeper into the
specifics of this breath of life and the dimension Samuel
was trapped in. You've got it all right here," he said, passing her Omni back.

Rae eyed the device with suspicion. "Okay." Through
the headache she assembled the pieces of information
and slowly remembered how they had gotten on this
topic. "And today was a good day at the lab? You didn't
play the recording for them, did you?"

"God, of course not!"

"Then how were you able to get them to keep working
on preserving the death frequency?"

"I think what we've been calling the 'death frequency' is the same thing that Samuel calls a 'point of crossover.' But to answer your question: I combined the ideas
that Samuel talks about with the research we've been doing on the PS and left them a note from you saying that
you've—"

"You did WHAT?" she shouted.

It stung, but Ashley shook it off. "To explain your
grossly unprofessional absence, I told them you've been
working nights, and that you wanted them to build a
Helmholtz resonator."

"Since grad school I've had to work twice as hard as
any man to get to where I am now. Generations of sexism compacted with being a minority here on Mars has
forced me to think strategically about every move I make,
but in one move you've undermined all that."

"Rae—"

"I'm not finished. Everything I do, everything I say,
reflects not only upon me as a scientist, but upon the

reputation of all women scientists. You assumed I needed help, and, without consulting me, stepped in to fix it."

"But I did. I asked you this morning after I tried to get you out of bed, but you didn't seem interested in coming to work, so I—"

"I would have said anything this morning to get you out of my hair. What were my words exactly?"

"Rae, I'm sorry. I swear I wasn't trying to undermine you or take advantage of the situation, I just wanted to get the team back on track."

"No, I'm sure you didn't. Just like you don't realize that now you have the power to either claim whatever success your note brings or shrug off whatever ruin it causes."

He held out his hands. "I'll—" *Don't say "fix it."* "I'll tell them it was me. I'll tell them you've been sick and I was covering for you."

"It's not about just that." She leaned in closer. "Ever since I was a little girl I've known that emotions make you weak, so I have always done my best not to have them. Last night, it felt like you unlocked every emotion I've ever pushed aside."

Ashley smiled, but she wasn't smiling.

"I can't be like that. I can't be this emotional and taken seriously at the same time. Lab Seven will turn on me like wild dogs."

"What are you talking about?"

It seemed as if Rae's entire face had hardened. "I think you should leave."

*Is she for real? What is this really about?* Ashley stared at her but couldn't manage more than a dry swallow.

"I think you should leave," she repeated. Her gaze burned holes in his heart.

"Rae—"

The Amazon warrior returned. "Get the fuck OUT!"

"You should have seen the way the team talked about you on Monday; they have so much respect for you. Evermore—"

"Evermore is using me as the poster girl for faster-than-light whether I discover it or not."

Ashley stood and squared his shoulders to her. "Then you'd better start paying attention to me, because the FTL engine isn't even the goal."

"Pay attention or else what?" she challenged him, and Ashley's moment of resolve crumpled under her force. "Ashley, get the fuck out of my house!"

# CHAPTER EIGHTEEN

# Black Holes

### Rae

Ashley looked as if she'd stomped on his heart. He turned, walked from her suite, and slammed the door behind him. Rae swallowed her tears and thought, *Where are you going, dumbass? Don't leave me alone like this.* The thought echoed across the vast cavernous hollow that opened up inside her. The void pressed against her insides painfully, as if it wanted to extend beyond her physical form and didn't mind ripping her apart in the process.

Rae stared at the door for a long time, wishing he would return. Eventually she realized that he wouldn't come knocking, the intercom call would come from her Omni, and she shifted her gaze. She checked to see that the device wasn't silenced and noticed that a new file had completed downloading: Samuel_Reznick.mp3. Disconnectedly, she opened the file, but her mind wandered off, and when it returned she had no recollection of what had happened in the recording. She tried again.

"October 31ˢᵗ, 2024. I may still be dreaming, but I have been awakened by a ghost."

Ashley had already told her as much.

*Goddamn it, how could he have used my name like that, doesn't he realize that I'm in control of the situation?*

*"Are you really?"* Deborah's voice asked.

*Yes. Evermore was right; I was putting too much pressure on them. The only way to know for sure was to leave for a few days.*

"And what are you offering in return?" Evermore said.

*Damn it!* She'd gotten distracted again and had no idea what Evermore was talking about. She stopped the recording and went to her address book.

Combing through the numbers in her list of contacts, she realized how long it had been since she last spoke with the few people she considered friends. It would have been easy to blame it on the annoyance of communicating between worlds and the minutes that passed between question and response, forcing her to speak in chunks as if leaving a series of voice messages. But the truth was that she had left those friends behind long before leaving for Mars. Her move to San Diego had altered most relationships from face-to-face updates to online catch-ups. She followed a link in her address book to each of their profile pages, one by one, and realized that all of them were married, and many of them had kids. She examined her own profile and realized that her last update was from during her first semester at UMars. She thought of the friends she'd made at the university and realized that most were male and hadn't stuck around once they received the "just friends" talk.

Systematically, Rae deleted the friends she had either lost touch with or knew she wouldn't call again; the contacts that remained were colleagues she'd worked with recently, hard-earned contacts from the scientific community, the Chemist, and Ashley. She tried to delete the Chemist's number, but her finger seemed unable to descend on the confirmation button. *I'm going to lose control of the lab if I don't get better.*

"But I'll lose Ashley if I keep using, and probably lose my job."

She shook her head. *I've already lost Ashley. I just sent him away, and he's a good boy who does what he's told.*

Reaching across the table, she jammed a cube of Ashley's unfinished steak into her mouth and played the next vid in her playlist. Forcing all thoughts of Ashley and work from her mind, she planted herself on the couch and tried to relax. It was a foreign romance, and before long the subtitles began to blur, and she realized she was crying. Unsure of what exactly was happening, she assumed it must have been sad and didn't stop herself. The tears poured down her face, surprising her with their volume and making her cry even more. She let out a tiny moan of self-pity, and it felt so wonderfully terrible she let her body convulse with ever-amplifying sobs. Her throat hurt after a while, but there was still more. Rae wanted to vomit the sadness out of her. She pressed her face hard into the couch cushions and screamed into them until the shell, the armor, the wall surrounding the hollow was just as empty as the hollow itself. Panting and out of breath, Rae emerged from the cushions for fresh air. Her headache had subsided to a dull throb, her hands no longer shook, and her mind felt sharp and clear, but her body felt awful. It had been abused, and it knew how to hold a grudge.

Rae brushed her hair and pulled on a pair of jeans and something with spaghetti straps she hadn't even known she owned. Venturing outside her apartment like an agoraphobe, she checked to see if anyone was there before cautiously stepping into the hall and walking outdoors. On her way out, the guard, whom she didn't recognize, said, "Glad to see you're feeling better, Dr. Dahlia, have a good evening."

Her first thought was to punch him in the throat and demand to know how he knew she was sick, but then she realized that he didn't actually care how she was feeling.

*Where am I going?* she thought after the automated rickshaw prompted her for the fifth time, but then she decided that the more important question was: *How fast do I want to get there?*

After walking for half a mile, Rae realized that although she hadn't had a destination in mind, her fucked-up autopilot was taking her to one of the cafés where the Chemist liked to meet. She stopped walking, took out her Omni, and opened his profile in her contact list. Her finger again hovered over the delete option but fell on "message" instead.

> **R.Dahlia:** We need to talk.

**T.Chemist:** You know how it works, doctor. Besides, I thought you were done with me.

> **R.Dahlia:** I am. I'm calling to tell you that the last batch of ingredients was rotten.

**T.Chemist:** Not likely. You didn't try to smell them, did you?

> **R.Dahlia:** No. I just ate one, but it didn't work. I fucking crashed!

**T.Chemist:** Based on your heavy diet there's bound to be a few headaches, and maybe, *maybe* a little nausea. But the ingredients were good.

> **R.Dahlia:** I'm not being a sissy. I ate one Friday evening then slept until Monday night.

**T.Chemist:** Impossible!

You'd have to be eating them for years to build up that kind of tolerance. You didn't... eat it with anything else did you?

**R.Dahlia:** NO.

**T.Chemist:** Are you on any medication?

**R.Dahlia:** Birth control and the occasional aspirin.

**T.Chemist:** Neither one of those would affect my ingredients, but it sounds like you didn't get the intended amount of endorphins. You're sure you're not on any medication? Nothing that might restrict pituitary function?

**R.Dahlia:** Positive.

**T.Chemist:** Well, maybe there's something wrong with your pituitary gland.

**R.Dahlia:** Yeah, or more likely there's something wrong with your fucking formula.

She silenced her Omni and stuffed it back into her pocket, ignoring all future messages. "Fuck him, he's not an MD."

*No, he's a lowly doctor of neuropsycho-pharmacology.* She turned around and walked home.

Feeling her control and resolution return, Rae set her alarm for 6 a.m. and tried listening the Samuel_Reznick. mp3 again.

"October 31st, 2024. I may still be dreaming, but I have been awakened by a ghost."

There was a long pause, but as she listened harder she caught the last of Evermore's whisper, "—eternal life."

*Ashley was right. Evermore's just messing with him. Right?*

"Well, then, if you are not a ghost, who are you?" Evermore said, replying to himself.

Rae synced the recording with her OmniWatch smart TV and turned up the volume.

"October 31$^{st}$, 2024. I may still be dreaming, but I have been awakened by a ghost."

Evermore's throaty whisper followed. "I am not a ghost. I am an energetic being that refuses to relinquish my consciousness. To do that is to die, and I was promised eternal life."

"Well, then, if you are not a ghost, who are you?"

"You may call me Samuel."

"What can I do for you, Samuel?"

"Within the space where I am confined I have noticed an energetic coalescence congruent with the birth of a human; however, this one has developed consciousness traits that shouldn't exist until later. Furthermore, the traits were written in a nonrandom perfection that you don't find in the natural world. I have identified you as its creator, in more ways than one. I would like to commission you to build me a body."

*If this is when Evermore got the idea to build a synthetic body, what is Samuel talking about? How can Evermore create a human "in more ways than one"?* Then it hit her. There was only one way to make a human before Evermore's synthetic man. *He's a father.*

"And what are you offering in return?" Evermore challenged.

"Fame, money, power: take your pick."

There was a long pause before Evermore asked, "Would an empty body work? Perhaps a coma victim?"

"No, the container must match the contents."

"Building a body will ruin my reputation."

"But think, Evermore, of what could be achieved with a complete understanding of life and death."

"Immortality is not a pill I want to swallow."

"You are lying."

"I'll do it, but you have miscalculated my motives; I do not serve myself; I am a servant to all humankind."

Each session between Evermore and the ghost Samuel came one year after the previous. Each time, Evermore would all but beg Samuel for one of the secrets he had promised, and Samuel would refuse: "When I have a body and a voice, I will tell you in person."

Three and a half hours later, Rae heard Samuel's voice for the first time. He sounded like a baby just learning to use his voice box, but instead of developing over months, Samuel was able to rein in his wild cords after a few minutes.

"All life aspirates the breath of God."

"I don't believe in God," said Evermore

"This is not some bearded white guy living in a gated community of clouds and pearls; it does not need you to believe. It only needs you to live. Life is God's chest rising and falling. As we breathe in life, light, and new energy, we convert the light to shadow. After the in-breath peaks, it is followed by an out-breath. But do not picture this out-breath moving out, away from you; it does not. It, too, moves through all life, carrying with it a shadow. And at the bottom of the out-breath the shadow is transformed into light."

"Are you saying we're the source of these two energies?" Evermore asked.

"No, and there are not two energies. It is one energy with two qualities. The breath can be light, and it can be shadow. As soon as you create two, those that were one become opposites, enemies bent on annihilating the other."

"So even if we separated them, they would just destroy each other?"

"There is nothing to separate. If you stand outside on

a sunny day, you will cast a shadow. Can you think of a way to separate yourself from your shadow?"

"No." Evermore confessed.

"Can I move on? Do you understand?"

There was a long pause before Evermore spoke. "No."

"You are such a man of science, but I know nothing about the world which I cannot see: electricity, cells, viruses. So it is hard for me to find something that fits. Imagine this: There are two men, both goldsmiths, both work for the same noble for the same amount of pay, everything about them is the same, except one man's job is to take raw gold and smith it into something new, while the other man's job is to take beautiful golden trinkets, dismantle them, and melt the form back into raw material. Without these two goldsmiths, life would have no purpose beyond multiplying until in direct competition with itself, and God would not exist. Life, living, pumping, jumping, dreaming, swaying, eating, screaming, fucking... all of it moves energy and makes the heart of God beat."

"So that bible verse 'my body is a temple of the holy spirit,' you're saying that's true?"

"No. If Saulos had spent more time with the astronomers of Babylon, he might have been able to grasp the concept that your body is less like a house and more like a constellation of a thousand stars, each star part of a web that invites, attracts, and reflects the in- and out-breath of God."

"Is that why you were so specific about the mitochondria?" Evermore asked.

"Yes, I couldn't see the constellation until it was alive."

Evermore's question seemed to come from nowhere; there had been no description of anything scientific, or biological, until this point. But Rae listened on as Evermore asked Samuel question after question, until the doctor constructed a hypothesis for proving the existence of a human soul.

Rae had never much liked the idea of a soul. At one extreme it was a childish white-sheet ghost yelling 'trick-or-treat!,' and at the other it was karmic capitalism. Yet more than once she had scratched at a nagging itch that there must be something else out there that made her greater than the sum of her parts. The *self* couldn't just be the holograph of a self-aware mind. What else could explain why religion had helped so many people find happiness? *That many people can't be that simple-minded. Maybe I don't have the right opioid receptors?*

By Evermore's third or fourth mention of mitochondria, Rae realized why Ashley was talking about building a resonating chamber. "If the PS lichen is in a symbiotic relationship with an out-breath mycobiont surrounding an in-breath cyanobacterium, and arranged within a piezo-electric crystal, then that lichen will produce a vibrating frequency equal to the alternating current of the breath of God." She reached into her pocket and removed the same PS crystal that she had shown to Evermore. It seemed to be buzzing with the same excitement she felt. "But why did Evermore ask if you were related?"

The recordings ended in the year 2046, with Evermore and Samuel's final words.

"Damn you, Everett, must you record everything?" Samuel said.

"Once there is proof of this agreement, you will have the ability to—"

"This new body of mine is enough proof that you are a man of your word."

"Nonetheless, my friend, I swear that once I establish my new company, Evermore Research Labs, or Evermore Systems—"

"Does it matter what it's called?"

Evermore said, "It absolutely does matter, but not for the purpose of this recording. Once I establish a new

R&D company on Mars, I will send for you before long. I'm sorry I miscalculated our timeline, and I promise that I will do everything in my power to see our project through to completion before it's too late."

Without so much as a sign-off, the .mp3 ended.

"Too late?" Rae asked no one. She sat in silence for a long time, exhausted but buzzing with excitement. It was too elaborate and would be too insane to fake something of this volume. There were so many ideas to proof, so many new truths — as Evermore called them — that pointed toward the creation of something that was less like an FTL engine and more like an event.

*This is it, this is what Evermore has been hiding from me yet steering me toward.* Rae glanced at the clock, fearing what she would find. Her alarm would go off in an hour, yet she didn't feel tired. *How many days have I lost to sleep, I don't need one more hour.* As her foggy memories of faded in and out she remembered Ashley, which sent a quick stab into her chest, but she pushed the thought away, got dressed, and returned to Lab Seven.

The lab had been redesigned. The genome printer, the disassembler, the other machines and the crystal grow chambers had been pushed to the walls of the clean room, though it couldn't presently be considered clean, as a crew of men in construction hats were moving huge pieces of plywood and metal around the lab and assembling something in the center of the room.

Peeking inside, she found two halves of a 183-centimeter-tall dome of plywood, separated by a hand's width.

She walked around the construction zone to the conference table on the south wall and started browsing through the notes and to-do lists the lab had constructed. She browsed through its history, starting with the note Ashley had written in her name, then moved forward to the most recent. There was a list of five experiments to proof; she crossed out two of them, knowing they would reveal nothing, and next to the others she wrote, "*Try these first.*"

Suddenly she had an idea that would take their research in a whole new direction. *Evermore had to make a constellation before Samuel could cross over. What happens to the shadow after it's been cut from the caster?*

Searching through Ma'at's workstation she found the Rochelle salt, the original bacterium crystal that had inspired all of their research thus far, and picked it up. She held it to her face to look at it through the small vial it inhabited. "You're related to our PSs, but their inside is the same as your outside."

She grabbed three PS crystal sample dishes and a metal device the size of a softball and headed to K&J Labs. The metal device was a cantilever that Lab Seven used to measure the exact number of vibrations at 6,828 yottahertz while protecting the crystal from the synchrotron's deadly delta rays.

Knowing that Lockheed Martin had scheduled the synchrotron lab but probably wouldn't be using it, Rae snuck into the small and thankfully empty lab and carefully inserted Ma'at's Rochelle salt into the cantilever, reset its counter, and set it up in front of the delta ray. Next she stole the microwave from the break room down the hall and set it up on a stool in the shielded synchrotron control booth that took up the other half of the lab. Placing one of the PS crystal samples in the microwave, she double and triple checked the calculations she'd made on the rickshaw ride from E.I., to make sure the delta ray was blasting the cantilever at the precise moment the microwave nuked her PS crystal. Everything checked out. Rae set her timers and took a deep breath. She positioned both fingers over "start" and pressed both buttons at once.

The microwave hummed pleasantly, and the smell of the butter from someone's overcooked popcorn filled the control room. Rae was wishing she had a bag of Insta-Pop, and wondering if they carried the double-butter variety in the vending machine, when a globe of nothingness enveloped the microwave. Rae was yanked from her center of gravity toward it, but the hole only lasted a sliver of an instant. It disappeared, and she fell, careening into the microwave and the stool; she tripped over the cord, ripping it from the wall.

Rae lay on her back staring up at the ceiling, wondering what had just happened. She replayed the events in her mind. The ball of darkness wasn't just a sphere of impenetrable light: it had a weight, a gravity, and an emotion to it. It had startled her, to be sure, but remembering it filled her with dread.

*Am I going crazy? Did I just trip on the cord and make the whole thing up?*

Rae tried not to think about being crazy, focused on the physical, and took stock of her injuries. She slid herself back to the wall, noticed that her wrist was sore. *I must have reached out to break my fall.* Her shin was burning, and she rolled up her pant leg to find a slight abrasion where she'd tripped on the cord. Then her attention left the things that hurt and went to her stomach, which felt nothing at all. *It's gone, my stomach is gone!* Fumbling with the buttons of her lab coat she tore through the layers of clothing until she was staring down at her own belly. Or *a* belly. It felt substantial, fleshy, warm, but it was absent in some metaphysical sense that her logical mind couldn't comprehend, and the more she wrestled with a reality that contradicted her sense of self, the more she panicked.

The door to the synchrotron lab opened. "Hello? Is anyone in here?"

"I'm in here. I need help!"

A short, red-haired technician with a K&J Particle Physics Lab patch on his jacket rushed into the control room and surveyed the scene. "Dr. Dahlia? What are you doing in here? Are you okay?"

"My stomach is missing," she cried.

He knelt beside her. "Looks like you tripped. Did you hit your head when you fell?"

*Why is he checking my pulse! I need him to find my stomach!*
"My stomach," she mumbled.

"Omni, call 911. It's going to be okay, Rachael, you've just had a little fall." A third voice came from the technician's Omni. "Hello, what's your emergency?"

"Hi, this is Todd, I've got a woman here. I think she fell and hit her head. There's no blood, but she's going into shock."

"Stay on the line, Todd, help will arrive at your location shortly."

Rae was only vaguely aware that something outside of her was happening. Inside she could feel the hollow. Not only as the shadow of some emotional event, but as a physical part of her. As if the emptiness had finally clawed out of its cage in her psyche and found a permanent home in her stomach.

# CHAPTER NINETEEN

# Pass the Salt

## Ashley

Ashley drank himself to sleep watching an old movie from before the turn about erasing the memory of someone from your mind. He had started watching it for its amazing and completely CGI-free camera tricks but had entirely forgotten it was a breakup flick. He dreamed that he and Samuel were brothers. That he was being haunted by his mother; she would chase him around his suite while he climbed through a series of secret passages trying to find the exit.

He was exhausted by the time his alarm jarred him awake, and he had a crick in his neck from sleeping on the couch. Ashley double-checked to make absolutely sure it wasn't the weekend and hit the snooze button. After the fifth snooze, he pulled himself to his feet. His body was angry with him. He sloshed across the suite feeling weak and uncoordinated, as if his bones were dissolving. A long, hot shower gave him a thin layer of exoskeleton, but as he rode the elevator to Lab Seven he still felt spineless. As the doors parted, he immediately noticed two things. The first was that he was the last to arrive, almost; Rae was still missing. Second, he saw that the contractors had been hard at work last night. He nodded his approval of the size of the plywood dome they had built. No sooner had he stepped from the elevator than Ma'at called from his workstation. "Ashley," he hesitated for a moment to remember if he'd said the right name. "Were you here with Dr. Dahlia last night?" He looked concerned.

He glanced back to the plywood dome. "No. Why?"

Ma'at crossed the lab to Ashley's workstation. "I don't want to jump to any conclusions, but someone took the Rochelle salt crystal from my station. It's the only one I have, and the only physical evidence that remains from my research of spiritual resonance. I was the first one here this morning, and I can't imagine what the contractors would have wanted with it."

"I can't believe Rae... Dahlia was here; it would have been impossible to get anything done."

"She may have only popped in for a moment; she left a note on the conference table."

"Sorry, I haven't seen her. Could it have fallen off your desk when the workers were moving things around last night?"

"My desk didn't get moved." Ma'at frowned.

"I'll look into it."

Ma'at seemed unsatisfied but also unsure of what else he could do, and he walked away.

Ashley messaged Julius at the front desk.

> **A.Rephaireal:** Is there a way you can check the entrance records? I need a list of everyone who entered Lab Seven last night.

> **J.Amand:** Nope, only Dr. E can do that.

> **A.Rephaireal:** Okay, thanks anyway.

*Ugh. Seeing the Doc means walking past the Thing. Unless...*

Ashley stretched and turned to the nearest doctor, who happened to be Joseph Allan. "Will you text me when Dr. Dahlia arrives? I'm going for a swim."

"You mean *'if'* she arrives?" said Allan.

Though he went straight to the pool area, Ashley wasn't planning on swimming. Behind the slop sink in the janitor's closet was a hidden door, and behind it a long stair leading up.

*All this just to avoid Samuel,* Ashley thought as he climbed the fourteen flights. *What is it about him that bothers me so much? Other than that he stole my job and is inherently creepy.* Around the tenth floor he realized what it was: *Samuel is living proof of something I don't want to believe.* He thought back to his dream of being chased by the ghost of his mother. The hairs on the back of his neck stood on end, and he had to look over his shoulder at the nothing in the stairwell behind him.

Just as he was about to knock on Evermore's secret door, he heard voices coming from the other side.

"...you're not a rising star anymore, Everett; you're an unstable sun about to supernova."

Ashley pressed his eye to the peephole. Evermore and Dr. Clyde Kander were sitting in the two high-backed leather chairs.

Kander seemed concerned as he said, "It was cute the first time she tried to manipulate me into letting her use the synchrotron for her 'secret project,' but last night was unequivocal trespassing. If you need to use the synchrotron, just let me know and we can work something out."

Evermore, too, looked grim. "I'd rather keep the media thinking we're enemies, and use UMars's. She's worked on her own these past two times, and I hate to say it, but I suspect drugs were involved this time. Tell me how you found her?"

Kander sighed and switched which legs were crossed. "Todd, one of my collider technicians, claims to have seen something out of the corner of his eye early this morning that 'perplexed' him. Most likely he got bored and had wandered from his post, and that's when he found her on the floor of the delta-ray control chamber. For some reason she had dragged a microwave in with her. EMS got there before I did, but Todd said she was in shock, and all she wanted to talk about was how her stomach was missing.

"I mean, none of that matters now that we know she was high. Do you think you'll—"

"Everything matters!" the Doc said. "Insignificance only occurs after an inability to perceive correlation.

"Why would she bring a microwave into the control room?"

"To cook herself a little snack?" Kander guessed.

"What snack?" Evermore pressed.

"Todd said it was empty except for a small petri dish. Clearly, she was confused. Will you fire her? I know I'm going to."

Evermore ignored the question and leaned forward to pick up a chunk of metal the size of a softball. It was the cantilever device Lab Seven used to protect the crystal from the delta rays and count its vibrations. "Where was this?"

"In front of the aperture."

Evermore looked directly into Kander's eyes and said, "You're sure the cantilever was empty when you found it? You didn't take anything out?"

Kander opened his hands innocently. "Arnold. How long have we been friends?"

Evermore pointed at him threateningly. "*Never* call me by that name! *Did you take anything out?*"

Kander frowned. "No, *Dr. Evermore*, I did not."

"I'm sorry, Clyde, I had to be sure. The prior presence or absence of the crystal that should be in here indicates a world of difference in Dr. Dahlia's mental capacity.

"I'm terribly sorry this has happened, and I apologize for asking for a favor in the same breath."

Kander rolled his eyes, stood and stuck out his hand.

Evermore remained seated. "You will not fire Dr. Dahlia. You will instruct Todd to remain silent when the media comes to interview him, and you will do the same. If you must, tell them she fainted and hit her head."

"You're not going to fire her?" Kander exploded. "I think you know I agree with you about gender equality, but let it happen at its own pace. Protecting her because she's a woman is just as discriminatory. You really need her that much?"

"Maybe if you can get her to tell you the significance of 6,828 times $10^{24}$ you'll understand this has nothing to do with her sex."

Clyde raised an eyebrow. "Where'd you get that number from?"

The Doc shook the device at him. "This is a digital cantilever for measuring crystal vibrations."

Kander looked confused. "I know what it is; K&J probably made it and sold it to you."

Evermore's eyes twinkled.

"You're a supernova, I tell you," Kander said, and started walking away from Evermore. Ashley's heart leapt in his chest as he realized that Kander was planning to leave through the secret passage. *He's going to walk right into me!*

Thinking fast, Ashley jumped down to the landing on the previous floor and started walking up the moment he heard the door open.

"Oh! Ashley. You startled me. I didn't expect anyone to be back here. But of course Everett never keeps any secrets from you."

"Dr. Kander," Ashley said, "what are you doing here?" *God, could you be more obvious?*

"Ah... just visiting. Good to see you, Ashley."

Ashley stepped over the threshold into Evermore's office as the Doc was opening up the cantilever device.

"Come in, my boy. Come in."

Ashley, pretending to pant, said, "Ma'at thinks his crystal was stolen by the work crew. Can you get the entry logs for Lab Seven to see if anyone else was poking around there last night?" Evermore listened but didn't immediately answer. His attention was on opening the device. When the delicate crystal housing was fully exposed and obviously empty, Ashley said, "That's one of Lab Seven's cantilevers, isn't it?"

"It is; Rae was running a test at K&J last night." Still distracted by the device, the Doc grabbed his Omni from the edge of his workstation and took a picture of the black and white data code on its side. His Omni synced with the cantilever and downloaded the information stored within. Evermore showed his screen to Ashley. It said: "$6,828 \times 10^{24}$"

Ashley looked confused. "That's the death frequency, but where's the crystal?"

Evermore jumped back to answer Ashley's previous question. "Before we go accusing people, we should make sure that Lab Seven is adequately searched. Look again and let me know if it doesn't show up." Evermore's eyes twinkled with some hidden amusement. *There's something he knows but I don't.*

"How are you, my boy? You look as if you're being run ragged."

*Damn, I forgot he might try to ask me about Rae. Fuck. It wouldn't hurt to tell him what he already knows.*

Ashley nodded. "I'm exhausted, Doc. Rae hasn't been in since Monday. I think what you were afraid of has happened; I think she may be using again. Without Rae the team has been spinning its wheels, and I've been trying to carry them. So yeah, I'm tired."

Evermore smiled. "Kander assumed the same thing, but I didn't correct him."

*That's a bald-faced lie.* "Why?" Ashley asked.

The Doc gave him the look that meant, *Did you even bother to think about it yourself before asking me?*

"You want him to assume she's messed up because the alternative would get him asking about the fifth fundamental interaction?" Ashley had meant to say it as a statement, but his intonation rose into a question anyway.

Evermore smiled and put a hand on Ashley's shoulder. "Take care of *yourself*, my boy. You're there to learn from her genius, not to rescue her. You know better than anyone how an addict can draw—"

"I know," he said, turning away and walking out through the passage.

"Let me know if you don't find Ma'at's missing crystal," Evermore shouted after him.


As Ashley descended the stairwell, he thought of his mother and how hard she had tried to push him away, how badly she had abused him, and how much he had wanted to save her. But he couldn't then, and he certainly couldn't now. Even before she had died she had been dead, since long before he was born, and a piece of her death was inside him. He thought of how much he'd drunk last night trying to forget but inadvertently feeding that piece of death. He started to cry. For ten stories he sobbed as quietly as he could. For himself, for his mother, and for Rae. The hollow she talked about, he was sure it was piece of death like his, which her parents — one or both of them, he didn't know which — had put inside her.

"I wish I could help you," he whispered to her. "I wish I could bury that death and show you how amazing you are."

He replayed the conversation between Kander and Evermore. *What did Dr. Kander say about her missing stomach?*

As much as he hated himself for caring about her when she clearly didn't give a fuck about him, he also had to know if she was okay. Somewhere around the first floor he texted her:

> **A.Rephaireal:** Are you okay?

> What happened to your stomach?

There was no response. Ashley assumed she was either ignoring him, still in the hospital, or passed out on her couch again.

When he reached the cafeteria level, his Omni buzzed with an incoming call from Cyrus Ma'at.

"Hello, this is Ashley," he answered without video, and tried to surf the line between suspiciously quiet and loud enough to hear through the walls.

"Ashley, this is Cyrus; when you're done taking advantage of the company benefits, we could use your help reprogramming the genome printer. One of the proofs Dr. Dahlia suggested we explore is beyond what Washington is capable of, and she suggested we ask you."

*Shit, they needed me and I wasn't there.* Ashley couldn't quite tell if Ma'at was affably giving him a hard time or if he was annoyed that Ashley had the gall to go for a swim during working hours. "Dr. Dahlia suggested you use me? Is she there? I'll be right up."

"She's not here." Ma'at took a breath. "We just found out she's in the hospital."

Ashely was overcome at the delicious feeling of being needed. *I possess an important skill that six highly trained doctors don't have!* He was so busy doing a happy victory dance that he almost forgot to respond to what Ma'at had said about the hospital.

"Oh my God, what happened?"

Ma'at said, "Nothing serious; she fainted from fatigue and hit her head. They're holding her to make sure there isn't something else going on."

"Thanks for letting me know. I'll be right up."

Ashley threw himself down the remaining flights of

stairs and dunked his head in the pool, and not just to keep up appearances: he imagined that his face was still tearstained and his eyes puffy and red.

The water was a perfect seventy-eight degrees, and the way it filled his ears and deadened the sound was comforting. He felt removed from the world. He opened his eyes and watched the lines of light play off the bottom. *Now I wish I actually had time for a swim.*

The tiny bubbles clicking out of his nose slowed, and his nasal passages started to sting as they filled with water. From somewhere a long way away, his body sent him a message, and it was taking a long time traveling up his leg and up his spine before he registered that his Omni was buzzing again. *Rae!*

Ashley pulled his head from the pool, blew water and mucus from his nose, and walked over to a pile of towels with his head bent over so he wouldn't get his pants wet. After quickly drying his hair, he opened his Omni.

> **R.Dahlia:** Everyone's asking about my head. How do you know about my stomach?

> **A.Rephaireal:** I overheard Kander and Evermore talking about you. What happened?

> **R.Dahlia:** He promised he wouldn't tell. Why were they talking to you?

> **A.Rephaireal:** They didn't know I could hear them.

The explanation required too much writing; he called her and waited a long time while she considered picking up. Just before her Omnibox was about to offer to send his message as a text, she answered with video. She was still wearing her clothes, but she was half reclined in a hospital bed. "Kander promised he wouldn't tell," she said, bypassing any sort of greeting or explanation.

Ashley, still feeling excited and playful, said, "Don't you remember being seventeen? Making pinky promises to never tell your secret? Then turning around and telling your *other* best friend? That's basically Kander and Evermore, but with less pillow fights."

She half-smiled. "Where are you? Did you just get out of the shower? No. You're at the pool. Do you realize I just recommended that my team get your help programming the genome printer?"

Ashley almost said he was confused about whether or not he was supposed to be running her team for her, but she looked so alone and vulnerable. *She's clutching at any shred of power she can.* "Ma'at just told me. I'm on my way back upstairs. What happened to you, are you okay?"

He watched as she struggled with what or *if* she would tell him. "I'm... not sure what happened," she said with a cold certainty that made her sound absolutely sure that she wasn't sure.

"I went back to the delta-ray synchrotron lab late last night, or early this morning, technically. I wanted to see if Ma'at's crystal would vibrate at the same frequency, or if something about it would make it different."

*It's nice to know she's coming back to work.* "But what happened?"

"I'm not... *entirely* sure. I put Ma'at's crystal in front of the delta ray, and set up a PS crystal in a microwave I found down the hall. But something went wrong, and it exploded."

"The microwave exploded?" Ashley assumed that Kander would have spoken about the microwave a little differently if it had been blown to bits.

"Sort of... It didn't explode, like *puushhh*—" she made a sound effect poorly and a gesture like parts flying everywhere. "There was a flash." Ashley couldn't tell whether she was struggling to describe it or fabricating it. "There was this flash of darkness. A globe of black nothingness exploded out of the microwave and... it yanked me toward it." Her eyes began to water. "I think part of me went with it."

Ashley was dumbfounded. Every part of him wanted to be with her, to comfort her and to take care of her. Before he could say anything, she wiped her eyes and said, "I feel..." her throat clamped down on the emotions and wouldn't let them be felt. "I feel strange. Like my stomach has been replaced. It's like I'm looking at a photograph of me. I'm able to recognize myself, but it's also not me. It's like that 3D animation you showed me. No matter how good it looks, you can still tell it's fake, but it's impossible to name that quality that lets you know it's not human. That's how I feel about my stomach. There's something indescribably fake about it—" she realized she was rambling. "Was Evermore angry?"

"No, he seemed curious and excited. Ma'at, on the other hand — he's been panicking about his missing crystal all morning. You should let him know you have it."

She shook her head. "I don't have it. It's in the cantilever device."

"No, it's not. I just heard Kander promise that he didn't have it. Evermore opened the device right in front of me. It was empty, and you forgot to reset it. It still had the 6,828 number from the last time we used it. Think, Rae, where did you put Ma'at's Rochelle salt?"

Rae held something up to the screen. It was an empty, tiny glass vial with Ma'at's handwriting on it. "I'm positive I wiped the data before the test this morning."

Ashley didn't want to say what he had to; he didn't want her to hang up him; but he also thought another possibility about what happened might give her some emotional relief. He sucked it up and said, "Is it possible you were hallucinating?"

"From what?" It was a challenge. "Ashley, I'm clean. Remember seeing me in withdrawal the other day?"

*I can't stop thinking about it.*

"You think I could've had the willpower to go through that hell, and then snuggle back up with Queen Anne?"

"I just want you to be thinking about *all* the possibilities. Why is the cantilever empty if you're positive that's where you put the Rochelle salt?"

Rae lowered her voice. "That's what I've been trying to figure out."

Someone walked into the room and said, "Hi Rae, my name is Dr. Santino, I'm here to talk with you about that shadow we saw on your—"

The line went dead.

Ashley called back but it went straight to Omnibox. Any concern he had for her was burned to a crisp by a flash of anger. *That's right, Rae, just keep pushing me away.*

Ashley finished drying off and headed upstairs. As soon as he walked through the doors, Ma'at looked at him and said, "We found it!"

"Found what?"

"The Rochelle salt. Somehow it ended up in the growth chamber. When Mora went in to examine the largest of the PS crystals, he found my Rochelle salt right beside it in the same petri dish."

*Did Evermore move it? How the fuck did he know it was here?*

When Rae called back, Ashley was alone in the lab working late on a custom code for the genome printer. Evermore's caution came to mind. *"You know better than anyone how an addict can draw you in."* He almost didn't answer, but then again he was an addict, too.

"Is now a convenient time for you?" he asked.

A wind was blowing through her hair, and the whine of the automated rickshaw's electric motor could be heard in the background. This was a very different Rae than he'd been talking to before; her face was focused, hardened. She seemed angry at him, or annoyed that she'd called him at all. "I guess I deserve that. It was private stuff. Maybe I'll tell you about it if..." she trailed off.

He wouldn't bite. "What do you want, Rae?"

"I want to get back to work, and you're the only one I can talk to about the Samuel stuff."

*Okay, so this is "first day at E.I." Rae.*

She didn't wait for him to approve. "I listened to the .mp3 of Samuel and Evermore. That's how I ended up at K&J last... this morning."

"So it's *my* fault?"

"No. That's not at all what I was saying. God, Ashley, don't be such a girl! Just help me think out loud for a bit, and I'll let you get back to work.

"Before Samuel could leave his dimension and enter our world, Evermore had to make a body that fit his spiritual constellation exactly. I keep thinking of the PS crystals as an organism, which they are, but each part of it is the exact same constellation repeated over and over, and each distinct crystal isn't at all distinct. They're exact clones of each other."

"That's all true. I agree."

She smiled at the love of the discovery, and Ashley's heart began to ache. "What I didn't tell you before is that I had another PS crystal in a petri dish in the pocket of my lab coat right over my stomach. Granted, the coat wasn't in my possession the whole time, but when I got it back, the dish was empty."

"I'm not sure what you're saying."

"You should have felt this black sphere pull me toward it. Only it wasn't pulling me, it was pulling the *Lepraria ptilisaccharon*. We've never run an experiment with two crystals so close together.

"Ashley, I don't think some stray EM signal is triggering the 6,828 vibration. I think when one PS dies, it crosses over, and the other PS crystals flicker in and out of existence as some sympathetic reaction. If the PS crystal in my pocket disappeared, I bet Ma'at's Rochelle salt is wherever the PS in my pocket went."

"No fucking way! Ma'at found his salt crystal. It was in the incubator right beside the largest PS."

"Oh shit! We've been trying to figure out why that one has been getting bigger. What if it's been happening this entire time?!"

"Slow down," Ashley said. "What if *what's* been happening?"

"Don't you see?" she said excitedly.

"I see something," he said, "but I want *you* to say it so I don't get laughed at."

"If the exterior of the PS crystal signals the crossover point, and every other PS is blinking in and out of reality at the exact same moment, what if the inside of the crystal is escaping. Slipping from one point in reality to another, right beside the biggest PS crystal in the incubation chamber."

"You think you've discovered teleportation," Ashley said skeptically.

"This is what Evermore has been driving us toward. This is the faster-than-light he was imagining would be possible with Samuel's information."

Ashley frowned.

"Still not convinced? I'm coming back to the lab. Stay there."

"Shouldn't you get some rest?"

"I wouldn't be able to if I tried," Rae said, and hung up.

Part of him wanted to wait for her, but another part knew he was weak, and if she was using again he didn't want to be available to be dragged back into her gravity well. Ashley finished writing the line of code he had been working on, packed up his things, and left.

## Rae

Rae arrived at Lab Seven to find it empty. She walked up to Ashley's workstation and stared at his empty chair. "Why didn't you wait for me? Are you getting back at me for hanging up on you?"

She remembered that look on his face when she'd said she'd been dealing with 'private stuff', "Are you punishing me because I didn't tell you that the hospital wouldn't let me leave until they'd subjected me to every test ever invented? Well fuck you! Some things are better shared it person, and it is fucking private and you'll be lucky if I share it with you at all!"

The chair reacted the same way Ashley would have, by being silent and maintaining its rigid posture. She was hit with an enormous loneliness, and knew she'd feel this way regardless of whether or not he occupied that chair. "Ashley, I want so badly to share myself with someone. I wish you were here to go over our next hypothesis together. I wish I could have taken you home, snuggled up on the couch and told you about how Evermore sent Julius to sneak me out the back of the hospital to avoid the media drones, but I can't. Because then you'll ask why they were testing me for so long."

*I'll have to tell him sometime.*

# CHAPTER TWENTY

# Resonance

### Rae

The next morning, as the elevator leapt seven stories up, Rae held her stomach. Not because of the speed, or because she'd drunk two cups of coffee on an empty stomach; she couldn't get over the sensation that her core felt as if it were missing, and it wore on her attention like a stubbed toe that won't stop throbbing.

Ashley hadn't waited for her last night, and as the excitement wore off, the hollow welled up within her, making itself at home in her empty abdomen. *How likely is it really that I forgot to reset the cantilever and left the Rochelle salt back in the lab? After all, that's the only proof I have that the crystal actually teleported.* And while she was measuring likelihood, even though she was sure of her own actions, when compared with the idea that she had accidentally teleported matter, the probability that she was simply confused seemed astronomically high.

*If I'm wrong, I'll look like the biggest idiot in front of my team.* In her mind, Deborah's voice added, *"Not to mention that you ran the experiment without even considering your own safety. What if it had been worse? Would you really want to put your dear old mother in the position of caretaking her vegetable daughter?"*

Even though she had seen the lab since the change,

the half dome of plywood and metal now dominated the center of the lab and demanded attention.

"So this the Helmholtz resonator," she said, exaggerating her awe as she circled around the outside of the clean room.

Benjamin Washington was the first to notice her. "Good morning, Dr. Dahlia."

Rae positioned herself at the southeastern edge of the clean room, where she would be visible from all of their workstations, and addressed the room.

"Everyone, I want to apologize for my absence. I heard some disturbing news at the beginning of last week, and I started to panic, working late trying to get us to a place we just weren't at. I felt like I had to carry it alone because you guys are already under so much pressure." Her eyes fell to the floor for a moment. "I'm so used to doing things on my own that I forgot to trust my team." She took a deep breath, hoping she wouldn't regret telling them: "Evermore has been secretly pitting three of his labs against each other. Three of us here at E.I. were tasked with the same assignment, and I can only imagine what happens to the labs who come in second and third." She raised her voice over the murmur. "The only thing that should concern us is our team efficiency, and our trust in each other. If we are strong in both those areas, we will be the first to meet his goal. I feel like we're close to something, and I hope you feel it too."

The team stared at her. Rae imagined they were watching their careers flash before their eyes, all except Ma'at, who turned his back to her and returned to his desk. She went around awarding verbal doggy biscuits to each of her team members until they were all happily wagging their tails. Only Ma'at seemed unable to be swayed. To him she asked, "What's the next step with the chamber?"

Without looking up, Ma'at said, "Ashley reprogrammed the genome printer to produce a sprayable PS slurry, which should be ready in half an hour; then we can start the first coat."

"Ashley did?" Rae asked looking around the lab and not seeing him. "Where is he now?"

Ma'at shrugged.

*That's for the best. I don't want whatever's going on with him contaminating the lab.*

"Good, let's make that the first thing we do today." Rae glanced at the time. It was 8:10. *God, I can't start watching time pass already.*

After donning their clean-room suits and carefully going through the sterilization process, Doctors Washington, Hubert and Brando entered the clean room. Washington started the process of printing the PS slurry, and the other two started covering all the sensitive machines in plastic sheeting and hermetic tape.

At 8:25, two delivery men from K&J arrived and wheeled a total of eight tanks out of the elevator. Each tank was the size of a two-liter soda bottle but twice as tall. Rae met them and double-checked that Lab Seven had received everything she had asked for. Each tank contained a collection of tightly packed molecules, which the genome printer used like ink to assemble more complex nucleic acids, genes, cells and tissue. After nodding and sending the delivery men on their way, Rae instructed Doctors Ma'at and Allan to move the tanks into the clean room beside the printer.

At 8:51 the rest of the team joined them in the clean room, and the PS slurry was loaded into the same lichen applicator that Evermore had designed years before. Even though Rae had politely told him that his support was no longer needed, the fact that his discoveries were still helping them along was not lost on her.

The team gave Rae the honor of applying the first coat. Ma'at handed her the applicator. "It's just like spray-painting," he instructed. "Don't point it at what you want to cover; you'll get a heavy glob. Start spraying off the form, then evenly cover in long strokes. Don't try to hide the form, just get a good even layer on first, and we'll worry about full coverage on the second layer."

Rae fought off a gut reaction to reject his help and assert her independence. Her artistic experience didn't extended to spray-painting, and once she realized she actually wanted his advice, she could only be angry at herself for needing it.

Rae approached the circular form that would make up the bottom of the resonator, and squeezed the trigger, painting a line of lichen 15 centimeters wide across the very edge of the circle. She moved down and painted another line just beneath it. As Rae focused on the task, an old desire awakened in her. Though applying the lichen in an even layer barely resembled painting, it was enough to remind her how much she loved the process of creating. She lost herself in the Zen of spray-painting, and for a moment the hollow was forgotten. But as soon as she realized her freedom from it, it returned even stronger, howling from deep inside her, raging at the pain of being forgotten.

Rae finished her third row and took a step back. She handed the applicator to whomever would take it. She wanted to cry but forced it down. Her hand tried to find comfort in her pocket, but the clean room suit denied her access, and in any case her pockets were empty.

Ma'at took the applicator and started using it so naturally Rae wondered if there was anything he wasn't good it. After a minute, he began absentmindedly telling a story.

"I was in a gang when I was a young teenager—"

Brando whispered something to which Hubert replied, "Egypt."

"We didn't call ourselves a 'gang,' even though we were breaking the law. There was something about the word we didn't want to associate with. We liked to think we were something more pure. Like a street artists' club. We all went on strike, at first because it was what everyone else was doing, but after, we felt like we were part of something and became full-time 'artists.' At first it was just defacing anything with Mubarak's face on it. We played around with different slogans late into the fall. Writing things like 'freedom' and 'justice' in colorful, stylized Arabic. We finally settled on the word 'think.' I remember the fear tying my guts in knots the first night we broke curfew. But the fear went away after we were caught by a pair of police officers, who grabbed us, saw what we had written, and laughed. They shook our hands and told us to be more careful. After Mubarak resigned, I left to join the watch group that was patrolling the area around my parents' home, while my brothers saw themselves as the defenders of freedom and took it upon themselves to make sure the elections were fair." Ma'at stood back and examined his work. The floor of the dome was perfectly covered.

"Freedom," Rae repeated aloud. The doctors turned to look at her. "How many people are there back on Earth — 10.2 billion?" A few of them nodded, but the rest were trying to puzzle out where she was going.

Everyone knew the end result of overpopulation, but no one wanted to think about it. The UN's current plan for overpopulation was to buy plots of land from the Martian government and resell them to corporations based on Earth to encourage the construction of more terradomes. But they were having trouble overcoming the cost of shipping materials. A terradome big enough to support a billion people wasn't economically viable if no one could afford to live there.

"Imagine what would change if we could instantly reach one of the hundreds of Goldilocks planets that have been discovered. No life-support infrastructure required. We'd have another world at our disposal, and suddenly Earth's population is down to five billion. Then we expand out to other Earth-like planets. Each time we colonize, the population of Earth halves. The frantic race to avoid global destruction ends. The implications expand out from there in all directions, but the end result is freedom."

They were still looking at her. "Since I took this job, I've been trying to figure out why so many of us, myself included, took such a big risk working for Evermore. I was just realizing that freedom is the dream he sold us — that he sold me. We should be proud to be part of making that happen. Even if we fail, at least we'll know we were working on the solution and not just hiding from the problem in our bubble in the sky."

There was a long silence.

Covering the dome took the entire day, and when they were finished, Rae wished them all a good weekend and repeated her previous statement: "Be proud knowing that you're working on a solution."

With no other way to mark the passing of the moment, the doctors shook hands with each other, stripped off their clean-room suits, gathered their things, and left.

Rae looked around the empty lab. She thought back to her first week at E.I. She and Ashley had fallen into a routine of leaving at the same time. But she had messed that up, and now it seemed that he didn't have the nerve to face her. *He's a sensitive boy. He must have taken it pretty personally when I yelled at him for impersonating me.* It felt real as she said it, but then she remembered how concerned he had sounded over the phone.

"Are you okay?" she mocked. "What happened to your stomach?" *Ashley, if you're concerned... about me or about Lab Seven, why the fuck were you absent?*

She shook her head. *No, fuck you for getting under my skin like this. I've got better things to worry about.*

Rae's hand had squirmed itself into her pocket, and she became aware of it searching for a stim. Her stomach still felt strange, and she felt alone. More alone than she had been at Chasma Australe.

She sat back down at her workstation, pulled a scrap of ePaper from a drawer and began to write:

> Dear Deborah,
>
> I've made my first real friend up here at Nili Terradome. His name is Ashley. The problem is that he's also my employee. I need him to do menial tasks that are important to the progress of our research, but it makes him feel useless. I also need him to be my friend. I need someone to talk to. Working for Evermore is amazing but confusing, and the pressure has been getting to me. He sucks at being both. Or maybe I suck at asking him to.
>
> I don't want it to be a big deal, but I want to tell him about what the doctors found. It's not confirmed yet, I still need to see an oncologist...

Rae looked up from the ePaper. *God, I would never tell Deborah anything until I knew for sure.* She opened the ePaper options, hit "select all," and deleted it. Rae placed the page back in its drawer, opened the messaging app, and selected Ashley.

> **R.Dahlia:** Hey, great job programming the genome printer. We sprayed on the slurry today. It was actually pretty fun.

She let a minute pass before changing her tack and trying again.

**R.Dahlia:** I missed you.

**A.Rephaireal:** You missed me? I'm sorry, who is this? I think I'm having a problem with my Omni.

**R.Dahlia:** Don't be like that.

**A.Rephaireal:** What do you need, Rae?

**R.Dahlia:** I don't *need* you for anything. But I like working with you.

He didn't say anything for a long time. Rae tried to call him, but he didn't answer.

**R.Dahlia:** You want to hide behind the text? Fine. And if I'm being honest, I *was* pissed you were a no-show, and a little worried. But I assumed you needed some personal time.

**A.Rephaireal:** I can't work with you anymore. I quit.

**R.Dahlia:** I don't accept. I'm sorry I've been a bitch lately. Obviously I was going through some tough shit, but I don't want to hide behind that excuse.

I owe you an apology, can I come over?

**A.Rephaireal:** I undermined you. Hijacked your project, and you need to get back control. I didn't even give a reason for being absent today, so now you've got a reason to fire me.

**R.Dahlia:** Ashley, I'm not upset about you forging my name anymore. It was the right thing to do. You saved my ass! You saved Lab Seven from shitting the bed!

**A.Rephaireal:** I can't go back and forth anymore. Your life's work is Lab Seven, and I don't have the emotional fortitude to keep surviving the moments when you crush me to preserve yourself.

**R.Dahlia:** You're right, Ashley, you don't deserve to be treated that way. And you've shown me that anyone could do the personal assistant job but the role you play in Lab Seven is irreplaceable.

**A.Rephaireal:** I appreciate that, but I'm still quitting.

**R.Dahlia:** Your last assignment as my personal assistant is to hire your own replacement.

I told Evermore that I'd look out for you, so I can't accept your resignation. Instead I'd like to offer you a position as research assistant.

**A.Rephaireal:** You'd really do that just to keep me around?

**R.Dahlia:** I'm not doing anything. You've earned this by proving that you are an indispensable part of this team.

**A.Rephaireal:** Thank you. Really thank you, but I need you to do something else before I'll consider coming back.

*Oh god, are you going to make me say I'll be your girlfriend?*

**R.Dahlia:** ?? Are you waiting for me to agree before you tell me what it is?

**A.Rephaireal:** No, I'm working up the courage to hit "send."

**R.Dahlia:** Take your time; meanwhile, you're killing me with suspense. ;)

A moment later, Ashley called her Omni.

Rae answered. As the call connected, Ashley's face filled the frame and in the background the familiar neon lights of the Relativity Lounge reflected off the "windows," beyond which the beautiful simulated singularity pulsed with dark intent. Ashley's eyes were watery. He looked so much older than he had a mere month ago, but maybe it was just because he hadn't shaved today. "Hey," she said trying to ride the line between excitement and concern. "So you decided to call after all."

"Yeah. I, uh... This is a face-to-face question."

She waited.

"Last time we talked you said you were sure it wasn't a hallucination... Rae, look me in the eyes and tell me you're not back on stims."

*God, Ashley, you are all work and no play! I can't believe I thought you were going to force me to go out with you.* "Ashley, I'm not on stims. I'm not going *back* on stims. I hadn't ever felt withdrawal before, and frankly, I've never experienced anything so awful. I think I lost more time on recovery than I gained. I've got... something wrong with me that makes it so the CrashPads don't have any affect."

"What are crash pads? Never mind, I just need you to promise you'll never use again."

She brought the Omni closer to her face and looked deep into his eyes. They were like big round pools of concern. She stared deep into the lens and said, "I promise."

His expression didn't change; if anything, he seemed more concerned.

"So I'll see you back in work on Monday?"

He nodded.

On Monday morning, Rae was pleased to see that the *Lepraria ptilisaccharon* on the forms had grown a thin layer of blue-green sugar. It was still too thin and fragile to move, but the coverage looked good. By the end of the week the work crew could return with curved aluminum panels that would eventually surround and vacuum-seal the PS and force it into cryptobiosis.

The elevator doors opened, and Ashley stepped out. Rae surprised herself by giving him a big smile. He returned one that was half-hearted. "Yep, I'm here."

She wanted to say more, but he broke eye contact and settled into his personal-assistant's workstation facing the elevator. Rae pushed him and their drama from her mind and checked on Lab Seven's list of tasks. *After we build the chamber, we'll need to test more crystals. Kaspar Mora has designed one variation, but it would helpful to have many so we can discern if there's a specific part of the crystal that reacts to the 6,828 frequency.*

Normally, she would have given the crystal building project to her team, but spray-painting the PS on Friday had felt so good, she wanted to remember that feeling of creation. In addition, she had been fantasizing about the XR-25,000 genome printer as soon as she had heard it was available. Settling into her workstation, she linked to the printer and felt her heart flutter as she downloaded their original *Lepraria ptilisaccharon*'s gene map. The deeper Rae peered into the genetic code, the more her chest was filled with a yellow joy that she had all but forgotten. The controls were identical to the Hakaru app, but the XR allowed her an exponential degree of control over the genome. Her hands moved with the precision and passion of a first-chair violinist, starting softly, but then pulsing with waves of intensity. When she extracted the packets of genetic code in the nucleus of the cyanobacteria that directed the mitochondria, she remembered Ashley's suggestion and began designing a new species from within the mitochondrial DNA.

Her process was interrupted as Doctors Hubert and Brando and Ma'at stepped from the elevator. The first two were engrossed in a conversation, and Ma'at seemed frustrated.

"We mustn't forget about the rule of threes," Hubert said. "The Christian trinity recognizes the Father, the Son, and the Holy Spirit, which are symbolic representations of consciousness (*mens*), living matter (*corpus*), and spirit (*spiritus*); body, mind, and breath; that which makes us live."

"The—" Ma'at began, but Hubert cut him off.

"Within body, arguably the most heavily studied of the three, we find a further breakdown into threes with the organs that control homeostasis: the brain, liver, and kidneys; those that organize circulation: the lungs, heart, and blood vessels; and those that promote reproduction: the..." His eyes landed on Rae then took off again like a nervous fly. "There we also find three."

An MD wouldn't have given a second thought to naming her organs aloud. Organs were organs and there was nothing dirty about them. She wanted to say "Uterus, vagina, and ovaries" aloud just to break taboo, but she didn't want to face the disgusted looks she knew she'd receive in return. Instead, Rae did her best to ignore them. And failed.

Hubert continued, "The mind has long been divided into three: the id, ego, and superego; perception, cognition, and behavior; and Plato (though he was talking about the spirit) also defined three: feminine, masculine, and reason, which Jung later adapted into anima, animus, and the self.

"With the new force, I believe we're dealing with something betwee—"

"What about yin and yang?" Dr. Brando interrupted.

"There's no trinity in the Qur'an," Ma'at offered skeptically.

"Taoism breaks the rule of threes," Brando restated, louder than Ma'at and bearing a look that was decidedly smug.

Samuel had rejected Evermore's labeling of the in- and out-breaths as two energies, yet he defined the role of life as transforming one to another. *Samuel said he couldn't see the constellation until it was alive.* She knew Samuel had been guiding Evermore to build an invisible puzzle in three dimensions, but he couldn't have used trial and error on every cell in the human body. They must have discovered some formula to guide the process. *I can't imagine there's any way to ask Samuel or Evermore what that formula might be without revealing how much I know about the breath.*

"No." Hubert wrung his hands in frustration, then wrapped them around each other. "Yin and yang are only halves of the *taijitu*, or the diagram of ultimate power, which represents the flow of the natural world. One could either count the whole as being the third aspect, or — and this is the option that I prefer — one could count the black and white dots, which represent the *transformation* each half is constantly going through."

Brando shrugged. "Admittedly, I was playing the devil's advocate."

Rae smirked at how awkwardly the expression fit into their philosophical conversation as she tried to find the third. If God is the ultimate good and Satan the ultimate evil, shouldn't there be an ultimate neutral? *I don't know enough about Christianity to even guess at that answer.*

Hubert frowned. "To the Taoists, nature consisted of darkness, light, and transformation. The Hindus similarly believed in creation (*Brahma*), destruction (*Shiva*), and preservation (*Vishnu*), which coincidently — and synchronistically — aligns with physics; atoms are built out of protons and neutrons and persevered by electromagnetic force, and subatomic particles are built out of two types of quarks held together by gluons. Three again... and again... and again!"

Rae had given up on ignoring them and was now actively listening.

Ma'at rubbed his temples. "Hubert, what's your point?"

"I'm surprised at your impatience, Ma'at. I thought you were interested in bridging the physical and the spiritual, and this project is the perfect opportunity to do that."

Ma'at was lost in introspective silence. Rather than wait for another grumpy contradiction, Hubert continued, "I think our time would be better spent not discussing how to sustain the 6,828 frequency but speculating on this force's opposite. Then with both types in hand, we can find the gluon that unites the two."

Brando nodded. "Well said, Hubert. I'm on board. Ma'at? Judging by the look on your face, you couldn't care less." He grinned, but Ma'at was not roused by his levity.

Instead, he shook his head. "Name me a force that has an opposite. Are delta rays the opposite of radio waves? Everything science measures is from zero to infinity." His tone left an uncomfortable silence in the air. "I'm sorry. I know you were having fun with your philosophical conversation, but Allah has no opposite. Hate is not the opposite of love; it's the absence of it. Impurity is not the opposite of purity. You cannot be pure without piety, which by definition must include reverence *for* impurity! Though how to be reverent without castigation or self-elevation eludes me."

Hubert was taken aback. "Well spoken, Cyrus."

Feeling that the possibility of conflict had passed, Rae turned back to her work. *It's helpful to remember that death is not the opposite of life. In fact, if every cell that died created a blast like the one from that microwave, it would be catastrophic for the body, since programmed cell death occurs billions of times every day.* The logical answer was that there was some failsafe or something that naturally balanced the system. Whatever had caused the Rochelle salt to slip through reality was an aberrant event. *If I can figure out what caused Ma'at's crystal to slip, maybe we can sustain the 6,828 frequency by creating a chain reaction where one cell slips in an endless loop?* Looking at the mitochondria on the metaphorical dissection table before her, Rae thought of loops, and loops implied direction.

"We need a way of distinguishing in-type mitochondria," she mused aloud. The other four doctors had just arrived at Lab Seven and were now staring at her. There was no stifling her embarrassment. "I'm working on a new hypothesis," she explained.

"What's 'in-type mitochondria'?" Ma'at asked, brightening a little.

Without missing a beat, Rae said, "Hmmm... What's a good analogy?" but she was actually considering how to say anything without sounding off-the rails crazy.

Ashley stood and called over to her, "The way you described it the other day made sense to me." The team glanced at Ashley, then back to Rae, waiting for her reaction.

*Did we actually talk about this the other day?* She combed her memory, but everything during withdrawal was fuzzy. But the smile and excitement on Ashley's face told her that he wasn't just messing with her. He had a plan.

## Ashley

*The found-object laboratory in Evermore's garage was swelter-ing hot. The small air conditioner chugging away at the back of the room couldn't keep up with the number of computers Evermore was running. The Doc was seated and scratching an itch under the electronic shackle the state of California had slapped around his ankle, which kept him under house arrest.*

*"Look at the code, my boy, search for the six markers I taught you. Each one has a different 'spin.' The left is called NAat-gc1—"*

*"I remember all that," Ashley said, his sixteen-year old voice cracking and undermining his angry tone. "What I just don't understand is how something can spin toward, or away."*

*"Think of it like a foam ball with a hole through the center. Spinning toward would be like forcing the ball inside its own center with your thumbs. Away would be the inverse from the back."*

*Ashley nodded. "And what are we building?"*

*"We're looking for a cure for our friend Samuel."*

*"He's not my friend, and I've never even met him."*

*"He has only been here a few times during the day. You've been in school. Now, Clyde Kander showed you how to program the genome printer, right?" Ashley nodded. "Your first assignment is to write a program that can identify the six markers in a line of mtDNA I'm going to give you. Once you do that, we'll start finding the attracted marker pairs."*

## Rae

Ashley crossed the lab to the conference table, and, gesturing to open a drawing program, he drew two lines in a ninety-degree cross, then bisected the upper right and lower left quadrants with a third line so that six lines all originated from the same point. "Stop me if Dr. Dahlia already explained this on Friday, but she has found at least six genetic similarities within the mitochondrial DNA of our PS, and it's funny you should mention the rule of threes, Dr. Hubert, because the six share three common-alities, best thought of as axes." He labeled the up-down axis "y" and "-y" and the left-right "x" and "-x." After la-beling the final line "z" and "-z," Ashley said, "If this were algebra, the z-axis would represent forward and back, but for our purposes it's better to think of it as 'in' and 'out.' That's what Dr. Dahlia was talking about, 'in-type.'"

*How the fuck does he know all that? Is this Evermore continu-ing to offer me help via Ashley?* Rae stared at his drawing and tried to pretend this wasn't her first time seeing it.

"Okay," Ma'at said, his brightness fading, "But what defines an 'in-type' mitochondrion?"

*It's too soon to tell them about the breath of life*, Rae thought. *We don't have the research to back it up, and they'll assume I'm ei-ther keeping information from them or making assumptions, both of which make me appear untrustworthy.* "The six markers are still an unconfirmed observation, but the hypothesis I want to test is whether the number and type of markers have an effect on the crystal's natural oscillations. Please keep working through your assigned experiments on the to-do list, and I'll let you know when I've got a solid theory for us to work off of." The team seemed content with that, and before they could think to ask her any questions that only Ashley could answer, she said, "I've also got an ex-citing announcement, now that you're all here."

"Evermore's decided to keep us over Lab Eight?" Dr. Allan guessed.

Rae shook her head and smiled. "Not *that* exciting. As you know, since Xepher was asked to move on, there has been an opening on our team. I was reluctant to fill it since you six have really found your flow with each other, and rather than hire someone from outside, I've decided to promote Ashley to assistant researcher, and I believe he'll be a good addition and a great fit on our team."

To his great surprise, the team broke into enthusiastic applause. Ma'at gave him a hearty slap on the back. But before the clapping had entirely died down, Joseph Allan said, "Speech!"

Ashley shrugged. "I don't really know what to say."

To which Allan replied, "Tell us why Dr. Dahlia's right."

Ashley looked as if Allan had slapped him, and Rae stepped in to defend him as much as herself. "It was actually Ashley who came up with the idea to build a Helmholtz resonator. So if it turns out to be a useful tool in our discovery of this fifth fundamental interaction, we'll have him to thank."

Ashley had shaken off the attack and almost stepped on her final word as he hurried to defend himself.

"Many of you know that I was once Evermore's personal assistant, but what you may not know is that before that he used to mentor me out of the lab in his garage. The slurry program I wrote for you all last week was taught to me by Dr. Kander himself, back before any of the K&J genome manipulators had a visual user interface. Back then you had to know C++.

"I may not be a doctor of philosophy like the rest of you, but I'm no amateur either. In fact, Dr. Dahlia, I think I may have a theory about where we can find your six mitochondrial markers. It's not just the presence or absence of the MT-ND enzymes: I believe it may be a cross-reference between them."

"That's interesting, Ashley; let's talk about it later. I'd like everyone to get back to their projects."

Ashley nodded. "Thank you all so much for the warm welcome. I'm still technically Rae's personal assistant until I can find a replacement, so... yeah, I'll be back at my workstation."

Allan followed Ashley back to his workstation, and the two shared a few quiet words. Beyond all odds, it looked to Rae as if Allan might be apologizing. After he'd said whatever he wanted to, Ashley smiled, and the two shook hands.

Rae, too, returned to her workstation and messaged Ashley.

> **R.Dahlia:** The markers are our new top priority. Be prepared to stay late tonight.

Rae waited, expecting a negative response, hoping for some flirtatious quip about how she was trying to seduce him, but all he wrote was, "Okay."

Ashley wasn't the only one to stay after most of the rest of the team had left. Dr. Allan chose the moment after Ma'at had stepped into the elevator to approach Rae at her workstation.

"Dr. Dahlia, may I have a word?"

Rae looked up at him and nodded.

"I know I'm seen around here as the skeptic and the critic, but I just wanted to let you know that I'm fully on board with our research. In fact, I've been doing some of my own around how a third dimension of time could allow for shortcuts through space-time and allow for travel that doesn't precede its own causality. Though no such dimension has ever been proven," Allan said, "being able to prove that would not only forward my career, but the concept interests me greatly." He shrugged. "I just wanted to let you know what I'm up to when I'm not participating in those philosophical brainstorming sessions. I may not be able to play along with most exotic concepts, but I've got your back as far as natural sciences are concerned."

"I know you do, Dr. Allan, and being the skeptic shouldn't be seen as a negative thing. But from many of these speculative scientists' perspective, all they ever get is skepticism."

"Well, they should understand that it gets frustrating how people can hang on to one scientific theory and abuse it to shape their opinions and ideas." Rae could tell he had more to say but was trying to behave himself. As he walked away, he seemed to be considering what she'd said.

Over the course of the day, Ashley had been busily writing code, which he later revealed was a program he had written for Evermore back in the days when they were working out of the garage lab. Even before the doors of the elevator closed on Allan, Ashley uploaded the program into the genome assembler and used it to open the genome of the original *Lepraria ptilisaccharon.* Minutes later he and Rae were poring over the colorful genome covering the conference table. Each of the six markers were displayed in a different color. "Down," "right," and "toward" were identified as in-type mitochondria and were associated with warm colors, and the opposites with out-type.

Ashley said, "The original PS lichen has nineteen markers, twelve in the mycobiont, and seven in the cyanobacterium. I think it kinda looks like an hourglass." He turned to Rae. "Your intuition was right, the cyanobacterium in our PS is mostly in-type."

"Ashley, this is amazing! You were seventeen when you made this?"

The praise seemed to make him uncomfortable. "No. Well… sort of. I used the basic framework from then, but I've learned a lot since. The constellation lines, the colors, and the other visual elements were written today."

Rae said, "Give yourself some credit; you didn't have the recording helping you out then."

He shrugged.

She looked at the hourglass constellation of the PS for a long time. Eventually, she said, "Everything is so balanced and symmetrical. I want to unbalance it." She added, "I want to design a chain reaction like a particle accelerator and crank it up to 6,828."

"Before we try that," Ashley said, "I want to make sure the Helmholtz chamber works. We need something that can block this breath of life before we start opening doors we don't know how to close."

Rae nodded, but the tone in his voice implied he was talking about them. *I don't want to close this door, Ashley. I'm just scared I can't control it.*

# CHAPTER TWENTY-ONE

# The Chamber

## Rae

Two weeks passed. It was the Friday before the Martian holiday Feast of Thanks, also known as Hex-giving, when everyone would gather with their closest colleagues, friends, and/or family around a vaguely chicken-flavored and -shaped loaf of hexapoda protein, or hexapro meat. Then whoever was hosting would recount the tale of how our civilization had been born from a sort of ancient terradome called the Fertile Crescent. Rae remembered Thanksgiving on Earth as something to get out of, something she needed a rock-solid alibi for in order to avoid the prison of spending the day with Deborah and the divorced ladies from her online life simulator.

The Feast of Thanks upheld the same kind of illusion as the VR screens of Nili Terradome: thin bucolic imagery draped over reality to fabricate the feeling that we belong here. And speaking of the dome, the scenery had recently shifted to somewhere in the Grand Caucasus, which she only knew because someone had pointed out the tallest peak and called it Mount Elbrus, and she had looked it up on her Omni.

In the lab, every experiment that could be done without the resonator, had. Dr. Kaspar Mora had designed five variants on the PS crystal on his own and five with Ashley's input, and Ashley and Rae had together designed another three. Today marked the day that they could safely say the *Lepraria ptilisaccharon* had fully entered the meta-bolic stasis known as cryptobiosis, and excitement was running high.

Everyone arrived to work in high spirits and five to ten minutes early. The first crystal they placed in the chamber was the original PS, or, now that they had thirteen vari-ants, PS00. Rae seated it in the cantilever device herself and sealed the door. The team watched the oscilloscope on the outside of the chamber twitching in response to the crystal's random fluctuations.

"How long will it take to stop?" Brando asked.

"How long does it take a refrigerator to go dark after the light switches off?" Allan responded.

Hubert nodded appreciatively. "A koan for our gen-eration."

"It wasn't a—"

Hubert put a hand on Allan's shoulder. "I'm joking, Allan."

They all agreed that if the chamber were effectively trapping the unknown radiation inside, the effect should be either steadily increasing oscillations or the absence of numinous energy. They spent fifteen minutes fearing the worst. The PS00 showed no change. Next they tried iso-lating a PS01 and arrived at the same results. After wait-ing five minutes, Rae said, "I want you to shut me inside. There must be some leak somewhere; the first thing we can do is check for any light coming through the cracks."

"Are you sure?" Ashley said.

Rae nodded, but she could feel a fear welling up inside her as she approached the dark chamber. She paused at the threshold of the door. "I'll let you know through the cantilever when I want out."

As soon as the door closed, her Omni chirped a net-work disconnection alert; she was absorbed by the dark-ness and struck with a fear she had only felt once before in her life. She was transported back to the memory of being in the delta-ray control room with the sphere of utter blackness reaching out and pulling her toward it. In reality it had only lasted a second, but in her mind it was still pulling at her skin like a thousand hungry leeches. She took her Omni out and lit up the space. The smooth aluminum walls reflected the light, but although the space was lit, the darkness hadn't left. *What the fuck is wrong with me? Was that event really so traumatic that I'm reliving it now? This feeling is so tangible. I've never felt so alone. God, that sounds so melodramatic, but I objectively have a sensation that no one is outside. No one is in this building, or this terradome, and I'm on Mars all by my—. No, I can't take it anymore.* She tapped on the cantilever with quick frenetic jabs, terrified that everyone had left and she would suffocate. A moment later the door opened, and she hurried out in the most professional manner she could, but of course Ashley had to point out, "Rae, you're shaking."

She looked down at her hands, and tried to play it off. "Yeah, I guess I had one too many cups of coffee this morning.

"Alright, team," she said, ignoring the concerned looks they were giving her. "I couldn't see any light coming through, and I know we've got a uniform layer of PS, so the only other possibility is that some of the PS was killed during construction. Just in case, let's test the rest of the PS crystals; then we'll see if it at least blocks the 6,828 frequency."

There is a mindset one slips into when performing a series of nearly identical proofs, and Rae watched as most of the team switched off their excitement and shifted into a mechanical routine. For Ma'at, it seemed as if something else had switched off. He wandered off to his workstation.

Rae followed him, passing the whiteboard app on the conference table that overflowed with ideas, none of them viable now that the chamber was useless.

"Ma'at," Rae said quietly, "Can I talk with you for a moment?"

After Ma'at slumped into the chair in front of her workstation, she wheeled her chair around to sit beside him. Without meeting her eyes, he said, "I... don't think I can do this anymore."

"You can't do what anymore?" she asked, trying to hide her fear that he was about to quit.

Eventually he shook his head and said, "I can no longer motivate myself with the progress of science, or the betterment of humankind, or strengthening my connection to the *Ruhhil-Qudus*. All that I am is back on Earth, and all I want is my old life back." His eyes glistened with unshed tears.

Her Omni chirped with two texts in succession, and Rae gave Ma'at a moment to collect himself while she checked it.

> **Mom:** Rachael, are you alright? I had such a terrible feeling that something had happened to you.

> Please don't ignore my texts like you always do.

*Leave it to Deborah to interrupt an intimate moment with her neediness.* Rae quickly typed:

> **R.Dahlia:** I'm fine, Deborah. Let's talk later.

As she hit "send," she noticed that she had typed the exact same thing about two weeks ago.

Without looking to see if she was paying attention or not, Ma'at said, "My wife misses her family, and I'm the one keeping her here. I'm so thankful we have each other, at least, but it's not enough. She needs to be with her people. I mean, I do too, but my work has always trumped that. I'm sorry, Dahlia, I guess the Feast of Thanks gets me thinking about the nieces and nephews who won't remember us when we return. I'm afraid our heartstrings are weakening under the strain."

Ma'at made a gesture with his hand as if he were pulling a thread from his heart. It was hard for Rae to relate; the only people she'd left behind were old friends she'd lost touch with, and her mother. She scrolled up through their text history:

> **Mom:** Are you alright? I just woke up from a nap thinking about you. Mother's instincts never go away I guess.

> Of course you're too busy to talk to your old mom.

The texts had arrived moments after Rae's stomach had been consumed in the sphere of blackness, but she hadn't even seen the message until the hospital had given her back her Omni, and she had responded with the same message:

> **R.Dahlia:** I'm fine, Deborah. Let's talk later.

"Heartstrings!" Rae gasped. "Ma'at, if there is a God, it just spoke through you." She called across the lab. "Which sample is in the chamber?"

"The PS06," Mora answered. "But we were just about to swap it out."

"Leave it." Rae commanded. The team watched her with eager curiosity as she collected all of the PS06 samples in the crystal growth chamber and tossed every single specimen into the molecular dismantler, basically the laboratory equivalent of a microwave, where, at the press of a button, the lichen was melted into a puddle of sugary sludge.

Dr. Brando was manning the oscilloscope, and as Rae pressed the button and turned back to the awaiting team, he spun around and checked the frequency. Luther Brando's eyebrows raised. "It's still!"

Dr. Allan pushed in beside Brando. "There's no frequency!"

The significance of the nothing that was happening was a strange lull to begin celebrating from. But slowly it dawned on everyone present that they had succeeded.

Rae announced victoriously, "Our chamber is shielding the PS06 from... well, what should we call this new force?"

"*Numen*," Hubert suggested.

"That's a little on the nose," Brando said, smiling.

"I like it, but there's no denying that name will cause some trouble," said Ma'at, who had returned to see the flatline on the oscilloscope for himself.

"Is that a reference to something?" Ashley asked.

Hubert nodded. "It's a Latin term for the divine will, or divine force."

Allan smiled. "Those religious fanatics have had it out for us for centuries, and I love the idea of reappropriating one of their words!"

Ma'at grimaced. "I liked 'numen' until Allan reminded me that its roots are Roman and not Arabic, and since I'm a fanatic I insist we call it *sakinah*."

Rae had never heard Ma'at use sarcasm before, and she found it didn't fit him. "Allan—"

He didn't even wait for her to finish. "I'm sorry, Cyrus, I'm... That was insensitive. I didn't mean anything by it."

"Thanks, Joseph, but," he turned to Rae, "you're the one who invited it with your comment 'if there's a God.' How can you even deny that's what we've encountered?"

Rae was entirely taken aback. "I..." she thought for a moment. "Fear," she said truthfully. "We've stumbled deep into the unknown. Connecting it to some vengeful old guy in the clouds doesn't make any sense in my mind. I'm sorry, I was just raised with a very different idea of God, and I don't want anything to do with that. What I will concede is that something just spoke through you and told me why our anti-numen chamber wasn't working." Rae gestured at it with both arms. "There's something connecting identical crystals to each other. The PS06s all had a link that could not be cut or blocked, so whatever the 06s were experiencing outside the chamber was telegraphed, via some invisible strings, to the PS06 inside the anti-numen chamber. It wasn't until I killed every 06 except our test sample, that it was truly isolated from this numen source." Before anyone could ask another question, she turned to Ashley and said, "It's time to test the PS12."

A worried look crossed his face, but he obediently walked to his desk and returned with a small glass vial that contained a crystal bead the color of lime juice and the size and length of a pencil eraser. Rae explained, "With Ashley's help, I built another series of PS lichen: PS11, 12, and 13. But the PS12 is the most relevant.

"Because the 6,828 frequency is caused by the death of a crystal and felt by all the PS crystals we have built, I believe that this 6,828 number is not something we have created but something that occurs naturally every day. But I've wondered how can it be that trillions of life forms across the universe are dying at every moment, yet our crystal only reacts to the death of its brothers."

Ma'at's interest slowly stirred. "Perhaps the other deaths *are* felt. Since we have been measuring their vibrations, there has been no moment when the crystals are still. Until now."

Rae continued, "Once I understood about the six types of mitochondria, I decided to design the PS12 with all in-types arranged in a repeating pattern. If I'm correct, when we kill the PS11, its 6,828 frequency will start a chain reaction in the PS12, which, if we seal it in our anti-numen chamber, will have no escape, and its vibration will be sustained."

Joseph Allan crossed his arms skeptically. "That's assuming this numen is unaffected by entropy. Are you sure that no other lichen we've created has energetic ties to the PS12?"

"Only the PS11, which we'll be killing." Ashley answered.

The doctors looked hungrily at the PS12 as if it might hold all the answers.

Mora asked, "What's the PS13 for?"

Ashley explained proudly, "We only had two options to destabilize the PS12's reaction. One was to print another PS12, but then it would take roughly thirty-five minutes to stop the chain reaction. The other option was to dissect another PS species so that it becomes a PS12. Meet the PS13. It's built in two layers separated by a Faraday cage to block the microwave radiation. When we nuke the outside layer, its death triggers the autophagy of the inner lichen. Across the entire organism certain parts of its DNA are cut out, and some of its cells wilt and die, until the inner layer decays into a structure identical to the PS12, which creates an energetic tie to its identical twin in the chamber, giving it an exit and destabilizing the reaction."

"And you want to try that now?" asked Brando, with more than a little worry on his face.

"What's the matter, Luther?" Hubert's tone was concerned yet jovial, as if calling him chicken yet egging him on at the same time.

Brando seemed unsure of himself. "Archaemimeology suggests that a great innovation preceded the downfall of every empire, and I just had the thought that this might be ours."

Without pause, Hubert said, "Don't be absurd, our

downfall came long ago with the invention of electricity. Every great innovation since has simply prolonged our collapse. Dr. Dahlia, please proceed."

Rae smiled, laced her fingers together and cracked her knuckles. "Washington, please secure the PS11 in the molecular dismantler. Ashley, give Dr. Mora the PS12. Make sure it's securely in the cantilever device in the chamber: we only get one shot at this. Brando and Hubert, please observe the oscilloscope."

After everything was in place, and the door to the chamber closed, Brando said, "The oscillations just stopped."

Rae nodded at Washington, who destroyed the PS11. Immediately Brando called out, "The PS12 is holding stable at 361 Y-hertz!"

There was an explosion of cheer, after which Mora said, "But it's still shy of the 6,828 yottahertz Evermore is asking for. Can we kill another PS11 to double the signal?"

Rae said, "We don't have another PS11. Its existence would give the energy trapped in the chamber an exit and destabilize the reaction."

"Ah, right. I forgot about the invisible strings."

"Ashley, put the PS13 in the dismantler." After he finished and gave her a thumbs-up, she said, "Kill it."

Everyone had left. Rae sat at her desk in the empty lab feeling incredible. Normally, if she was able to accomplish anything it was because it was too easy, but her design for the PS12 and the way its genetic structure sympathized with the death of the PS11 was objectively brilliant. She felt like Amazonian warrior women must have felt after a raid: powerful, brilliant, and, if she was being honest with herself, horny. She wanted more than anything to call up Ashley. *It figures; I'm doing my best to be nice to him, and he's been avoiding me. You know what? I don't even care.* She imagined showing up at his apartment and taking him whether he wanted it or not. She sighed. *But let's be honest, I'd never do that in a million years. I'd only chase Ashley away if I were actually that forward.* Then she realized she'd never even bothered to ask where he lived.

*Good thing I've got personnel files on everyone!* Not that she would ever actually show up unannounced, but now that she was curious, she had to know. But when she awakened her workstation she found that Evermore had sent her a message:

> **E.Evermore:** Time is growing short. If you don't make measurable progress on your assignment soon, I will replace you.

Her smile never faded as she wrote her reply:

> **R.Dahlia:** This afternoon we were able to sustain a frequency of 361 yottahertz.

> You could try to replace me, but I suspect it's too late for you to start over at the beginning. We're close.

The following morning, as Rae was getting her things together to leave for a weekend shift at K&J, a sudden nausea overcame her. She ignored it and fought it off as long as she could, but eventually it bent her over and she puked coffee in the hedges outside her building. The stream of people pouring out of the apartment complex were kind enough to give her a wide berth, but no one ventured to kneel beside her and ask if she was alright. Thankfully. If they had, she might have burst into tears. *I don't even know what I'd tell them.* The tests the doctors had run after the delta-ray accident at K&J had uncovered a "troubling" shadow on her pituitary gland, but the oncologist who ran another series of tests gave her a clean bill of health. But she didn't feel normal. *Who knows what kind of damage that numinous blast might have caused?* She shook her head, disappointed with herself. *I never even considered the health risks of working for Evermore. Not even when I was reading that whole "in the event of your death" line in the E.I. contract.*

Slowly she climbed into an automated rickshaw, her stomach still churning.

"What is your destination?" The rickshaw asked.

But she was still thinking about the exact wording on the contract: "In the event of your death, any discoveries you've made at Evermore Industries will pass on to your next of kin. If none such exists, Evermore Industries claims all discovery rights and ownership."

*Is someone poisoning me?* The thought was crazy. The only person who stood to gain anything from her death was Evermore, and while he could be manipulative she didn't think he was capable of murder. But what had her first assignment said? *"Do not directly lick the DNA sampler, it could have been tampered with or poisoned."*

"What is your destination?" the rickshaw asked again.

Rae still couldn't believe that he would or could have poisoned her. The Chemist had asked if she was on medication that might restrict pituitary function. A strange coincidence, since her first MRI had shown a shadow there.

"Evermore Industries," she said, and the rickshaw backed out of its charging station and picked up speed at a rate that upset her stomach.

Rae didn't spend long at Lab Seven. She simply collected each of Evermore's ePaper assignments from her desk and left. Once she felt outside the range of the building's cameras she called up her roommate at UMars, a clever but boorish young woman who often bragged about "cheating" her way through her computer science classes by speed-hacking the ePaper their tests were written on.

## Ashley

For his own protection he'd been keeping Rae at a distance, but his promotion changed everything. It was as
if the team at Lab Seven saw him for the first time. Rae
was treating him differently as well. Instead of double-
checking everything he said, or crushing him under her
authority, she treated him more like a peer. But he got the
sense that it didn't come without a favor she had yet to
ask. He still couldn't tell if she liked him or not, but she
almost seemed happy. *She's finally running the lab she has been
envisioning since the team was hired,* he thought. It was amazing
just to watch her work. She had an uncanny ability to keep
multiple details in her head at the same time. He never saw
her take any notes, but she could reference some particular from weeks ago as if she'd just been thinking about it.

Against his better judgment he found himself thinking
about her all weekend, wondering how terrible it would be
to hold a Feast of Thanks gathering at his place. The only
person he really wanted there was Rae, but he felt that
would be too forward for her. Extending the invitation
to the Lab Seven team would be a safe bet; not everyone
would come, and then it could be a coincidence that he
and Rae spent the night talking. *Although, if the team is there,
she might feel as if she has to uphold her precious professionalism.*
He almost worked up his courage to invite her, but when
Monday morning rolled around Rae was two hours late
to work and showed up looking like she had a little too
much alcohol, drugs, or both. For a brief moment he felt
his heart reach out to her, but he stopped himself from
being pulled into her darkness, and canceled the dinner
even before anyone had been invited.

When she eventually decided to show up on Tuesday,
looking clean but worn down, Ashley was fuming with anger and anxiety that a second fall was coming. The apprehension soured into resentment; every time someone in

the lab referenced the six markers as "Rae's numen markers," he was tempted to discredit her and reveal how much he knew about this fifth force they were calling numen. He also wished they had called it something else; "numen" made him uncomfortable. In one word it seemed to acknowledge the presence of a divine being, and yet none of them showed any concern for the consequences of using It as a free-energy power source.

Rae was late again on Wednesday. Her mood was reserved and lacked the excitement the rest of the team was experiencing. It physically hurt him to see her so melancholy after finally seeing her in her element. He avoided her as best he could and held initial job interviews at a café a block from the E.I. building. The RSS fliers on the café window advertised a number of different holiday parties, and though he dreaded the thought of spending the holiday with strangers, he also didn't want to spend it alone. The Relativity Lounge, Ashley noticed, was throwing something they called a Singles Collider, offering free drinks for those who "identify as women."

After his last interview late Wednesday afternoon, Ashley took his Omni out of airplane mode and reflected on meeting Mitch, or Rich, or whatever his name had been. Unfortunately for both of them, the meeting had felt like a waste of time from the moment the young freshman introduced himself.

As soon as his Omni found Cloud9, it chirped: Rae had called. In spite of himself, his heart freaked out and started jumping around excitedly. The calls came three minutes apart and were followed by a text message:

> **R.Dahlia:** The team is taking the holiday early. Can you come over when you get a chance? I need to talk to you about something.

*"Something"? Goddamn text! That could mean anything with-*

*out tone and inflection. Whatever it is, it's clear that it's not an over-the-phone kind of talk.*

**A.Rephaireal:** Sure.

**A.Rephaireal:** My interview was a bust.

Is everything okay?

She never responded.

# CHAPTER TWENTY-TWO

# Gravity

**Ashley**

Rae buzzed him in without responding to his greeting over the intercom. As he entered, the security guard smiled at him. "Haven't see you in a while; thought maybe things hadn't worked out between you two."

Ashley forced a smile. "We'll see."

Outside her suite, he rapped his knuckle against the door, and Rae opened it before the third tap. She looked tired, but not withdrawal tired. Her left hand rested on her stomach. Without a word she stepped aside behind the door. The gesture pulled Ashley into her apartment before he was sure he wanted to enter.

"Rae, you're kind of freaking me out; what's on your mind?"

She closed the door behind him and stood in front of it, blocking his exit. He turned around, and she locked her gaze on him. It was the look of an angry animal, and every muscle in Ashley tightened, not poised in anticipation, but petrified, rooted to the spot. It felt all too similar to another time he'd been cornered.

*His mother was towering over him, blocking the exit of his room. He knew she couldn't see him though her brown-bottle cataracts. Even sober, they distorted her world with disdain and hatred, and Ashley had become an expert at avoiding her when she couldn't recognize him as her son.*

*She cornered him in his room that day, but no matter how much he was afraid he couldn't bring himself to abandon her.*

Ashley forced himself back into the present, though Rae continued to stare at him. *No matter how hard I try, I think I'll always be attracted to her.* She seemed to be scrutinizing him. He knew that look; he'd done something wrong, and now he was supposed to apologize. *Is it worth finding out what I'm saying sorry for before I say it? Maybe she's going to apologize to me?* Then he heard Evermore's voice: *"Do you want to be a great man, or a cowering plebian who distinguishes himself through his willingness to abandon his own path and serve another's?"*

"I am here," he said, straightening his spine. "Do you want to tell me why you called me over, or... ?"

Ashley watched her lips sneer before opening to say, "You're here so I can decide if you're incredibly talented or fucking clueless."

His spine collapsed, and his instincts told him to run. This time it was his resolve that hardened him to the spot. "Was that a thank-you?" His voice quavered. "I mean, I appreciate the promotion, and I see how it was your way of thanking me for saving Lab Seven by covering for you when you were 'sick,' by sharing the recording of Samuel with you, and telling you about the six markers."

"*That's* why you covered for me, is it? Are you sure it wasn't because Evermore told you to? I know all that information didn't come from you, all that was Evermore. I just don't know why he waited so long instead of giving it to us right away. And all that shit about hiring three labs to work on the same problem; was that supposed to make me feel cornered?"

Ashley forced back tears. "Oh goody, a new side of Rae! Who's this tweaky paranoid?"

Rae flashed him a mean smile. "It's good to see you

fighting back. Doesn't feel so good to be cornered, does it?"

Ashley's knees felt week; they wanted to collapse and drop him to the floor. Even though the Doc was at the root of all this drama, he was the one Ashley imagined standing behind him. A hand lightly on his shoulder holding him upright. "Rae, I don't know why we're fighting. Or even what we're fighting about."

"You know!" Her mouth moved as if she were about to say something else, but the conversation was going on in her head. A long time passed. She stood there assessing him until her eyes grew watery, her shoulders deflated, and she said, "I know you know! Stop torturing me and just fucking tell me: What does Evermore want from me?"

Ashley shook his head. "I'm lost, Rae. You think he wants something other than some means of faster-than-light travel?"

Rae threw her hands in the air. "Sure, I get it. You don't want to accidentally reveal something I haven't figured out. Where do I start? Maybe with the phone call where you acted all sweet and innocent to lure me to work for him."

Ashley interjected, "The one where you used your feminine wiles to distract me and influence my decision?"

Rae ignored him. "When I declined to get involved with you, Evermore personally asked me to 'take care of you' and fed me some line about how you were a 'survivor.' He painted you as this simple and naive boy to trick me into trusting and even protecting you. He knew he couldn't manipulate me directly, so he used you to give me the recording of Samuel and tell me about the six numen markers. I don't know how he found out about the stims, but I know he sent you to clean me up."

Ashley's heart hurt. "Rae, I stole the Samuel recording because I wanted to expose him. Everything else I've done of my own free will for you. A— and Lab Seven."

"Give it up Ashley, I know all about you two."

"You only know what I've told you about us, and that has all been the truth! When he fired me, he said I needed to work with someone other than him and gave me three choices: Ma'at, Voss, and obviously I picked you." Ashley starting unbuttoning his shirt.

"Keep your clothes on, freak, what do you think this is?"

"I didn't tell Evermore anything, and I wouldn't have. I was so pissed off at him; he could have made me an assistant researcher, but instead he made me your bitch! Don't get me wrong, I'm not saying he's not manipulative. I know now that he wanted me that mad; he wanted me to steal that file. Why else would he have left it in plain sight on his workstation desktop? But he's not controlling me, and I'm not spying for him."

She was doing her best to seem unfazed, but he could tell she was changing her mind.

"So... in reference to my original question, you're telling me you're fucking clueless?"

Ashley finished unbuttoning his shirt, but he left it hanging from his shoulders. Under it he wore a white T-shirt. "During that first interview, you seemed weird in the same way I've always felt; I've always had this thing for strong women. The Doc knew that, he thought I'd probably choose you, but if he absolutely wanted me working with you he wouldn't have given me the choice. He's always looked out for me. He saved me from—" Instead of telling her, he pulled up his T-shirt. On the left side of his rib cage was a cluster of small cigarette burns. When she saw them, her shell cracked. Her fists unclenched, and her fingers extended, but she didn't touch him.

"I remember those," she said. "That first night we spent together, as I lay on your chest, my fingertips traced circles around those smooth spots until I fell asleep. I can't believe I forgot. I *am* out of my mind. I'm fucking crazy, I get that, and I understand why you've been avoiding me, but you're wrong: I didn't promote you out of gratitude. Ashley, I need a friend I can trust."

Ashley let his shirt fall back into place. "So you promoted me to be your friend?" He sighed. "Rae, you are out of your mind, but you don't even know *why.*"

"Well, please enlighten me, then, since you know me so well."

"Fuck, I... That was supposed to be a sweet thing. I do know you. I know it hasn't been long but... fuck, I'm just going to say it: Rae, after the immense amount of determination and willpower you've used to get where you are, you still think you're not worthy of the very thing you're chasing." He awaited her reaction, expected tears, but it didn't even seem to penetrate her armor.

"Rae, I really like you, but you and I don't fit together so well."

With all his heart he wanted her to deny it, to reject his assertion and finally admit her feelings for him. She looked at him for a long moment and said, "Don't I know it."

Ashley couldn't meet her eyes. His gaze fell on the couch, where he saw a memory of her falling into him as she slept.

Rae continued, "Everyone who meets me either treats me like one of their peers or like a piece of imported steak. I've gotten so adept at countering those hungry stares and fitting into this masculine world that I've gotten exactly want I wanted: to be left alone. But I never considered how lonely I'd be."

"So basically you're only with me when you get lonely?"

She shook her head. "No, I'm trying to say that I've heard every pickup line there is, but you surprised me, Ashley Rephaireal. You probably don't even know what you did."

He wanted to smile, but something felt wrong. He shrugged. "Did I wear you down with my persistence?"

"No. Maybe. Rather than hunting me, you opened a door and posed an invitation. Even after you found out I was your boss and I told you off, I could still feel you making yourself available no matter how cruel I may have... I was to you." Rae's eyes drifted off. "Even though you did it in your own clumsy way, you cut through my layers of armor and bullshit. And in appreciation I've either hit you or punished you in some other way." Her eyes glistened with the first hint of tears. "But then you saw too much of who I am, and I freaked you out."

Ashley's frustration peaked, and he put a heavy spin on his sarcastic tone. "Yeah, it freaked me out when you yelled 'get the fuck out of my house'!"

"And like a *moron* you listened to me. Don't you know anything? You left me alone when I was at my lowest. It may not all be on you, but man up, Rephaireal, why haven't you brought it up?"

"You said it yourself, you've hit and punished me for my impudence. Did it ever occur to you that I've been protecting myself?"

"Uh-huh." She wanted more.

Ashley closed his eyes and tried to calm down. "I'm scared of everything. I have trouble sleeping through the night. I'm afraid of being alone. I'm afraid of anything that can leave or break or be taken away. Evermore is the only stability I've ever known; when he left for Mars, I didn't know what to do with myself. That moment when I walked in with soup and saw you crashed out on the couch... I know what that's like. Not the withdrawal, but I've been there.

"I wanted to die when he replaced me with Samuel. Like, crawl up inside myself and disappear without a trace. I, too, needed a friend I could trust, and I went to you because I thought we'd made a special connection, but again you shook me off because I made you weak." He took a deep breath and opened his eyes. Her eyes were wet and angry, but not at him. "It took all of my will to stand back up, but I've been doing pretty good on my own. But goddamn it, I can't spend the rest of my life alone, and I can't spend it with another addict. Every time I see you I don't know which Rae I'm going to meet, and it's wearing me the fuck out.

"After we... fucked and you pushed me away the next day, I drew the line and took control of my own protection. Since you promoted me, you've been actually kind, and like a fool I softened up, and now you're using again."

"Ashley, I told you the other day. I'm clean."

"You've been late to work all week, and you come in looking pale and sick. If you're clean, I'm Evermore's spy."

"Ashley, I'm so fucking tired." A juicy tear rolled down her cheek. "I'm tired of being numb. I'm tired of being alone, and I'm tired of constantly questioning every move I make. I'm tired of juggling so many lies."

"I can't help you detox again. But maybe there's a rehab—"

"Ashley, I'm not high, I'm pregnant."

A flood of memories from their night together slammed into Ashley's brain. "The pill dispenser on the sink in the bathroom — I thought you were on the pill."

"Me too. That day you broke in and found me. That's the first time I'd ever experienced stim withdrawal. There's a little red pill, kind of like an antidote, which has always worked for me, but last time it didn't."

"What does this have to do—?"

"Just hear me out."

Ashley crossed his arms.

"When I complained to my Chemist, he asked if I was taking any medications that might affect pituitary function, which I wasn't, so I didn't think anything of it. But after the accident at K&J, they saw a shadow on my MRI scan and thought it was possibly pituitary microadenoma.

"You have cancer?! Holy fucking shit!"

She put her hands out to calm him. "I don't have cancer. They just *thought* they saw something on my pituitary gland. I've had it double-checked by an oncologist. Before she sent me in for another MRI, she asked if I'd been experiencing heavy mood swings, and if I was on the pill. She told me that in rare cases a pituitary tumor can increase estrogen levels beyond what birth control can handle, and that I should be careful."

"I don't understand how you can be so calm about this. You've got a tumor! Are you going to need surgery? Or radiation? They can't do that when you're pregnant, can they?"

"Ashley, calm down. The higher resolution MRI didn't find anything. Nothing. Whatever was there earlier was gone. She said it was an error."

"I don't understand. If you didn't have a tumor, then your birth control was working. Right?"

Rae pulled a piece of paper (real paper that required real ink) from her pocket, unfolded it ,and handed it to him. Ashley recognized it as micro-magnetic response language, the programming language that controlled ePaper. As a whole, it didn't mean anything to him, but there were two parts that were underlined. "This is from the ePaper document you handed me on the first day. I had a classmate of mine hack it. This line here—" she pointed to an underlined stream of letters and symbols, "—changes the date and frequency of my performance reviews, based on my saliva sample." She pointed to another underlined section. "Here it shows that it was measuring my estrogen levels."

"...the fuck? Why?"

She sighed. "That's what I was hoping to beat out of

you, but—"

"You think I've been helping Evermore impregnate you? As if all this bullshit I've been dealing with with him was a front. Jesus, no wonder you haven't been more supportive!"

She looked at him apologetically. "Ashley, I'm sorry for all of that, but this next part might be even harder for you to swallow." She handed him another piece of paper. "This is my second assignment from Evermore. When I licked the DNA lock, it released a chemical called NPA01838617. This is the proof that Evermore drugged me."

"Not possible." Ashley shook his head and stumbled backward until he ran into the back of the couch.

"The beauty of it is that whatever was wrong with my pituitary did its damage and disappeared. The only clue that there was ever anything wrong is a shadow on an MRI scan and this line of code."

"Okay, but I know for a fact that Evermore can't code. Sure, he could have gotten Ariel to write it, but there's no way he'd trust anyone to keep a secret like that!"

Rae looked as if she pitied him. "At first I assumed you wrote it. But then I realized he outsourced the project: The first week in September the weekly Hakaru puzzle was a self-destructing pituitary microadenoma. He had a hundred winning possibilities to choose from."

Ashley rubbed his face. "Why would he do that?" Ashley could feel his heart breaking, and a deep self-loathing rise in him. *I can't believe I ever trusted Evermore!* "What does Evermore gain by you being pregnant?"

Rae closed her eyes. "I've been asking myself the same thing and have come up with different possibilities depending on whether I keep it or—"

"You have to keep it," Ashley commanded, surprising even himself at the tone he conjured.

"I'm not discussing that with you!" New tears flowed

down the trails the previous set had drawn.

"You have to keep it," he said again, moving in close. "You and I made this being together, and maybe it wasn't a conscious decision, but it's our responsibility as parents—"

"We're not parents yet." She kept him at arm's length. "It's barely a coalescence of mucus. I'm not talking about keeping it or not keeping it, I'm just trying to figure out what the fuck Evermore is up to!"

Ashley ground his teeth together. *Damnit, if we don't talk about this now... No, forcing the issue is only going to push her away.* "I used to think I could read Evermore, but maybe I've only noticed what he's been broadcasting. What I *do* know is that he's been watching you since the trial; he knew your personality profile long before I ever interviewed you, and I think it's a safe bet he's expecting you to terminate."

Rae finished the thought, "—which means that getting me pregnant in the first place was futile unless he wants the embryo. Isn't it obvious? Samuel's sick, and Evermore's building him a new body."

"No." Ashley shook his head. "In the recording Samuel says, 'the container must match the contents'; unless you happen to be a direct descendant of Samuel, our child is useless to him."

"I can't fucking believe this is happening to me! I don't care how shallow it is: I know Lab Seven is on to something big, and I want all the fame and glory that comes with it. I want my name up there beside Jeannette Piccard, Rosalind Franklin, and Valentina Tereshkova as one of the most influential women in history. If there's any chance this will prevent me from getting that, then there's no way I'm going to keep it."

He wrapped his arms around her in a furious and passionate embrace.

"Get off of me." She pushed against his chest. "I'm

serious!" She pushed harder. "Get the fuck off me!"

Ashley spoke as softly as he could over her protests. "I know what it's like to grow up without a dad, and I *swear to God* I will not be like that!"

She squirmed and fought until she was actively trying to wrestle out of his grasp. She ground her teeth together and growled into his ear, "Get... away... from... me." She pulled his ears and dug her nails into the back of his neck, but still he held on. "Let me go, you fucking pussy!"

"I'm not going anywhere," he promised. "I won't leave you." It spurred her into another round of thrashing, cursing, and scratching. She wiggled an arm free and snaked it down his pants. Her thankfully short nails scratched at his inner thighs until they found his balls. She squeezed and twisted, as if she were punishing *them* for her predicament. Ablaze with pain, Ashley's eyes rolled up and his teeth clenched together, but he refused to let go. He kissed her neck tenderly, and whispered, "We're going to be alright. You know that, right? We are what our empty places have always hungered for." His words cut through her, severing her spine, and she went limp. "You don't need to earn goodness. You are good. You are enough."

Draped over his body, she shook with heaving sobs. "Ashley, I'm going to be sick!" He released his hold, and she took two steps toward the bathroom before collapsing onto her knees and vomiting onto floor. He knelt beside her and rubbed her back while she alternated between sobbing and dry heaving that shook and contorted her body in unnatural and necessary ways. When she had finished she looked exhausted and empty.

"I'm a ghost," she said, wiping her mouth with the wad of paper towels Ashley had brought her. "I'm Samuel." She started to laugh. "I'm simultaneously trying to get some proof that I exist and disappear at the same time."

"Do you love me?" he asked. It felt a too soon and a little forced.

She shook her head, searching for something to say. "Love is messy."

He gestured at the mess of yellow-stained towels contaminating the floor of her apartment. "I'm not afraid of messy."

She smiled.

## Rae

In the morning Rae awoke to the smell of pancakes. As Ashley set a warm mug of syrup in front of her, she said, "There's pluot jam in the drawer next to the sink."

As they cut through the pancakes, the screech of silverware punctuated the silence between them. Finally Rae said, "I hope you're not just making me breakfast in hopes of changing my mind."

"Of course not." He seemed disappointed. "This is me showing you how supportive I am. Maybe at the very least you'd let me come with you."

"Well, that's part of the problem; my options for trained doctors are pretty limited, as you can imagine; most MDs up here are more interested in studying the effects of Mars on the body than actually treating patients."

Ashley was lost in his thoughts for a moment. "If the options are limited, that must apply to Evermore as well. The question is, does he already have someone in mind? Or is he going to convince whoever you chose?"

Rae set down her fork. "Last night I decided that I have enough on my mind without worrying about Evermore's secret plans. Ashley, we can't let the things he *might* do affect what we want to do. If he does have some grand scheme, he's been planning it for years. The only way to totally avoid it is to quit and go back to Earth, and I'm not quitting. What I do know is that Seven is the only lab working on FTL now, and Evermore's lost his leverage over us. If he tries anything we don't like, we're in a position to walk away. It's too late for him to start over, and even if we have to threaten him with bankruptcy he's not going to win."

Ashley raised an eyebrow and smiled. "So you are still planning a contingency?"

She sighed. "Yeah, I guess so."

"Well, if we're already at it, let's plan something that will actually work. You don't have any breakthrough or unknown information locked in your head. The moment you threaten to walk away, he'll let you go and put Ma'at in charge."

Rae said, "We've got unknown information."

"What, the recording? It wouldn't be hard for Evermore to devise a way to leak that to Ma'at."

Rae was silent for a long time. "I'm afraid of moving forward. Evermore has used every assignment I've been given to subtly manipulate or drug me, and I can only imagine what fucked-up shit awaits me in the next one. If he uses it to find out I'm pregnant, he'll have so much leverage over me... I'd work here for free if it would prevent him from telling the news media, but who knows what he actually has in mind.

"On the other hand, no one will notice if I stall for a few weeks. I mean, it's feasible that we're years away from FTL."

"Seriously, Rae? You already figured out how to sustain a 361 yottahertz signal. With all the Hakaru you've solved, no one's going to believe that you're hung up on a multiplication problem." Ashley scoffed.

*Held back by pregnancy, cornered by Evermore. I never should have left K&J; the more I try to fight the system, the tighter my bonds get.*

Ashley ran a finger through a trail of jam and sucked it off. "The new assignment might only test if you're pregnant."

"I've taken a bunch of sick days, and I've been coming

in late. He probably has a good idea about that already, but just in case, I'm going to stall until I can find a doctor who'll—" After seeing the pained look on Ashley's face, she didn't finish the thought.

Ashley smiled, trying to reassure her. "We'll figure something out."

# CHAPTER TWENTY-THREE

# Spin

## Rae

"Eight weeks? I have to be nauseous for the next eight weeks!"

Though the exam room was surely soundproof due to the thick rammed-earth walls, as were all of the first-floor and subterranean buildings in the terradome, Dr. Isaac looked uncomfortable at Rae's volume and waited a moment before responding. "Eight weeks total, Dr. Dahlia. Remember, you're already three weeks in."

"But still, five weeks!"

"If your desire is to free yourself of the responsibility of motherhood—"

"It's not," Rae interrupted. "It's to save my child from a terrible life because of my parenting."

"Dr. Dahlia, if you're concerned you won't make a good parent—"

"If you met my mother you'd know I barely have the skills to be an adult, and have exactly none of the skills required to be a parent."

Isaac sighed and tried again. "I can see that you've got your mind made up, but whatever your reasons, I simply can't do the procedure until it is of an age where it can be safely transplanted."

Rae leaned forward. "Safe for whom?"

"For *both* of you."

Rae folded her arms. "But especially for — I don't even know what to call it — the *sample*, the *fetus*?"

"Dr. Dahlia," Isaac said in a tone that was meant to calm her. "You're upset. You should be, this is a hard decision to make, but you're still thinking about this like a woman. Think about it like a doctor. You have some very special, very unique tissue inside you that can bring us closer to solving some of the most complicated medical questions of our time. I understand you want to get back to work as quickly as possible, but there are doctors up here just sitting around waiting for their jobs to *begin*.

"The other day you mentioned your time at Chasma Australe. Well, just imagine what it would be like to have to wait for your ice samples before you could begin your work."

Not thinking, Rae shot back, "That's not hard; there were storms down there that would last for days."

Isaac nodded. "These doctors have been waiting *years* for someone to donate tissue."

"And what if I choose not to donate?"

Dr. Isaac chose his words carefully. "That is your right up until the moment you enter the operating suite."

"But you're not just talking about taking the tissue, you're talking about keeping it alive. Shouldn't I have the right to choose what happens with the tissue?"

"That is true on Earth, but here..." Isaac gave Rae an "empathic" look, which only served to infuriate her. "One of the principal agreements between Earth and Mars is that all resources brought here belong to Mars."

"I'm well aware of the Liberation Accord." Rae loosened her jaw and pulled her tone back from the edge of yelling, "But I had no idea it extended *into* my body. This is forced surrogacy!"

He looked apologetic. "I'm sorry, I assumed you knew. You seemed so confident that you wanted the procedure. I take responsibility for that oversight." He leaned in, elbows on his desk, and asked, "You are an organ donor, aren't you?"

"Dr. Isaac, I'm not opposed to my tissue being used; what concerns me is who's getting it and what it's being used for."

"The tissue will unequivocally stay right here in the UMars medical lab, and what it *may* be used for ranges from stem cell research to cancer cures. No matter how it gets used, you will be helping to advance medical science."

*But is it safe from Evermore?*

"I understand your concern, Dr. Dahlia, and I want to assure you again that the choice is entirely up to you."

"Sounds like there's not really much of a choice." She stood to leave.

"Thank you for being so understanding." Dr. Isaac pulled out his Omni, tapped and swiped a few times, then extended it toward her. "In about five weeks, you can schedule an appointment with Dr. Emilio Huarez, the ob-gyn."

Rae touched his Omni with her own to accept the contact. *Why do I know that name?* she wondered, but shrugged it off. *I must have come across it when trying to figure out who to talk to.*

Rae shook the doctor's hand and thanked him a second time before leaving. As she walked away, she felt lighter. Until she remembered Ashley. *He's going to be upset that I didn't bring him along.*

In the back of her mind she heard her mother's voice: *"What he doesn't know can't hurt him."*

*Well, thank you for that poignant adage, Deborah. It's nice to receive some good advice for a change.*

Walking through the halls of the UMars medical center, she noticed she was turning a lot of heads, and not because women were a rarity. Each set of eyes that watched her held a look of recognition. *Seems as if I'm already a minor celebrity.*

Through the glass doors of the foyer Rae saw a small crowd of people milling around, seemingly without purpose. *Worried loved ones?* she guessed, but as the doors parted and she stepped among them, their eyes all locked on her and a swarm of camera drones descended from nowhere.

"Dr. Dahlia! What's wrong with you?"

"Dr. Dahlia, a few questions?"

"Dr. Dahlia!"

"Dr. Dahlia!"

Panic boiled up inside her. *How did they know I was here? Do they know why? No. They have no idea.* And as soon as she realized that, some other part of her took over. Rae stood on a bench by the rickshaw charging station and held out her hands to silence them. "I'll take three questions, and then I'm leaving!" She pointed at one of them.

"Did your appointment today have to do with your accident at K&J labs?"

"Against all assurances that I'm fine, Dr. Kander insisted that I go in for a follow-up. I'm as good as new." She pointed at another.

"Can you give us a hint as to what you're working on over at Evermore Industries?"

She seemed to consider it, teasing them with her devious smile, and said, "You know I can't."

"Was the doctor able to give you any more insight as to why you fainted?"

*Which was it? Dehydration or anemia? Oh, wait, thanks for the loophole!* "Yes." Rae stepped off the bench to a chorus of groans. "I'm sorry, that's all! What else can I say? Hexapro just doesn't cut it; I need my red meat!" She climbed into a rickshaw and said, "Home." Even as it sped away the questions kept coming.

Rae breathed a sigh of relief. They could have trapped her there if they had wanted to by blocking the rickshaw with their bodies. *Maybe they would have if they really knew what I was doing there. That I was meeting with the same doctor who checked on me before fits my story, but when I meet with the ob-gyn they'll know. You didn't think of this angle, did you, Evermore?* Long ago, back in Chasma Australe, Kander had suggested that Evermore wanted to use her as the face of E.I., but its slogan, "Making a Future Possible," was the antithesis of abortion. She wrapped her hands around the abdomen that felt as if it didn't belong to her, and imagined she could feel something growing inside that space. *Either I keep you and I'm forever imprisoned in motherhood, or I destroy you and I become useless to Evermore — which I don't care about except the favoritism grants me a power I can't yet acquire on my own — and the media paints me as...* She actually didn't know how they would spin it. Rae took it as a point of pride that she knew nothing about celebrity gossip, and had only a vague awareness that mothers were celebrated and abortions were scandalous. *They can only call it scandalous if I make it a scandal.*

Her Omni rang. It was Ashley, and she answered with video.

"I heard you might need some red meat," he said, grinning.

"God, you saw that already?"

"Can I come over and cook for you tonight?"

"Absolutely, if you're bringing steak!"

"You know, spinach is high in iron, too. Fuck, I never should have said that; you'll turn me down for sure now."

"I'll pretend I didn't hear that. It's a date."


Ashley met her at her apartment, and after cooking a dinner of braised spinach and chickpeas with lemon, they curled up on the couch together and watched a movie. As the credits rolled, Ashley kissed her softly and confessed, "On our first date, you asked me what my UMars application essay was about. It was about genetic trauma."

She gave him a confused look. "I remember that, but

it wasn't during our date, it was during our interview."

He smiled. "What is a date, really, but an intimate interview?"

"You set me up for that one. Nerd. You got a lot further on that date than the one at the Relativity Lounge." It still bothered her that Evermore had succeeded in getting them together. That she could be so predictable made her as nervous as she felt about the idea of fate. Or ghosts, for that matter. "What about genetic trauma?"

"Unlocking the human genome birthed the field of molecular genetics around the turn. Geneticists mapped the human chromosome into genetic sequences, genes into genotypes, and when I was a kid they finished sorting genotypes into predispositions. For example, they could have predicted your inclination to become a scientist."

"I'm quite a bit smarter than the women you usually take home from the bar; I know about predispositions."

"Don't talk about my mother like that," Ashley said, smiling like an idiot.

"Wha— Ugh, that's not funny. Anyway, they didn't 'finish' predisposition sorting, they hit a dead end."

"Yeah, they had taken apart and reassembled the entire genetic puzzle, but they were left with extra pieces: 'Vestigial packets,' or 'junk packets.' My essay was a hypothesis on those junk packets."

Pulling herself back from the edge of sleep, Rae asked, "Junk packets? Is this your idea of nerd foreplay?"

"What? Oh, because I said 'junk'? Yeah, never mind, if you're going to—"

"Oh, don't be so sensitive! You just did the same shit to me. I'm listening, really, you were about to tell me that junk packets are genetic trauma."

He shook his head. "No. Not by themselves anyway. My first argument was that basically — and I know I'm bastardizing this, but fuck it — emotions are neurotransmitters released in reaction to something: fear, stress, lust, what have you. Over the course of your life your brain essentially teaches your body to enjoy — or avoid — experiences by feeding it dopamine doggy biscuits.

"Argument two was that certain psychedelic chemicals can become stored in fat and then experienced later in a 'flashback' when the fat is burned. It has been shown that trauma can also be stored in fat and reexperienced in the case of post-traumatic-stress-disorder patients. It has also been proven that susceptibility to PTSD is hereditary." He paused as Rae yawned.

"I'm with you so far. Emotions are chemicals, and chemicals can get stored in fat..."

"From these two points I hypothesized that traumatic flashbacks are not the only kind of event that can become stored in cells."

She had closed her eyes and was resting her head on his shoulder. "What's that mean in physiological terms?"

"I think that if there are enough of the same kind of chemical instructions throughout your body, when your body creates fatty acids and proteins, the instructions can become stored within the proteins that make up our DNA. Just like the way the brain remembers things using clusters of neurons, I believe these genetic memories or tiny instruction booklets are holographically encoded throughout our bodies. I think these junk packets are actually ancestral memories that have helped guide our evolution."

Though his words still made sense, drowsiness had smudged her comprehension of his argument. "Is that a point for nature versus nurture, or another layer of the theory of evolution?"

"Both. Your parents built on their genetic memories and passed them down to you. It's like an oral tradition on a physiological level." He might have said more, but for her, time skipped directly to when Ashley lifted her into his arms and carried her to bed; the last thing she remembered saying was, "That doesn't seem so farfetched; why didn't UMars accept you?" But she couldn't remember his reply.

\* \* \* \* \* \*

The Gregorian New Year was approaching when Evermore made a building-wide announcement that Labs Eight and Nine were being liquidated due to "a lack of progress." The news media took what little information they could find and ran a news cycle about how Evermore was reaching the bottom of his seemingly bottomless wallet. While James Jansen fanned the flames of the rumor, it was neither confirmed nor denied by Evermore himself.

That Lab Seven had been spared from the chopping block was taken as a minor victory and encouraged almost everyone to keep working at Rae's breakneck pace. By repeating a cycle of building a new PS lichen, waiting for the crystals to form, and trapping more and more numen in the resonator, the team pushed the sustained frequency further up the spectrum and kept most of the team interested, involved and optimistic. Cyrus Ma'at was not among the excited. Ever since he had admitted to missing his family, he had been flagging like a tile of heat shielding on the D4 space plane. It seemed that at any moment he might break off and endanger the entire ship. Rae had been searching for something that would rekindle Ma'at's passion, and for a time he was her favorite puzzle to work on.

One afternoon as Ma'at and the other doctors returned from lunch, she said, "Dr. Ma'at, can I have a word?" His gaze fell to the floor as he guessed what was coming. "I've noticed that you've been having a hard time these last few weeks. I know you think you want to return to Earth, but I don't think you'll be happy there."

He looked confused and on the edge of anger. "How

can you know that?"

"Look, I know we haven't had many heart-to-hearts, but I think I have a good idea what you're going through."

"You do?" He was getting defensive, but she kept pressing forward.

"Yeah. It's the *terra firma* blues. A few weeks ago you told me your wife was missing her nephews and nieces. You two are starting to realize how small Nili Terradome really is. But all that goes away with time. You've only been here a few months; give it some time, meet some new people. Either way, you've got a year and a half until the next shuttle to Earth, so you might as well make the best of it."

Ma'at seemed to be considering her words, but she was wrong. He was considering whether or not to say what was really on his mind. "Aziza and I have been trying to have children for a long time. We found out before the Feast of Thanks that... we... can't." He held back tears. "Without the option of having my own family, my life's work seems pointless. This is the end of the Ma'at line."

"But you could adopt."

"Martian law won't let us adopt until we renounce our Earth citizenship, and neither one of us wants to spend the rest of our lives here."

"I..." Rae began. "I'm sorry."

Ma'at said nothing. Rae imagined how he would react if he knew she had an abortion scheduled. *He won't be able to see it from my side of things. He'll walk away right when Seven needs him most. Is there a way to acclimate him to the idea?*

Her moment of pause seemed to be making Ma'at anxious. "Was there something else?"

Rae nodded. "Yes, actually. I didn't call you over here to tell you to suck it up. I wanted to tell you that after Lab Eight was cleaned out, I asked Evermore to give it to us. He just let me know it's ours. In fact, it's *your* new lab. While you'll still be under my supervision, and working toward Seven's goals, the eighth floor will be your personal area."

Ma'at's eyes relaxed as he realized he wasn't fired, but the rest of the news seemed to wash over him.

Rae continued, "I appreciate how much you've given to this project. So, thank you."

Ma'at nodded. "No. I want to thank you for the opportunity. Since day one you've been exploring questions I had long given up on. And I want to apologize for my recent behavior."

"No apology needed. Now that I know what you've been dealing with, I understand. Take some time if you need it."

"That won't be necessary."

Rae said, "Now that we have confirmed the existence of numen, we need a way to prove that our research... that *your* research on spiritual inertia belongs with the other natural sciences. We need a way to observe the phenomenon so we can begin to predict, quantify, and measure its potential. Your task is to build such a tool. You have all of the machines and staff of Lab Seven at your disposal. I'll have your desk moved up there as soon as you're ready."

While Rae waited for his answer, she thought of Émilie Du Châtelet, who predicted infrared light but died before she could prove it, leaving the prize available to William Hershel. She wondered if she were placing herself in the same situation; although she assumed she wasn't about to die any time soon, Rae still worried that Ma'at would edge her out and get the credit for their discovery. *I suppose that would be poetic justice, since I never would have* made *that discovery without Evermore.*

"I am at your disposal," Ma'at said, but Rae got the sense he was speaking not to her, but toward some higher power.

\* \* \* \* \* \*

Rae split her days between overseeing her team's personal experiments, pushing the PS12s toward the crossover point, and working with Ma'at in Lab Eight on a numen sensor. During the second week of the New Year, Lab Seven had strung together a bracelet of nineteen PS12 beads, and while the oscilloscope inside the antinumen chamber read a stable 6,859 yottahertz, nothing extraordinary seemed to be happening. It was clear to everyone in Lab Seven that there was something special about the 6,828 mark, and they couldn't wait to discover what it was.

As Rae entered Lab Seven early the next morning, she looked through the bulletproof glass walls of the clean room at the bracelet of nineteen PS12 beads in the growth chamber. In her mind she deconstructed the bracelet and reassembled it with the missing PS bead. It was so easy to do, and she was so sure it would work. Success tasted so close, and she longed to chew, swallow, and be done with it.

Her stomach started to churn, and she hurried to sit in the closest chair. *On the subject of being done with things...* Rae held her roiling stomach as if that would calm it. *I seriously can't wait to be done with you,* she thought. And while she was looking forward to being done with her accidental project, she reminded herself that sustaining the crossover point wasn't really her end goal, it was Evermore's. She thought back to her conversation with Evermore in his rooftop garden. *I told him I wanted to do something great for Earth, and he didn't believe me.* She tried to imagine what that would even look like. *I don't even believe me. I became a scientist because I wanted to be Victoria Crellinger. Once I create the crossover point, there's nothing Evermore can do to stop me. No, that's only true if the public* knows *it was me. It wasn't until Crellinger made her breakthrough discovery at NMC that she was able to get enough funding to start up her own research firm.* She thought of Kander's warning: *"I wouldn't be surprised if Evermore will try to use you as the new face of Evermore Industries, not because you're a talented scientist, but just because you're a woman."*

*If I want to become a force in the scientific community, it can't be because Evermore has given me that power. I have to achieve it in spite of him. The media needs to see that I created the gate.*

But then she thought, *Do I really want to be the head of my own firm? What is it I'm so interested in discovering? The fifth fundamental force and the crossover point are the fucking hottest things going on in science right now!* Her forehead broke out in a thin layer of sweat as a gentle pressure constricted her stomach and threatened to eject its contents, reminding her exactly what Evermore had done to her, but it was so hard to hate him completely when he wanted to give her everything she wanted for herself. *Why the fuck did Evermore want me pregnant? I'd ask him, but I know I wouldn't swallow any answer he'd try to feed me.* The nausea got so intense that Rae knew this wouldn't be one of the days she'd be able to fight it back, and she rushed into the bathroom.

On Friday, after a week of trying different combinations of PS species, Rae gathered her team together and announced, "Nineteen PS12s caused us to overshoot the 6,828 mark, as Dr. Allan predicted." She looked elsewhere so as not to unconsciously shoot him an annoyed glance. "After this week I don't believe any combination of the PS crystals we currently possess will bring us to our goal. Ashley and Mora, I want you two to design a new series of crystals we can swap into the bracelet of eighteen to hit our mark." She glared at Ashley, trying to silently remind him that she didn't actually want him to create the missing piece, and to his credit he only looked confused for a moment before nodding. She smiled and headed to the elevator. "I'll be upstairs working with Ma'at if you have any questions."

The numen sensor Rae and Ma'at had designed had six tubes arranged in a hexagonal pattern. Each was based on the anti-numen chamber and had an aluminum vacuum chamber with dormant PS crystals lining the inside. The ends of each tube would be capped with a special lens of PS crystal they had yet to design, which would refract indirect numen. At the back of each tube they mounted a single PS crystal from a special batch Ma'at dubbed "the twenty series." The twenties crystals were connected to piezoelectric sensors, a mass of wires that wove their way through a condenser coil to the innards of a six-inch color cathode-ray tube they'd custom ordered from the fabrication department at K&J.

Midway through the morning, Ma'at looked up from his workstation and said, "If you do not mind my asking, Dr. Dahlia, I have had the sense that something has been bothering you ever since we started working up here."

Rae ran through every lie and excuse that came to mind and threw them all out. "There is something, but it's personal."

He returned to his work, to break the tension. "I assumed as much, and did not want to press you. My only intention was to clear the air, as it seemed to be something between us."

Rae swallowed hard. "It's not *between* us exactly, but I'm afraid it might negatively affect our relationship."

He looked back up, worried.

"I just want you to hear it from me and not from some clickbait journalism site... I wasn't careful enough, and I got myself pregnant."

As Ma'at's expression peaked at elation, he said, "That is fantastic news! Did you think I would be jealous?" She watched a realization enter his mind, and his features dropped below baseline into the trough of melancholy. "You're not planning to keep it."

Rae shook her head. "Cyrus, I—"

"UMars medical center performs an average of seven abortions per year; most of the patients are young girls from the entertainment district, but the scientists who study the embryos are desperate enough that they have been bribing general practitioners to *recommend* abortions. I know you've got a good head on your shoulders, and I can't imagine anyone pushing you around, but parenthood is a very emotional decision... were you at all pressured by the father or your doctor?"

"Cyrus, I'm so sorry, I know you and Aziza have been trying for so long, and this must feel like a slap in the face, but can you imagine me as a mother? How could I treat that child with anything but resentment?"

Ma'at was clearly doing his best to calm himself and keep his tone even. "A mother's love is not something that is planned; it is biological."

Rae thought of Ashley's scars and almost shouted back at him, but she caught herself. *Remember, I'm here because I'm trying to keep him on the Lab Seven team. I've got nothing to prove to Ma'at.* "Yeeeah... you know what, Ma'at, I'm not any less of a woman just because I don't want to be a mother."

"But are you any less of a human after you choose to kill something?"

Rae stared into his face searching for some hint of anger, some reason he would lash out at her so coldly, but he was sad, not angry, and the question was posed philosophically.

"Ma'at, death is part of life. You're not a vegetarian, you kill things through your purchase of them as food. You kill your native bacteria when you wash your hands!"

"I agree: death is part of life when that death *feeds* the life and allows it to live or thrive."

Rae took a deep breath. *Don't say anything you'll regret. You need him. You need him.* "That's exactly what I'm doing. If I have a kid, I won't be able to do my job at E.I., then I'll be homeless on Mars, and both of us will starve."

"Evermore can't fire you for being a mother."

"That's not the point. The point is I don't want to have a kid!" She wasn't yelling, per se, but someone who hadn't ever heard her yell might incorrectly classify it as such.

Ma'at said nothing in return, and the awkward silence stretched on. Rae felt she couldn't leave; they still had work to do, and they hadn't quite arrived at the end of the conversation.

"Do you already have an appointment scheduled?" he asked. "Our ob-gyn was a friend of Evermore's, really nice guy, and he helped us understand how they do things on Mars. You know they're going to force you to keep it until it's big enough to *harvest*." He leaned into the last word with a disgust his even temper couldn't hide.

Finally, something they could agree on. "I feel just as disgusted about that, believe me, if I had any choice..." sensing his response she pivoted to a different topic. "My appointment is with Emilio Huarez."

Ma'at nodded. "Small world. I think you'll like him."

"Rae, what's the matter? You don't look well."

She didn't feel well. *If Huarez is a friend of Evermore's, there no guarantee that the fetus is safe from whatever that monster has in mind.*

"Is it morning sickness?" Ma'at guessed.

Rae nodded and excused herself to the restroom, where she balled up her coat and sobbed into it until her throat was raw.

# CHAPTER TWENTY-FOUR

# Crossover

### Rae

The following morning, Ashley cooked breakfast while Rae sipped from a hot cup of something she called "pregnancy tea." She needed something to replace her morning ritual since caffeine had become off limits. She savored the acidic memory of the blacklisted beverage, and her thoughts drifted as she watched a few crumbs of leaves that had escaped the bag swirl around and eventually settle on the bottom. "So I was talking with Ma'at yesterday... apparently he and Aziza have had trouble getting pregnant, and Evermore sent them to an ob-gyn friend of his."

While Ashley dropped a piece of bread into a mixture of raw eggs, milk and nutmeg, she could see him trying to figure out what she was saying. As the eggy bread sizzled in the hot buttery pan, he asked, "Do you find that surprising? He knows a lot of people up here, and I know one of his strategies about FTL travel was not actually getting a ship to travel faster than light but creating an experience that felt instantaneous. He had a South American guy pretty interested in long-term cold storage of living humans."

"Was his name Huarez?"

"Yeah, that sounds familiar."

"I have an appointment with him this afternoon."

Ashley set down the spatula and gave her his full attention. He made no attempt to hide his worry and sadness. "Is it *the* appointment?"

She nodded.

He shook his head and turned away from her. "I did my part. You asked me not to talk about it, and so I haven't. I guess I had some fantasy that you were considering keeping it, and that you'd change your mind if I gave you space." A burning smell started to drift from the pan, and Ashley flipped the toast onto its other side. "So Evermore gets our child after all?"

Rae spent a long time choosing her words. "Ashley, motherhood will take everything I've got. And not just for nine months, for the rest of my life—"

"Rae, I'm not going anywhere. Granted, growing it inside you and giving birth will take a lot of your energy, but as for the rest of its life, there'll be two of us."

"I didn't mean to imply otherwise, just that it's going to take a lot of energy. Can we agree on that?" Ashley nodded, and she continued, "Once this fifth interaction theory gets released, it's going to take everything I've got just to keep up with it. I know you want it, but I'm not willing to give up on my life."

"What if I am?"

"Then you need to find someone else to make a baby with." Rae could tell her words had hit hard, but she didn't feel the least bit sorry. "We are at such a crucial moment. If I'm out of the lab for... I don't even know how long a baby will need me, or how soon I can be back in the lab — a year? Eighteen months? There won't be any place for me on the team; the qualities of numinous energy will have been measured, or at least I'll need so much catching up, and the field will be moving so fast, I don't know if it will even be possible to catch up."

Ashley flipped the French toast onto her plate. "But don't you feel responsible for what Evermore might do to the fetus?"

"No. It was out of my control when the Martian government taped a 'Property of Mars' sticker to my uterus."

"But you still have the power to keep it from them."

Rae took a sip of tea. Swishing it around in her mouth, she scowled and swallowed. "Any response other than 'Okay, let's keep it' sounds impossibly cold. I don't have any attachment to this thing. I know it's got tiny arms and a tiny heartbeat, but I don't have that whole 'protect the tiny cute thing' response, and that should tell you something."

Ashley dropped another piece of eggy bread into the pan. He looked to be sitting on something he didn't want to say.

"What was that thought?"

A tear rolled down his face. "Before today I'd been working up the courage to ask you if we could name it Sean."

"It won't even have genitals until like sixteen to twenty weeks."

"I was thinking S-E-A-N. I think it would work for both. It was my father's name."

Rae frowned and changed the subject. "You've never told me anything about your father."

Ashley drifted off to some distant place and said, "There's nothing to tell. He left before I could remember. I can't even picture his face."

"What about photographs?"

"My mother hated him. Any trace of him was destroyed when he left, and asking about him just made her angry."

Rae glanced at the time. "Shit, we're going to be late!" She lathered her French toast in pluot jam and stuffed bite after bite into her mouth.

Even "late," they reached Lab Seven before anyone

else. Before settling into her workstation, Rae stood at the southernmost point of the lab's curved windows that looked out over the city, and took a moment to watch the sunrise over the... *That's funny,* she thought, *They changed the mountain range.* Rae tried to remember what the view had looked like yesterday, but couldn't. The slopes, still in shadow, did not wear the Alps' modest dark-green skirt of spruce but a sparse bikini of juniper and high desert shrub. *Was it different yesterday, or is this the first time I've noticed?* Regardless, it was beautiful, and for a time Rae was held stationary by it.

The change of scenery gave her the sensation that she was somewhere else, as if they'd moved the terradome while everyone slept. Her hand idly held her stomach, which still felt as if it belonged to someone else. For a moment she had the sensation that not only had someone moved the terradome, but that she had also been moved to a new body, possessing a new life. It was the way she'd always expected to feel on her birthdays when she was young. As if the clock would tick and she would be a different, older version of herself.

*I've been walking through the world backward,* she thought. *Always looking at who I was and waiting to become the person I want to be.* She turned slightly toward the west. *Who am I? Now, in this moment, who am I?*

The light of the sun slowly crept down the wall of the dome, lighting the unknown granite-gray mountain range.

*I am a respected doctor of synthetic bioengineering.*

The skyline of Nili Terradome rose from the shadows, the first and tallest of which belonged to the E.I. building.

*I am a powerful woman.*

Rae became aware that she was still holding her abdomen.

*And I am a mother.*

It didn't feel true, or she didn't want it to be.

*For however much longer, today I am a mother.*

Afraid of her own coldness, she tried to feel the connection to that living being inside her, but all she felt was hollow. "I am a mother," she said quietly.

Rae felt the kiss of sunlight as it broke the horizon to the east, but its warmth was all wrong. She could feel the radiation but not the heat. She turned to face it. It looked just as big and bright as ever but as fake as a treasure chest in a fishbowl.

"You ready, baby?" she asked the hollow. "Good, then let's make some history."

Rae spent the morning carefully lacing PS beads on a thin copper armature. As the doctors arrived they might have said something to her, but she couldn't hear though her intense focus. Sometime later, without so much as a hello, Rae addressed the lab. "We're going try another numinous chain reaction. I want all of you focused on getting the experiment set up and ready to test by this afternoon."

Joseph Allan sighed loudly as he headed toward his work station. "Do you have something to add, Dr. Allan?"

"Nothing at all, Dr. Dahlia."

"No, please, if you have anything at all that will help us or hold us back, please let's get it out now before we've got some potentially dangerous energy field eating up half the lab."

Allan looked horrified. "What exactly are we testing today?"

Brando spoke up. "She means your negative attitude."

"Oh." He made a show of calming himself. "I'm sorry, doctor. I'm getting... impatient. In the past our experiments have revealed exactly what we wanted them to, but lately it just feels like..." He struggled for the right word. "Let there be no misunderstanding: I don't have the solution by any means. Hell, most of the stuff we've been dealing with is science fiction, and I'm embarrassingly uncreative. But I feel like we've been spinning our wheels."

Rae locked him in her stare. "Is there a question you would like to ask?"

Allan couldn't back down from a challenge, regardless of how it made him look. "I guess I'm wondering if you're truly stumped, or if we've been intentionally wasting time for some reason?"

From the corner of her eye she saw Ashley freeze, and she hoped no one noticed. She kept Allan locked in her gaze, smiled, and said, "We're done wasting time."

By early afternoon Rae had finished assembling the bracelet, which consisted of 18 PS12 beads and three new PS crystals. The rest of the team had gotten everything ready, including the setup of another wireless cantilever alongside the bracelet inside the anti-numen chamber. This second cantilever housed a single PS12 crystal. Everyone anxiously held their positions while Rae secured the bracelet and attached it to its array of sensors. Ma'at was called down to watch. Additionally, Rae had the team record the event on their personal Omnis, which were propped up and positioned around the lab.

Dr. Washington was manning the molecular dismantler. With a nod from Rae, he destroyed the PS11 within. In the same instant, the bracelet and the PS12 inside the chamber buzzed once at the 6,828 frequency, and then their vibrations diverged. While the PS12 slowed down to the 361 Y-hertz its identical PS12s in the bracelet were individually experiencing, the bracelet as a whole held steady at a perfect 6,828 yottahertz. The team held its collective breath as Rae checked and double-checked the readings. *I expected something more, something epic!*

Allan broke the silence. "That's it, then. We've got a sustained 6,828 yottahertz frequency. Shouldn't we get Dr. Evermore down here?"

The team broke into chorus of cheers, but the rounds of congratulations were quelled when Rae didn't join them. The room grew quiet as they all watched Rae watching the anti-numen chamber. "It's not enough just to know it's there," Rae said. "Don't you want to see it?"

"Dr. Dahlia, do not—" Allan began,

Not breaking her stride, she said, "I told you before: I'm done wasting time."

"Rae, NO!" Ashley called, and rushed forward to stop her, but there was too much equipment in the way; he couldn't reach her before she had grasped the handle of the chamber and yanked it wide.

Someone else yelled, but the sound was interrupted by a brilliant explosion of darkness whose throbbing force reverberated reality itself into two versions. In one lab, the hole of darkness in the center of the numinous bracelet seemed to pull light toward it, and for an instant they were blinded as visual perception was pulled from their eyes. And yet, in another sense there was nothing wrong with their eyes. They could perceive (while also being blinded) that the actual level of light in the room was unchanged, as was everything else physical about the space. But at the same time, the hole of absolute darkness had grown, opening up beneath them, and was warping the room so that all points led down toward the hole. The team stumbled forward. Some fell to the floor and began to slide. Rae was on her knees mere feet from the dark anomaly. She reached out to it, and her voice rose above the chaos. "That's my son!" she called. "Give him back!"

Ashley scrambled toward her on all fours, and as he threw an arm around her to pull her back, she felt him stop. *I'm not crazy*, she told herself. *He can see it too.*

In front of her was the transparent form of a middle-aged man in a business suit. He was barely visible, but she checked his features to see if she knew him before focusing on the naked infant he was holding. Like a hologram shifting in the light, the child was many ages at once. At one angle the infant was smaller than a newborn, but at another it was older, more developed. At yet another he was a boy, still less than a year old, but able to hold up the weight of his own head. He clutched the lapels of the man's suit as if he might slip.

There was no question that the child was hers. The boy had Rae's eyes and facial structure but Ashley's thin lips and hard, triangular nose. Rae writhed and fought against Ashley, reaching out for the ghostly child, but before she could escape his grasp the hole disappeared as if it had never existed. The light returned, even though it had never left, and the only hint that something had even happened was a buzzing throughout her entire body.

Dr. Washington stepped away from the molecular dismantler. "What the hell were you thinking?! What did you just expose us to?"

Hubert stepped from behind the chamber. With a look of disbelief on his face, he said, "I could see all of you even though my sight was physically blocked."

Rae couldn't speak. Her body was overwhelmed by a grief that was not limited to one thought or event but was a direct current of pure emotion that surged through her. And even as the emotion dissipated, her body continued to buzz. When it had passed, Rae had no idea how much time had elapsed. The team had collected themselves around her and were waiting. *This is it. It's over. I took a risk and broke their trust. I don't regret anything. It had to be done.*

She stood and faced their disparate reactions. Those who were concerned for her assumed she was weak. Those who worried for their own safety burned her with their wordless accusations. "We made history here today. This is what you signed up for, so stop looking at me like that."

The elevator doors parted, and Samuel held them open with one hand and leaned heavily on his cane. The look on his face was part excitement and part fear. He looked directly at Rae and said, "Dr. Evermore wants to talk with you. Now."

A deeply uncomfortable silence hung between Rae and Samuel as the elevator jumped to the twelfth floor. Samuel seemed anxious, and Rae imagined him to be burning with questions, while all she could think about was the recording of him and Evermore.

"You're dying, aren't you?"

The doors opened, and he gestured for her to exit first.

"No. I must have caught that stomach bug that's been going around." He didn't smile, and when she didn't, either, he said, "Leukemia. I've still got a few months to live." As her eyebrows rose and her shoulders slouched, he barked, "Don't pity me."

She knew exactly how he felt.

His voice softened. "We are everlasting, and the pain of this life is just an illusion."

She stepped out of the elevator and walked through the small waiting room and Evermore's open office door. Samuel followed her to the threshold of the office and pulled the door shut behind her. Evermore was pacing when she entered. For the first time since she had started working for him, he was wearing a perfectly white lab coat.

"Dr. Dahlia." He walked the edge of the Mexican rug that outlined his library but stopped when he reached the corner. "On my desktop is a bill of labor from the builders' union."

*He wants me to explain it.* Rae leaned over his workstation, which he kept in tabletop/tablet mode, or flattened for meetings, and read the pink bill in the topmost window. The itemized description listed various plywood and aluminum fabrication jobs. In another line at the top, the form mentioned Lab Seven. "These are the materials for the anti-numen chamber. It was my understanding—"

"In your reports," he interrupted, turned on his heel,

and traced the edge of the rug back in the other direction, "you claimed that this 'anti-numen chamber' was being built to create a space to contain this new force." He reached the opposite corner. "It was my understanding that your anti-numen chamber was capable of blocking the numen energy."

Rae had never seen Evermore like this; she had entered without her armor and now it was too late, he was inside her, poking at her every weakness. She couldn't hold eye contact with him and looked back down at the workstation. "I don't understand; are you asking if it works? Yeah, it works."

As her eyes focused on Evermore's mess of open files she realized that there was an engineering schematic in the window beneath the pink invoice. She could only see a fraction of it, but it was enough to guess that it was some kind of spaceship. The label said, "E.I.S.S. Godspeed."

"If it works," Evermore shouted, spun, and left the boundaries of his rug to stand on the opposite side of his desk, "then why could I see a black hole of nothingness open up beneath my feet?"

"You saw it through the floor?" she stared at him. *Did he catch me looking? Is that SS like 'Space Ship'? Why does he have plans for a ship before we've designed the engine?*

"Answer me," he growled.

It took Rae a moment to remember his question. "I take responsibility for that. We were able to create a sustained 6,828 yottahertz anomaly within the chamber, but I had to see it; I had to know what it looked like."

"So you exposed the entire terradome to an unknown energy, radiating at double the strength of a high-energy gamma ray?"

"Yes, but we are surrounded by this numinous radiation all the time."

"Where is your proof of that?"

*Don't you know the answer to that?* "Remember the *Lep-*

*raria ptilisaccharon* crystal I showed you? The crystals buzz and fluctuate all the time. There's never a moment they're still."

"That's a thin excuse, Dr. Dahlia."

Rae sat in the cold plastic chair across from Evermore; she took a deep breath and a long moment to construct a psychic wall between them. As she finished, Evermore's energy also seemed to shift, and he sat as well. She said, "This was not the first time I've seen that dark anomaly. During that accident at K&J labs back in December, I inadvertently caused a numinous event, which caused a crystal to jump from the delta-ray accelerator to the crystal incubator back in Lab Seven. The anomaly wasn't captured on any of the cameras or sensors at K&J; my eyes were the only instruments capable of measuring the 6,828 yottahertz event." She took out her Omni and re-played the video from moments ago. It was unimpressive: the Lab Seven team was standing around, then celebrating, then yelling at Rae. When she opened the chamber door there was no blackness, no warping of space; the only strange event the device had recorded was everyone falling to the ground in the same synchronized moment. Rae stopped the video before it showed her screaming into the chamber. "That's why I had to open the door. I had to see if both events were the same."

Evermore began to say something, but she cut him off. "Give me six months, and I'll build you a gate big enough to step through and appear miles away in an instant."

Evermore was silent. His eyes were blank. His mind was elsewhere. Some grand multidimensional puzzle was being solved behind those eyes.

After a lingering silence, Rae tried another strategy to sell him on her idea. "Do you want to put DuPont out of business? Just make their space elevator obsolete. E.I. could make the trip to Chasma Australe as simple as step-ping through the Dahlia Gate. Forget airports and space shuttles, step through a Dahlia Gate to get to Phobos. Or," her eyes grew wide with possibility, "step through and return to Earth."

Evermore finally spoke, perturbed. "Dr. Dahlia, you have no idea just how many things my attention is coordinating at the moment. I have a contract with our investors holding me responsible for trillions of dollars' worth of investments. They have trusted me with this money because I have proven one thing: the capability to think big, and think of everything. Before we attempt to use this numinous anomaly to fulfill our every desire, we must weigh the consequences."

Rae had a flashback to the man holding her child and struggled to hold back tears; she wanted to run out and demand that Samuel tell her what it meant. *Was that one of his friends?* Then she was struck with a realization: *What if the sustained crossover point is a way for Samuel to get his friends here? Does Evermore already suspect that?*

There was a quick knock, and Samuel opened the door, "Doctor, you're getting a number of calls about the recent event. I know you told me to hold them, but the Public Health Service just called; they're sending over an inspection team to shut down the building."

"They're welcome to do whatever they please as soon as they can prove that the event originated in our building."

Samuel looked genuinely worried; it was the first time Rae had seen him look anything other than bored. "It's beyond that point; they're on their way."

"Then let me know when they've arrived. *Out.*" Samuel scowled and pulled the door shut with a loud thud.

"Aren't you afraid they'll find something?" she asked.

"No. They'll be looking high up; say, somewhere around the seventh floor. That should keep them away from my secret labs in the—" He pressed both hands over his mouth as if to shut himself up.

Rae rolled her eyes as she realized he was teasing her. "Very funny, but there's really nothing here you don't want the government to see?"

"Sounds like you suspect there is." Evermore leaned back in his chair and interlaced his fingers. "If I'm the evil villain you assume me to be, oughtn't I wait to unveil my grand scheme until I have you bound in some vile contraption?"

Rae pressed her arms to the sides of the chair. "Then tie me up and let's get this over with. You're the closest thing to an evil villain I've ever met. I'm *done* playing games with you," she said, wishing she could hate him absolutely.

"Okay. Here's what I had in mind: First of all, we're not calling it a Dahlia Gate, and the problem with just stepping through is that there isn't enough technology involved: If it doesn't seem expensive, I'll never make those investments back."

And there it was; now she hated him. "Last time I was here you were picking apart my desire to save the world, now I know why you were so critical — you're just thinking about your profits."

He laughed good-naturedly. "Rae, how would you like to be on the first ship to travel light years in an instant? And, if you can imagine it, the first person to set foot on an alien world?"

"I—" she began, but it wasn't her turn yet, and Evermore kept talking.

"Samuel has been researching Goldilocks planets all across the galaxy—"

"Not too hot, not too cold."

"He's got his heart set on one in the constellation of Hercules."

Rae's heart rate increased; her mouth dried up and hung open. She thought she said something and waited for him to answer. Impatiently she said it louder, "Why me?"

"My primary reason is the practicality of it. If anything goes wrong during gate construction on the other side, I would want the *inventor* present." Evermore broke eye contact. There was something else, and he was trying to figure out how to say it. "My secondary reason... I don't want to do this forever. Running various iterations of the same R&D company is not my life's work. Evermore Industries will be the forever corporation — well, forever as far as humankind is concerned — but I do not want to be its forever CEO. My dear, your testimony during the trial reminded me that I have a responsibility to the future generations, not just in how I conduct myself and my business, but in how I shape the future of science. I don't want E.I. to be everyone's competition, I want it to be an incubator of brilliance. But..."

Rae let out the breath she'd been holding and gasped for a fresh one. She groped for that hate she had felt moments before as she said, "...but you want something in exchange?" Her tone had no emotion.

"Yes, I want great science to be the goal, not great power. I've seen so many of Kander's employees climbing up his corporate structure so that they might one day be at the top. I want to build a structure akin to the divine right of kings; if owning the company is out of reach, if principal researcher is the highest level within the organization, there can be no struggle for power, only the struggle to produce brilliance."

Rae frowned. "You're talking about a dictatorship."

"No, people know how to handle dictators. I'm talking about a dynasty. Think of what you could have achieved in your first week if your Lab Seven team hadn't been focused on one-upmanship. Think about how it would have felt if K&J Labs had given you a choice about who to work with. How much happier, how much more free would you have felt?"

*He's right: it would have been incredible. All I ever wanted was the freedom to explore the things I'm interested in. If I left to start my own R&D company, all my time would go toward running the company.* Then the word "dynasty" struck her.

"It was a test!" *There it is, there's the anger.*

Evermore looked startled. "My dear, I knew you would find the solution to FTL travel. If there was any 'test,' it was sink or swim."

"That's not what I'm talking about, and you know it. Kander once told me you wanted me to be the face of E.I., but that wasn't quite it: you want me to be the mother of your dynasty, and now you get what you want either way!"

Evermore held his open hands out to her. "This is a gift, my dear; you get what you want either way."

"I don't want to be pregnant! Fix that!"

His face lit up. "Oh my goodness that's—" His face fell. "You weren't expecting it. Is that what all this is about? Are you holding me responsible for putting you and Ashley together?"

She scrutinized his features. *Does he really not know? Have I been wrong this whole time?*

He clutched his heart as if she'd injured him. "That's it, isn't it: you think I've forced you two together for some dark purpose; that's why you've been treating me like some evil villain. I'm not so righteous as to think I'm a good guy, but I thought you had forgiven me for all that cloning nonsense." His features grew sad. "Do I look like a man in need of progeny? Besides, the inheritance of junk packets is far too random and inefficient for my needs." For a fraction of an instant, Evermore's face showed alarm, as if he'd been pricked, but it passed so quickly Rae wasn't sure she'd seen anything at all. "What do you imagine I would *do* with your child?"

She almost took his bait but waited and tried to remember what he'd said before. "How do you know?"

There was that flash of fear, and then it was gone. She pressed him. "How do you know genetic inheritance is too inefficient?"

"Ashley wrote a paper once about genetic inheritance and junk packets. It was quite the idea—"

"But it was just an idea," she said sarcastically, playing along, "After all, UMars didn't even find it interesting. Yet somehow, for a moment there you spoke as if that random idea had been tested and proven inefficient."

Evermore was frowning at her. *I'm not playing his game and he hates it.*

"Normally I wouldn't answer a question so tactlessly asked, but I might make an exception if I knew you'd accepted my gift."

"I might accept if you would be clear on the terms."

"Very well, my dear. Part one, you will not repeat anything I'm about to tell you to anyone, especially Ashley. Part two, you will complete this assignment before taking family leave." Evermore took a classified folder from the top drawer and slid it across the desk.

Instead of reaching for it, Rae crossed her arms. "I've learned my lesson about those. What's it say?"

"I'll leave that for you to discover on your own time."

Her arms remained crossed. "What if I don't keep the child?"

"No child, no dynasty." But he continued as if that weren't an option. "After you complete that assignment, I will begin training you as the vice-CEO; I guarantee that you will receive the deed to E.I. upon my death and that you will be the first person to set foot on the planet in Virgo."

Rae narrowed her eyes. "I thought you said we were going to Hercules."

"I need your help, and time is short, please stop interrupting. If Samuel were driving, that's where we'd go. I'm *hoping* it won't be up to him."

*Hoping? Evermore doesn't hope, he manipulates the chaos of possibility into the inevitability of fate.* Rae shook her head. "I don't understand. Can't you just tell him to go to Virgo?"

"That, too, I will leave for you to discover on your own time. Do you accept?" he stuck out his hand.

Without hesitation she shook it and said, "Yes. Now, tell me why you're so sure about the randomness of genetic inheritance."

Evermore took a deep breath. "My highest priority is the liberation of humanity. Many years ago I formed a plan that I thought would take multiple generations to complete." He was talking much faster now. "In my mind this plan is a delicate blossom that will only have one chance to bloom. It is a meaningful vision quickly fading as the dreamer wakes. Therefore, my second priority has been the protection of the vision. I cannot predict what might tempt others to stray from its path, and I cannot trust anyone who does not fully realize its impact on humankind. I have not had the pleasure of meeting such a person." His eyes glanced at the clock, and he scowled. "To the end of protecting that vision, I have experimented with genetically inherited knowledge."

"You're talking about junk packets. That was Ashley's research!"

Evermore sighed, and his eyes fell in shame. "No. It was mine."

"You let him plagiarize your work? No wonder he didn't get into UMars."

"I wish that were the case. I was his age when I came up with the idea. It wasn't until after Kander and I designed the first genome printer that I had the resources to try it. After five years of self-administered gene therapy, I found a woman who would," he cleared his throat to protect her modesty, "...help me with the experiment."

Rae shook her head as she solved the equation. "No."

"The genetic memory I encoded in myself was the

desire to discover the existence of genetic memories, as well as a drive to protect my mother. Something I regret not doing, and that I regret passing on."

"You fucking monster." She squeezed her hands into fists.

"Yes, and I have regretted it every day since. I didn't know how terrible she was until I was living there full-time under house arrest, but by then he was fifteen and it was too late." Something subtle shifted in Evermore's face and body language, and Rae felt she was seeing the man beneath the mantle. He sighed and said, "If I am a monster, it's through association with her. She treated Ashley like garbage, and all he wanted to do was protect her. He loved the sanctuary of my garage, but he would never leave her. I trapped him there!"

She wept but refused to free him from her gaze. "He told me his father's name was Sean." She wrapped her arms around her stomach.

"Were I his father, he would have resented me for always leaving for so long, and for prioritizing my vision over my family. But as his mentor I could be gone for years without contact, and the day I returned would be the same as the day I left. I tried," his voice was quavering, "to spend as much time with him as I could. I wasn't around when he was a baby. I promised myself I would make up for lost time, but when Ashley was about four, Samuel came into my life, and I know you already know this part, but I got distracted. Using what Samuel knew I could shorten the timeline of my plan and at least see part of it come to fruition."

"I'm not the one you need to explain yourself to."

"Ashley *cannot* know. Imagine one day you found out that you were not the product of all your experience but a train on a track. Bound to a schedule beyond your control."

"I'd kill myself." *Never. I would never do that.*

"Ashley came up with the same solution after his mother died. Thankfully, he failed. He needs someone to protect, and that's why I put him with you." Evermore swallowed his sadness, and the cold, objective doctor was back in control despite his red eyes. "UMars never saw his application; I couldn't risk him studying genetic inheritance and finding my old work. I forged the rejection letter."

"You're a horrible human being!" she shouted at him.

"The evidence for that is plentiful, but I hope in the end that the gifts I given to humankind will outweigh all of the wrongs I have caused."

"The gift of another monopolizing corporation?" Her eyes burst into flame. "You think you're Ashley's father, but no father would *ever* do that to his child."

Evermore stood and leaned over his desk. Despite his short stature, he towered over her. "I'm finished with this conversation. If any of these secrets are revealed, you will not set foot aboard the *Godspeed*, you will never see the planet in Virgo through anything but screens, I will rescind the gift of E.I., and I will ruin you."

"You wouldn't risk the truth coming out," Rae growled.

The fire alarm went off, and the hidden door in Evermore's library sprang open automatically.

Evermore took a step back and threw up his hands. "I have already taken that risk. Please forgive me; I need your help."

Samuel burst in through Evermore's office door and said, "They're here."

# CHAPTER TWENTY-FIVE

# Interlocking Puzzles

## Rae

Rae, Evermore and Samuel turned toward the open passage in Evermore's library. The sound of heavy feet pounding up the stairs could be heard over the blaring alarm. In the next moment two huge figures emerged from the door, wearing thick, metallic-orange fabric, which Rae had heard was hermetically sealed, lined with lead, and fireproof to 1,000 Celsius. Both health servants loomed over them at the exact same height in the titanium armature of their skeletal-assist suits. While one pointed an NBC (nuclear, biological, and chemical) detector around the room, the other approached them. Behind the huge plexi faceplate, an unidentifiable person wearing a gas mask started yelling at Evermore in an electronically amplified voice that boomed over the alarm, "Evacuate the building in an orderly manner."

Rae felt so exposed next to their bulky protective gear. Her lizard brain, thinking she was in danger, dumped a cocktail of fear into her bloodstream.

"What's this all about?" Evermore demanded. "Did Kander call you? There's no hazardous material here."

*Oh right*, she thought, feeling stupid. Evermore's assurance extinguished all the images of being trapped in a burning building, and she took control of the panic her heart insisted on pumping through her body. Evermore and Samuel both had their backs to her, and she realized that an opportunity had opened up. She licked her thumb and smeared it on the DNA sampler, unlocking her latest assignment from Evermore. She laid it on Evermore's desk, which was still synced with the ePaper, and it only took her a second to grab the schematic labeled "E.I.S.S. Godspeed" and drag it into her assignment.

"Dr. Everett Evermore, the PHS has received multiple witness accounts of a black hole, and we have a warrant to shut you down until you can prove otherwise. If you do not leave the building, I have permission to remove you by force."

By this time the second health servant had finished the sweep of the room and was approaching the two from the side. "This floor's clean."

"Hear that?" shouted Evermore. "It's clean!"

In one quick motion, the orange giant stooped forward, pressed Evermore's stomach into its shoulder, and tossed him over its back. The health servant seemed to notice Rae for the first time. "Ma'am," it said, "I'm well equipped to carry you both." Rae grabbed the assignment folder from the workstation and hurried out the door.

Behind her she heard Samuel shout over the blaring alarm, "Be careful, my bones are—" followed by a scream.

The stairwell was clattering with a hundred bodies evacuating the E.I. building. The health servants had had no trouble clearing the other floors, as most employees left as fast as they could when the alarm went off. When Rae reached the lobby she was herded by two part-mechanical health servants directly up the ass crack of an opaque hermetic-plastic caterpillar that was sealing the front door. The sterilized air in the inflatable plastic corridors burned her nose as those two health servants passed her off to two normal-height health servants in hazmat suits, who led her to a hot quarantine trailer.

"We need to test your clothes for any harmful materials. Put all of your clothes and belongings in this box. There are jumpsuits hanging there. You have 5 minutes to change."

After returning to collect the clear plastic shoebox they left her to wait out the next hour or so alone.

*I thought Chasma Australe was boring, but I don't even know what to do without my Omni. Am I just supposed to fucking SIT here?*

Finally another faceless hazmat servant entered her trailer.

"Hi, um. Can you tell me what time it is? I've got a really important doctor's appointment today at four."

The servant made a gesture of looking at a wrist watch and shook its head before going on to inspect her with ultraviolet lights and multiple hazard detectors.

Another hour later and the same, or perhaps a different, hazmat servant came to collect saliva and blood samples. Again she asked for the time and how long it would take, but no answer was given, and she was left to wait.

Finally she was collected, walked down a winding plastic corridor to an opaque plastic room, and seated before a plastic folding table. Her escort then stepped back and waited. A moment later another health servant entered and sat across from her.

"How long is this whole thing going to take?" Rae asked. "I've got a really important appointment with my doctor at four."

"You're going to have to reschedule. I apologize, but our technicians are overtaxed." The voice was distinctly feminine, and Rae peered into the hazmat mask. Beyond the gas mask within she found a pair of brown eyes lightly traced with eyeliner.

"You're a woman," Rae said, relieved. Behind the mask the eyebrow raised slightly, and Rae said, "I need to see my ob-gyn, and the timing is *really* important!"

"The safety of everyone in Nili Terradome is also *really* important. Were you hoping to appeal to my emotional feminine side? Dr. Dahlia, how long this takes depends entirely on your cooperation. Tell me what you know about the black hole."

Rae frowned. "I know it wasn't a black hole."

"We know that, too. We've got hundreds of eyewitnesses who say they saw it, and around eighty Omni video recordings that show nothing. Besides all that, there isn't a trace of Hawking radiation anywhere; 'black hole' is just what everyone's been calling it."

"I signed a proprietary information agreement, I can't—"

The brown-eyed woman interrupted, "We're the Public Health Service, we've got an open subpoena, meaning if you withhold information you could be deported back to Earth and serve up to twenty years in federal prison."

"Am I under arrest?"

"Not yet. You're under quarantine."

"Contaminated until proven nonhazardous," Rae grumbled. "Show me some documentation, and I'll tell you whatever you want."

The woman reached into the clear plastic box she'd brought with her and laid a plastic bag in front of Rae. The badge inside it said "PHS Captain Katara Fitzpatrick." While Rae read it, Captain Fitzpatrick took an ePaper from the clear box and set it beside the badge. "Subpoena" was written along the top.

"I'll ask you again: tell me what you know about the black hole."

Rae sighed. "I can't tell you much. The reason we're experimenting with this energy is to find out what it can do. And one thing it can do is create a bridge between the dimensions theorized in supersymmetry."

Captain Fitzpatrick shook her head. "But what kind of energy are we talking about? Electromagnetic? Nuclear?"

"None of the above. It behaves like a boson carrying a force to certain particles, but unlike a boson, it transfers its energy specifically to living cells." The health servant sat up straighter, which Rae interpreted as concern. "I know; a radiation that interacts with living cells rings all kinds of alarm bells, but we believe that the interaction between this energy and living cells is happening all the time. We have also proven that this energy's radiation cannot be blocked by any chemical element. Meaning that hazmat suit is useless."

"And you're sure that the black hole was caused by your experiment?"

"Absolutely. It was Lab Seven's project. I stood within feet of it. There's no damage done, nothing to clean up, and nothing you can do to affect whatever it has caused."

After a moment, Katara Fitzpatrick pulled back her hazmat hood and laid her gas mask on the table. Her brown eyes stared off to a distant thought and eventually circled back around to land on Rae.

"I don't know whether to be relieved or terrified." Rae raised an eyebrow. "I spoke with each of the members on your research team separately, and they each shared a similar account. Each of them told me that the frequency... the radiation... the energy... can't be blocked. Each of them told me it comes from another dimension and that none of them were adversely affected. What is it for, Dr. Dahlia? What are you working on?"

*How can I explain what we're doing without seeming crazy or dangerous?* "We're testing communication beyond the electromagnetic spectrum." *If she knows anything she'll think we're working with nuclear materials, or quantum particles. If I keep it esoteric...*

Fitzpatrick seemed to notice her squirming. "I remind you, you're under subpoena. What was the hypothesis you were trying to prove?"

Rae's mind drifted back to something she'd heard Dr.

Hubert say and stole it. "*Prima causa*. Nothing can cause itself to change. If the Big Bang caused everything we know, what caused that? We're looking for an integration beyond the standard model."

Captain Fitzpatrick looked confused. "Officer, take her back to quarantine."

"What? Wait, I told you everything! I need to go!"

"This is all just protocol, Dr. Dahlia. Unless you skipped your mandatory PHS hazardous response orientation at UMars, you should be well aware that we need to hold you until we get your blood panel results," she said, and Rae was escorted back to her trailer to wait.

Rae remembered PHS HAZ-OR-01 as the class that everyone attended but no one took. Rae had spent the forty minutes each Wednesday afternoon studying for other classes.

In her trailer, Rae paced a slow circle, trying to outrun her boredom, and resigned herself that she was going to miss her appointment with Dr. Huarez. When she complained of thirst, they brought her fruity electrolyte water. When she complained of hunger, they brought her a box labeled "Self-Heating Meal, Ready-to-Eat," which, after a few bites, she realized was not for addressing hunger but for suppressing her appetite. When they finally gave her back her things, at quarter to six, Rae was informed that she was on a no-fly list for the next two weeks and that they were going to shut down Evermore Industries for the next month to conduct a "probable latent effects" protocol.

"That's outrageous!" Rae began, but curbed her rage; she didn't want them to put her back in the quarantine trailer. Surely Evermore would understand that they weren't going to meet the deadline for assignment three. *Is that why he was so quick to make that agreement?*

"People in the terradome are really afraid of whatever you're building in there," said a short health servant in a tone that suggested Rae think about what she'd done.

Restraining her temper, Rae picked up her Omni and the manila ePaper folder and left.

Her Omni buzzed with concerned messages and missed calls. A few acquaintances from UMars, Dr. Manfield, and Rockwell from Chasma Australe wondered if she was all right. There was a missed call from the office of Emilio Huarez, but the most texts were from Ashley, and they all asked a variation of "How's our baby?"

Ashley met her outside the quarantine area. He was visibly vibrating with excitement at seeing her, and as she approached he practically jumped on her like a puppy left inside all day. "Man, they sure took their time with you. I was out of there hours ago! What did Evermore have to say? Did he yell?"

She pushed him back. "Ashley, I've got so much on my mind right now. I just want to go home."

He backed up. "Of course. I actually thought you'd need a break, which is why I planned a date for us to take our minds of everything."

"A date? Ashley, I've got work to do."

He shook his head and smiled. "Babe, E.I.'s going to be closed for weeks. I think we can take a night off."

"I can't do any more sitting around doing nothing," she said.

"Okay." He looked a little crushed. "Another night, then. Aside from the boredom, how are you doing?"

Rae was looking at her Omni, and as she put it to her ear she said, "I've got to make a phone call."

"To who?"

"Dr. Huarez; I missed my appointment."

"Oh shit, with all the excitement I forgot that was this evening. Did you—"

"Shhhh."

They were both silent until she hung up and said, "No

answer."

"You misunderstand me. I'm not happy because you missed your appointment. I'm happy because you chose to."

"Ridiculous. I did everything I could short of fighting off the servants in their skeletal-assist suits."

Ashley shook his head. "No, you knew today was the day, and you chose to open the gate."

"How could I have known the PHS would raid the building?"

"Did you sleep through the hazardous response orientation? No, and you don't forget anything!"

*Is he right? Did I choose this?* She looked into Ashley's eyes, waiting for some unconscious answer, but was distracted as she saw hints of Evermore. It was subtle, but it was in the spacing of his brow, the width of his nose, and the fathomless depths of those green eyes.

"What? Am I wrong?"

"Did you see him in the crossover point?"

Ashley's body stiffened, and his eyes glazed over with the memory. "Not until I got close to you. I could see him in the light cast by the darkness. There was some guy in a business suit... did he take Sean from you?"

She shook her head, "I don't think so. I don't think he's been inside me yet. It hasn't been safe for him."

"You saw Sean as a boy too?"

"Yeah."

A wave of excitement crossed Ashley's face, but he stifled it when she didn't join him. "How does your stomach feel? Is it still..."

"Missing? Yeah. This crossover was farther away. The one at K&J was right on me."

There was a long silence, which the automated voice of the rickshaw broke to announce their arrival.

Once inside her apartment, Rae opened the folder, selected the "Godspeed" file and sent the image to her

OmniWatch smart TV. An image appeared on her screen that looked like a load schematic for a container ship, except it was very narrow, and there was only one row of shipping containers on either side of a narrow corridor.

Ashley stared at the screen. "What is that? Is that our assignment?"

"Not exactly. This is the E.I.S.S. *Godspeed*, the ship that will carry us through the gate, which I'm assuming our assignment tells us to build."

"It's an Asbjorn Breivik design, must have taken him months, but why did Evermore give us the blueprints?"

Rae was studying the screen. "He didn't, exactly. I was still in Evermore's office during the raid, and he left it right out in the open on his desk. He even made a show of drawing my attention to it."

"You stole it from him," Ashley said.

"It's pretty much his go-to method of info dispersion." Rae grinned.

At the fore of the ship was a small room labeled "control room." Mid-ship there was a seating area for passengers, but the seats were installed on the forward wall. On either side of the passenger cabin were private quarters; past them toward the aft was a room marked "construction bay" and a wide-open space labeled "helicopter pad." Along the right side of the schematic was a bar of colored boxes that Rae had first assumed was a key to some color codes. After a second look she realized they were interactive buttons; she could select one and view another layer of the *Godspeed*.

Rae shook her head in disbelief. "Where is he planning on building this huge ship?" But before Ashley had a chance to answer she remembered hearing the news that Evermore had bought the Lockheed Martin facility during her final semester at UMars. The general assumption was that the LHM facility would be the home of Evermore Industries, but that wasn't the case. Long before he broke ground for the E.I. dome-scraper, it seemed that Evermore knew that at some point he would need the manufacturing capability of the Lockheed Martin facility. *How does Evermore seem to have a plan for everything?* Rae shook her head. *No, I'm giving him too much credit. It's always been Evermore's plan to build the starship.* She selected the exterior view of the *Godspeed*, and something between a crystal millipede and a Civil War ironclad appeared. The exterior was built out of hundreds of interlocking crystal plates of different shapes and sizes. Each one was the greenish color of melted ice cubes at the bottom of a glass of limeade.

"It's a crystal cucumber," Ashley laughed, but Rae felt sick.

"It's our PS crystal. If Asbjorn Breivik's been working on this for months, how did he know to use our crystal?"

Ashley sat back down on the couch, but only on the edge. "This is not something Evermore cooked up overnight; he must have started working on this as soon as we decided to use a lichen to grow crystals." Ashley made a gesture that spun the ship around on its x-axis, searching for something. "It doesn't have any rockets. What kind of rocket ship doesn't have rockets?"

"E.I. isn't building a FTL ship, remember?"

"Okay... but it still has to move forward, and I can't even find an engine room."

Rae selected the visible layer menu, which listed five options: Exterior, Interior, Structural, Electronics, and Plumbing. She selected "Electronics," and they traced most exterior wires to a larger electric artery which led within to a generator and battery bank in the nose of the ship.

"There," she said.

"I see it, but all that does is run the lights." Ashley switched the layer to "Exterior" and selected a random plate. A box popped up with the plate's specifications:

weight, volume, vector expression for 3D printing, genetic code, and numen markers. The name of the plate was simply 09.12; it was a unique species of their *Lepraria ptilisaccharon,* and it had five markers. Yet only two markers faced each other; the other three pointed off into space like satellite dishes awaiting a signal from somewhere else.

"Two ups, one in, a left and a right. Only two of them are connected," Rae mused.

Ashley said, "We're just looking at one piece of a larger organism. I'll bet all of the plates combine to form one individual lichen species."

She shook her head, unconvinced. "He knows that it's possible to spray a species onto a form and make a perfect shape. These are designed to be 3D printed. This is far too complicated not to have a specific purpose. Look at this, there are hundreds of plates!"

"Hundreds," Ashley mused. "Could there be 238?"

Rae spun the Godspeed around diagonally on its x- and y-axes. "It's hard to estimate. Their sizes vary so much, but I would say it's possible. Why 238?"

"It's Evermore's favorite number. It's the most common isotope of uranium."

She scowled at him. "Do you really think that Evermore would demand 238 plates because it's his favorite number?" Rae sat up a little straighter. "Here we go. I found a build report which lists all the plate groups and numbers. Damn it, the groups all have a different number of plates: Group 1 goes up to eight, Group 2 goes up to fourteen... Ugh, Group 9 has twenty-seven plates."

As she counted Ashley started adding up the total number of plates on his Omni. After a time he said, "There are exactly two hundred plates." He ran through the list again, double-checking his work. "No, I skipped Group 3 somehow." Returning to his Omni, Ashley added 6 to 200.

Rae shook her head. "I'm glad we're not in the lab right

now. I'm embarrassed that you just used your calculator to add six to two hundred," she teased.

He reddened and looked at his Omni. "Sometimes I just count on this thing to do everything for me."

"Could be worse, you could have gotten the glucose bio-app installed and let *it* tell you when *you're* hungry."

"Speaking of hungry..." Ashley rubbed his stomach.

"Are you stumped by Evermore's puzzle already?"

"No, I'm just hungry." Ashley sighed, and it rang melancholy. The look she gave him must have been concerned; he nuzzled up to her and said, "This is what I've been waiting for: you and me puzzling out some mystery together until late into the night."

"Don't get ahead of yourself, it's only seven. But... it is kind of exciting." She smiled.

"Evermore used to tap on my window late at night when he wanted my help with something. Sometimes he'd be gone for months, and that *tap-tap-tap* would be the first I'd know he was home. We'd stay up all night working. I'd be ruined for school the next day, but it was always worth it."

Rae's guts twisted themselves around the secret she had buried there.

"Rae, what's the matter?"

"This is the guy who got me pregnant, and I can't forget that. Ever. I'll order food; you run a search for anything 206," she said.

For a moment there was silence as they pulled out their Omnis and started gesturing at them.

"It's the area code for Seattle," he said.

"Yes, hi. Delivery for Maplecrest Apartments suite 18A..." she moved the Omni from her face and shushed him.

"It's the model number of a Cessna single-engine plane," he whispered loudly.

"One order of the eggplant lasagna." She moved the

Omni from her face again and turned to Ashley. "What do you want?"

"It's a stable isotope of lead, Pb-206. Chicken Parm."

To the Omni, Rae said, "Chicken Parm. Yes, we'll pay extra for the real thing."

Ashley spoke over her, saying, "Tell them no bones; last time I nearly broke my tooth on some bone fragments."

The Omni fell with her arm, and she stared back at the *Godspeed* schematic.

"Did you tell them?" Ashley asked, but then he saw her face. "What?"

"There are 206 bones in the human body. Each plate is a bone," she said.

There was a long silence as they both sat looking at the crystal schematic. "Remember when I was telling you about junk packets and genetic memories?" Ashley said. "I assumed the red blood cell was the main carrier of the junk packets, but they only last from 100 to 120 days. Now it makes sense: though blood cells may carry the information, it's the bone marrow that makes those cells and the osteoblasts that build our bones. What if our consciousness lives in our bones?"

"Evermore designed a complete consciousness constellation like Samuel talked about in the recording. Holy shit!" Rae stood, unable to contain the energy of epiphany that had just hit her. The jumble of Evermore's goals, his deceptions, and his hints were all there in plain view, but up until now she hadn't been able to make the pieces fit. Now she realized that Evermore's puzzle was not one but three jigsaw puzzles all mixed into the same box. The idea that the ship itself could contain a soul sorted one of the puzzles from the others.

"I know why Evermore only gave us three months. It would be suspicious if the ship that was designed to fly through the jump gates was built *before* the gates themselves had even been invented, but Samuel's got leukemia. Evermore is building the ship as a container for him, and he has promised that it will get finished before Samuel dies."

Ashley shook his head. "Leukemia? Impossible. Evermore Biomedical Systems holds the patent on the predisposition tracker; because of Evermore you can *know* if your child will have leukemia long before birth. If Evermore truly built Samuel's body, there's no way he could have missed the protein predisposition."

"I heard it from Samuel himself. He's got leukemia."

"Evermore, you sneaky bastard." Ashley shook his head. "Do you agree that there's only two ways the Doc could have generated this 3D map of numen markers?"

Rae nodded. "Yes. Either he took a marrow sample from every bone in Samuel's body—"

Ashley finished her sentence, "Or he already had that information because he built Samuel's body, in which case he intentionally limited his lifespan with chronic leukemia."

Scouring through the pieces, she found and separated out the third puzzle in the box. A calm came over her as it had in the moments when she realized she had solved a Hakaru puzzle, or was five moves from beating an opponent in chess. She assembled all three puzzles in her mind and said, "While I was in Evermore's office, he mentioned that Samuel had his heart set on an Earth-like planet in the constellation Hercules, but later he promised that I would be the first person to set foot on a planet in Virgo, and then he added the caveat that he hoped it wasn't up to Samuel. He asked for my help twice but wouldn't say what he needed help with. I think building a body wasn't the only deal he made with Samuel; I think he promised Samuel something else, but he needs my help in making sure he can't deliver."

"So what do we do? Can we delay building the gate

until Samuel dies?"

"No," Rae said. "That will only force Evermore to replace me. Ma'at and I are close to finishing a prototype numen scanner, but we'll also need it to detect the location and type of numen markers in each bone in the human skeleton so we can map out new consciousness constellations. When we have another constellation, you'll hack into Evermore's computer and switch the crystal plate build order."

Rae's instincts warned her that she was missing a piece, or maybe an entire puzzle, but she forced the thought to the back of her mind. Hidden out of sight, it fed a monster that also lurked there; a secret wish that something terrible would happen.

Evermore didn't lose a day. The morning following the Public Health Service raid, the majority of the staff was placed on paid leave, but Labs Seven and One were relocated two miles northeast of the Nili dome to the underground Lockheed Martin facility, which was only accessible through the tunnels that followed a twenty-three–mile loop of the K&J Labs delta-ray accelerator.

A small foyer connected the delta-ray access tunnel to the spiderweb of tight corridors that led deeper to vaulted chambers and caverns containing robotic assembly lines and rows upon rows of CNC machines and 3D printers. In the center of the web was an enormous thermite generator that powered the entire facility. The rust-brown rammed-earth floors of the Lockheed Martin facility shone like marble; the walls and ceilings were finished with large pink tiles of Martian ceramic. Accenting the ceiling every thirty paces were full-spectrum virtual skylights that gave the feeling of being mere feet under a beautiful blue sky. Puffy white marshmallow clouds lent perspective to the illusion.

Rae and Ashley strode down corridors and took their

first left, their second right and the fourth door down, entering a chamber half the size of their lab at Evermore Industries with ceilings twice as high and vaulted like the Conciergerie in France. But whether this was the seventh chamber or the twenty-seventh didn't matter: this was the new Lab Seven. Its denizens were the Lab Seven team.

"Listen up, team," she called as they filed into their new lab. They stopped their preliminary explorations and turned to face her. They looked tired and their commitment was strained. *I betrayed their trust when I opened the anti-numen chamber. God, I hope I haven't undone all of the work I put into them.*

"Dr. Evermore chose us to be one of the few labs to continue working during the PHS shut down. He has made it clear to me that we're on a tight time schedule." She paused. "In the next few months, we're going to transform this room, and room G1-3847 on the other side of the Lockheed Martin facility, into anti-numen chambers. Inside each of these chambers we are going to build another bracelet of PS crystals, but on a much larger scale." The level of side chatter grew. Rae raised her voice above it and added a reprimanding edge to her words. "We are going to build two hoops—" The chatter stopped. "—244 centimeters in diameter to test whether a living object can safely pass through the dimension within."

"What kind of living object?"

"First a PS crystal. Then a human."

"That's insane!" Joseph Allan wailed. "Where did you get the impression that we could enter this dimension? Didn't you see that black hole? That's a one-way trip!"

"It's not sane, I'll grant you that, but it's an order from Evermore himself. Let's get to work."

No one spoke during the ten-minute tram ride back to the terradome; perhaps it was because Rae had run the team ragged that day, keeping them an extra two hours. Or perhaps it was the persistent, annoying whine of the tram's electric motor, made louder by the enclosed space, that made any conversation laborious. Yet the silence remained even after the tram stopped and they boarded a long escalator which carried them to the sidewalk level of the dome. Ashley was the first to break the silence by pointing, slack-jawed, toward the western edge of the dome. "Oh my God, look at that." Sinking toward the horizon, the virtual image of the sun, yellow and enlarged to an Earth-like scale, was accompanied in the virtual sky by a black hole half as big. As they watched, it began to affect the sun, pulling at the rightmost edge and dimming it as if under partial eclipse.

Ashley laughed. "I wonder if someone went to the trouble of hacking the VR screen, or if the environmental designers programmed it in."

"I don't like it," Rae said. "It's a passive-aggressive attack on E.I. Everyone thinks we're a safety threat, but they're ignorant of what we're trying to do. I wish Evermore would release a statement about what we actually created."

In alliance with her interpretation, the sun, rather than setting behind the scrub-brush mountain range to the west, was swallowed by the black hole at an exponential rate. For the first time since the VR environment had been installed there was no sunset. No artistic rendition of pink sky, or grey dusk, just a quick fade, and it took a moment for their eyes to adjust to the dim glow from Nili Terradome's light pollution.

# CHAPTER TWENTY-SIX

# Mother

**Rae**

With camera drones hovering around his head, Evermore said, "The anomaly that people are calling a black hole has nothing to do with its namesake; there was no singularity involved; it did not affect gravity or any frequency on the electromagnetic spectrum, which is why the many Omni recordings were unable to capture what your eyes could see. I'd like to invite Dr. Rae Dahlia to speak with you more about this force she has discovered."

"That's kind of you, Dr. Evermore, but the discovery of this energy was a team effort. In a perfect world, we'd be making this announcement having had more time to confirm what I'm about to tell you, but given the scare we've caused everyone here in the dome, I wanted to make sure everyone knew they were safe.

"The force we've been testing is called 'numen,' after the Latin word meaning 'divine will.' Unlike the other elementary particles like electrons or protons, the numen particle's influence can only affect and be affected on a cellular scale. Though we do not yet know what information it is carrying, or its purpose or relationship to the standard model of physics, we do know that it moves faster than light. At the request of the PHS, our continuing experiments on this new force will be conducted outside the dome. But as someone who has stood beside the event, I can testify that this energy is terrifying but perfectly safe."

The news conference seemed to put Evermore Industries on everyone's radar again. E.I.'s research stocks were doubling each day. Everyone Rae talked to was getting either emails or, if their Omni number got leaked, text messages and phone calls, ranging from adoration to death threats. Rae hadn't checked her email in months, as she had no reason to bother with the outdated technology, but after hearing about what others were getting, she decided to give hers a peek. She had 1,463 unread messages. She filtered out everything from before the crossover event, and anything with attached malware or common hate-mail words. One hundred and thirty-four emails remained. She perused through the subject lines and clicked anything that sounded interesting. There were religious figures from Earth who had various boring things to say about the spirit/power of Jesus/God/Satan, and the occasional clickbait tempting her to check her credit score for free, and then she came across one from a twelve-year-old girl in Florida.

> Dear Doctor Rae,
>
> My name is Valerie, and I'm in seventh grade. My favorite classes are math and chemistry, but our teacher moves so slow. I started a math club at our school, just for girls, so that we'd have an excuse to play around with some more complicated algebra. Last year for my birthday my mom drove me up to Gainesville to hear Victoria Crellinger speak at the University of Florida. I've always looked up to her as a role model, but I never knew that Dr. Crellinger didn't have kids. I want to have a boy and a

girl when I'm ready. Do you think it's possible
to have time for both a family and a career in
chemistry? Do you think you'll ever have kids?

There was more, but Rae couldn't bring herself to
read further. *The goal of being famous was to bask in the glow
of recognition. I never considered the responsibility. Ugh, responsibility, the smallest prison of all.* Rae ran a search for a list of
famous scientists who had families. There was a long list
of men, and very, very few women. Rae thought of Val-
erie finding out that she had gotten an abortion, and the
message she'd be sending. She wondered how many girls
out there felt the same way. *But isn't keeping it to be a good
role model just as fucked up as deciding to keep the baby to inherit
E.I.? No,* she decided. *It's way nobler.* Yet since Evermore's
ultimatum, she'd been seriously considering it.

Rae scrolled through her short list of contacts and selected her mother's number. A minute passed before she
decided to type out: "I know it's been a while since we've
spoken, but I need to tell you something." Her finger
paused over the "send" button as she remembered the
last time they had spoken in person.

*As she sorted the laundry, Rae's mother turned to her with a
different sock in each hand. "Well, I'm sorry that I haven't been
more supportive; it's hard for me to support you when you don't
even know what you're doing. First it was zoology, then almost art?
Then biology — now it's bioengineering? What happens when you
get to Mars and you suddenly realize that you've always wanted to
be a mechanic like your father?"*

*"At least I'm doing something with my life."*

*"Giving up everything you know and leaving your family be-
hind to chase some dream of becoming something you're not is the
opposite of doing something."*

*"Right, and sticking it out at the same boring job until the day
you die, is that doing something?"*

"*Rachael Michelle Dahlia! That 'boring job' is what kept our heads above water all those years. And it's not boring if I'm doing it for a good reason. You can't just keep changing your mind about what you want to do. Someday you'll realize that eventually you'll get tired of anything you try. You just have to just pick something and find what it is that you love about it.*"

"*Is that how you stayed with Dad for so long?*"

*Her mother's lips snapped tightly together, only parting to say four final words: "Good luck on Mars."*

*The taxi ride to the launch pad took forever, and Rae had managed to find the only driver who didn't want to talk.*

> **R.Dahlia:** I know it's been a while since we've spoken, but I need to ask you something.

Almost seven minutes later, her mother's reply chirped in her hand. She took a deep breath and read it.

> **Mom:** Oh my God! I saw the news; do you need money to come home?

Ten seconds later she received three more:

> **Mom:** Are you there?

> Where'd you go?

> OMG! You're in some back alley homeless shelter and all they can afford is a 3G network from the turn.

> **R.Dahlia:** Relax. I'm still on Mars. There's a seven-minute delay.

> It doesn't matter how many Gs I have: Light can't travel any faster. I'm pregnant and I don't know what I should do.

During the next seven minutes, Rae tried to think of a way to use the crystals to communicate instantly from Earth to Mars, but without the ability to produce numen, there wasn't any way to send a signal.

**Mom:** My baby's pregnant! Do you know who the father is?

**R.Dahlia:** Yes. He's a very nice man who will support me either way. But I'm afraid I won't be able to do my job and be a mother at the same time.

Seven minutes.

**Mom:** Oh honey, come back to Earth and I'll help you.

**R.Dahlia:** Wow, no! But thanks for helping me realize I really hadn't considered all the options.

**Mom:** And then we'll be together again. I know my condo isn't very big, but it's on the first floor, so you wouldn't have to worry about stairs.

Deborah sent a series of attempts to convince her to move back to Earth, but they only served as interruptions as Rae tried to type in her response:

**R.Dahlia:** We're not coming back to Earth.

I've got a real shot at running Evermore Industries someday, but I'd have to marry Ashley and start a family.

As the next seven minutes passed, Rae considered why she had even written to Deborah in the first place. *There's no reality where she would tell me anything other than "Come home and let me see the baby." Maybe that's what I wanted to hear?* And then she wondered, *What was the answer I wanted her to give?* Rae played around with typing out her ideal message:

No one's ever ready to have a kid. But it'll keep you busy, and even when you get tired of whatever project you're working on, you'll never get tired of being a mom, and you'll never do anything as rewarding.

That was just about perfect; it had the right amounts of regurgitated wisdom, sentimentality, and hope. Instead her mother said:

> **Mom:** That's my girl! Willing to do anything to get what she wants. Maybe if the boss likes family so much he'd fly me out there? I know I'd hate Mars, but I can't bear the thought of you depriving me of seeing my grandchild. When are you due?

She had never asked, and she counted out the months on her fingers.

> **R.Dahlia:** August 25th.

> And hopefully the technology I'm working on will make the trip back to Earth shorter, and we'll come visit you.

When the PHS finally allowed Evermore Industries to reopen, Ma'at was the only one to return to the E.I. building. All of his crystal lenses and the pieces of the numen sensor were still on the eighth floor. Rae split her time between Lab Eight at the E.I. building and the new Lab Seven at the old LHM facility. But toward the end of her first trimester, Rae and Ashley realized they weren't going to be able to hide her pregnancy any longer, and she messaged the Lab Seven team.

> **R.Dahlia:** Meet me tomorrow morning at the old Lab Seven; I've got an exciting announcement.

When the moment came, Rae gathered her team together as she often did when she was about to give them a pep talk, but this announcement wasn't another assignment from Evermore, and it wasn't even Dr. Dahlia standing up at the front of the room. It was Rae. She stood there for a moment gathering her will before gesturing at Ashley to come over, and the two wrapped arms around each other in a sideways embrace. The look that crossed many of the doctor's faces as Ashley came to stand beside Rae was a warm confusion that broke into either disbelief, approval, or deeper confusion.

"You can tell them," Rae said, trying to hide her smile of anticipation.

Ashley's chest inflated with pride as he said, "Rae and I are pregnant."

Luther Brando was the first to break the shocked silence as he smacked Hubert's arm and said, "I knew it! Is it a boy? Sorry, I'm just… Congratulations!"

Ma'at let out a huge sigh and seemed on the brink of tears, yet he was smiling so wide it would have been comical if it weren't so beautiful. "Congratulations to both of you!"

Each of the other doctors followed in the gesture of congratulations, and when they had all finished, Rae said, "That's it," trying to dismiss them. "We just wanted to let you all know before I started to show."

The attention was uncomfortable for her. *It seems so*

*disproportional to the appreciation I've received for the things I've actually earned.* She could feel herself backsliding into a stereotype that was not "brilliant and powerful head of research." "Pregnant lady" was brilliant in a vivacious way, but her only power came from an array of unstable hormones and a Cold War-era threat to unleash them at the first sign of attack.

A few days later she received a friendly e-pamphlet from the HR department telling her about her rights as a pregnant woman and dumbing down some of the bolder points of the International Family Medical Leave Act. Rae took this as a reminder from Evermore that they were both on a tight time line.

The first day Rae noticed her small baby bump, August felt so far away, and the passage of time seemed nonexistent. It was February, but the days weren't getting any longer. The sun hadn't grown any brighter or higher in the sky. It was a warm day, exactly the same temperature as it would be in August. Rae bent over the incubation chamber and realized that rather than in seasons, she was accustomed to measuring time in micrometers of crystal growth.

One afternoon the door to Lab Seven slammed open, and Ma'at stepped in shouting, "It works!" He held a device that looked like a mutated six-shooter. Benjamin Washington and Joseph Allan jumped up and seemed to consider diving for cover. As Rae approached, Ma'at said, "I'm sorry, Dr. Dahlia, but I couldn't wait; our directional numen marker lenses reached their optimal thickness today, and I went ahead and installed them without you."

"And it works?" Rae grinned at him.

"It works," he said. Handshakes and congratulations surrounded him as the doctors took turns looking at each other through the lens. Their numinous images were composed of highly pixelated blotches of color, like watching weather radar with a high refresh rate. It was mesmerizing to watch the colors that swirled within each of them slowly adjust. Ma'at swelled with pride as the sensor was excitedly passed around. However, not everyone was amused. Allan seemed greatly unsettled by this discovery, and he aimed the numen sensor around the room wearing concern on his face.

## Ashley

Ashley could hardly wait for his turn. All of the other scientists were looking at each other, or examining the PS crystals, or the resonating chamber, but he wanted to see what his son might look like. When the device was finally placed in his hands, he aimed it at Rae. The numinous energy radiating from her was an excited, fluttering orange and yellow, but her stomach was a cold, slowly churning gray. Not black like the walls and machines around the lab, but the whitish-gray of dead skin around an infection.

All eyes were on Ma'at, and no one noticed the shadow that crossed his face. He held out the device. "The image could be cleaned up with a demosaicing algorithm," he said, but no one seemed to be listening.

A moment later, Dr. Washington was pointing the sensor generally upward when a look of confusion crossed his face. "Ma'at, what's this?"

Ma'at took a quick glance at the black sensor screen. "We're underground, and there's nothing living above us."

"But there is!" Washington said, pointing to a tiny orange spot, only a few pixels wide, which was almost invisible in the black background.

"Is there something wrong with the screen?" someone suggested.

"Oh my God, I know what it is," Washington said.

Hubert squinted at the ceiling. "Is there a little bug up there?"

Rae crossed her arms. "Not in my clean room."

Washington shook his head. "No, it's Earth." He grinned and pivoted toward the north, and the sensor lit up. "Look at all the people in Nili Terradome!"

Hubert pointed the device around the room, repeating the actions that each of them had taken, and suddenly stopped. The blood drained from his face as he looked back and forth between the screen and an empty space by Rae's workstation.

Ashley said, "What is it, Hubert?"

"Something's watching us," he said, pointing at nothing. Ashley looked over Hubert's shoulder at the sensor and saw the gray flickering shape of a person drift backward through the walls and corridors of the LHM facility.

They shared a look between them. "Was that a..?" but Hubert couldn't finish the word.

"I think so."

"What? What did you see?" Ma'at asked.

Hubert gave the device back to Ma'at and sat in the nearest chair. "I... I can't believe it. I shouldn't be surprised. All native cultures everywhere have known this truth for thousands of years, but without proof the idea could only be speculation in ours." He chuckled. "I think transitional metaphysics just became a natural science!"

"What did you see?" Ma'at asked Ashley.

Hubert answered first. "It was a ghost. It was floating right over there," he pointed.

"What color was it?" Ma'at asked?

"No color, just a churning whitish-gray."

*The color of death.*

"Ashley, what's wrong?" Rae asked.

Ashley's hands shot up to his face to wipe away the tears. "Just give me a—" he started to say, but couldn't without breaking down entirely. His mouth opened to say something else, but no words came out. He stumbled across the room and out the open door. Rae followed after him. "Ashley, talk to me. What's wrong?"

She followed him down the corridor a ways before he slid down the pink ceramic wall to the floor.

"When's the last time you had a checkup with Dr. Huarez?"

"Last week. I got to see his tiny heart beating away on the sonogram. What happened back there?"

There was a pause as Ashley considered whether to tell her or not. "When I was looking through Ma'at's sensor, I looked at your stomach. Rae, Sean's the same color as the ghost. I'm sorry to run out like that, but I thought our son had... I thought he was. . ."

Rae embraced him. "The baby's fine."

"You're sure?" He asked, but the moment was interrupted as Allan entered the corridor and, oblivious, demanded Rae's attention.


At the end of the day, the Lab Seven team boarded the tram back to Nili Terradome. Ashley looked down the nearly full three-car tram and wondered where all these other people had come from. They wore navy coveralls, and at first he assumed they must be the maintenance crew for K&J's delta-ray accelerator pipeline. But they didn't wear K&J ID tags, or in fact any ID tags at all.

When the team emerged from the access tunnels, the sun was setting behind the mountains to the west.

"That's Mount Whitney," Dr. Hubert said, pointing out toward the western wall of the Nili Fossae. Speaking to no one in particular, he continued, "I was part of an ayahuasca ceremony at the foot of that beautiful grandmother."

Rae didn't ask who or what the i-yo-waska were/was, as the word "ceremony" was enough to put her off the topic. "That's in California, right?" She had been in southern California for school but had never traveled. The only mountain range she had seen was the San Bernardinos.

"Yes," he said. "It looks like they moved the dome to the Sierra Nevadas."

Rae's hands held her stomach as if cradling the child within, and she got a strange, almost pained expression on her face. "There are so many places in the states — in the world, really — that I've never been to."

Hubert, climbing aboard a rickshaw, said, "You're still young; there's plenty of time to explore."

Rae looked at Ashley. "Do you think we'll ever see those mountains in real life?"

Ashley scanned the snaggle-toothed mountain range as it gnawed on the western edge of the dome. He shook his head. "We're going that way," he said, pointing toward the darkening edge of the sky, out toward the constellation Virgo.

# CHAPTER TWENTY-SEVEN

# Of Dark Space

**Rae**

By June the team had built two matching anti-numen chambers, each containing *Lepraria ptilisaccharon* crystal rings that were big enough for a human to step through. The anti-numen chambers were located at either side of the huge underground LHM facility, one in the new Lab Seven and the other in room G1-3847, which they had taken to calling Seven and a Half.

"Today," Rae said, addressing her team. "We'll be testing whether the gates are actually two connected points, or two identical crystal rings responding to the same stimulus." She paused to watch her nervous excitement trickle out through the rest of the group. "Doctors Allan, Hubert, and Brando, you will stay here and monitor this chamber, while Ashley and Doctors Ma'at, Mora, and Washington, you'll head over to Seven and a Half. Washington, I want you on the molecular dismantler. Ashley, I want you assisting the doctors from outside the chamber. Let's start small and safe. Ashley, let me know when you've arrived."

He nodded, took out his Omni, brought up a map of the facility, and lead the procession of doctors down the web of identical corridors. The moment they were gone, she said, "By the way, I forgot to mention that 'small and safe' means that I'm going through first. No. Stop, I don't want to see that face. I'm not going to throw a handful of PS crystals through. If for some reason it requires some force of will to push oneself to the other side, throwing a few unintelligent crystals in might cause us to draw the conclusion that the gates aren't connected, so unless anyone has a pet cat or dog handy..."

Hubert and Brando both looked at each other, but it was Allan who spoke. "Dr. Dahlia, you're pregnant."

Rae wrapped her hands around the roundness of her belly. "If the baby could be injured by numinous energy, it has already happened. I'm doing you the courtesy of telling you so you'll be prepared. Don't make me regret this decision to keep you in the loop."

Hubert spoke: "Brando and I have been playing with a thought experiment. Because the properties of numen are still largely unknown, we've been overlaying theologies on top of it. The one we keep going back to is Hinduism, which posits that nature consists of creation, destruction, and preservation. If numen maps to it, then this gate of destruction leads to a place where consciousness comes unglued from corpus. I agree with Dr. Dahlia's assumption that the traveler needs to exert a force of will, and, if not, they will unravel." He turned and spoke directly to Rae. "If there is any symmetry to the universe, I believe that if you step through, you will encounter a force that we have yet to measure. If this numinous force phase shifts from conscious to unconscious, then it follows there must be an analog of entropy; there must be a Kali to undo what the creator has made and your consciousness has preserved. I believe you will encounter a destroyer."

*What if this is it for me? Am I really willing to risk my life for this?* she asked herself. She nodded and steeled her resolve. *Besides, Evermore plans to send Ashley through here; if it weren't safe, he wouldn't risk the life of his only son.* Even as she thought it, she only put four-to-three odds on Evermore's morality, and a gentle kick from the baby made her wonder if she was any better.

Allan put a hand on her shoulder. "Don't think I can't see what you've done here: you've sent everyone who you think cares about you to Seven and a Half. Frankly, I'm offended you think so little of me, and if you think I'm letting you risk the lives of yourself and your child, you're wrong."

Rae faked a loving smile. "Thank you, Allan, but *you're* wrong. The groups are based on who values logic over emotion, but I see I've misjudged you. Surely you must understand that *someone* has to test the gate, and since I've had the most up-close exposure to the dark anomaly, it should be me."

"I'm not disagreeing that you have the most experience, I'm saying that you objectively have the most to lose."

Rae raised her eyebrow at him. "Are you volunteering to go in my place?"

Allan swallowed and stood up straighter. "Yes."

"Fine, then let's stop this debate and get the gates ready."


Rae braced herself for that feeling of absolute aloneness that she had experienced the first time she was shut in the anti-numen chamber, but as she and Allan's Omnis chirped a network disconnection alert, she didn't feel it in the same way. It could have been because of the battery-powered work lights illuminating the space, but whatever the reason, instead of feeling absorbed by the loneliness, she felt a pressure, as if Allan's psychic energy extended beyond his body, filling the space and squeezing against hers.

As the gate was activated, the crystal ring leaked tendrils of darkness that couldn't be chased away with their lights. Like a fog blown by a subtle wind, the tendrils were swept around the edges of the ring clockwise. Rae could tell the moment the second gate was activated because a tiny shimmering circle appeared in the center of the gate, like the microscopically thin film that divides two soap bubbles. The film spread out across the mouth of the gate and surprised both Rae and Allan by showing them their reflections.

Everything was being recorded, but Rae knew the cameras couldn't see what she could. "Both gates have activated, and a reflective film in the center is showing a non-mirror image of us. When I raise my right hand, my reflection raises the hand on my left."

Allan took a deep breath and summoned his courage, but before he could take a step, Rae switched off the lights, slipped past him, and grabbed hold of the edge of the gate.

"Rae, what are you doing?" Allan called out.

"I built this thing, and I have responsibilities."

Allan, groping in the darkness, found the collar of her lab coat, but she hadn't been able to button it since March, and as she stepped forward she let it slip off her shoulders.

The oppressive dark that plugged her eyes and forced itself into her ears was what she imagined it would be like to be underwater in a cave. Without the pull of gravity she lost all sense of direction. Thick nothingness rushed into her lungs to drown her. Suffocating on it, she panicked and tried to draw air, but nothing happened. She couldn't inhale. She screamed but it made no sound. Flailing her arms and legs she reached blindly into the void to find something to pull herself along and found nothing. Stretching out into nothingness, she lost contact with herself and grabbed her own hands as evidence that she hadn't ceased to exist. Still gasping for a breath she couldn't catch she reached into her mouth and searched for the thing that was choking her. Systematically she searched her throat and neck for an unseen strangler and found none.

Long after she should have asphyxiated her mind refused to lose consciousness. She grew too tired to flail and hung in space suspended by nothing.

She tried to remember where she was, but it was all too hard to hold on to. *I am nowhere.* She disconnected from all parts of her past and her conscious projection into the future. Her name lost its meaning. All that remained was the present, and here there was nothing, and slowly that's what she became. *I am nowhere.* There was a comfort and a freedom in the nothingness. There was no pain to avoid or mitigate, no ego to maintain, no relationships to preserve, no appointments, deadlines, or responsibilities. The being released its hold on its own identity and started to forget even the fact that it was physical. Then, out of the nothing, it became aware of a thumping pressure, which was echoed by a faster, weaker rhythm, and it remembered: there was one responsibility left, and it was to the second heartbeat inside her. As she remembered that she was a mother, she became aware of something else, a small and insignificant light in the darkness; the very idea that something could exist external to herself was to multiply the size of infinity. Curiosity drew her closer, and slowly the light grew in size from a pin-hole to a far-off star.

She reached out to it, only to realize that it was enormously far away. Centuries passed, and she drew closer, until it was the size of the sun. She reached out to the penetratingly bright light again, but it was still too far away. Time passed. The kind of time it takes for a solar system to form a star, and for the planets around that star to cool, form an atmosphere, and give birth to advanced lifeforms. The light grew bigger and brighter until she was blinded by it. There was pressure that reached out to her and threatened to break her bones and squish the blood from her skin, yet the pressure of being squeezed was the most comforting feeling in the world. Beyond the comfort was life, and she could smell its sweetness like overripe fruit begging with its lusty aroma for its flesh to be torn and devoured. She reached out to bite into it with parched lips and famished teeth...

Everything returned at once. Air, gravity, light, and identity. The first words she heard after eons of silence came from Dr. Ma'at: "Who is that? What the fuck?!"

Rachael was falling. She reached out with a naked foot as the cold metal floor rose up to meet her, stumbled, and was caught by a very surprised Ma'at. Kaspar Mora was also there, and he pounded on the wall twice, and the glowing crystalline gateway of sucking nothingness disappeared a moment later.

As soon as she regained her balance, Ma'at released her, took off his long lab coat and draped it over her shoulders while looking elsewhere. She made no attempt to cover herself. For all her years of modesty, she had just experienced an eternity of loneliness, and that they wouldn't look at her hurt far more than the shame of her nakedness. Even with the lab coat draped over her shoulders, her round belly and swollen breasts prevented it from covering anything. "Look at me!" She demanded. Slowly they raised their gaze and faced her, joining the bank of UV, IR, and numinous cameras whose eyes were all pointed at her, obediently watching.

Ma'at smiled weakly. "I didn't recognize you at first. Your hair..."

She reached up and ran her hand across her perfectly smooth head and across her face. Her eyebrows were also missing. She checked her eyelashes. Gone. Rachael was marveling that even the smallest hairs on the back of her hand were gone when she stopped. "My fingernails." Her hands began to shake, and the doctors realized that she had not painted her fingers and toes red, but what they were looking at was her exposed nail beds.

Calmly, she said, "Someone get the first aid kit."

Moments later, as her fingers and toes were each being carefully bandaged, the anti-numen chamber was unsealed, and Ashley burst into the room. "Oh my God, Rae, are you okay?" He embraced her, then stepped back to button the oversize lab coat. She looked straight into the eyes of the young man before her and saw him as just that. She saw his concern, but it was the fear of losing her, of losing that which defined him that was so worrisome. Inside dark space she had felt more alone, hollow, and empty than she had ever felt before, but now she realized that that's why she loved him. Ashley wanted an outline, a border drawn around himself that defined the contents, while she had a definition but wanted something deeper to fill it. It was a perfect fit. "Yes, I'm fine," she said flatly.

"How could you do that to me? You could've been killed. The baby could've... What if your skin had... What if... Could've..." but he was alone in his hysterics.

"Ashley." She didn't mean to, but her tone was as if she were addressing a lost puppy. "I'm alive, and Sean's alive."

Dr. Mora put a hand on Ashley's shoulder. "Ashley, Dr. Dahlia's right, this is a time for celebration!"

"Please call me Rachael. Just so I can hear the sound of it."

Dr. Washington entered the chamber and excitedly asked, "What was it like?"

Rachael shook her head and said, "On the other side of the gate is darkness. There is no air, and no vacuum state to pull it from my body. There is no temperature, and no particles to facilitate conduction or convection. There is no sound, no light, and no gravity. That dark space is not a place for living things." Rachael remembered the way the past and future became irrelevant and how her identity bled out of her.

Ashley left the room in a hurry, and Rachael continued, "I'm afraid this is a failure. The time it takes to travel between gates rules this out as a viable means of transportation." It had taken centuries. How were they all still alive? "How long was I gone?"

Ma'at cleared his throat and said, "The experiment lasted less than twenty seconds."

"Eight, actually," Dr. Washington said, looking at his Omni. The door to the chamber in Lab Seven must have been opened, and the recording footage updated to all their Omnis. As he flicked through the footage, he said, "Five seconds for countdown, one where Dr. Allan hesitated, three seconds of darkness, and then Dr. — Rachael stepped out."

"But how long was I actually in the gate?" Rachael asked.

"Hard to say, because you killed the lights in the Lab Seven chamber, but by the time Allan switched them back on, you'd already been here for a few seconds."

Allan burst into the room. Panting, he said, "Oh, thank God you're alright! Dr. Dahlia, this goes beyond anything I could've imagined. I'm sorry I ever doubted you. How could I have possibly known that months ago, when we destroyed that first *Lepraria ptilisaccharon* crystal, we were actually observing a fifth fundamental force?"

Rachael shook the astrophysicist's hand and said, "I'm glad to see you're finally on board, Dr. Allan."

Allan smiled and shook his head. "What amazes me is that this force can only affect living matter. Imagine if we'd attempted this experiment in outer space like the Public Health Service wanted. I can't imagine how terrible it would have been to find your space suit empty after it drifted through the gate."

Ashley returned with an armload of Rachael's clothes and set them on the workstation beside her. "Everyone out," he commanded, and raced around the room turning off all the cameras and recording devices. Rachael couldn't help but smile at him.

Almost as soon as the last doctor had left the room Ashley said, "I know why the *Godspeed* doesn't have thrusters!"

Rachael nodded, pulling on her clothes. "It can't. The entire ship will need to be shielded in crystal plates. Any chink or crack in the armor, and all nonliving material will be left behind."

"How long have you known?"

"When we figured out that the *Godspeed's* crystal plates are Samuel's bones, I had the thought that the passengers would be like funny little parasites moving around inside of Samuel's body; then I realized I have a funny little parasite in me too. I'm a perfect analog to the *Godspeed*. That's why Evermore wanted me to get pregnant. He knew I'd want to be first, that I'd want to test it myself. Ashley, Sean is what kept me sane in there."

Ashley did not smile. "I'm so mad at you."

"Well, get over it, because it already happened, and it turns out I was right. Or is that why you're mad?"

## Ashley

"Hey, no running," Julius called. As Ashley entered Evermore Industries and hurried across the lobby.

His tone seemed to be joking, but he wasn't smiling.

"Good evening, Julius."

"Hey, seriously, buddy, slow down. I haven't seen you in a while. I heard you were there when Dr. Dahlia stepped through the portal." Julius was not one to be so conversational, and often their talks degraded into him talking about himself. Ashley did his best to keep things short. "Yep."

"Slow down," Julius mouthed, and gave Ashley the strangest look. Aloud he said, "'They're calling her the

Mother of Dark Space." The open, inviting elevator doors began to close. Ashley made a dash to catch the edge; the sensor stopped the door with a clunk and it opened to let him in. "I'll catch up with you later, Julius," he said. *Why is he looking at me like that? Is he going to treat me like I'm something special now?* As the doors closed he found out: standing beside the panel of buttons, supporting himself on the handrail and a white aluminum cane, was Samuel.

Ashley's eyes glanced from Samuel's adjustable-height cane, to his sickly pale skin and bald, eyebrow-less head. The combination of old and young that occupied his body at the same time was unsettling.

In a weak, tired voice, Samuel said, "You no longer have a lab here, so I'm assuming you're here to see Evermore. By the way, congratulations on the breakthrough at the Lockheed Martin facility," he added. "It's a victory for all of us."

Ashley smiled halfheartedly and said, "Actually, I'm here to help Ma'at." With only a brief awkward hesitation he reached between Samuel and the wall and pressed the button for the eighth floor. "By the way, I was sorry to hear about your cancer. Leukemia, wow. So you must be preparing a lawsuit against the company that did your prenatal screening. Or did your parents use Evermore Biomedical? Boy, that would be awkward."

"Ashley, you forget that the world hasn't always been the way it is." Samuel's tone dripped with condescending ichor. "In 2003 prenatal screening didn't exist to the extent it does today. Sure, it may have been possible, but uncommon. I'm grateful I wasn't born in 1903; with my condition I would have been hidden in the basement so my parents didn't have to bear the shame of giving birth to a freak."

Samuel's eyes seemed as if they were about to water when the emotions disappeared from his face as if they'd never existed. "There's no need to keep mincing words; at this point the endgame is inevitable, so let's stop pretending you don't know exactly what I am."

Ashley clenched his teeth. "Tell me then, what do you get out of all this?"

Samuel shook his head. "No, that's the wrong question. If I were you, I'd be asking myself, 'Why didn't my good friend Evermore tell me the truth about Samuel?'"

The elevator slowed to a stop as it reached the eighth floor, but the doors refused to open. Ashley looked around and realized that Samuel was intentionally leaning into the "close doors" button with the head of his cane.

*He wants me to think we aren't as close as I thought. Evermore has been keeping me at an arm's length since we got to Mars.* Ashley had attributed it to the mentoring relationship, but maybe he was just the only willing intern during a rough spot in Evermore's life, and his usefulness had faded when things turned around. *Then why bring me to Mars at all? For the same reason Samuel has leukemia. Evermore needs my help.* Ashley shrugged. "I already know the answer to that: I'm a terrible liar. If the Doc had let me in on the secret, I wouldn't have been able to keep quiet about it. For example, when I found out he *intentionally* gave you leukemia, the first thing I did was tell Rachael. So maybe you're the one who should be asking, 'Why did my good friend give me cancer?'"

"I like what you did there, throwing my phrasing in my face like that, but I can tell you're guessing. Evermore's biggest weakness is that he gets focus locked. He just missed it. That's the simple truth."

Ashley shook his head. "Yeah, the Doc gets focused, but he couldn't have missed the predisposition. Not a chance."

Samuel shifted his weight and released the button. The doors opened, and Ashley held them with his hand and said, "Tell me: what's so great about the planet in Hercules? Why go eighty light years away when there are better options within thirty?"

"It's the eternal everlasting we were all promised."

Ashley stepped out into Lab Eight and turned back to toss in the final word like a grenade as the doors closed. "Everlasting life sounds boring," he said.

The doors hung open a second longer than he expected, and Samuel said, "Just wait until you experience purgatory."

The look Samuel gave him worked its way under his skin like a worrisome rash.

Ma'at called across the lab, "Ashley, is that you?"

Dominating the center of Lab Eight was the numen scanner. The machine was a three-meter-long octagonal cylinder laid on its side. In the center was a manhole-size opening. Each of the eight quadrants around the opening held racks of circuit boards crammed with wires and laced with plastic lines of coolant.

Ashley navigated counterclockwise around the machine, careful not to upset any of the piles of spare parts stacked around it. He found Ma'at seated at his workstation, which faced south and overlooked the city of Nili Terradome. "Hello, Ashley," Ma'at said, shielding his eyes against the setting sun, "Dr. Dahlia mentioned she'd be sending you along. I have almost finished compiling the data from the test scenarios I have been running."

"I thought you said the scanner was finished."

"It is finished. I am just trying to balance the safety to efficacy ratio. It is looking optimistic. The biggest issue is that it runs hot from the circuit boards processing three numen scanners operating at the same time. Spacing the octagonal quadrants farther away would require a whole new armature."

Ashley shook his head. "We don't have time for that."

"Dr. Dahlia said the same."

Ashley took out his Omni and ordered the janitorial crew to bring up four of their biggest fans. Then he turned his attention to the controls on the side of the numen scanner. Upon waking the interface screen its first question was, "Full- or subsystem scan?"

Ma'at stood from his desk. "I cannot guarantee your safety."

"How many of your scenarios have ended in death?" Ashley followed a tree of submenus until he arrived at "full skeletal scan".

"None," Ma'at admitted, "But—"

"But you're too afraid?" Ashley said.

"I was going to say: but it's likely to get up above fifty-six degrees."

Ashley was confused for a moment before realizing that Ma'at meant Celsius. *What's that conversion? One-point-eight plus thirty-two... Jesus, that's something around 120 to 130 Fahrenheit.*

"I hope you don't mind, but I'm taking my clothes off."


After the janitors arrived, wheeling their fans out of the elevator, Ashley directed them to set them up around the machine. As they left, he stripped down to his underwear and crawled into the hollow center of the numen scanner, where Ma'at had installed a coffin-size polycarbon tray.

"The scan will take two hours to complete," Ma'at yelled over the fans. "I'll be here if anything goes wrong."

As the machine spooled up, Ashley felt his heart rate increase with it. The higher-pitched sound of CPU fans and coolant circulators cut through the throbbing hum of the industrial fans. The air moving over him was not unpleasant, but around minute fifteen he began shivering, and he hoped it wasn't blurring the image. Ten minutes later he felt the heat of the machine beginning to warm up the tray. At minute forty Ashley had gone from shivering to sweating and wasn't sure which he preferred. One hundred minutes in, the sound seemed to be part of his body. He *was* the pulsing thrum. The heat continued to rise, and he felt like he was actually starting to bake, and the wind from the fans was merely adding to the convection. He alternated between breathing from his nose and mouth, switching as one dried out, then the other, until his tongue felt like it would crack and bleed, and every breath burned his nostrils and throat. "Water," Ashley called out pitifully, and when there was no reply he yelled it louder. A few seconds later, Ma'at called up into the machine.

"The markers are defined by their network of connections; we'll lose everything if we interrupt the process. Do you want to abort?"

"How much longer?"

"Twenty minutes. Do you want to abort?"

He heard Rachael's voice: *If there's any chance this will prevent me from getting what I want, then there's no way I'm going to keep it.*

*Sean didn't ruin her life. I did. If she can keep going, I can too.* "Don't abort!" he yelled.

"Got it. Hang in there!"

The next twenty minutes passed in hours. He would have lost consciousness, but every bead of sweat that ran down his face felt like heaven. As the machine wound down and the air blowing on him cooled, Ma'at called in, "We're done. How're you doing in there?"

He tried crawling out, but his body felt like rubber. He was light-headed and delirious. "I can't get out," he whimpered.

Ma'at grabbed Ashley by the ankles and pulled until his feet were on the floor, but even then Ashley slid out like toothpaste from a tube into a white pile on the floor. "Here," Ma'at said, handing Ashley a half-full bottle of water. Ashley reached for it, but his arm felt impossibly heavy. He made a weak attempt to grab it but was unable to do so. Ma'at placed the bottle to Ashley's lips.

After a while, Ashley was able to drink for himself and sit up. "Take your time," Ma'at cautioned. Sitting on the floor beside Ashley, Ma'at held up his Omni and showed him the constellation the machine had produced. It was perfect. As a whole its hundreds of points could have belonged to anyone. Not even Evermore would know it didn't belong to Samuel without close examination.

"Ma'at, you're amazing!"

He shrugged off the compliment and said, "I have the feeling you and Dr. Dahlia already have a purpose in mind for this?"

Ashley nodded weakly.

"You used to work for him; you know him best." Ma'at stood and sighed. "Well, I should be getting home. Aziza expected me hours ago. Are you going to be okay?"

Ashley nodded again and tipped the empty bottle over his mouth, savoring the last drops that fell warm on his tongue. "Ma'at, thank you for staying late."

Ma'at was gathering his things to go, but he stopped and his eyes grew sad. "I regret that I wrote you off so quickly, Ashley. After spending all these months in Lab Seven together, I have come to know you better, and I have to say I have enjoyed working together."

"You sound like you're leaving forever. Oh man, are you quitting?"

"Not exactly." Ma'at pressed the elevator button. "Dr. Evermore has created a new branch of E.I., and he has asked me to run it."

*Why Ma'at and not Rae?* Ashley tried not to look shocked. "Congratulations!"

The doors opened. Ma'at nodded and stepped through.

# CHAPTER TWENTY-EIGHT

# Changes

## Ashley

Lab Seven had completed their final assignment from Evermore, to "design two linked crossover points and measure the time it takes to pass between them." They had succeeded in completing Evermore's far-reaching goal of extending their tools and truths so that humankind could begin to understand numen and incorporate it into the global community. At least, that's what Evermore told them in their exit interviews. Those who wanted to continue with E.I. were welcome, as there were more job openings every day, and those who cared to move on were given a generous thank-you bonus.

Dr. Joseph Allan returned to Earth, where he secluded himself, subscribed to *Speculative Science,* dreamed of becoming the next Einstein, and began trying to use quantum field theory to describe the fifth fundamental interaction of the numen particle.

Dr. Kaspar Mora was hired by UMars (in lieu of Doctors Dahlia and Ma'at, who both turned down the position) to teach a biomaterials class that focused on living crystals.

Dr. Luther Brando became a legal citizen of Mars, bought an apartment, and dedicated himself to writing a book using archaememeology to predict and prepare for cultural trends and technological advances in the twenty-second century. Once a week he met with Dr. Raymond Hubert to argue philosophy at a café downtown that had the best pluot jam.

Dr. Hubert continued living his philosophy throughout the transition, patiently waiting and watching for the next mystery he would dedicate himself to. In his mind, the most important piece he had taken away from working at Evermore Industries was the idea of tools and truths, or more importantly, the truth that shifted in himself after understanding the idea of tools and truths. As Hubert heard it, our reality is limited by the tools we use to build it, and, inversely, the tools we build to manipulate reality are shaped by what we believe to be true about the world, so on and so forth in a closed loop. Every part of him believed that it was indeed a closed loop, especially with the cost of research and development of the immensely powerful tools that humankind was producing, but still Evermore's gamble vexed him. The man had risked trillions of dollars to build a tool that didn't exist to enable an event (traveling faster than the speed of light) that was not supported by any truth. By Hubert's reasoning it was impossible, but the possibility the impossible thought created through its association was this: "Crazy is believing in a reality that doesn't exist; genius is getting others to believe in that reality until it exists."

Dr. Cyrus Ma'at accepted a position as director at a new division of Evermore Industries called the Department of Numinous Cosmology, which included oversight of a crystal incubator the size of a football field. His lead man was the molecular physicist Dr. Benjamin Washington, and Ashley accepted a position as programmer for the industrial-size genome printer on the condition that he could work from home whenever possible.

The department was located in a spoke of the Lockheed Martin facility that had previously been used for roto-casting silica polymers. When Ma'at and the DNC took over, their first task was to prepare for a large series of PS crystal plates. They retrofitted the huge spinning and rotating machines with a gigantic clear mold. Instead of squirting molten silica into the mold, the same machinery was altered to inject a liquid slurry of PS lichen, coating the inside of the mold. And the whole mold would be stored in an incubation room big enough to hold two C-130J Hercules aircraft.

Rachael had been growing more and more distant since the day she stepped through the gates. Ashley knew she had had an exit interview with Evermore, but she wouldn't say if or where she was placed. The day before the DNC moved in to begin creating a version of the gates that was large enough for the E.I.S.S. *Godspeed*, Rachael had thrown a farewell party in Lab Seven and a Half. More than once Ashley had overheard one of the doctors asking Rachael what she was going to do next, and yet she never answered their question.

Afterward he had brought it up again. "Allan was right, you know: you can work anywhere you want. I mean, I know you're getting tons of offers. UMars can't be the only one. Are you overwhelmed by your options?"

"No."

"Well, you must be pissed that Ma'at got his own facility."

"No, I'm happy for him."

"What is it, then? I know parsing out where each crystal plate aligns with my skeleton isn't feeding you creatively."

The crystal plate puzzle may not have been mentally stimulating, but their relationship worked best when they were working together. It hadn't taken long before sheets of ePaper of the *Godspeed's* 206 crystal plates had taken over Rachael's home, and they had decided to rent an office cube a few blocks from her apartment. On his way home from the DNC, Ashley would pick up some takeout and meet her at the office.

"Hey babe, how was your day?"

"It was fine."

"You're sure?"

"Damn it, Ashley! Why don't you ever believe me that I'm fine?"

*Because I can see you, remember?* "Please talk to me," he begged. "I love you and I want to know what's going on. Is there a problem with the baby? Is he making you feel ill?"

"Nothing's wrong. Sean's healthy. I feel fine."

"You don't feel fine to me."

"You're right, I don't feel fine. I feel like an irrational bitch because I'm angry in one moment and sad the next, and sometimes I can't even tell what I'm feeling. I feel like a weirdo because I can still smell the Thai food we ate last night, and I've taken out the garbage twice. I feel like a freak because I spend all day in the bathroom since there's a tiny alien in my uterus constantly standing on my bladder. But worst of all I feel like a beached whale rotting in the hot summer sun, like any day now the gasses inside me are going to reach a critical point and I'm going to explode. So I'm sorry if I feel 'off' to you, but I'm literally not myself; I'm transforming into something that I can't control and wasn't excited to become in the first place!"

He was sure it was more than that, but there was no way he was going to contradict her. And then again, he'd never been pregnant. His persistence only drove them apart, and he stopped asking. One day he was walking downtown and passed someone sucking on a vaporizer and blowing thick clouds that smelled like a doughnut shop. He had a moment of empathy for how horrible it would be to be addicted to something. He had lived with addiction as an external monster that fed on his family, and he knew it never really went away; it just hibernated and woke up hungrier than ever. Then he realized there was only one thing Rachael would hide from him, and one night he worked up his courage and asked, "Tell me the truth: are you back on stims?"

Ashley watched her eyes for any hint of shame, but all he saw was pity as she calmly said, "No." And that was it. There was no defensiveness, no anger, and no fire behind her words.

"Rachael, you're scaring me. I don't know what's going on between us."

"Nothing's changed; nothing's going on," she offered.

"I miss you," he said.

"I'm right here."

But she wasn't right there, she was empty. Not sad or depressed, just hollow and complacent. After he eliminated the other possibilities, he felt it had something to do with the gate. He briefly considered opening the gate by himself and stepping through so he could know what she had seen. In his mind he heard Samuel's voice: *"Just wait until you experience purgatory."*

According to Rachael, he wouldn't survive it unless he had a passenger, and if everything went according to their plan, he would see that nothingness soon enough.

In late July, Rachael was called into Lab Seven and a Half, though the DNC called it ANC-2, to meet with Asbjorn Breivik. Ashley, excited for the distraction from coding, took the tram across the LHM facility to meet her.

When Rachael entered, Asbjorn leaned slightly toward her with his shoulders, and his two wheeled "chair" (which currently held him in a standing position) headed toward her. "Asbjorn Breivik," he said, extending a hand and carefully leaning back to counter-balance himself.

Rachael took it, and Asbjorn said, "Thanks for coming all the way out here to help."

"Not a problem. Do you mind if I sit?"

"Not at all," Asbjorn said, then rolled past them and through the open door of the anti-numen chamber, where he stopped and stared. Ashley followed his gaze to the 244-centimeter-tall gate, but all he could see was a reminder of the day Rae left.

"It's gorgeous," Asbjorn said. "This is the room where no numen particle can enter?"

"That's right. So if you don't mind me asking, you've been working at E.I. since the beginning?"

Asbjorn nodded. "Even before the groundbreaking of the E.I. building, I've been out here overseeing the *Godspeed* build. Since E.I. went up, Dr. Evermore has had me designing upgrades on the DuPont dry dock station. It's been a depressingly utilitarian project. Tell me about the gate."

Ashley listened while the two of them workshopped the design of one gate that was large enough for the E.I.S.S. *Godspeed* to pass through and another they could carry with them and assemble at the journey's end.

It was August 18th, and though Ashley's workday at the DNC had ended, Rachael and Ashley's was just beginning. After grabbing some Thai takeout, Ashley wound his way through the maze of halls entombed in the office cube. Dropping the plastic bag of food containers on the workstation, whose screen had been flattened so they could both work on it from either side, he kissed Rachael and asked how her day was.

Hiding his disappointment at another answer of "fine," he glanced out the VR "window" of a live image from the exterior of the building, then turned to the wall perpendicular, which was covered with an OmniWatch whiteboard crowded with two groups of crystal plates numbered 09.01 through 09.27, and 10.01 through 10.27.

"We got into a good flow last night; I think if we can keep working systematically like that we should be able to go a little faster."

Rachael didn't answer. Her singular focus was on unpacking the takeout. Ignoring her ignoring him, Ashley opened the stolen *Godspeed* schematic. Their saving grace was that Evermore, or whoever had built the work order, had arranged the plates within coherent skeletal groups: 09 and 10 both had 27 plates and were located along the left and right flanks of the ship; with 27 bones each, these could only be the hands. The other clue they were allowed was that each plate had distinct numbers of numinous markers that were lock-and-keyed to the bones that that plate was attached to; therefore, it only took Ashley a few minutes to figure out that 09.01 through 09.05 were fingertips because they each were only connected to one plate; from here he could assume that the next four were intermediate phalanges, and so on until he would reach the confusing configuration of carpals.

As Ashley was transferring the build order into a codified list of his numen markers from Ma'at's scan, Rachael tossed a paper plate of takeout onto the workstation, directly in the center of his screen. "Eat," she said, pushing a wad of hexapro pad Thai into her mouth. Ashley raised his head to retort, but just then she let out a whimper around her mouthful of food and the expression on her face drove away whatever he was about to say. "What's wrong? Did they make it too spicy?"

She shook her head, swallowed, and said, "No. The contractions are getting worse."

"The... contractions? —sss? As in, more than one?"

She frowned. "I hate it when you second-guess me like that."

"What are we even doing here? Let's get you to the hospital!"

"It's too soon; our birthing appointment isn't for another week. Honestly, they aren't that bad. I thought the first one was a cramp from being so hungry."

Ashley looked back down to his food. Worried but unsure of what to do, he twisted his plastic fork around in the rice noodles. "Are you going to eat?" he asked, before wrapping his cheeks around the mouthful.

She moved her plate to the floor and rotated the desktop view so that it was facing her. "I lost my appetite." She leaned heavily on the desk and stared intently at the list of crystal plates.

After swallowing, Ashley said, "Those are the right-hand fingertips, starting with the thumb."

Rachael nodded and relaxed into the work. She sat up, her hands fell in sync with the desktop, and she began carefully labeling the plate with the code Ashley had taught her.

Just as Ashley had sucked down the last bite of pad Thai, Rachael doubled over the desk, groaning.

"I'm calling the hospital," he said.

"No," she growled. "It's too soon."

"Well, we should at least call your doctor."

Through a few deep breaths she was able to collect herself and sit upright again. "It's on my Omni."

Dr. Huarez's line rang until the voicemail picked it up: "You've reached Options and the office of Emilio Huarez, ob-gyn, please leave your name, number, and a brief message, or call back during regular business hours. For emergencies call 10-3645..." if there was more to the message, Ashley didn't hear it. He dialed the emergency number and waited as it rang a few times before a tired young man who sounded the same age as Ashley answered, "Hello, this is Dr. Huarez's emergency line, what seems to be the problem?"

Ashley already hated this guy from the way he said "seems." In the background he could hear the fast rhythm and low pitch of a bass guitar churning furiously away like a giant hummingbird's heartbeat. "I need to get in touch with Dr. Huarez,"

"Unless this is an emergency, Dr. Huarez is unavailable." The young man wasn't tired, Ashley realized: he was impatient.

"This *is* an emergency," he said, sounding frantic even to himself. "My girlfriend's going into labor!" Even though he had leveled his tone, it still fishtailed into panic as he said "labor."

"I'm not going into labor; I just had a few small contractions. He's overreacting," Rachael said calmly. Ashley glared at her.

"Which—" The young man paused, took a breath, and asked, "How far apart are the contractions?" In the background someone tried to congratulate the young man. There was the sound of a finger covering the receiver and his muffled voice telling that same someone to "piss off."

"Maybe twenty minutes between the first and second, and ten between the last two," Rachael guessed.

"If you *are* going into labor, Miss Dahlia, you've got plenty of time. Dr. Huarez should have given you a package of white, oval, adhesive monitors. Are you wearing one?" As soon as he started talking to Rachael, his tone became patronizing.

"No. The doctor said to start wearing them when we got close to the due date."

Ashley shot her a questioning look. She hadn't wanted him to tag along during her monthly appointments, but now he wished he had insisted.

"Why don't you go ahead and put one on now. The important thing is to relax and make sure you read the application instructions carefully before putting it on. The monitors collect data from your contractions; they measure the frequency and duration, and they will automatically alert the doctor when you have gone into labor."

Ashley expected her to explode at this nobody for treating her like a moron, but to his surprise she didn't seem to notice his condescending tone and nodded.

"Do you have any with you?" Ashley asked.

"No, I thought I still had a week—"

"Listen," Ashley said to Huarez's secretary or whoever he was. "She doesn't have one on, and they're back at the apartment, so will you please give us Dr. Huarez's number?!"

"It's fine, Ashley," Rachael said. "He said I've got plenty of time. Why don't you just run back home and get them for me?"

"All right, folks, I'm going to hang up, and Miss Dahlia, start wearing the monitors daily, please."

"Okay, thank you."

*Rachael being cheerful and friendly to a stranger? God, she must be terrified!* As the line went dead, Ashley jammed his Omni into his pocket and said, "Let's go!"

"Nonsense. I'm going to keep working."

There was no reasoning with her. "Okay, I love you. I'll be back as soon as I can!"

Ashley ran down the winding corridors of the office cube, getting turned around and lost twice in his panic. Once outside, he snagged a rickshaw and headed back to the apartment at an unbearably slow speed.

Now that he was on the significant-other list, the doors of the Maplecrest Apartments detected his Omni and automatically opened for him. He nodded to the night guard, who waved back, and rushed to her door. A part of him expected the smell he'd experienced the first time he'd entered her place, but since she'd been pregnant every little scent that she couldn't control either made her nauseous or drove her insane. The moment some residue from old take-out containers started to go bad, she made him take out the trash, and as such, her suite was wonderfully clean and had a faint aroma of orange blossoms to help mask any intruding odor. It was the fourth scent they'd gone through, and Ashley gave it a week before it would start to remind Rachael of something unpleasant and they'd need to switch to a new scent.

Ashley went straight to the cabinet in the bathroom where the adhesive monitors were kept and grabbed the entire box. Then, just in case this was it, he grabbed their toothbrushes, a travel-size tube of toothpaste he'd bought at the convenience store on Phobos, some bottles of water, and a couple of protein bars, tossed the lot in a plastic take-out bag with a big yellow smiley face on it that read "China Delite 88. Enjoy Your Delivery!" and rushed out the door.

# CHAPTER TWENTY-NINE

# The Second Gate

## Ashley

Hurrying down the tangled corridors of the office cube, Ashley heard a scream that tore through him. "Rachael!" he called and broke into a run, slamming into the corners as he made his way to their office suite. Rachael was curled up on the floor holding her stomach and moaning in abating agony. Ashley fell to his knees beside her.

"Breathe," he reminded her.

After a few minutes she slowly stood up, clinging to Ashley's arm, not for support, but in case the pain might suddenly return. "Whooo, that one was intense." She released her grip on him and turned her attention to the workstation. "I'm going to need your help with the last eight wrist bones."

"Okay, but first we're going to put one of these monitors on you."

"Obviously. I'll handle that; you start working on the wrist."

While she skimmed the application directions, Ashley searched Cloud9 for "skeletal human wrist" and began comparing it to the numen markers that had no pair. Rachael affixed the stretchy contraction monitor and said, "Looks like the lunate bone is the only bone in the wrist with six connections." She compared it to the only six-marker match: 09.16.

Ashley smiled. "I was working from the other direction; the triquetrum is the only two-connection match."

After inputting the final carpal bone, Rachael let out another soul-shivering moan.

"How long was that?" Ashley asked.

"GodDAMNit who the FUCK cares! Oh Ffff-UCK!"

"Breeeeee!" Ashley reached out to comfort her, and she grabbed his hand and squeezed. He let out a cry of pain and tried to remove it from the vice. Rachael smiled, and through gasps of pain she said, "That makes me feel so much better."

In a short while the pain lessened, and Ashley marveled, *That's miraculous. I can't believe how quickly she returns to her normal self. Or, more accurately, the most recent baseline version of her emotionally cloistered, workaholic self.* They slowly worked their way through the finger bones, pausing every eight minutes to brace for another contraction, and after the third, Rachael's Omni rang with a private number requesting video chat. Her initial response was to ignore it, especially since it was across the room and she had yet to fully recover. Ashley moved to silence it but realized it was Dr. Huarez. He hit "accept" and had managed to say "Hello?" twice before video connected.

"Ashley, is Rachael there?" Dr. Emilio Huarez wore no facial hair and looked old enough that his hair had no right to be so thick and so uniformly black. Ashley had only met the man in passing but recognized him nonetheless.

"She's right here." Ashley held the Omni so that she and the doctor could see each other, but far enough away that she wouldn't crush it in the event of another contraction.

"Dr. Dahlia, how are you? I see that your hair is growing back nicely."

Rachael forced the ebbing pain deep within her and said, "Depends which minute you catch me in."

"I'm glad you're wearing your monitor, and I see you're having contractions at regular eight-minute intervals. But I'm only getting data from the last half hour; how long have you been experiencing contractions?"

Ashley's mind drifted off. *It's really happening: I'm going to be a father. Unless something happens during... no, don't even think it. Sean, I can't wait to see your face. I'm going to have to learn how to change diapers. Where are we going to live? Will we try to raise him on Mars? We'd have to school him ourselves. We haven't even talked about moving in together.*

"Ashley," Rachael said, and by her inflection he guessed it wasn't for the first time. "The doctor says I'm going into labor." Immediately Ashley felt the color draining from his face.

"Wh-what should I do?"

"Breathe," she said, and Ashley took a deep breath before realizing that the advice had been sardonic. "Good job, now call an ambulance and help me out of this stupid office cube."

Ashley walked beside her, holding her arm as if she were a fragile thing he was afraid to break, but when her next contraction struck he wasn't ready for her, and she slipped from his grasp. She didn't fall per se, but teetered to the right, away from him and into the wall. She slid slowly down it, and Ashley caught her on the way to the floor. Rachael fought the pain and when it had passed she turned her head and threw up. After spitting the last of it into the existing puddle, she looked up at Ashley with eyes that were helpless and afraid.

"Oh my God." He hadn't meant to say it out loud, and he managed to suppress the rest of his thought process. *Is vomiting normal? Either way, she's the Amazon, and anything she can't handle is over my head.*

Ashley knelt down beside her and gingerly wiped her mouth and chin with some takeout napkins. "Do you feel ready to walk a little farther?"

She nodded and reached for him, and he bent and pulled her up into a sideways embrace; she weighed a ton. Martian gravity should have made her easier to lift, but maybe his muscles were beginning to atrophy. *We can't raise Sean on Mars; his bones would be useless.*

Once outside, he guided her to a bench beside the almost empty rickshaw docking station, and there they waited for a short while and listed to the wails of the ambulance growing closer. "I love you, Rachael," he said.

She turned to him, pale and sweaty in the bluish-white glow of the simulated million billion stars and said, "I know. Thank you for being here. I..." there was the briefest of pauses before she finished, "love you, too." That pause could have been anything — the whisper of another contraction, a sudden wave of nausea, an odd smell catching her off guard — and Ashley refused to look into it. She loved him, and that was all that mattered. She put her head on his shoulder and said, "I'm so tired, Ashley. I don't know how I'm possibly going to deliver a baby tonight."

"Okay, I'll let the baby know. You call off the ambulance."

Rachael started to smile, but then another wave of pain rolled across her and she leaned back into the bench and closed her eyes.

Perhaps it was the EMTs treating him like he was invisible, or perhaps he was entranced by the flashing lights, but something seemed to disconnect time from its usual course. Some moments would stretch thin as time raced forward faster than he could comprehend it, while other moments would pile up behind each other in a traffic jam as time slammed on the brakes. Dr. Huarez beat them to the hospital and was the most comforting to Rachael when he was commanding his staff like a general while also giving her the illusion that she was in control.

As the labor progressed, Ashley came to realize that the pain he had seen on Rachael's face earlier was merely discomfort, a lumpy pull-out couch compared to the fear and desperation that crossed her face in the hours following the moment her water broke.

Ashley hated the tension, hated feeling like he was constantly in the way, hated not knowing the timeline; the doctors refused to tell them how dilated she was. Most of all, Ashley hated the helplessness. There was no way for him to help her.

At some point late into the night, Ashley realized his bladder was screaming, though he didn't want to let go of her hand. "Rachael, I... I have to pee, I'll be right back."

"Don't go." Her short hair was matted to her head with sweat. In the dim light of the birthing suite she looked exhausted and somehow the most beautiful he had ever seen her. *How can I say no to that?*

"I'm about to pee on the floor. I'll be right back. Technically, I'm not even leaving the room."

Dr. Huarez entered the room just as Ashley stepped into the bathroom, and he overheard him say, "You're doing a great job, Rachael, I just want to—" and the rest was obscured for almost a full minute. "Your body normally produces that chemical to help your cervix get all nice and relaxed, but you're not progressing. So I'd like to help your body out with an extra dose." Huarez said.

"Ashley? Where's Ashley?" Rachael called.

"I'll be right there," Ashley called as he washed his hands. When he exited the bathroom, it took his eyes a second to adjust, and then he saw Huarez standing over Rachael holding a needle. An animal awakened in Ashley, and he rushed the doctor with raised fists. One of the nurses moved to intercept, and Ashley crashed into him. Huarez took a few steps away from Rachael and said something that couldn't be heard over Rachael's scream, which rattled out of her throat like a freight train, and for a moment nothing happened.

Huarez put the needle away and said, "Mr. Rephaireal, will you step outside with me for a moment?"

As the two of them stepped outside, Rachael said, "Don't let him drug me."

Ashley spoke first, "What the fuck do you think you're—"

"I'm sorry," Huarez said. "I should have waited for you. Rachael isn't progressing; we need to help her body with a little boost of oxytocin, or we going to have to discuss a C-section."

"Can't we just give her more time?"

"Ashley, it's 10 a.m. It's been seventeen hours; we need to move this along."

When they returned, the two of them convinced Rachael to accept the oxytocin. Through warbling moans of pain, she said, "No C-section; he needs to come through the gate."

By eleven Rachael had reached full dilation and the real birth began. Ashley's concept of pain was rewritten as he witnessed the real animal emerge, and there was nothing that could hold back the raging tempest of Her. Ashley coached and helped her relax in between contractions; he poured his energy and strength into her tired, pale, immensely powerful body. And she pushed. The room seemed to contract with each mounting effort to eject the boy from her body, and shake with her exhaustion in the moments in between.

He heard the nurse say, "Keep going, Rachael, one more big push and he's going to come right out."

Ashley couldn't hold back his curiosity and pulled back the cloth that was attempting to cover a miracle, and there was his boy. There was his head, anyway. Covered in fluid and turned away from him so only his big ears and tuft of light brown hair was showing. *Purple. He's turning purple*. Ashley suddenly felt as if there wasn't enough air in his lungs, and he gasped for a breath, then another, and another. The room started to tilt and darken. Rachael mumbled in an exhausted pant, "Something's wrong. I can't increase the frequency. He's trapped. He's trapped."

Ashley turned to Rachael to comfort her, but someone shook him awake. He was slouched in a polyester arm-chair, and a nurse he didn't recognize was squatting beside him with a hand on his shoulder. Ashley gave the nurse a long confused stare, and the nurse repeated, "Hey there, Papa, come meet your son."

Ashley stood slowly, with no concept of how long he had been asleep. Whatever the nurse had said still hadn't sunk in. He looked across the birthing chamber with a sudden jerk and there she was. Beautiful and glowing even brighter than the afternoon light that shone through the curtained windows. Ashley's chest stirred with an elation unlike anything he'd ever felt. His son was bundled in a soft, white cloth sleeping on her chest. One of Sean's tiny hands was curled sweetly under his chin, but he was as pale and lifeless as a doll. Ashley felt the blood drain from his face as a feeling of déjà vu sent him reeling. This wasn't the first time he'd seen this boy. The day Rachael had opened the chamber door and he'd reached in to pull her back, he had seen a balding, spectral man in a business suit holding a baby. This was that boy.

Ashley went and carefully placed his hand on the ba-by's back and felt his tiny heartbeat. He leaned in and kissed Rachael on the forehead.

"Here." She moved her hands to lift the child but was too weak. "Pick him up. One hand on either side... support his head."

Sean felt so fragile in his arms. "He so tiny." Sean's little hand raised and dragged itself across his eyes, and they opened sleepily. His wide, wet eyes were the green of fresh grass and fathoms deep. They pulled Ashley into them, and he was lost in another place for a moment. "Hi, Sean. I'm your father."

He rocked his boy until the verdant pools of green slid closed.

"Did I faint just before he was born?"

A sleepy smile crossed Rachael's face. "Yeah, you did. Don't get me wrong: I'm still pissed at you for abandoning me right when I needed you most." She smiled again. "But you looked so excited right before you went down. You were so cute I think I'll forgive you."

He hid a bashful smile. "Babe, you did such a great job. You were so great!"

Even though they had been spending all of their time together, neither one of them had fully suggested moving in together until after Sean was born, Rachael had gotten some rest, and Ashley worked up the courage to ask, "The doctor said you'll be released soon, and I've been assuming you'll want to return to your suite, but where do we want to make Sean's home?"

Adjusting Sean, she reached for her Omni on the over-bed table, which was littered with bioplastic cups, the remains of her light afternoon lunch. Rachael pointed the screen at Ashley.

"This is on Phobos. Oh God, it's only 350 square feet, that's not enough room for both..."

Rachael reached out and touched his hand. "Oh, honey, no, that's not a suggestion that we keep living separately. That's one of the larger ones that are still in the affordable range."

"But why Phobos?"

"I told you. Huarez said that we'd need to relocate to Phobos."

Ashley shook his head. "No, you didn't. Was that while I was napping?"

"No, it was weeks ago. Huarez said that the Martian

gravity would affect Sean's growth, but the CNSA centrifuge station on Phobos spins at one-G."

"Is this your way of asking me to move in?" he joked, but his face betrayed that he was still hurt at being left out of the plan.

"I swear we already talked about this, but I'm sorry you don't remember that we're moving off planet in a week. But—" she changed the subject, "—I think you should keep your current place, just in case you ever have to work late and can't make the commuter shuttle."

Between relocating off planet and figuring out how to parent a newborn, Ashley and Rachael had their hands full, at least that's the line he fed to anyone who asked to visit. In truth, Sean slept all the time, and Rachael's belongings were being cleaned out by a moving crew. Every hour they didn't spend watching Sean sleep, went toward re-writing the Godspeed's crystal build order. Using the numen constellation that Ma'at's machine had mapped, they carefully replaced the instructions in each of the 206 crystal plates, with the information in Ashley's bones.

At the end of the week Ashley entered the E.I. building after hours and uploaded the file to the Doc's workstation. Though his heart pounded nonstop the whole time, the only resistance he encountered was a question posed by Evermore's workstation, "There is already a file with that same name in this folder. Do you want to replace the old one?"

He didn't hesitate to select, "Yes."

\* \* \* \* \* \*

The apartment on the centrifuge station had barely enough room for them both, but the size was the one thing Rachael never complained about. She hated that they didn't have a bathtub, that there was zero natural light, and that she felt like the neighbors were judging her. Ashley found the apartment community of Chinese station workers charming, though only a few of them spoke enough English to carry on a conversation. Mandarin didn't fit well in his Midwesterner mouth, but that didn't stop him from trying. For Ashley, the size seemed to highlight how much non-work time they now spent together. He was surprised at how many hours they passed simply staring at Sean.

On their fourth day in the apartment Ashley let out a big sigh and said, "I can't help it. I'm bored. I'm sorry, but after working so hard to finish the crystal build order, this is getting…" He paused to see how Rachael would react.

She gave an exasperated sigh and dropped a façade of contentment he didn't even know she'd been holding. "I've been working non-stop since high school! And I don't know what to do either. I'm going stir crazy looking at my Omni, we can't fuck until I'm all healed up, and I'm already uninterested by our restaurant options; this is essentially airport food."

"Heeey, you should know that here on CNSA lunar station Màoxiǎn is where Nili Terradome gets 90 percent of its hexapro; in theory, it should taste extra fresh up here."

Ashley gestured at the OmniWatch and selected their unwatched movie list. It had taken Rachael some time to warm up to his obsession with 2D classics from before the turn, but he got the impression that she could finally see past the flat, paper figures and really absorb the brilliance of the limitations of twentieth-century film. He selected *Scent of a Woman*.

The other thing they watched together was the latest announcement from Evermore. Ashley couldn't help but compare the Doc to the man who had appeared in the press conference over a year ago announcing that he was moving to Mars. Evermore looked older, but he spoke with so much more conviction.

"Over the next few months, Evermore Industries will be building a transgalactic vessel capable of taking that short step through dark space and traveling light years in an instant." Evermore turned and introduced Asbjorn Breivik, who seemed so comfortable in front of the cameras that he came off as slightly annoyed. Breivik shared some technical information, thanked the engineers at Lockheed Martin for building such tight machinery, and turned to introduce the lead foreman, a broad, stubble-faced man's man in navy coveralls who was not given a chance to speak but waved proudly.

Ashley recognized him. Well, not him specifically, but he remembered riding the tram from the LHM building with a bunch of workers in navy coveralls. He shook his head. "Evermore didn't just start building the *Godspeed*; he's been working on it since the facility switched hands."

Rachael said, "I didn't think it made much sense to fire up the thermite generators just for our tiny lab."

If Evermore's first announcement of a physics-shattering hole in space-time had felt like a slap in the face for the scientific community, the second must have felt like a punch to the gut. It was the equivalent of JFK telling the Soviets, "We choose to go to the moon!" And then following it up with, "To be sure, we'll be landing there next week and building a nuclear missile base by the end of the year!"

Another month went by. Ashley was hanging out on the bed with Sean, realizing for the first time that Sean was tracking Ashley's face. Though he still didn't seem to be able to see much or focus on anything specific, Sean was clearly interested in him, and it felt amazing. "Hey, babe," he called across the apartment. Rachael was working on a Hakaru on the couch and didn't look up. He was about to try again when his Omni rang.

"Hey, Dr. Ma'at," Ashley said. The background behind Ma'at was his office at the Department of Numinous Cosmology.

"Ashley, I— Oh, and Sean! Hi there, buddy. We should have you over for dinner one of these nights."

Over the screen Ashley could see that Rachael had cocked an ear toward them and was paying attention to their conversation. "Yeah, that'd be nice. You don't need me to come back in, do you?"

"No no, Evermore told me to give you all the time you needed. But about a month ago E.I. gave us our first build order, for a bunch of small crystal plates. Nothing that seemed anywhere near big enough to cover the *Godspeed*, and... well, I thought you two would know something about them, but I didn't want to bother Dr. Dahlia with work questions."

"No, no, I'm sure she'd love to be bothered. Hang on. Hey babe," Ashley, scooped Sean up in one arm, and started walking over to Rachael. "You want to spoil our secret about the crystal plates to Ma'at?"

Rachael looked up and forced a smile, as if she knew it was something she should be pleased about, but she shook her head and went back to her puzzle. Ashley stopped. "Then do you mind if I take a trip down to the DNC for the afternoon?"

She gave him a dispassionate head shake without looking up, and he walked back to the bed. Into his Omni he said, "I'd rather show you than tell you over the phone, and honestly, I'd love to see the plate roto-casters in action. If I rush I'll make the next flight."

He kissed Sean on the forehead, inhaling the smell of him. Doing his best Pacino impersonation, he said, "God must have been a fuckin' genius. The hair... They say the hair is everything, you know?"

Rachael scrunched up her face. "What are you doing,

what's that?"

"It's from the movie! When they're... never mind." He kissed her and said, "I'll be back tonight."

She gave him a pained look. "Okay, we'll just wait here for you to get back." She grabbed Sean's hand and waved it at Ashley. "Bye, Daddy, I'll miss you," she said in a baby voice, but the effect was disturbing. Even though he loved him with every ounce of his being, there was something about the way Sean acted and moved that reminded Ashley of some hyper-realistic doll.

## Rachael

As soon as Ashley left, Rachael felt alone. Even though Sean was right there, he never complained or made any noise unless she deliberately let him get hungry. Huarez had stressed the importance of breastfeeding, but she hated the feeling of him attached to her breast like some tiny alien sucking away her life.

*This isn't normal. What I'm feeling can't be right,* she often thought, but she felt too guilty to tell Ashley or anyone else.

# CHAPTER THIRTY

# The Hand

**Ashley**

While Ashley had not fully intended to go back to work, after his afternoon with Ma'at explaining the purpose of the crystal plates, he found more and more ways he could assist the DNC with its various projects. The day after Ma'at announced to Evermore that the plates he had ordered were ready, Evermore showed up to give himself a tour of the incubator room. He wandered around the huge and largely empty space for half an hour. He ran his hands along the crystal plates but asked no questions until they were back in Ma'at's office. Evermore spent another long silent moment staring at the crystal plate schematic on the OmniWatch whiteboard before bringing up a map of the DNC facility. "I want you to move that group of plates here," he said, circling a small unused sub-basement. He looked into Ma'at's face as if daring him to challenge his authority or ask a question.

Ma'at nodded and said, "That shouldn't be a problem. The twenty-seven hand plates are each small enough to fit into the cargo elevator."

Evermore had started to turn away when his gaze snapped back. A strange smile crossed his face, followed by a surge of excitement, but then both were stuffed away by a look of concern. Furrowing his brow, he casually closed the door to Ma'at's office, sealing the three of them inside. Before he said anything, his gaze wandered around the office and fell on a doodle drawn on a scrap of ePaper showing the eight cranial bones of the skull unfolded like a box and labeled 01.01 through 01.08. Evermore picked up the doodle and said, "This drawing is labeled with plate numbers." Ma'at seemed unsure whether to answer, and then he didn't seem to know the question, until Evermore asked it: "How do you know that the plates correspond to bones?"

Ashley and Ma'at stood there like a couple of boys who'd just broken something while playing baseball in the house, yet Evermore's intensity seemed to exist only to cover his joy. He gestured toward Ma'at's chair and sat in one of the two on the other side of the workstation. "Please, everyone sit. I'm sorry, I'm a little caught off guard: I took a gamble when I decided not to tell you the real purpose of the crystal plates. People are still growing accustomed to the idea of dark space, and there is a psychological pinch we experience when our reality is expanded. The fear is that if I expand it too fast, I'll have to answer to the inquisition. Once regulators and lawmakers get involved, scientific facts, which *should* be infallible, get muddied by mistrust and politics and money."

"You could have told us to keep it a secret," suggested Ma'at.

Evermore shook his head. "Secrets invite suspicion and mistrust."

"By your logic, then, shouldn't we mistrust you?" Ashley said.

"Why?" Evermore shrugged. "I merely kept you on a need-to-know basis. I have not obfuscated anything."

Ma'at frowned. "That's a fine line."

"But a line nonetheless. I would have told you had you asked."

Ma'at let out a frustrated sigh. One thing Ashley liked about working for Ma'at was that he never tried to hide what he was thinking or feeling. "Then why not tell us from the start?"

Ashley answered, "Because the next question is, 'Why bones?' and after that, 'Who's the pilot?' and 'Why him?'"

Evermore chuckled. "Quite right, my boy."

Ma'at gave Ashley a look he'd become familiar with, which asked: *How do you know so much?* Then he turned to Evermore, who was also looking at Ashley, with some combination of pride and relief. "Who's the pilot?" Ma'at asked.

Evermore said, "I want to answer that, but first we need to conduct one more experiment. I need those twenty-seven hand plates down in that sub-basement. Out of curiosity," Evermore scanned the ceiling as if contemplating the color choice, "how'd you find out?"

Ma'at redirected the question to Ashley, who said, "When Rachael walked through the gate, two things happened: everything that didn't contain living matter stayed behind, and, while she was in there, something was trying to dismantle her consciousness. It proved that only living matter can enter dark space, so obviously that's what the crystal plates are for, but I know you, and I know that nothing you create is ever just doing one thing unless it does it incredibly well."

"My boy, flattery is not an answer."

"I'm not your boy, and I wasn't finished." Ashley's tone was flat. "When I saw the schematic for the *Godspeed,* I noticed two things: 206 plates and no engines or thrusters. Engines made me think about the pilot; thinking about the pilot, I was faced with the problem that no thrusters means no way to steer, but of course the answer is simple when one remembers that Rachael didn't have thrusters either. I can only imagine what human-to-crystal interface you've come up with, but having 206 plates substantiated not only that it was the pilot, but that each plate must have the approximate numen constellation of a typical bone."

"Not approximate," Evermore corrected. "Every crystal genome and every plate location I've given you must be *exact*."

Cyrus Ma'at looked guilty and opened his hands as if to show he had nothing to hide. "Everything has been fabricated as specified by the build order you provided."

"Good," Evermore said, yet he seemed disappointed. "Additionally, there are six systems that need to be in place before launch. I was going to wait until after you saw the purpose of the hand plates in action, but you already know enough and may have other questions then. Now seems a better time."

Ma'at rose and stood poised beside the whiteboard; as Evermore spoke, Ma'at audio-captured the list. "One, the DNC will need to hire and train a crew of eight gate builders to build the exit gate in dark space at our destination. Two, they will need a way to leave the *Godspeed* without compromising the crystal shield. Three, they will need tools; contact Asbjorn Breivik about the specifications. Four, we need a way to control opening and closing the gates that won't be blocked by our own crystal armor. Five, if our gates inadvertently let ghosts out, we will need a way to get them back in."

"Like a proton pack!" Ashley said excitedly, drawing their attention, but when they expected him to say more, he had to admit, "That was a joke. It's a reference to an old movie about ghost... exterminators. Sorry, Doc."

"No no, you've heard me say it before, the imagination of science fiction is one of the things science often lacks. Tell us about this proton pack."

"Umm... It's like a big backpack with a hose coming out the back that shoots out a stream of protons. The theory being that ghost are made of electrons or like... charged anti-protons or something."

"A stream of protons?" Ma'at scoffed. "Is there a particle accelerator in the backpack?"

"It's not *in* the backpack; that's what the proton pack does," Ashley said, but Ma'at crossed his arms and clearly wasn't going to play along.

"So the protons and the anti-protons annihilate each other, killing the ghost?" Evermore asked.

"No, you can't kill a ghost — I can't believe I'm trying to describe this silly tech — the beam drains the ghost's energy so they can catch it in a ghost trap, which they empty into a big containment unit."

Evermore grasped his chin in a show of interest. "And how does this trap work?"

Ashley could tell Evermore was straining to come up with some cutting-edge piece of technology and tried not to smile as he said, "Lasers."

Evermore let out a barking laugh.

"This is ridiculous!" complained Ma'at. "Don't you feel the weight of the situation?"

"Of course I do, Dr. Ma'at. That's why I'm laughing; the only other option is to be crushed under the weight. But enough of that. Six, we need a method of allowing a separate landing craft to detach from the *Godspeed* and reattach before returning home."

Ma'at was editing the whiteboard capture and deleting the aside about the proton pack. Evermore added, "The DNC is not responsible for creating all of these systems, merely expanding the truths of the numinous cosmos. What I expect from you is to experiment with the limitations and possibilities of dark space and help predict the problems that will arise from these six systems, and solve them." Evermore looked down the list. "Excuse me, I may have misspoken; there is an item on that list which I expect the DNC to construct in-house."

Ma'at looked the list over once again, but Ashley beat him to the answer. "The proton pack."

Ma'at pinched the bridge of his nose and said, "Ashley, why don't you take that one on as a personal project."

"Really?!" Ashley grinned. "Am I really the Egon of this team?"

Ma'at shrugged. "I guess so."

A few days later, Ashley was getting ready to leave for work and rushing to make his flight. Sean was getting some tummy-time, and attempting to grab a yellow plastic block bigger than both his hands put together, but it was just outside the reach of his chubby little arms.

Rachael, pretending to be interested in baby Sean, said, "You seem nervous."

Ashley finished packing his lunch. "I am nervous," he confessed. "Today's the day Evermore and Samuel are going to find out that we rewrote the crystal plate build order."

She nudged the block within Sean's reach. "I think there's something wrong with Sean."

Ashley crossed the room and checked the temperature of Sean's forehead with the back of his hand.

"That's not what I'm not talking about. There's something wrong with his temperament."

He pinched the boy's fatty thighs and smiled. "He's perfect. He sleeps through the night, and he never cries." Sean's chubby cheeks parted as he smiled back. Or his mouth smiled back in an odd, fake, "smile for the camera" sort of way.

"Then there's something wrong with me," she said.

Ashley kissed her on the forehead. "Tell him nursery rhymes. I'm going to be late for my flight. I'll see you tonight!" He grabbed his lunch, and rushed out the door.

"I really could have used some encouragement back there," he whispered to her as he rushed up the escalator and exited the Yīgè Qī apartment complex. "This is a big day for me — for both of us, really."

He left one walkway and entered another that would load him onto the Skylon D4. But the more he thought

about it, Sean was one of the reasons he was so enthusiastic to return to work at the DNC. Over the weekend
Ashley had run out of things to do with the baby. They
were painfully short on toys, and Rachael said screens
weren't good for Sean's eyes or his brain. As a last resort
Ashley had forced himself to remember all the nursery
rhymes he could. Halfway through "Little Bo-Peep," he
had paused, trying to remember what rhymed with "tuffet," before he realized she hadn't ever sat on a tuffet. Not
in that rhyme at least. Maybe after Ms. Peep went home,
took a warm shower, and washed the smell of sheep out
of her hair, she would sit down on a on soft lambskin tuffet and give her aching feet a rest. But it was that Muffet
dame who did all the tuffet sitting. At least he had gotten
"Humpty-Dumpty" right. Not that "right" mattered. Sean
loved being talked to; he seemed content to watch their
faces no matter what they were saying. Ashley longed to
ask his mother what he had been like as a baby. *She wouldn't
remember even if she were alive.*

   The sub-basement ancillary room at the DNC was lit
with caged work lights that gave off a harsh white light.
The lower level had even lower ceilings, and though it was
wide and long, it felt as if it barely contained the small
group consisting of Ashley, Ma'at, Samuel, and Evermore, who stood around a rectangular puzzle of twenty-
seven slightly convex plates of PS crystal. Never before
would the thought have occurred to Ashley, but as he
looked at the plates he pictured Humpty's shell fragments
scattered across the floor. He wondered who among them
was the king and who were the king's horses and men. It
had been months since he had seen Samuel. *How long has
he been in a wheelchair attached to all those tubes and wires?* In
some ways, Samuel inhabited the chair like a throne and
Evermore stood behind him at his right hand. But unlike the skeletal-assist chair that Asbjorn used, Samuel's

was a geriatric go-kart. *He looks a bit like a rice cake,* Ashley thought. *Pale, frail, and helpless, yet crunchy and puffed with an air of self-importance.*

To Evermore, Ma'at said, "Here are the twenty-seven plates arranged and laid out exactly as you specified." There was poorly concealed annoyance in his tone. In the days leading up to this moment, Ashley had seen Ma'at pacing around his office, complaining that there were so many things to do, he shouldn't be bothered with bringing the plates all the way down to that remote room. "And why bother laying it out? Why couldn't he just look at the computer models?" For the most part, Ma'at was comfortable knowing there were things he wasn't supposed to know, and he trusted Evermore to keep him on a need-to-know basis. But every so often he would ask rhetorical questions while pacing to see if Ashley wanted to share anything with him. Ashley guessed Ma'at wanted to avoid pulling rank and demanding it from him.

Evermore nodded. "Thank you, Dr. Ma'at. I trust you brought numen detectors for each of us?"

Ma'at shook his head. "Manufacturing is still working out mass-production kinks." He gestured to the northern corners of the room, where two small numen detectors were mounted on tripods like tiny six-barreled turrets. He pulled out his Omni and said, "This model is wireless. I'm sending each of you the link so you can watch the feed from your Omnis."

"Are you ready, Samuel?" Evermore asked.

"Can I get some explanation of how these unconnected plates are going to help us determine the pilot?" Ma'at said.

"This *is* the explanation," Samuel said, closing his eyes.

Ashley's chest felt tight, and his mouth went dry. While Samuel seemed to be attempting to fall asleep, Evermore took out two pieces of heavy-stock ePaper, drag-and-drop installed a program from his Omni, and handed them to

Ma'at and Ashley. The paper turned black, and a rainbow of six parallel lines raced horizontally across the page, leaving a trail of sine and spike waves in their wake. "The top spike line is Samuel's pulse," Evermore said. "The next three sine waves correspond with Samuel's conscious neural activity." Even as he spoke they were calming and decreasing. "The bottom two lines correspond with his primary somatosensory cortex and his nociceptor, which reacts to potentially damaging stimulus and translates the sensation to pain." The pain lines were thrumming with constant noise where Ashley expected them to be flat. *If those are pain receptors...* Ashley realized with a wave of empathy how much pain Samuel dealt with day to day.

As Samuel's consciousness dropped, the muddy somatosensory waves spread out and relaxed. After a few minutes, every line but two, his heart and one of the consciousness lines, had gone flat. Ashley looked at his Omni for a numinous view of the room. In the center he could see the twenty-seven crystal plates holding a steady chlorophyll green. He could see each of the spectators' consciousness states pulsating with red and orange apprehension and dancing with yellow curiosity. Additionally, Ma'at's signature was laced with threads of malachite green that Ashley read as annoyance. Samuel's had started hot but was quickly cooling toward a steady frigid blue when it dimmed, and a grayish-white color began swirling around itself like a hurricane and condensing into a ball in his chest. One tendril of gray reached down his right arm and extended beyond his fingertips in five, then ten, then twenty, then twenty-seven tendrils, which reached out and into the twenty-seven crystal plates on the floor.

Keeping his voice low so as not to disturb Samuel, Evermore said, "As you can see from your Omnis, Samuel has projected his consciousness into these twenty-seven crystal plates, which are matched exactly to the numen constellation of his hand."

*Something went wrong,* Ashley thought, panicking. *Fuck! The build order was never on the Doc's workstation. That was all a misdirection; he was just keeping us busy and out of the way.*

"While this isn't much use in our world, in dark space, it will allow him to guide the ship at will, at speeds exceeding light by exponential factors of imagination. However, it leaves him extremely vulnerable..." Evermore bent and picked up the smallest plate from the wrist, a trapezoid the size of a medieval shield. Lifting with his knees, he raised it to his waist. "Watch his brain waves," he said, then dropped it suddenly. It hit the floor with a loud crack, and a spiderweb fracture blossomed across the face. The somatosensory lines didn't budge.

"Nothing happened," observed Ma'at.

Evermore was still staring at the flat line with disbelief. He pulled out his Omni, and Ashley looked back to his. Groping the floor like some blind octopus was one of the gray tendrils, still trying to find the plate Evermore had removed. Suddenly it gave up; the tendrils retreated from the crystals and unified into one ghostly vine extending from Samuel's chest. Slowly it pointed itself at Ma'at, then at Evermore, and finally at Ashley. It crept toward him like a phantom anaconda slithering through the air toward his bright red outline. Ashley looked up from his Omni and terrified himself at the nothing he saw. He backed away, refusing to look at his Omni, afraid of what he would see.

"Samuel," Evermore said in a loud commanding voice. "It's time to wake up."

Ashley saw that Ma'at's eyes were locked, unblinking, on his Omni screen. "It's coming for you," he said. Ashley hadn't stopped backing away.

"Samuel, wake up." Evermore said, louder.

Ashley felt the cold wall of the room pressing into his back. He took a step right, and the other wall touched his shoulder.

Evermore slapped Samuel's across the cheek. "Wake

up!"

Ma'at yelled, "Ashley look out!" as something cold slipped into his body like the pins-and-needles of a waking limb.

He passed out, but things didn't go black, they went somewhere else.

*In Ashley and Rachael's office suite the VR "window" showed a twilight gray terradome cooling down after a long day. The wall perpendicular was covered with an OmniWatch whiteboard crowded with two groups of crystal plates numbered 09.01 through 09.27, and 10.01 through 10.27.*

*Dropping a bag of Thai takeout on the workstation, Ashley kissed Rachael and asked, "How was your day?"*

*"Fine." She didn't look up.*

*"We got into a good flow last night; I think if we can keep working systematically like that we should be able to go a little faster."*

*Rachael's focus was on unpacking the takeout. "Eat," she said, pushing a wad of pad Thai chicken into her mouth.*

*As he was transferring the build order into a codified list of his numen markers from Ma'at's scan, she let out a whimper.*

*"What's wrong? Did they make it too spicy?"*

*She shook her head and said, "The contractions are getting worse."*

**\* \* \* \* \* \***

*Ashley found himself in a room back on Earth. It had to be on Earth, because it was populated by too many useless things. A fake fireplace, an upright electric heater, three antique wooden chairs, a big wooden desk covered with stacks of unsorted paper, and a huge bed where Evermore was sleeping. It was night, but the aged hotel towel he was using as a curtain didn't quite cover the whole window, and the orange glow of street lamps lit the room.*

*A gray-white ball of numen hovered above the bed, draping its tendrils over Evermore. They slithered through his covers and bit into him while he slept. He whispered in his sleep, "Evermore, wake up!"*

*Half asleep and half-awake, Evermore couldn't seem to decide if he'd really just heard something, until the voice, using his own throat, called out to him again, "Evermore!"*

*Ashley watched a chill run down the Doc's spine. He sat up and looked around the room, glancing through Ashley and through the gray ball of numen. Yet the voice called to him a third time, "Evermore, do not be afraid. I am what you would think of as a spirit."*

*In his normal voice, Evermore said to the emptiness of his room, "Is that supposed to calm me down?"*

*"I don't want you calm, I want you alert."*

*The Doc felt around the nightstand until his fingers found his bulky cellphone. He set it to record and said, "October 31$^{st}$, 2024. I may still be dreaming, but I have been awakened by a ghost."*

*The quieter voice from his own mouth said, "I am not a ghost. I am an energetic being that refuses to relinquish my consciousness. To do that is to die, and I was promised eternal life."*

*"Well, then, if you are not a ghost, who are you?"*

*"You may call me Samuel."*

*"What can I do for you, Samuel?"*

*"Within the space where I am confined I have noticed an energetic coalescence congruent with the birth of a human; however, this one has developed consciousness traits that shouldn't exist until later. Furthermore, the traits were written in a nonrandom perfection that you don't find in the natural world. I have identified you as its creator, in more ways than one. I would like to commission you to build me a body."*

*That's odd, Ashley thought, I don't remember that part. But I only listened to this section once. He had spent most of his time past the fifteen-minute mark, listening to the specifics of numen energetics.*

*"And what are you offering in return?" Evermore asked.*

*"Fame, money, power: take your pick."*

*Evermore paused and considered something. "Would an empty*

*body work? Perhaps a coma victim?"*

"*No, the container must match the contents.*"

"*Don't do it!*" *Ashley called, but his voice sounded muffled, like he was underwater. Samuel's amused laughter echoed off the walls of his mind, and Evermore didn't seem to notice Ashley standing there in his room.*

## \* \* \* \* \* \*

*Ma'at walked to the front of the numinous scanner and grabbed Ashley by the ankles, and pulled until his feet were on the floor. Though Ashley's thoughts bordered on delirium, he clearly saw Samuel standing in the corner of the room.*

"*Here,*" *Ma'at said, handing Ashley a half-full bottle of water. He made a weak attempt to grab it, but was unable, and Ma'at placed the bottle to Ashley's lips.*

*Once Ashley was able to drink for himself and sit up, Ma'at said, "Take your time."*

*Ma'at held his Omni up in front of Ashley's face and showed him the constellation his machine had produced.*

*Ashley clamped his mouth shut. In the past he had told Ma'at he was amazing, but it didn't change anything.*

*Ma'at kept up his end of the performance: He shrugged and said, "I have the feeling you and Dr. Dahlia already have a purpose in mind for this."*

*Ashley looked to where Samuel stood in the corner of Lab Eight. "You bet I do."*

"*You will regret this!*" *Samuel growled as Lab Eight faded to black, but Ashley and Samuel remained floating in nowhere.*

*Squaring off against each other Ashley smiled. "Remember this day? Just a few hours earlier you had me locked in the elevator. You wanted so badly to tell me your grand plan. What was it you said? 'The endgame is inevitable.'" Ashley laughed. "Did you forget that pawns don't attack head on?"*

*Ashley felt the numinous chords of Samuel's consciousness slipping as he released his grip, but Ashley wasn't finished; he laced*

*his fingers through Samuel's net and held on to fistfuls of strings.*
*"Let go," Samuel commanded.*

**\* \* \* \* \* \***

*Ashley found himself in a small hut where torchlight chased long shadows across the poorly crafted walls. Herbs tied into small bundles with ribbons of faded cloth hung from the rafters, and the acrid smoke of an extinguished cook fire, foul incense, and lamp oil hung in the air. Four people were crowded into the small space: two men who wore beards and rich flowing robes of fine fabric, a third whose robes hid the glint of gold beneath them, and a gray-haired woman. Tattered rags, which were likely as old as she, were wrapped around her waist, leaving her pale breasts exposed like tiny rough-barked oak burls. She chanted something in a language Ashley didn't understand, and the darkness on the far wall of the room stirred, parted, and allowed the cloudy gray figure of Samuel to emerge from the shadows. It didn't look anything like the twelve-year-old body he currently possessed, but it was undeniably him. The woman greeted him, but Samuel responded with angry words.*

*The old woman said something to the oldest and fairest of the men, and Samuel spit forth a long tirade that caused the old man to become increasingly distraught, and finally he threw himself prostrate on the ground.*

*"I don't understand," Ashley said.*

*"Saul wanted to know his fate. Would you like me to do the same for you?"*

*Ashely shook his head.*

*"Guess you're not as dumb as you look; he killed himself the next day."*

*Samuel tried to shake Ashley loose and, when his grip didn't weaken, pulled him into another memory that consisted of an eternal blackness. A color beyond the mere absence of light. It was the absence of thought, and it shriveled his heart and burned his eyes. Without thinking, Ashley knew it was dark space. Samuel might have wanted him to let go, but instead he clung tighter, like a child afraid of becoming lost in a crowd.*

Evermore yelled, "Wake up!" and Ashley startled so hard he might have jumped off his feet if not for the wall directly behind him.

Ma'at looked up from his Omni to Ashley with wide round eyes. "Could you feel him touch you?"

Realizing that no time had passed, Ashley gave a slight nod. The black ePaper in his hand showed Samuel's neural activity and heartbeat increasing, and the somatosensory lines of pain began to shiver. Samuel's heart rate was considerably higher than before as his eyes opened. He was glaring directly at Ashley. Samuel flexed and massaged his right hand as if it had fallen asleep. With wrath screaming from his eyes, he grabbed the joystick control and turned his chair around to face to Evermore. "You promised me that they couldn't figure out the numen markers. You said it was like building a puzzle in six dimensions." His voice turned raspy, and he started to cough uncontrollably. Either the frustration at his disease, the situation, or both made him whimper painfully through the barking coughs, and the somatosensory lines flared.

Ashley had never seen the Doc at such a loss for words. Evermore stammered, "I... I don't understand what happened."

*He must know.* Ashley thought, not even allowing the possibility that he had outfoxed Evermore.

"Well, that's a first," Samuel spat, his voice suddenly hoarse.

"The constellation is coherent and complete. I checked it myself. Especially these!" Evermore said.

Ashely found himself disgusted at how practiced Evermore was as lying.

"The problem is not that it is incomplete; the problem is this is not my consciousness," Samuel whispered in that same eerie voice Ashley had heard on the stolen .mp3.

Evermore stared at him dumbly. "Impossible. The DNC started building plates the day I sent out the build order. It took me years to map out and design your consciousness, and three long months to write the codes into the *Lepraria ptilisaccharon*'s DNA. There's no way to make a fake—"

"There is a way. And it isn't fake," Samuel interrupted, but he was shivering with so much anger he couldn't bring himself to say how Ashley had outsmarted them.

"If the constellation isn't fake and it isn't yours, then whose is it?"

Ashley stepped forward and said, "It's mine."

At the same time Samuel spun his chair and said, "It's *his*." He pointed at Ashley.

Evermore stared at Ashley with disbelief and a shade of sadness on his face. "You? How can that be? It should have taken years to complete. The process of sampling marrow from each of your bones is not only painful but time-consuming. You would have needed the *Godspeed* schematics long before you ever came to Mars and long before the plates would have had any significance to you. And besides all of that," he turned back to Samuel, "the boy is terrified of breaking the rules. If we use Occam's razor, it's more likely that *I* messed something up."

"I'm not a fucking *boy*, and these are my bones!" Ashley said, pointing to the plates. But Samuel howled over him.

"You gave me your word that he didn't know enough to figure this out." Samuel pushed the joystick forward and tried to ram Evermore with his chair.

The Doc dodged to the side and said, "He didn't!"

"Liar. Your word is useless. They built a consciousness constellation with the machine *he* made." He pointed at Ma'at, who seemed unsure of what to say or which side of the argument to weigh in on.

Evermore gave up trying to figure out how Ashley had

done it and said, "I've already invested too much to back out; if these really are your bones—"

"Like hell you can't back out!" Samuel said. "You promised me..." he didn't finish his own sentence.

Evermore opened his hands in a helpless gesture and shrugged. "What would you have me do? The *Godspeed* is ready for her armor. The plates are built and waiting to crystallize. If we stop construction to build more plates, E.I. will lose millions just keeping the dry dock station aloft, and then the launch date will be too close to when Earth and Mars are blind to each other behind the sun."

"Goddamnit," yelled Samuel. Ripping the IV out of his arm, he whipped Evermore across the face with the dripping tube. "We had a deal!"

Evermore held one hand to his face and kept the other outstretched to shield himself from future lashings. "The deal isn't off; it just needs altering due to uncontrollable circumstances. Teach Ashley your projection technique."

Ma'at spoke up, trying to deescalate the situation. "If projecting oneself into the crystal is what it takes to maneuver in dark space, then I'm already going to need your help training the gate construction crew."

Samuel threw the IV tube at Evermore as the Doc backed out of his range. "This was supposed to be my escape from this... this iron maiden of human frailty." He gestured at himself. "Now what do you have to offer me? What do I get if I train all your peons for you?"

There was an awkward silence as everyone waited for Evermore to say something. He picked up the IV tube from the floor and coiled it, carefully avoiding the needle. When he had finished, he looked at Dr. Ma'at and said, "I think that about covers today's demonstration. Do you have any questions?"

"Answer ME!" Samuel bellowed. Evermore continued to ignore him and kept his gaze firmly on Ma'at.

Cyrus Ma'at looked back and forth between Samuel

and Evermore and shook his head.

"Good." Evermore ran a hand through his salt and pepper hair. "Good." He turned and walked out. "Samuel, we will continue this conversation in private."

Samuel glared at Ashley one more time before wrapping his fist around the joystick and driving himself out.

# CHAPTER THIRTY-ONE

# The Company

### Ashley

When Ashley entered their studio apartment at Phobos, Sean was the first to greet him. The chubby baby was dressed in one of Ashley's favorite onesies upcycled from XL T-shirts. A friend of Julius's was a costume designer for the dancers at the entertainment complex, and he had gladly agreed to make Sean's clothes. This one was faded red and had an oversize *1* from some sports jersey sewn on the front.

Sean had been on a blanket on his stomach staring under the couch, but when Ashley opened the door he turned his head and went into Superman by lifting his arms and legs off the floor. As he focused his X-ray stare on his papa's face, Ashley saw recognition, but no emotion. Rachael, barely turning her head from her movie, said, "How'd it go?" Her voice also held no emotion.

*Breakfast Club,* Ashley thought. "This is a good scene coming up, I don't want to interrupt."

One of the characters was crushing cereal between two slices of white bread.

"Don't be passive aggressive."

The room resounded with the loud crunch of a cereal sandwich, and Sean's head swiveled around, trying to find the source of the noise. Ashley looked at the screen and paused the movie with a gesture. He picked up Sean and sat on the couch beside Rachael. Her eyes were glazed over, and she didn't take them from the TV.

"Remember how I told you that the Doc had us move the hand plates to a random sub-basement? Well, today we found out why. It was a demonstration of Samuel's powers and the reason for such a specific constellation. We guessed right, the *Godspeed* was designed for Samuel." He realized that Rachael wasn't really listening. She was staring at Sean, and she didn't look well. "Rachael, what's the matter?"

"I don't want to see him." She sounded close to tears.

Ashley lowered his voice and carefully said, "What do you mean? The Doc?"

"Sean. He creeps me out." She still wouldn't make eye contact. Her left tear duct overflowed, and a long drop ran down her cheek.

Ashley lowered his voice even more. "Yeah, like how his mouth smiles but his eyes don't."

Finally she looked at Ashley and relaxed slightly. "He's like some freaky animated doll that only responds to stimulus."

"Shhhh, keep your voice down."

"Are you afraid he'll find out?"

"No I... I don't want to hurt his feelings."

"He doesn't have any feelings. Like right now he should be starving, the last time he ate was five hours ago, but does he cry? No."

"Babe, that's not okay." Ashley got up and headed to the kitchen. Sean's eyes followed him like a haunted painting. "Is there milk?" he asked.

"Are you kidding? I've been producing like a prize Jersey."

Sure enough, there were many small plastic bottles of milk in the fridge, labeled and lined up like lab samples just waiting for a nuke and a nipple. He grabbed one, put it in the microwave and said, "Ninety-seven degrees."

When he returned to the couch, he plopped Sean onto his lap and stuck the bottle in his mouth. Sean sucked away hungrily. "Rae, I love you. I can only imagine that you've been keeping this to yourself because you were afraid of what I'd say. I'm on your side: Sean is different. Super different, but we can't just push him away. This thing you're feeling is bigger than you. Hell, it's bigger than both of us; we going to need some help on this one."

Finally she turned her tearstained cheeks to face him. "You keep saying 'we,' but I don't see you afraid to touch or even look at him."

"I'm not afraid of those things; I'm being crushed under the guilt of leaving you alone each day even though I know you hate it, and of putting you in this position."

Rachael shook her head, "You didn't make me do this. You helped me do it, and in many ways I still think it was the right choice: There are so many young girls watching me. I want to show them that having a family is not the end of your career. But I—" her words tripped, and she swallowed hard. "I may have been able to physically do both, but I can't do it emotionally. I can't even bring myself to fake it."

"Certainly not alone. Can I find us a therapist and get us some help?"

"Yeah."

Sean had drained the bottle and was gnawing on the silicone nipple. Rae shivered and looked away. Ashley stood and took Sean with him. As he picked up her Omni, he said, "I'll work from home tomorrow. You should go down to Nili Terradome and—" The Omni's screen awakened, showing her most recent conversation, a call with Evermore that had lasted just over two hours. The day before they had spoken for almost three, and the day before— He realized he never finished his sentence. "Heh, I suck at multitasking. You should have a day out at the terradome." *I can't get a twenty-minute conversation out of you, but you're spending how many hours with Evermore? Maybe you're worn out from talking to* him *all day?*

Ashley switched screens and searched for a list of therapists covered under their work insurance.

## Rachael

Their cognitive behavioral therapist called it postpartum depression. Telling the therapist the things she was afraid to tell Ashley helped alleviate some of her guilt and allowed her to sleep better at night, but the antidepressants he gave her made her nauseous, and after dealing with the discomfort for three weeks she still hated Sean. Ashley had been working from home and hanging out with Sean three days a week, but it didn't make her stop resenting Ashley on the days he left. The therapist also suggested she spend time with friends and family away from the baby, so on the days Ashley worked from home, Rachael flew down to the terradome. She worked in Evermore's office some of the time, but he only had an hour or two of attention for her. The rest of the time she worked as a private contractor at Kander and Jansen. But that, too, ended before she was ready to let it go. One day Doctor James Jansen offered her twenty million dollars to help them develop their own Department of Numen Studies. Twenty million was enough to pay off her school debt, return to Earth, buy a house, and still have fifteen million left. She could go on a cross-country trip. She could see Mount Whitney for real.

Or she could honor her contract with E.I. and become the first person to set foot on Second Earth, or whatever Evermore decided to call it.

She hadn't even finished shaking her head when Jansen said, "Fifty."

The number knocked the wind out of her. These super-science corporations were used to dealing with trillions, but even ten million was more than she ever thought she'd see in one place. *That's a lot, but no one will remember the woman who made fifty million in one day.* She shook her head.

Jansen scoffed, "Jesus, what's Evermore paying you?"

"It's not about the money," she said.

"What then, honor?" He seemed about to laugh when Rachael handed him her K&J ID badge. Jansen continued, "Evermore doesn't understand honor; he'll stab you in the back the first chance he gets. He has no morals! You should know, you were at the Synthetic Man Trial." But she made him say it to her back as she walked away, and she never turned back around.

## Ashley

Evermore had assured Ashley that Samuel had cooled off and was not a threat. As Ashley walked into the new Lab Seven at the DNC, to his surprise Samuel wasn't wearing the same dour look he had grown so used to; beneath the plastic tubes, he looked pleased to see him.

"Your first lesson," Samuel began without any word of greeting, "is to experience dark space."

"It's my understanding that I won't survive that without some tether to reality."

"That's true. All of you will be stripped away until I pull you out." When Ashley looked confused, Samuel continued, "We'll only be opening one gate, and I'm going to dunk you in."

"So my life will literally be in your hands?"

"Do you have a problem with that?"

"Only that you seem super weak, not to mention the last time we spoke you told me I'd regret changing the build order."

"So you will, and this will be your first lesson in understanding that."

The lesson hadn't been instructional so much as experiential, and at its end Ashley understood that Samuel hadn't been pleased to see him but had been looking forward to torturing him. Plunging him into dark space again and again. Nothing was so bad as that initial dunk. The dark blew through him like a cold wind. It sank its teeth into his bones and devoured him until only one speck of identity was left: *My father abandoned me*. Even when the "me" had forgotten its name and the concept of "father" had lost all meaning beyond the blurry throb of an ancient heartbreak. But when that heartbreak was all that was left, it smoldered and burned, coalescing into a white-hot point of light that burned until Samuel backed up his chair and pulled him out.

The temperature of the lab was cold on his bare skin, and though he was furious at Samuel for keeping him in dark space gasping for breath for so long, he wouldn't let go of his hand. The connection to another living person was the most important thing at the moment, and letting go was even more frightening than the thought of going back in.

That night he and Rachael lay in the darkness of their bedroom. She kept running her hands along his hairless body and scalp and giggling about how smooth he was. It was oddly emasculating. He'd never considered his hair to be part of his gender identity, but it was. Ashley reached out for her beneath the sheets. Beneath the bandages covering his exposed nail beds, his fingertips throbbed, but he ignored them and found her hand. Their fingers laced together, and he said, "After the initial shock and fear of utter nothingness, I felt my identity being stripped off of me in layers. I—" He swallowed back tears. "I feel so ashamed: the memories of you and Sean were some of the first to go."

Rachael had never talked about her experience in dark space. Ashley felt as if she was waiting until he figured out the right question to ask. But he never did, because it wasn't a question she was waiting to hear.

The sheets whispered as she turned toward him and said, "In the dark I realized that I've always carried something hollow inside me: a dread disguised as self-hatred, or doubt, or deep boredom. Dark space taught me... or reminded me that the hollow is the void that awaits us after life. For a long time I carried the hollow around as a reminder that life is meaningless. It made me even more desperate to leave my mark on the world and do something really meaningful so I won't be entirely forgotten."

Ashley knew exactly what she was talking about, but his hollow was the faceless memory of his father. *I don't ever want to go back in there. I've never been so afraid of dying. I don't have a choice. I can't let Rachael down, and right now I'm the only one who can give her her dream.*

After a long silence Rachael said, "I don't know, maybe that doesn't make sense."

Ashley pulled her close to him. "Yes it does. The only thing I don't understand is why you'd want to keep that to yourself?"

She thought for a moment. "I guess I didn't want to infect you with my existential nihilism."

"It's too late for that now. Luckily we have Sean, and we have each other. If there's *any* real purpose to life it's to do our best loving each other and raising Sean in this crazy new interstellar world."

When she started to cry, Ashley assumed it was because she had been touched by his words, but as he lay there trying to ignore the still-foreign sounds of the busy centrifuge station and relax into sleep, he remembered that Rachael didn't feel the same way about Sean and the guilt tore her apart.

Rachael wasn't going to get over her depression any time soon. When Ashley left her alone with Sean she would become angry and distant for an entire day after his return, and just as they got back to their mediocre baseline it would be time for him to return to the DNC. He loved helping Ma'at and the team of designers troubleshoot issues with the dark-space detachment seals, or (even though the man made his skin crawl) meeting with Samuel and the gate construction crew for astral projection training. But Ashley began questioning if it was worth leaving when it meant that for the next thirty-two to forty-eight hours Rachael would be unbearable. Lost in his thoughts, he entered the Department of Numinous Cosmology and headed to his workstation. On the way he walked past Dr. Ma'at without even noticing him.

"Ashley?"

Ashley startled, turned around, and said, "What's up, Doc?"

"Come step into my office for a moment."

As Ashley walked inside, Ma'at closed the door but said nothing. Holding the silence, Ashley watched him move a stack of ePapers from one place to another nervously, but just when he seemed about to speak he stopped.

"Is something wrong?" Ashley asked.

"Not... really, it can wait. What's going on with you?"

Ashley squirmed in his seat uncomfortably. "Nothing. It's personal. I'll focus up, I promise."

Ma'at sat on the corner of his desk so that he was closer to Ashley. "I understand if you don't want to tell me, but you look like someone stole your milk money."

Ashley scowled. "Are *you* going to start calling me 'boy' now?"

"Only if you keep calling me 'Doc.'" He smiled. "I'm sorry. I wasn't trying to minimize your problems, only attempting to keep it light. Obviously it's not light. I want you to know you can tell me everything in your heart if it'll help you relax and focus on the task at hand."

Ashley sighed. "Rachael and I aren't doing so well. I imagined the things that would stress our relationship would be fights about who would change the diapers, but Sean's—" *abnormal... strange* "—behavior is—" *robotic... freaky* "—different. I haven't spent much time around babies, but I get the feeling that Sean isn't normal. On top of that, Rachael has — please don't tell anyone this — Rachael has been dealing with postpartum depression, which is terrible for her... but also terrible for me because I'm the one she takes it out on. She resents me for coming here, and I don't know if it's worse being the butt of that, or giving it up and resenting her."

Ma'at frowned empathetically. "It sounds like you are between the plier's jaws."

"Things are really tense right now, and I'm afraid she'll—" *go back to using stims,* he thought, but he couldn't tell Ma'at that, so he said, "—leave me."

Cyrus Ma'at held the silence in case there was anything else Ashley had to say. When Ashley shrugged awkwardly, he said, "I'm simply trying to be an ear for you. But perhaps I can offer a distraction: Aziza has been having... I don't want to say similar, but *parallel* resentment issues around my small group of work friends; she hasn't made any friends since she's been up here. Maybe it would benefit both women if we have the three of you over for dinner."

Ashley was considering the logistics of flying Sean down in the space plane when Ma'at's eyes widened. "Oh my gosh, she could make *fatta*."

"What's that?"

"It's a Nubian dish traditionally made in celebration of a woman's first child. Imagine big hunks of stewed beef and garlic fried in ghee over fry-bread and rice. It's quite rich, so Aziza never makes it for me. But you have just had your first child, so she'll made *fatta* for you, and *konafah* for desert."

Ashley's mouth was watering just thinking about a dinner of something other than takeout. "That sounds great, but if you wouldn't mind coming up to our place? The G-force of re-entry is probably too intense for Sean."

"I don't know why that wouldn't work." Ma'at stood and walked behind his desk to make the call. As it rang, he put a finger to his lips.

Aziza answered: "Cy? Is everything alright?"

"Everything is fine, my moon, I was just thinking that we haven't had Ashley and Rachael over for dinner yet, and—"

"—and you want *fatta*. Do you have any idea how expensive real red meat is?"

Cyrus smiled at her lovingly. "I do, and your husband is a big shot who can afford it. This is their firstborn! Let's celebrate."

"Of course we should celebrate. I'll call Rachael to invite her. Would she want to cook with me?"

Rachael had started teaching herself how to cook a few months ago and was uncharacteristically shy about it. Ashley quickly shook his head, and Ma'at said, "I don't think she would, and the baby is still too small to make the flight back to Nili Terradome."

There was some trepidation, but Aziza said, "Okay... I'll see which nights they're available."

"Thank you for being flexible, my love; I've got to get back to work."

"In a while, my afternoon sun."

Ma'at hung up. "Now, Ashley, since you have self-proclaimed to be 'good at puzzles,' I wanted to pick your brain about the dark-space detachment seals." He pulled up a picture of the E.I.S.S. *Godspeed* and the eight construction crew workers.

"We keep running into this problem of how to get them outside the ship into dark space without breaking the crystal plate. Then I realized that they don't even need to be *in* their suits. If these pilots are projecting their spirits, couldn't the suits be attached by break-away connectors like we designed for the gate pieces?"

"Down the road I think it's a good idea," Ashley said, "but the eight engineers and I seem to be progressing much slower than Samuel was anticipating. The best I've been able to achieve is falling asleep in the sensory deprivation chamber and waking up in the crystal. It's a really bizarre sensation: possessing the crystal feels nothing like being in your own skin. There's a dull coldness to it.

"Anyway, all of us need the crystal plate to be directly on top of the chamber for initial possession, and even when Samuel moves the crystal away from our bodies, it forces our consciousness to retreat back to warm flesh. That's the worst. You ever dream you're falling and startle awake? That's what it feels like."

"Alright, back to the design board. Thanks, Ashley."

"Thank you, Dr. Ma'at."

## Rachael

A week later a knock sounded on the door of their apartment, and when Rachael opened it she was greeted by Aziza's deep brown eyes and full lips pronouncing her heart-shaped face, framed by her dark hair that seemed so long and silky in contrast with Rachael's inch of curly fuzz. Rachael stuck out her hand, which Aziza deflected with her hip as she leaned in for a long hug. She then walked past Rachael and introduced herself to Sean, who had been fumbling with the plastic button of the restraining belt that held him in his stroller.

"Hello, Sean," she said, smiling wide, but when he didn't look up, she seemed taken aback, as if she'd taken it personally.

Rachael explained, "He tends to get really focused on one thing. I guess I'm the same way."

"Can I hold him?" Aziza asked excitedly.

Rachael said, "Sure," but made no move to give him to her. "I'll grab your bags. Jesus, what's in here? Is this your whole kitchen?"

"I wasn't sure what you'd have and didn't want to come unprepared."

Aziza made big faces at Sean. Rachael set the bag of food beside the small kitchen counter. "You seem like you've spent time around kids."

Aziza nodded without taking her eyes off Sean. "Back in London I worked for the National Autistic Society as a volunteer coordinator. Part of the job was observing the volunteers and the clients and making sure they were a good match."

Barely able to contain her excitement, Rachael said, "I've often thought Sean might be autistic; what do you think?"

Aziza looked uncomfortable. Her mouth moved slightly as she considered exactly what to say.

"Please," Rachael said, looking as if she might cry depending on the answer. "They diagnosed me with postpartum depression — any concerns I've had about Sean have been dismissed without consideration. But you've worked with those children, you probably know the signs better than I do."

Aziza bounced tiny Sean in her arms and looked into his face. When he saw her, Sean coincidentally made the same expression, scowling back at her and seeming to inspect her. Aziza smiled at Sean, and he tried to smile back. "He's still too young for many of the signs to present," she said, "but he has good eye contact." She bounced him again and in a baby voice said, "You look just perfect to me."

## Ashley

Ma'at joined Ashley on the space plane flight to Phobos. At that time of day the corridors of the Yīgè Qī apartment complex were filled with the amazing smells of each family cooking their traditional food, but Ashley and Ma'at both could easily pick out Aziza's cooking before they'd even reached the small suite.

Aziza approached both men carrying Sean on her hip and greeted them. Ashley had met her once before when Ma'at had taken her on a tour of the DNC, but tonight she seemed more lovely than Ashley remembered, and seeing Cyrus and Aziza together, a couple in their forties, underlined Ashley and Rachael's youth and inexperience.

Rachael also greeted Ma'at and kissed Ashley as he entered.

"How's it going?" he asked.

"Great." She smiled, and to his relief it seemed genuine.

"God, it smells so good in here!" Ashley said.

"There are some appetizers in the living room."

The quintet moved deeper into the apartment and surrounded a plate of crisped pita triangles and homemade spinach hummus. Ashley gratefully selected a pita chip, dipped, and popped it in his mouth.

Sean's eyes drifted to Aziza's hair and found her earrings. Clumsily he swung his whole body at her, flinging his arm out as if casting a fishing line, which tangled in the weeds of her dark-brown hair.

*Oh my God, what if Aziza would be willing to babysit Sean during the day?* Ashley thought as he moved to Rachael and wrapped himself around her from the back. She didn't shrink away from him, and for a moment the two of them watched Aziza patiently, lovingly untangle Sean's hand to the sound of snapping hairs and Cyrus crunching pita chips.

"How old are your kids?" Ashley asked.

Rachael elbowed him not so subtly.

Ma'at looked uncomfortable, and with his mouth full, he glanced at Aziza before quickly swallowing and answered, "Oh, we don't have kids. We chose our careers over children."

*How were we supposed to...* Ashley started to tell Rachael in his mind, but then he realized that she knew. He watched Aziza's shoulders sink as she sighed and said, "Actually, we *can't* have kids." The look she gave them seemed to say: *We've tried and failed enough to know that we'll never have one of our own.* She looked back to Sean.

Ma'at popped the cork on the bottle he'd purchased from the duty-free store on Phobos. "Would either or both of you like a glass of wine? It's a California cab-sauv to prepare your tongues and bellies for the *fatta*."

Rachael answered for them both. "We'd love some."

Aziza said, "Can you tell he's excited? This is Cy's favorite meal."

A small timer sounded, and Aziza immediately jumped into action. "The *fatta*'s done. Here," she said, passing Sean off to Rachael, who hastily set him back in the stroller.

Cyrus headed into the kitchen as if to help but began searching for wine glasses.

"It's a celebration!" he said, pouring the dark-red wine. After passing around the glasses and raising his own over his head he made a toast: "To the miracle of life!"

"...and death," Rachael added.

The glasses still hung in the air as she tried to clarify. "I mean, to both. Like, the regenerating cycle of life and death."

"We—" Aziza began, but Cyrus cut her off.

"It's fine," he told her. "We know what it means to us." He raised his glass. "To the miracle of life and death."

They all took a sip, but Rachael drained her glass.

Aziza's cooking was amazing. Ashley hadn't eaten beef in over two years, and the *fatta* was buttery, garlicky, and so tender it melted in their mouths.

## Rachael

Ashley ate a little too much, and Rachael drank a little too much, and after Cyrus and Aziza left, Rachael said, "I really like them."

"I know; you told them the Chemo Guy story."

A few days after Rachael had lost her hair in dark space, a man, not a PhD or ScD, just some guy on the street of Nili Terradome, had stopped and informed her that chemotherapy was poisoning her child and that she was a murderer. Rachael tried to tell him that she didn't have cancer, but he called her a liar.

Rachael smiled. "I was pretty surprised to hear myself tell that one, but it was nice to get to know Cyrus in a more casual setting."

"I really feel like we got over the hump of getting to know them pretty fast."

They settled onto the couch where Sean slept.

"The wine helped." She shook her head in disbelief. *Maybe Sean is normal. and there is something wrong with me?* She started to cry, but before he could ask why she said, "Aziza is *so* good with Sean."

Ashley said, "There's nothing wrong with you. We're good parents and the transition we're going through is really fucking stressful. Give it some time."

"By 'we' you mean 'me.' From what I've seen you're calm and normal; where's the evidence that you're under stress?"

Ashley rubbed his fuzzy scalp and looked ashamed. "The evidence is broken, battered, and left to die some-place far away. My father left when I was Sean's age. I don't remember him; I've never seen a picture of his face. The point is, he left me nothing. I have *nothing* and no one to show me how the fuck to even *be* a father. I don't know how to do it. What I do have is the feeling that Sean is a different creature. A being so foreign to me that, although I love him, I can't honestly conjure any feeling of connection with him. That's the evidence. But if that's true than I'm as big a fucking dirtbag as my deadbeat dad." Ashley made his face seem angry, but under the thin mask was a deep sadness. "I *can't* let that be true, so every time I have the thought *Sean is odd,* I take that thought, break its knees, drive it out to the country, and abandon it. I throw it in a hole, leave it to die, and force myself to love him even harder. You don't see it because I'm trying to kill that part of myself. Until it dies, I'm a fucking terrible father like my father before me."

His mask cracked, and they were both crying. They reached out for each other across Sean sleeping on the couch between them.

Rachael said, "For all the time that you've been holding on to that, I've felt alone. I just need to feel like I'm not by myself in this."

"I don't want to be alone in this either, but something kept telling me you'd leave if I didn't man up."

"Is being a hard shell of self-inflected violence your definition of a man?"

"I wouldn't put it like that. A man is someone who's got it all under control."

"Babe, not even your hero Evermore has it all under control."

Some part of him was clearly still angry at Evermore. She saw him pull away from her just a bit. He was still holding something back. "I miss being close to you."

Ashley ran his fingers through her short hair, massaging her scalp. He inhaled a deep breath through his nose and looked down at Sean. "Damn it, but doesn't this little alien smell amazing?"

# CHAPTER THIRTY-TWO

# Into the Darkness

**Ashley**

Ashley kissed Sean on the head and inhaled the sweet smell of him. Someday that smell would fade. It was hard to imagine that he would ever be anything other than baby Sean. That he would be a lanky teen taller than them both, reeking of aerosol deodorant and sweaty shoes. Ashley closed his eyes and took another breath; this time he imagined the alien constellations from a vantage point on the planet in Virgo. He had connected the unnumbered stars himself and named each of those simple shapes. He visited this mental palace so often that he had come to know these constellations better than those of Earth, where he had only ever known Orion and the Big Dipper. This alien chart of stars was the intention coordinates that would propel the *Godspeed* to their destination.

"Are you alright?" Rachael asked.

Ashley opened his eyes. They were in the tight windowless room of a space elevator, which had been outfitted with rows of seats to lift the crew to the DuPont dry dock station. It was strange to think that this was the same route each piece of the E.I.S.S. *Godspeed* had taken. In many ways, he was the final piece that would complete the six-month construction project.

Ashley nodded and said, "Yeah, just a little nervous," hoping the ambient noise of the elevator would mask his voice from the rest of the crew.

Rachael sighed. "Yeah, me too. I'm nervous about entering dark space again. But it won't be like our first time. We'll be inside the ship, not naked and exposed."

He met her eyes and glanced down at Sean. "We're not bad parents for bringing Sean, are we?"

"You're still thinking about what that reporter said, huh? He didn't know what he was talking about. The *Godspeed* is perfectly safe; we know the gates work; there aren't any unsafe speeds or hazardous materials on board. The worst thing that can happen is that we can't build the second gate and we need to turn around. The most dangerous part of the mission is landing on the planet, and he'll be staying behind with Aziza."

"I know and agree," Ashley sighed. "And Evermore's right: bringing Sean helps us communicate how safe this new form of travel is. But I hate the thought that someone else may be judging how good a parent I am."

"Have you never worried about what people thought of you before? That must be nice."

Asbjorn met them aboard the DuPont dry dock station and took the crew on a short tour of the factory, which ended at a viewing window, where they met up with Evermore. He greeted each of them briefly before directing their attention out the window toward the E.I.S.S. *Godspeed*, carefully held in the delicate jaws of the dry dock station and surrounded by catwalks crowded with robotic arms programmed for every task imaginable. Rachael and Ashley had seen each part individually as it was moved to the base of the space elevator ribbon. Part one was visited by the governor of Mars, part four by envoys from thirteen countries, each carrying a live connection to their queen, prime minister, or president. Part five was the backdrop for a live-stream interview with the Mother of Dark Space herself. But now it was complete, and they were seeing the first ever transgalactic vessel in human history.

The *Godspeed* looked like the cocoon of some gigantic butterfly, with its long cylindrical shape and the way the greenish plates of crystal armor interlocked so perfectly. Ashley thought back to that first tiny crystal they had built in the lab and marveled that they had come so far in such a short amount of time.

"It looks fast, and safe," Aziza said, but her tone revealed that she had been harboring doubt.

Ma'at said, "It's so beautiful the way the plates all came together."

Aziza squeezed him and said, "You did such a great job, Cy!"

After giving them a long moment, Evermore addressed the crew and said, "Are you ready for the real tour?"

The boarding tube leading out into the center of the *Godspeed* opened with a *wisp* as the pressure equalized. Asbjorn wheeled himself to the edge and said, "Ladies and Gentlemen, welcome to the E.I.S.S. *Godspeed*. Unfortunately, I won't be able to join you, as I am needed out here."

The tube led through a heavy door that was not only airtight and numen-proof, but redundant, so that in the event that the exterior armor was compromised the passengers within would still be safe within a secondary bubble of crystal armor. The boarding tube led directly into the passenger cabin. The ceilings and floors were covered in long metallic blue and silver handrails, which were entirely unnecessary while they were still attached to the dry dock station and under the false gravity of its centrifugal force. Ninety-six blue and silver seats, identical to the ones on the Skylon space plane, were arranged in a circle around dark screens mounted to a wide cylinder that ran floor to ceiling. A door on the side led into the cylinder and connected the passenger cabin to the arterial passageway and the rest of the ship. Evermore ran his hands along the seats and seemed as excited as Ashley had ever seen him. As the crew poured into the space, Rachael carried Sean to the special seat made just for him to make sure he still fit. He did.

Aziza sat herself beside him and said to Rachael, "I know you're needed in other parts of the ship where I'm not allowed. I'm happy to stay here with Sean."

Ashley and Rachael thanked her with such profuse gratitude that it made her uncomfortable. *We must seem so desperate with how much we appreciate her, but she actually seems to like being with him. He makes her happy.*

For the next five hours the crew ran tests of the various systems. Rachael assisted Ma'at in a mock launch of a construction suit, Ashley inhabited the *Godspeed*'s crystal shell for the first time, and Evermore ran communications tests between the various parts of the ship and between the *Godspeed* and Asbjorn at the temporary mission command on the dry dock station. Every check and test came up green, and launch was confirmed for the following day.

### Rachael

The number fifty-two had been thrown around a lot. "Fifty-two, there will be fifty-two passengers on the maiden voyage of the E.I.S.S. *Godspeed*." Evermore had said that he could have filled it to capacity had they departed from Earth. The cost of living was simply too high in Nili Terradome, and unless you arrived with a half million US to spare, no one was going to tap into their personal ticket-back-to-Earth funds.

Rachael, Sean, and Ashley sat in the front row of seats that faced the pillar in the center of the room. Though Ashley's place was in the pilot's chamber, he sat beside Rachael, holding her hand so tight it almost hurt. He clearly wanted to soak up every moment of her attention, but she was only giving him half of it; the other half watched the famed fifty-two pour into the passenger cabin, curious to see who thought it was worth the ticket price. The majority of passengers had ID badges from Evermore Industries and the Department of Numinous Cosmology; they, along with their spouses, had been sold tickets at a huge discount. There was a smattering of press badges from each of the news syndicates. Then there were a few Mars-based envoys from the thirteen nations, whom she recognized from the press conference in front of the *Godspeed*'s fourth piece. The final group was a handful of eccentric millionaires who had bought their way on board. Among them, Rachael noticed a man she recognized. He caught her watching him and deviated from his route.

"Rae Dahlia," he said, reaching out and shaking her hand. "And you must be Ashley Rephaireal, and baby Sean." He stuck his hand toward Ashley, who did his best to pretend to be friendly, though he was clearly upset at the intrusion.

"Ashley, this is Valenci Meritani; I sat beside him once on a flight from Phobos to Nili Terradome."

"I can see you're having a moment here, and I'm sorry for ruining it. I just wanted to congratulate you," he turned to Sean, "for making such a beautiful boy."

Now it was her turn to fake affection. *I thought he was going to say "creating the gate."* "Thank you." She smiled. As Valenci returned to his seat, Aziza, who must have witnessed the whole thing, made a compassionate face at her from across the aisle.

Rachael listened to what quiet conversations she could hear. There was a nervous excitement among the passengers, but no one seemed adequately terrified in anticipation of dark space. Maybe it was the inherent faith in technology. Each of these people had spent months trusting science on the shuttle to Mars, and in many ways the room was designed to feel like just another airplane cabin. *Why would they be scared? No one has prepared them.* Evermore had had her speak at length about dark space, but he hadn't allowed her to share her subjective or emotional findings. *It will feel different in the* Godspeed, *and if it doesn't, will anyone ever want to take a second trip?*

As the passengers finished settling into their seats, one of the doors on the pillar slid open, and Evermore stepped out. He walked to the front of the cabin and addressed the seated passengers. "I would humbly like to welcome everyone to the maiden voyage of the E.I.S.S. *Godspeed*. Over the last year you've all watched each piece of this very ship being lifted up through the thin Martian atmosphere and assembled. The news stations said that crystal plate 14.26 was the final piece to be lifted, but they were wrong. *You* are the final piece. I hope your trip to the dry dock station was comfortable. I'd like to thank you all personally, but we're T minus five minutes to departure, so this will be regrettably brief. First, I'd like to acknowledge Asbjorn Breivik for designing this beautiful ship. The zero-G construction crew who built our entrance gate and who will build our exit." They raised their hands and were met a light applause. Evermore continued, "Next I'd like to thank our pilot and navigator, Ashley Rephaireal." Ashley stood and waved awkwardly. Evermore had insisted he wear the uniform, but Ashley had told Rachael that it made him feel like he was playing dress-up. She disagreed. He looked handsome, and the brass buttons and silver wings on navy blue commanded respect, and the applause recognized it.

Evermore said, "Finally, I'd like to thank someone who told me it was impossible to go faster than light, and who, might I add, was right." He grinned at Rachael. "Yet Dr. Dahlia returned to me with a solution so outside the box that quantum physics is still scrambling to catch up.

Everyone please put your hands together for Dr. Rachael Dahlia, the Mother of Dark Space."

The applause was loud. Rachael reached up and waved, but when it didn't die down, Evermore motioned for her to stand. *This is ridiculous.* When she unclipped her seatbelt and stood, the applause grew louder. She could see genuine awe on people's faces.

*I didn't do anything,* she wanted to tell them. *Evermore set it all up; all I did was solve the puzzles he put in front of me.* The people cheered until her ears were ringing and Sean began to wail at the noise. The applause faded into tinkling laughter. In a matter of seconds Rachael went from a celebrity to that terrible mother with the crying baby on the plane. *Please don't see me as a mother. Please.* She made quiet shushing sounds at Sean, but he barely quieted. Ashley removed his silver E.I. pilot's badge and handed it to Sean. The boy was instantly transfixed and clumsily reached out for the shiny wings.

"Ashley, he could choke on that," Rachael said quietly.

"Well, that would stop his crying, too," he joked. "I don't think he'll put it in his mouth. His eyes are enjoying it too much." As they watched, Sean moved the silvery wings back and forth in a repetitive, hypnotic motion.

Evermore approached them and to Ashley quietly said, "It's time."

Ashley bent over Sean and kissed him on the forehead, though he never looked up from the shiny wings. "I love you both so much," he said, kissing Rachael, before following Evermore out of the room.

A few minutes later the screens on the seat backs in front of each of their faces lit up, showing an external view of the *Godspeed* from the dry dock station from a stable point a quarter mile off. Sunlight shimmered off the space elevator tether as it stretched down to the surface of Mars like a spiderweb. Another moment passed, and Evermore's voice spoke over the intercom. "Launch in T minus ten... nine... eight..."

Every pair of eyes was glued to its personal screen. The *Godspeed* suddenly detached and was thrown from the station by the centrifugal force. A sensation like an elevator drop caused everyone to gasp and clutch their armrests as their hearts jumped with momentary panic. The silver pilot's wings were thrown up and out of Sean's grip. Rachael's heart leapt into her chest with everyone else's, but stayed there as the gate came into view.

"Seven... six... five..."

Around the radius of the gate were ion thrusters and proximity sensors. As the rocket-less *Godspeed* fell away from Mars and the dry dock station, the gate positioned itself to catch her.

"Three... two... one..." There was no visual clue as to whether or not the gate was functioning. In the video it simply appeared as a large ring of metal, but as the passengers watched on their monitors as the *Godspeed* drifted into the ring, the front of the ship silently slipped into nothingness. Rachael held her breath as the screen went black and a barely perceptible shadow fell across them.

## Ashley

In the moments after Ashley kissed his family goodbye, he hurried along the sleek white poly-carbon corridors of the *Godspeed* to a hatch off the main corridor that lead to a private locker room outside the pilot's chamber. He stripped down to the layer of Second Skin. The electromyographic nano-weave bodysuit made him feel even more naked than his bare skin and even more uncomfortable than the dress-up costume that was his pilot's uniform. Beside the pilot's chamber was a nine-number touch pad, into which he typed an eight-digit code. The windowless door clicked and slid aside. Unlike the white corridors and rooms of the *Godspeed*, the pilot's chamber was painted a matte black that seemed to drink light and piss darkness. From the ceiling hung a vacuum chair barely wider than two palms, which conformed to the shape of his spine. Ashley approached it and pressed his shoulders into the chair, which responded by suctioning itself to the spine of his Second Skin, rippling simultaneously up to the base of his skull and down to his tail bone.

Once the vacuum chair had secure contact with the suit, it lifted Ashley off the floor, giving him the sensation of weightlessness without the risk of him floating into the walls and hurting himself.

Tubes and cables climbed the walls from banks of hidden circuitry, clung to the ceiling like ivy, and wound their way down the arm of the vacuum chair to sensors covering Ashley's spine and skull. They monitored his pulse, blood pressure, neural activity, and mood. Two clear hermetic-plastic tubes hung from the ceiling: one was filled with a yellowish liquid, and the other was lime green. Both tubes ended in twenty-gauge IV needles, which Ashley plugged directly into ports in the left arm of his suit, wincing as the cold steel slid into his veins.

Aside from the chair and the wires, the room was empty. There was no external view of the ship, no steering wheel or joystick, no overwhelming bank of blinking buttons. Just a chair and a man.

As Ashley plugged in the needles, Evermore said through his earpiece, "We're ready to detach from the station. Are you in place?"

"Yes, start it up."

"Alright, my boy. I'll see you on the other side."

"I'm not your boy."

Evermore made no reply, and Ashley liked to imagine that he was searching for the right words without finding them.

The dim lights inside the chamber faded and Ashley closed his eyes and listened for the hiss-click of the door sliding shut. There was the hiss, but it ended with a blunt thud. Behind his eyelids Ashley could see the room wasn't completely dark. He opened them. The door hadn't closed all the way, and the light from the locker room was casting a line on the wall in front of him. With the chair attached to the base of his skull, he could only move his head an inch to either side, not enough to see what was blocking the door. Without warning the *Godspeed* detached from the dry dock station, and a falling sensation churned his stomach for a moment before weightlessness took over. A shadow floated through the line of light. *Someone's in the locker room.*

The DNC's psychoactive cocktail known as guide serum hit Ashley's veins, lancing paralysis down his limbs. At first it caused his skeletal muscles to tense so fiercely he could feel them burn with lactic acid, and his eyelids snapped wide open. The shadow passed in front of the light again; the line grew larger as the doors were forced open, and the amorphous shadow became a child.

A warm feeling washed over him as a deep tissue relaxant kicked in, making him instantly drowsy. His eyelids grew heavy as the visage of Samuel drifted into his field of vision, but there was nothing he could do to keep them open, and as they fell closed he couldn't find the animosity to care. He had relaxed into a chemical calm where the sum of the parts of his body melted into one continuous vessel.

He felt tiny, sharp somethings being forced into his mouth like a straw punched through the hole in a juice box. An ancient instinct said "swallow," and the small things were forced down his throat.

Drifting through the darkness of an approaching dream, Ashley floated through the walls like a ghost until he was caught by something, some sticky psychic web that seemed to stretch him, and his body took on a new shape.

Behind his eyelids he could see light, and upon opening them, he found himself in space.

The red planet loomed above him, and the dry dock station was drifting away, pulled by the rotation of the planet. Inside the ship he felt every living organism moving and breathing. He felt an empathic connection to each of the passengers, but the strength of it was based on how well he knew them. He could feel Evermore's nervousness, and Rachael's fear, but his connection to Sean was entirely different. Pharmaceutically released from the stories and desires of how he should feel or think about the boy, he understood who Sean genuinely was, and the boy was empty.

*Can they feel me in the same way I can feel them?* he wondered.

He could feel the foreign crystal pieces of the exit gate around his waist like a utility belt, and the nine construction suits stuck to his belly like little egg sacs.

Ashley looked ahead, and there loomed the empty gate to dark space. As they approached, Evermore triggered the gate to open, and Ashley watched a tiny ball of nothingness appear from nowhere in the center of the gate, as if something from the other side had bumped into our world. It spread across the mouth of the gate, but even when it had reached all the edges there was some shimmering that still separated the two universes, like the microscopically thin film that divides two soap bubbles.

The launch security crew in their tiny crystal armor construction suits guarded against escaping ghosts and saluted Ashley as he fell past them. Thrusters around the gate fired, and the hoop aligned itself toward him, showing him a reflection of the *Godspeed* where Ashley felt his face should be. He took a deep breath in anticipation of spending the next century in vacuum, and plunged face-first into darkness.

Dark space had felt much different in the prototype gate construction suit he had tried during his trainings with Samuel. While he was possessing the crystal shell of the suit, the penetrating cold didn't feel so dangerous, and carrying the bubble of reality with him gave him a touchstone to remember where he came from, who he was, and that he was a whole being, a complete conscious entity separate from the purposeless void.

Possessing the *Godspeed* was also different. If the gate construction suit was a one-size-fits-all basketball jersey, loose as hell but at least it had his name and number on the back, the *Godspeed* was a well-tailored suit. As soon as his astral body detached from his physical one and slipped into it, it felt as snug and comforting as being swaddled. The other difference was that rather than being a spirit traveling the empty shores of purgatory alone, Ashley was a bastion. He was a roving fortification surrounding his small nomadic tribe, and, like the nomads, his guidance was the stars. Yet none were visible. Arriving at their destination required Ashley to picture, with all of his being, the alien constellations at the location of the exit gate, and at the speed of his intention the *Godspeed* would plunge ever deeper into the icy depths of dark space. It was a task constantly interrupted by the twinkling lights of life that moved about inside him. He found it far easier to turn his attention inward toward the undulating chaos of his passengers' numinous energy as it echoed off his insides.

Days passed, and he felt their restlessness grow. They watched movies until they realized they had reached the end of each one and couldn't remember what it was about. They read until their loneliness became unbearable, but mostly they sat in the passenger cabin and made small talk. Ashley would steal glances at Rachael and Sean, but there was a rift growing in his connection with them.

Weeks passed, and the passengers' restlessness turned to depression. For a time he thought he would be able to move faster without their energy weighing him down, but as he felt their spirits dim he quickly realized that they had been feeding him, and as their numinous energy waned, the destination stretched farther away. Ashley forced himself toward their goal by picturing that Earth-like planet orbiting its orange sun, by imagining each constellation of stars that he'd had to learn and name himself: the top hat, the hook, the black widow, the lightning bolt, and many more. But they were dead in the water no matter how hard he tried, and then the revenants started to come.

At first Ashley had no idea what had happened, one moment he was there, imagining himself down on that green and blue world just waiting to be discovered, and the next he was somewhere and someone else.

*The darkness of slumber slid aside, replaced by a drowsy world gray with predawn light. Ashley was no longer in the pilot's chamber. No longer on the Godspeed. There were birds loudly singing their dawn chorus, and it was enough to tell him that he was somehow back on Earth. The bed in which he slept was soft, silken, and enormously comfortable. As he peered around the dimness of his room, the shadows of his furnishings began to take shape. He propped himself up on his elbow and felt old bones creaking out their first complaints of the day. When did I get so old? he wondered, but the thought was interrupted as one of the shadows bled from the outline of his wardrobe and moved across the room. "Who's there?" he whispered around the fear that clenched his throat. The language felt like Mandarin to Ashley's tongue, but he understood it, whatever it was. A sleeve the color of night ending in a hand of ghostly white shot out from the darkness and pressed itself across his mouth with a force that made his skull ache. "Ming Chongyan," the voice whispered, "The prince needs you removed." He felt something cold slither into his chest, expertly dodging between his ribs. He tried to gasp, but the hand prevented it. He tried to cry out, and again the hand held back his words. Something warm spread across his chest and ran down his sides.*

*His body grew cold and limp much faster than he would have expected. The shadow released him and disappeared into the darkness. "My heart has stopped," he thought, but some last shed of strength seemed available to him. So he rose and followed after the assassin, running out into the darkness, but never reaching the opposite side of his room.*

In an instant Ashley knew and remembered it as if it had happened to him. He felt the foolishness, the betrayal, and the lust for revenge. At the same time he recognized the ghost of Ming Chongyan as it fumbled at him. It tried to walk along the edge of the *Godspeed* searching for the door, as if it had finally, after all these centuries, found the opposite wall of the room. Around and around it paced like some desperate animal walking the boundaries of its cage.

A few moments later Ashley became or remembered being a woman who had followed her forbidden lover over the cliffs' edge. He felt the crushing, tearing sensation so vividly as she was disfigured by the rocks and swallowed by the sea, and the heartbroken desperation with which she was still swimming through the darkness in search of Him.

Hours or days later a hapless man, struck by lightning but still thinking he had survived, asked him something in some Slavic language that grew increasingly desperate.

The dead grew in number the longer they spent in dark space. The ghosts seemed unable to interact with each other, but they clung to him like psychic barnacles, distracting him more and more from their destination.

Turning his attention inward, he heard one of the passengers telling a story. It was Valenci Meritani, and he was telling the story of Herman Melville's *Moby Dick* from memory. It took hours and days, and Meritani told it without stopping. The more connected they became to the characters, the faster the *Godspeed* seemed to travel, but although Ashley outdistanced the wandering revenants, he never really felt free of the psychic scars they left behind.

The first time they actually seemed to be getting somewhere was as the story and the journey fell into a cadence. As the white whale was discovered, Ashley saw an image of those alien stars he recognized flash before his eyes. He was inside the constellation Virgo, heading toward an orange sun.

When the harpoons sank deep into the white flesh of the whale, Ashley received another flash: the sun was bigger, and he could almost feel its warmth beaconing out to him. And when the sea, churning with blood, foam, and flotsam, settled into its final conclusion and faded, Ashley felt a twinge in his gut. A fluttering of hope like crocuses forcing their blossoming heads through the final vestiges of winter snow. An instinct that, in spite of the absoluteness of nothing that surrounded him, let him know that their destination waited on the other side of the veil.

Three months ago, the Doc had told him to pick three of his most vivid memories from various stages of his life.

*Ashley was strapped into an early version of the vacuum chair and asked to remember a memory over and over until the computer learned where it existed in his neural network. It took five hours before Ashley could open a text box on Evermore's computer by simply remembering. The computer took ten hours learning how to distinguish a second memory from the first, and the third took days.*

*"You don't need to tell me what the memories are," Evermore had explained, "But by using just these three memories in different combinations we can create twenty-seven unique signals. No, strike that. I don't want any memory twice in a row, so that only leaves..." He ran a hand through his hair. "...twelve.*

*"These mnemonic signals will be the only way you'll have of communicating with me while piloting. I'm going to give you a list of twelve useful signals and commands, and you're going to assign a memory order to each."*

*Evermore quizzed him daily using flash cards, then verbal cues, and finally situational cues. In their final test before launch, Evermore quizzed him one more time. "Abort mission?"*

*Ashley ran through the mnemonic signals, remembering each memory and triggering the pop-up to appear on Evermore's screen: "Abort mission."*

*"Good. 'I'm lost'?"*

*He heard the pop-up alert before he'd even finished remembering the third; the speed of thought still mystified him.*

*"Good, and what will you remember when we arrive at the exit gate location?"*

* * * * * *

Ashley remembered the white horse with mud up to its knees, balefully watching him through its rain-soaked mane.

He remembered the first time he'd seen Evermore, pushing an electric lawn mower around his yard. A green sports jersey hung off his belt, and his sweaty, pale-white skin was starting to pink on his shoulders with the first sunburn of the season.

He remembered his own shaking hands as he held his Omni between them. The screen scrolled the message "Connecting to Dr. Rae Dahlia." He propped the phone against a tall white take-out box with "88" written on one side in bright red. It rang and rang, and eventually she answered, saying, "Hello?"

Ashley remembered the feeling of butterflies in his stomach. The cloud of swallowtails that flew up to his chest and assaulted his heart with the flutter of a hundred thousand wings. Even though it was the nth time he remembered it, he could still feel his heart fluttering.

Back in the coffin of dark space, Evermore's voice found him and sounded as if it were coming from both inside him and all around him, "Ashley, I received the mnemonic signal that we arrived at the gate location. Please confirm."

*Rachael. Lawn mower. Rachael,* he thought.

"Wonderful," Evermore said, clenching his fists. Ashely had only seen Evermore this excited once before, on the eve of his first trip to Mars. "Ashley, stand by while I dispatch the gate construction crew."

# CHAPTER THIRTY-THREE

# Revenants

### Rachael

When they entered dark space, Rachael had been so afraid that her identity would be stripped away, or that the hollow would spread and consume her. When neither of those things happened and she finally allowed herself to relax, she let in another psychic enemy: boredom. She had always thought of boredom as the childish feeling of having nothing to do, but this was not the lethargy of idle hands, this was an anxiety named "eternity," whose nothingness extended infinitely and whose claustrophobic pressure increased with every passing moment. But once Meritani had started telling Melville's story of the white whale, she found she could settle into the story in a way that reading or watching movies didn't allow.

As Meritani's story ended, while its gravitas still hung in the air like a thick fog, Evermore's voice called over the intercom and dispelled the moment. "We have reached our destination. Ma'at and Rachael, please begin the construction sequence."

Rachael released a sigh of relief she hadn't even realized she'd been holding. *How long have we been in here?* she wondered. *How many movies did we watch? How many interviews have I been subjected to, and how many conversations have I had?* She could remember doing each of those things many times over, but she found that individual details and moments eluded her recollection. Chalking it up to an as-of-yet unexplained side-effect of dark space, she tried not to quantify anything and turned to Sean, who was asleep in Aziza's arms, as he had been for most of the journey.

"Thanks for keeping an eye on him," Rachael said.

Aziza declined her appreciation with a gesture. "I'm just thrilled to be getting all of the baby time I can."

Ma'at planted a kiss on his wife's forehead before he stood and looked out among the passengers, made eye contact with each member of the construction crew, and said, "I want the primary six suited and launched in the next ten minutes. Eta and Theta, you're on standby. Suit up and wait for my order. Go."

The eight young men who had signed their lives away to Evermore Industries pushed themselves to the handrails in the ceiling and down the corridors to the launch bay in the belly of the ship. Rachael and Ma'at followed.

During the many hours she and Ashley had spent looking at the blueprints of the *Godspeed*, she had imagined it configured lengthwise like a train. Moving down the corridor through the different numen-lock doors would have been comparable to moving between cars. But in zero-G the *Godspeed* felt more like climbing up the inside of a tower, regardless of whether she was climbing fore or aft.

In the foreman's control room, Ma'at and Rachael pushed themselves into two of the four vacuum chairs hanging from the ceiling. The seats faced a bank of monitors connected to a series of infrared cameras that allowed them to see through the protective crystal plating. Above the IR monitors was a series of bars and icons that monitored each construction suit pilot's biological status. Above that was a live feed of the long hexagonal launch-bay corridor. It had nine round hatches in the floor the size of sewer manholes. Soon the crew drifted into frame, pulling themselves along the handrails to wait in front of the closed hatches in the floor. The process was the same for each crew member: After a numen sensor scanned their marker signature and confirmed their identity, the hatch in the floor opened and they guided themselves through a short coupler and into their construction suit. Rachael watched the suit cams as each man pushed himself into the vacuum chair and plunged the yellow and lime-green needles into their arm ports. She watched their muscles constrict sickeningly before they went limp. Within minutes their eyes were moving rapidly as they arrived in the pilot's trance, and the hatch on either side of the coupler automatically closed.

Each of the construction crew knew that any crack or fracture in their crystal armor could cause their suit to wink out of dark space and appear randomly somewhere else in the universe, where their life-support would inevitably run out eons before Mars would ever receive their distress signal. Yet their independence from the Godspeed relied on that same principal; once both hatches were sealed, the coupler that connected ship and suit cut away its own crystal armor, and the instant it was exposed to dark space, the coupler disappeared as if winking out of existence, and the construction suit became its own vessel.

Rachael and Ma'at watched as the construction crew drifted free of the *Godspeed* and made their way to the ship's midsection, where eight huge pieces of the exit gate were attached. "Alright, just like we practiced, team," Ma'at said. "I want two bodies on each piece. Once you get a half circle, I want four of you to take the piece to the final build zone."

Each of their mnemonic signals indicated that they understood, except one. "Zeta, did you copy that?" Ma'at asked. He looked at the jockey's suit cam. "His brain activity is all over the place."

Rachael leaned over. "That's deep in his amygdala; he's

afraid of something."

Ma'at said, "Someone get me a visual on Zeta."

Through the mnemonic signals, Delta said, "Affirmative." Then a moment later, "Hostiles."

The construction crew had encountered a few drifting revenants during training, which had provided them with some impromptu target practice using their numinous countermeasures, but nothing they'd encountered had triggered this level of fear.

"Hold your fire," Ma'at commanded. "You'll catch Zeta in the blast."

"Affirmative," Delta returned. From the infrared camera, Ma'at and Rachael couldn't see the ghost, but it wasn't hard to guess what Delta was about to do. Each construction suit had a rack of crystal-coated tools. Each tool was attached to a grid of crystal rods, like a giant plastic model kit. He gave one of his wrenches a light twist and it cracked off of his tool wrack. As he flew over to Zeta, Delta took a big baseball swing, which stopped half-way through its arc, as if it had become lodged in whatever he'd hit. Placing his foot gingerly on Zeta's suit, Delta pulled until something seemed to give. He quickly threw the wrench, and it spun end over end away from the *Godspeed*, until it stopped, turned, and came flying back.

"Fire at will," Ma'at shouted. They watched the screen as three separate countermeasure charges exploded ahead, behind, and directly on top of the wrench, and it was gone. Zeta's brain pattern returned to normal, and Ma'at asked, "Zeta, are you okay?"

"Affirmative."

"New formation. I want Delta and Zeta on guard duty. Watch everyone's backs while they build the gate. Protect the gate at all cost." Even as they affirmed the message, both of them signaled, "Hostiles," and opened fire.

Ma'at looked back to the launch bay, where two of his crew were still waiting, and said, "Eta, Theta, plug into your suits and get out there. Use extreme caution; there are multiple hostiles in the area." The two looked nervously at each other before pulling themselves down the hatch and into their suits.

As the steady stream of revenants continued to haunt the build, Rachael felt increasingly helpless. She had heard from Ashley that the neural communication system had worked well during every training situation they had run through, but Ma'at couldn't see the ghosts and therefore couldn't direct his men. All he could do was watch the tiny bursts of heat as countermeasures detonated all around the ship. The construction crew dodged around and moved the gate farther from the *Godspeed*. The minutes crawled by, and the swarm of ghosts only seemed to be increasing. Though the suits were highly maneuverable, the crew's ability to see the revenants seemed limited to a short distance. During the battle, six of the eight crew members were attacked and frozen for a moment as the ghosts tried to enter their suits, but each was manually exorcised by someone else prying it off with the crystal-plated wrench, flinging it away, and catching it in the blast of a numinous countermeasure. Theta even managed to throw one wrench toward another revenant and catch both in the blast.

"What can I do?" Rachael asked, her eyes settled on the screen of the launch bay corridor and the unused ninth construction suit hatch.

Without looking up from the screens, Ma'at shook his head. "I feel so useless."

Rachael opened the intercom and spoke to the entire construction crew: "Focus on the build. If you aren't hauling or attaching gate pieces, try to distract the ghosts and lead them away from the builders."

After another ten minutes, Rachael noticed a pattern and said, "The bursts of numinous energy from the countermeasures is attracting the revenants!"

Ma'at nodded. "You're right." He opened the intercom and said, "As soon as this last piece is in place, Alpha, Beta, Gamma, I want you to grab hold of anything around the front of the ship; the remaining five position yourselves around the *Godspeed*'s midsection. From those positions, draw the revenants away from the gate and off the ship with countermeasure bursts at the same point in space. Delta, you're low on ammo; hold your fire until the last.

"Evermore is going to close the gate as soon as the *Godspeed* passes through, so hang on and don't get left behind."

"Affirmative," came the eight replies, and ten minutes later Alpha triggered his three most precious memories that sent the "Mission complete" signal to Ma'at.

"Dr. Evermore, this is Ma'at; the exit gate is complete."

Evermore's voice sounded over the intercoms. "Everyone please return to your seats. We will be leaving dark space momentarily."

From her chair in the foreman's control room, Rachael could feel the pressure in the room increasing exponentially, as if something was slowly squeezing the air out of her. She remembered the feeling from the first time she had stepped through the gate. A part of her even longed for it. Contrary to its intensity, the pressure felt comforting. The constriction rose to a crescendo she could only describe as a full-body pinch, and the quietness, the stillness, the smothering pillow of dark space was lifted from her face.

Rachael found herself in the passenger cabin strapped into her seat. She felt as if she'd forgotten to breathe, and so inhaled. That same gravelly gasp was repeated throughout the room. Sean was at her side, Aziza next to him, and Cyrus Ma'at beside her. Above her the silver pilot's wings bounced off the ceiling with a tiny plastic *tink*.

Worried that she'd blacked out and lost time, Rachael leaned toward Ma'at and asked, "How did we get here?" No sooner had she asked than she realized, by the look on his face, that he was puzzling out that same question.

Aziza also looked nervous. "I wasn't strapped in a second ago, and Mr. Meritani was over there."

Ma'at looked down at the live-feed magazine in his hand. "I haven't moved since we entered dark space."

"Yes, you have. A moment ago we were both in the foreman's control room."

The buzz in the passenger cabin grew, and Rachael realized that everyone was having the same conversation. Ma'at noticed it as well. "Yes, I remember that, but I don't think we were actually there." He unclipped himself and drifted to the ceiling. Above the rising clamor, he said, "During our experiments in dark space, it was well documented that time does not actually pass. The people we sent through didn't consume food or break down fluids. We did an experiment where we they inhaled some harmless vapor and stepped through, and even though they remembered breathing while they were there, on the other side there was a puff of vapor when they exhaled. We are three-dimensional creatures, and dark space is a very foreign dimension. This skip in reality we all just experienced was, I believe, some kind of shared dream-state."

One of the journalists raised a hand. "The eight-man construction crew is gone; where are they?"

"They are in autonomous ships called construction suits, edging their way around the outside of the *Godspeed* to an external cargo bay, where they will outfit themselves with thrusters and begin unfolding the solar array."

The raised hand was joined by another. "How or why were their actions permanent?"

Raymond Hubert cleared his throat and caught Ma'at's attention. Ma'at nodded, and Hubert rose to answer the question. "If there's one thing that the universe hates —

in all the dimensions of her multitudinous chaos — it's a paradox. How could we have left the dark space if no physical gate was built?" Hubert smiled. "I take it as proof that the human spirit is far more powerful than contemporary religions have led us to believe. Is it not the consciousness of a *plant* that has allowed us to *enter* the dark space? Perhaps the human mind can—" but he was cut off as Sean began to wail for no apparent reason.

Sean's sudden outburst startled Rachael. He was not a child who cried when he was hungry, or tired, or uncomfortable, and this wasn't his "pain" cry. She had never heard him wail like this. It conveyed torment. As she leaned over, first to make sure he was safe and then to comfort him, she couldn't shake the feeling that something bad had happened. "He must have gotten startled," she explained to the room. "Sean, what's wrong little man?"

"Dr. Shah!" Evermore's voice called out over the intercom, commanding but wavering with panic. "Get your medical team to the pilot's chamber as fast as you can."

Rachael felt as if she were falling backward and her heart had stopped. "Aziza, will you—"

"Go!" Aziza said.

Rachael unclipped her buckle and flung her body toward the door. Sensing her approach, the doors slid open, and she caught the edge of the frame and pulled herself through. She pulled herself as fast as she could up the corridors toward the nose of the ship. When she reached Ashley's private locker room, Evermore was frantically plugging his way through override codes on the nine-number keypad and referencing his Omni at the same time. The words "Trance in progress, Do NOT disturb," were projected on the door.

"Rachael," he said when he saw her. "Where's Dr. Shah?"

She ignored his question. "What's going on?" He

couldn't answer, and she asked again, "Evermore, what the fuck is going on?"

Tears burst from their ducts, and he attempted to swallow a lump of pain. "I don't know. Ashley... he's sick." He looked back to his Omni. "God*damn* this override sequence." He tossed his Omni to her. "Read this to me. No one can get through this door except the pilot."

"Hit nine four times to start the sequence."

Evermore jammed his finger into nine. "Nine-nine-nine-nine."

"Then put in the mission commander's five-digit ID number."

"I know that step, what's next?" Evermore shouted.

"Your private code!"

"Two hundred thirty-four. Four point four-six-eight times ten to the ninth," said Evermore, just as Dr. Shah and two other medical officers pulled themselves into the crowded locker room. The doors to the pilot's chamber slid open. It took all of Rachael's willpower not to follow Evermore into the cramped chamber where Ashley was hanging limp from the vacuum chair. Dr. Shah pulled himself into the chamber as Evermore ran his knuckles up and down Ashley's sternum and called, "Ashley. Wake up, my boy! Wake up!"

"Dr. Evermore, give me room," Shah said as he braced himself against the chair and the wall to keep steady. With one hand he grabbed Ashley's wrist to check his pulse and with the other he put the back of his hand under Ashley's nose.

"Do you feel anything?" Evermore asked, clinging to the arm of the vacuum chair.

One of Shah's staff, a young black man with close-cropped hair and a U.S. Navy tattoo partially hidden beneath his collar, said, "We need to get in there *now*!" with a cold urgency as he reached into the chamber and pulled Evermore out by the ankle.

Rachael reached out to Evermore and grabbed him by the hand. He looked back at her, and his face was awash with emotions. "Maybe the infusion pump malfunctioned," he said. "But even then, there isn't enough guide serum to..."

"He's in V-fib. Dex, get me an auto-compressor!" Shah quickly drifted around behind the chair and started violently squeezing Ashley's chest. The officer assisting in the locker room moved to a small compartment marked with a red cross and pulled out a roll of nylon bound with Velcro. As Dex unrolled something that looked like a wide red Wrestle Mania belt, the tattooed officer took a steel shoehorn from his kit and tried to force open Ashley's mouth. Rachael winced at the sound of metal scraping against teeth and gripped Evermore's hand tighter.

While Shah continued giving Ashley CPR from behind the chair, Dex wrapped the wide belt around both Ashley and the chair. After securing the Velcro, he said, "Auto-compressor attached."

The tattooed medic said, "His throat is clenched, I can't get an airway. Preparing to push an adult dose of Sux."

"No," Shah said. "He's already hyperkalemic from the guide serum, any more and we'll never get his heart—" the tattooed medic cast a glance at Rachael, and Shah cut himself off. "Sorry, Dr. Dahlia, you may want to leave for this next part." Shah stopped CPR and slapped the big orange button on the front of the belt, and it started compressing Ashley's chest at eighty beats per minute. "Get me the trach kit; we need to give him an airway."

Rachael was expecting some gadget of modern medicine until Dex handed Shah a scalpel. The doctor wiped a towelette across Ashley's throat and it came away red. Rachael gasped before she realized it was iodine.

Shah said, "At the end of this set, the auto-compressor is going to pause to instruct me to administer rescue breaths and give us five seconds. The moment it stops, I'll make the incision. Dex, you're going to insert the valve, and Adam," he looked at the tattooed Marine, "you're going to bandage before the auto-compressor starts pumping his blood all over the place. Get ready."

Adam tore through the medical bag, tossed a trachea valve to Dex, and armed himself with gauze.

A friendly, automated voice spoke from the auto-compressor: "Tilt the head back and give two, quick rescue breaths."

The medics snapped into action.

Evermore's Omni beeped with an urgency beyond a simple text or ring. He either ignored or didn't hear it as he focused on turning Rachael away. "My dear, you shouldn't watch."

Her eyes narrowed angrily, and she craned her neck around, but she couldn't see past the medics. "He needs us here," she said.

"We can't do anything to help him," Evermore said, and his Omni beeped again.

She tried to untangle herself from him, but the attempt was halfhearted. "I could feel him. No matter where I went in the ship I could feel him watching me." Her eyes were blurry with tears, but the look she wore was resolution. "We need to do that for him now. We need to be his lifeline so he knows how to get back."

The medics shifted, and for a moment she saw Shah squeezing a plastic bag of air into Ashley's throat, while Dex and Adam quickly cut away his electromyographic bodysuit. Before long they had Ashley's rigid body clear of all metal and strapped, as best they could manage, to a backboard. The CPR auto-compressor was replaced with a defibrillator.

"Analyzing," the machine said. The seconds it took the machine to complete whatever analysis it was doing crawled by like hours. While they waited in silence, Evermore's Omni beeped a third time, and the noise seemed to penetrate his attention.

Rachael felt useless. Watching. Knowing his heart wasn't beating.

"Stay clear of the patient and prepare for shock," the machine said, emitting a high-pitched whine that only grew higher.

Evermore pulled the Omni from his pocket and read the alert that covered his entire screen. The brightness of it attracted Rachael's attention. "What's wrong?"

"Nothing we have the power to change. We're caught in the planet's gravity well."

There was a low-bass thump as 120 joules of energy jumped across Ashley's heart. "Analyzing, do not touch patient."

"We're what?" Rachael pulled herself out of Evermore's grasp.

"Keep your voice down, my dear," Evermore whispered. "As we speak, the construction crew is outfitting each other with retrofit thrusters. When they've finished they'll nudge the *Godspeed* into orbit."

"Second shock recommended," said the machine.

Evermore continued, "If worse comes to worse, we'll load everyone in the lander and abandon ship." He looked back to his Omni to check the second alert.

"Stay clear of the patient and prepare for shock," the machine said, charging itself.

Rachael couldn't bear to watch Ashley's body make that sickening jolt a second time. She turned away and saw panic on Evermore's face. "Now what?" She asked.

Evermore quickly scanned the room, and his eyes landed on a small white sticker-cam stuck to the wall adjacent to the number pad.

There was another low-bass thump as Ashley's body was laced with 200 joules of electricity.

Evermore shook his head. "Samuel was watching as I

entered my code. He's in my command center."

"Analyzing, do not touch patient," said the machine.

"Why isn't it working?" Rachael yelled at the medics.

Shah shook his head. "We need to get him on life support. Prepare to evac. You two," he pointed at Evermore and Rachael. "You need to get out of our way. Out in the hall, now."

"Continue CPR and wait for emergency medical support," said the AED machine.

Shah yelled, "Dex, turn that thing that off!"

Evermore pulled himself out of the room, and Rachael followed. As she watched, the medical team quickly and effortlessly pulled Ashley's twisted body down the corridor. She started to follow when she noticed that Evermore was furiously gesturing at his Omni. "Evermore, are you coming?"

He shook his head. "I can't; Samuel is in my command center trying to shut off the atmosphere control and open all the doors."

"What!"

"He's not smart enough to lock me out of the system: I can reverse everything from my Omni, but if I take my eyes away for too long—" Evermore trailed off as his brain shifted focus on countering Samuel.

Rachael launched herself down the corridor, and yelled, "Open the command center door when I get there."

Evermore yelled after her, "Rachael, you can't kill him." If she had known Evermore any less, she might have mistaken his words as caution, but Rachael exactly what he meant; Samuel *couldn't* be killed. Not permanently, anyway.

# CHAPTER THIRTY-FOUR

# Countermeasures

### Rachael

Rachael had visited the command center during their initial tour of the ship. What she had seen then was a vacuum chair hanging at the end of a short walkway, which would presumably rotate to face the vertex of the half-sphere–shaped room. The curved walls had a radius of two meters and had been black glass upon her visit, but as she pulled herself into the doorway of the command center, the only thing she recognized was the vacuum chair. The virtual reality room seemed as big as an airplane hangar, and systems and subsystems of the *Godspeed* were scattered all over the space. Front and center were the rigid arteries of the atmospheric recycling system. From the chair, Samuel was manipulating the system with his bare hands like an orchestra conductor. Yet seconds after he clumsily closed off the airflow in the passenger cabin, it magically reopened again. He cursed Evermore under his breath and tossed the atmosphere system away.

As Samuel focused his attention on the *Godspeed*'s lighting system, Rachael launched herself at his side. Hoping to knock him out of the chairs, she slammed into him with both feet and felt the nauseating snap of ribs. Samuel cried out in pain, and as his body curled toward the injury, she flew off toward the hull of the virtual *Godspeed*. As long as she focused on where she was sure the wall should be, the illusion of the huge space couldn't confuse her, and she rebounded off the wall of the chamber, pushing herself back toward him. "What did you give him?" she growled.

With his arms cradling his ribs, he hissed, "Eternal life."

As she reached the chair, Rachael hit the emergency release button, took hold of his collar and pushed off toward the door, dragging him with her. Samuel still had one arm wrapped around his ribs, while the other alternated between flailing out for a handhold and weakly trying to fight her off. As their momentum carried them out into the corridor, Rachael grabbed at the handrail with one hand, and Samuel's head cracked against the side of the double airlock door. His body went limp. *Oops*, Rachael thought. A moment later Samuel's deadweight came crashing into her, knocking her off the rail and into the opposite wall.

She untangled herself from his limbs and grabbed his throat. *Breathe. Remember, you don't want to kill him.* Rachael forced herself to loosen her grip and feel for a pulse. *He's still alive.* She couldn't tell how she felt about it. Her hands around his throat felt so tempting. *Is it even murder if he was never born?* she wondered, remembering that Evermore had built Samuel's body from genetic synthesis.

Looking into his face, Rachael watched his eyes moving behind their lids, and a moment later, they groggily opened. It took Samuel a few seconds to remember and realize what was going on.

He croaked out, "Fucking kill me, you coward bitch." Droplets of bloody spittle flew from his mouth as he spat his venom at her. "Kill me. Or do you need Evermore to do that for you too, you cun-glnh." Rachael wrapped her fingers around his windpipe. He smiled, relaxed, and waited for death.

"I would like nothing more than to feel your diseased

bones snap between my fingers, but then I think of my son and wonder: How long will you stay dead this time? Will you find a way back in time to torment him, or will it be his—"

She felt his chest rattle with a laugh that had no escape. *He knew I was about to say "children."* But there was no reality where she could imagine Sean having children, and the hope that he would suddenly get better was a poison that prevented her from accepting who he was.

Their tangled bodies rotated around each other's axis, and when the ceiling came within reach, she let go of his throat and grabbed the handrails, arresting her own zero-G tumble. As Samuel drifted past, she wrapped an arm around his head and caught him in a headlock. Using one arm she side-crawled up the *Godspeed* toward the aft of the ship and dragged Samuel with her. She quickly got the hang of catching the rail and pushing off with one foot.

They picked up speed, but when her grip on Samuel relaxed, he whined at her in a strained, high-pitched voice that undulated with the pressure she was putting on his throat. "Trying to find a place to lock me up? There's no brig on the ship."

She said nothing, and when they reached the launch bay corridor, Samuel realized his fate and began struggling against her in earnest. Eight of the nine manhole-size hatches had "Suit Launched" displayed in red above the hatch. When Rachael moved in front of the ninth, she used her free knee to kick Samuel in his broken ribs, and she released him to writhe in agony while she positioned herself in front of the ninth numen scanner. When it finished reading her unique signature, the hatch slowly raised.

Of Evermore's many contingency plans, there was one where she would need her own construction suit to assist with the build. At first there had been nothing Evermore could say to convince her to take the dark space construction suit training. It had taken her months since her first eternity in dark space to shake the feeling that her entire life was empty and life itself was meaningless. Only Ashley had been able to convince her that traversing dark space in the suit was different.

Samuel's every movement lanced pain across his face and brought him no closer to escape. "You think you're going to be a celebrity when you return?" he hissed. "You're not: people are going to ask questions. They're calling you the Mother of Dark Space now, but if you do this they'll be calling you the Dark Space Killer!"

There was no human in there. All she could see was a a Frankensteinian science project falling apart.

"What do you think will happen to Sean? With you in prison and Ashley dead, they'll put him in an institution."

Rachael hooked a foot around the opening of the hatch, reached up, and pulled Samuel down to her. He punched at her weakly, not strong enough to cause damage, but to say it didn't hurt would be a lie. Rachael ignored the minor pain and pulled him down the hatch into the construction suit.

"Wait, listen to reason!" he begged. "This is all part of Evermore's plan. He's going to rally the passengers against you, and you'll be left behind while everyone else goes to the planet's surface."

"I guess you didn't get the alert. The planet is pulling this whole ship down to its surface, so I'll be getting there one way or another."

The suit was built for one, but she used the tightness of the space to pin Samuel's body and prevent his escape. After wrestling for a time, she forced Samuel's back into the vacuum chair, which activated and grabbed him.

"You stupid bitch," he laughed at her. "You're really going to sacrifice yourself, just to punish me? Or did you forget the suit won't launch without you in it?"

She loosened the screws to adjust the headrest but

pulled it completely off the chair. Its bundle of wires and vacuum tubes came with it. "You would have been such a dangerous man if you knew fucking anything about technology. Did you grow up in the Dark Ages?" Holding it to the back of her head she felt the cold electrodes kiss her scalp through her short hair. Rachael closed her eyes and remembered...

She remembered the night she was awakened by the sound of Lina, her older sister, crying in the bed next to hers. Rachael crawled into bed to comfort her, as she had done so many times before, and saw the sheets wet with blood. Her sister's foot lashed out at her, and the rough carpet rose up out of the darkness to bite her face.

She remembered the day she arrived at Nili Terradome. After her months of travel in the cramped space shuttle, the city seemed huge as the moving walkway carried her up to the street level. It smelled like a pottery studio from the unfinished buildings covered in pink ceramic bricks. The initial smell was followed by a lush bouquet of jungle, photosynthesis, and spring rain.

Finally, she remembered giving birth to Sean; not the pain, or anything about the room, but the overwhelming, orgasmic feeling of an outside energy moving through her as Sean came into the world, and the stark contrast of the following moment, where she felt so disconnected from the alien creature that lay motionless on her chest.

No feeble curse or attack from Samuel could make her forget that.

"Launch sequence confirmed," said an automated voice.

Pulling the lime-green IV tube from its holster on the side of the chair, she turned toward Samuel and opened her mouth, but nothing came out. She started to cry. "Ashley would have had a great one-liner for this." Her face contorted with the pain of loss and the rage of helplessness, and she said, "I hope you fucking suffer and never die." She stabbed the needle into the meat of Samuel's neck, and he let out a scream which dissolved into a sigh as his muscles were liquefied by the guide serum.

Above her Rachael heard the hatch start to move. She quickly pulled off the headrest, stuck it to the top of Samuel's chemo-bald scalp, and dove through the hatch before it slowly drifted shut. She listened to the sound of the crystal being cut away and the pop as the suit was ejected from the *Godspeed*.

As soon as Rachael drifted through the numen-lock door into the foreman's control room, Ma'at said, "Rachael, is Ashley okay?"

She had expected him to ask about what he'd undoubtedly seen and heard in the launch bay, and his personal tone caught her off guard. "I don't know," she said, her vision going blurry with tears. After she suctioned herself into the seat beside him, he reached out and put a hand on her shoulder. *That would have not been okay just a few months ago,* she reflected. Now Ma'at felt like family, and part of her wanted to curl up in his arms like a little girl and weep. She shook off the feeling and focused on the bank of monitors. "The *Godspeed* is falling into the planet's gravity well."

Ma'at nodded. "Evermore told me. The crew is installing the thrusters as fast as they can."

"What about the revenants?"

"Taken care of. Only a few made it out of dark space. I don't need you here; you should be with Ashley."

She shook her head and avoided looking at him. "There's something I need to do first." Rachael opened the communications channel to all eight crew members. "A revenant has just taken control of the ninth construction suit. If anyone has any numen countermeasures left, blast it back to dark space."

"Affirmative," said eight replies.

Rachael watched the screen as a cluster of counter-measures exploded around the ninth suit, and its status flashed the message: "Lost connection." She turned to Ma'at and gave him a questioning glance. "I just ordered your men to kill someone; why didn't you try to stop me?"

Ma'at said, "You are unstoppable." His dark brown eyes peered into her, attempting to penetrate the armor. "How's Ashley?"

She thickened the shell around her heart and coldly said, "Your guide serum stopped his heart. The medics—"

Ma'at shook his head. "Rachael, the serum is safe. It would take multiple bags..."

She pretended not to hear him. "The medics have him hooked into machines that are keeping his body alive, but he's gone."

Ma'at reached out to her again. "Shah is one of the best on Mars: it won't come to that. I understand why you would blame me, but you have to know I love Ashley like a little brother."

She pushed his hand away and released herself from the chair.

"Stop talking about it. Everyone's life is in danger right now; we need to focus."

"Leave all that to Evermore." Ma'at said.

*If anything, he's the most affected by this. Someone sane needs to be in charge.* She released the vacuum chair and pushed herself to the handrails.

"Rachael, wait!" Ma'at looked back and forth between her and the bank of monitors, considering if he should abandon his post to chase after her. "You need someone with you right now."

"I don't need anyone," she said, and pulled herself out of the room.

Rachael pulled herself along the corridors to her personal quarters. All the while she repeated, "I need to feel nothing and focus," as if it were a mantra. She tried to remember that feeling of being naked and alone in dark space, of having her identity stripped away until she was just an animal, but she couldn't. Ashley's face wouldn't let her forget. The antidepressants her therapist recommended had an excellent numbing quality. *I have to be careful, though; there's a risk I'll stop caring about life altogether.*

She hesitated before opening the door to their personal quarters. *Inside will be a hundred reminders of Ashley. I need to get my meds and get out. There's no time to grieve.*

When the door opened, she was struck with a wave of confusion. Their things were scattered and floating all around the room. She had already cleaned up this mess when they first entered dark space. *I assumed Ashley had forgotten to close the storage lockers, but this is exactly how I found it in dark space. Meaning it happened before we jumped, cleaning it created a paradox, and it reverted back when we exited.* Her curiosity wanted to know what paradox she had caused, but she forced it away and starting swimming through their things searching for the small orange bottle of antidepressants.

It wasn't in any of the lockers, and she hurried around the room collecting their personal effects piece by piece. The awful, oversize green sports jersey that Ashley loved so much in spite of the fact that he didn't watch sports. The suit-pants from her first designer lab suit. She plucked the clothing from the air and stuffed it into the accordion garment drawer. As she was chasing down one of Sean's baby shoes, the lights turned red and a loud klaxon blasted three times across the entirety of the ship. After the third blast, Evermore's voice spoke over the sound system.

"All passengers and personnel, please calmly make your way to the landing shuttle, where an E.I. representative will explain the situation."

Rachael's fingers curled around the shoe. *Why do they make shoes for kids who are too young to walk?* Admittedly this shoe was unlike any other: hand-sewn from white pleather with black-sequined Adidas stripes. The message repeated itself five more times before she was able to admit that the orange pill bottle wasn't there. *Did Samuel?* No, it was too easy to blame Samuel. All of her problems lead back to him, and she wanted to be sure. Things had to be calculated, not emotional and overreacting. But once she ruled out all the other possibilities, she realized, *Ashley didn't overdose on guide serum.* She dialed the medical bay on her Omni, and when no one answered she pushed herself back out into the corridor, pulling herself up the *Godspeed* as fast as she could. All the while the emergency klaxon blasted in her ears. She swung into the med bay and shouted, "It's not the guide serum!"

The room contained no doctors. They had evacuated long ago, leaving Ashley's body, still twisted in its horrifically rigid form and hooked up to a beeping, wheezing life-support system.

Evermore's voice instructed her for the nth time to evacuate the ship. She waited for it to quiet and yelled, "Ashley, wake up!" while she drifted across the room to his bedside. "Ashley!" she barked into his face.

Rachael searched his face for any signs of life.

"Damn it, Ashley, don't do this to me. Don't do this to Sean."

She lay down beside him. Wrapping her arms and legs around him, she let the straps that bound him to the table keep them both from floating away. Spooning him as best she could, she closed her eyes and imagined nothing had changed. This was just like any other night that she had held him and felt his body drifting off to sleep. She kept her eyes closed to preserve the illusion that they were back on Phobos, cradled by the noiseless vibrations of the centrifuge. The bass vibration of the *Godspeed*'s thrusters firing ineffectually were close enough.

She ran her fingers over the round scars on Ashley's chest and down his arm, where they found the IV taped to his skin. Rachael followed the line back to its bag. The name of it didn't mean anything to her, but the chemical list included benzodiazepine. *Perfect.* She set the drip to its lowest setting, stabbed the needle into her own arm, and laid back down beside him.

"All passengers and personnel..." said the recording of Evermore.

Faintly she thought she heard her name.

"...please calmly make your way to the shuttle bay..."

There it was again.

"...where an E.I. representative will explain the situation."

"Rachael!" It was Evermore's voice, but it was coming from the corridor. The door to the medical bay opened, and the Doc quickly stuck his head in and almost left before he noticed her curled up behind Ashley's body. "Rachael, we need to go. The *Godspeed* is falling into the planet. All the passengers are already in the shuttle."

"What about Ashley?"

Evermore seemed disgusted at his own answer. "There isn't room for the stretcher."

She didn't move.

"Rachael, everyone is risking their life waiting for you!"

"How could you just abandon him like this?" she shouted.

"Shah had to talk me into it, but there's nothing more we can do for him."

"So this is it? This is how we have to say goodbye?"

His voice strained to speak around the grief constricting his throat. "There isn't time, the living need us more."

There was an awful feeling in her chest, a horrible ache in her heart worse than— No, it was gone. The wall of rioting emotions she had been struggling to keep at bay dissipated and dissolved as the benzodiazepine reached wherever it needed to. She pulled the needle from her arm, untangled herself from Ashley, and turned to face Evermore.

"Hurry!" He reached out to her with one hand.

"What happens when we're in the shuttle?"

"I don't know yet. But I do know we last longer in there than we do in here."

"I'll tell you what happens. We float around out there overloading the shuttle's O2 recyclers while we wait for what? The government of Mars to build another crystal ship before we asphyxiate? Our best chance at survival is to activate the gate and fly the shuttle though. Obviously it's not coated in crystal, so it'll disappear, and we'll float around dark space for eternity hoping to someday be rescued."

The absolute horror on Evermore's face would have terrified her if not for her medicated calm. "Or, I have another idea. Remember my accident at Kander and Jansen Labs? When I killed a PS crystal in the microwave? The reason there was no crystal in the cantilever device was that a numinous explosion caused Ma'at's Rochelle salt to jump. It's the same theory Ashley used when he designed countermeasures. The death of the countermeasure causes an explosion of out-breath that pulls the soul back into dark space."

She looked at Ashley, and Evermore understood. "The whole ship will vibrate with his death frequency and pull us directly into dark space."

Rachael said, "Get to your command center, tell Ma'at to get back to the foreman's control room, and tell the construction crew to manually move the gate away from the planet and stay clear of the *Godspeed*." Evermore swung himself out of the room, and Rachael turned back to Ashley.

"I imagined we had the rest of our lives still ahead of

us. I'm sorry I acted so crazy after Sean was born. But I never stopped loving you. I don't think I ever will." She stared at his body for a long time before finally saying what she'd been trying to the whole time. "I love you, Ashley.

"Goodbye."

She kissed him on the mouth and pulled the tube from his throat. His chest deflated and the air they had pumped into his lungs gurgled out the hole in his trachea. A transdermal pacemaker was still running his heart until she untaped it and pulled the long conducting needles from his chest, but true death waited until the acute anoxia turned his skin a dark blue.

When that unnameable quality of life left him, the *Godspeed* slipped into dark space, and she felt a sensation of falling that had nothing to do with gravity, and the chill of a shadow that had nothing to do with light.

"Goodbye, my love."

Rachael pulled herself into the shuttle bay through a round, numen-lock door large enough for two people to enter side by side. The shuttle itself was hanging from magnetic restraining bolts on the ceiling, its ramp still extended. Every available seat had a passenger strapped into it, but many of them were left unaccommodated and stood in the isles, with their hands and feet stuffed into the rails. When she drifted in, everyone gave her the exact same condoling look. It make her feel a weakling who needed help taking care of herself. Then a pressure valve seemed to break, and the reporters and frightened passengers unleashed all their questions.

"Rachael, how's Ashley?"

"Where did Dr. Evermore and Ma'at go? Are we waiting for *them* now?"

Rachael hooked her feet into the footrails in front of Aziza and Sean.

"Are we still falling toward the planet?"

"We experienced a transition. Can you confirm that we're back in dark space?"

Rachael held up her hands to silence the room, then turned back to Sean. His eyes were red, and his shirt was wet from tears and drool. Aziza handed Sean to Rachael. It was clear she had something to say but was restraining herself. *Go ahead*, Rachael thought. *Just say what you're thinking: "Thank God you're back, I didn't want to be stuck with this freak forever."* But then Aziza reached up and pinched away a glob of snot from beneath Sean's nose with her fingers. Rachael didn't even want to hold her own child, especially now that he was a constant reminder of Ashley. Yet Aziza was willing to wipe his nose with her bare hand. She said, "He's been crying his little eyes out until just before that... shift."

Aziza's voice reminded the crowd that Rachael hadn't answered their questions.

"Rachael, for the record, can you confirm that one of the construction suits was intentionally destroyed?"

"Are we still in danger?"

With an unwavering scowl, she faced the crowd. *Fuck all of you for running like rats. I just risked my life for you. If even one of you had stayed maybe I wouldn't have had to be the one to kill my best friend. Now I know why Evermore doesn't trust humanity.* She almost said it; there was almost enough benzodiazepine in her blood that she didn't give a fuck. But she had had a child to preserve her media perception, and she wouldn't piss that sacrifice away for any amount of short-term satisfaction.

"We are safe," she said, and the room collectively released its held breath. "I want to thank Dr. Shah and his team for their tremendous response in that emergency."

Shah, like many of the passengers, had no assigned seat. He allowed himself to drift toward her. "Rachael, I'm so sorry we had to leave him. His condition was critical. I didn't think he would recover, much less be back in piloting condition—"

Rachael shook her head, and a hardened scowl still protected her face from emotion. "He didn't recover; his body is dead."

The room erupted with questions again; the loudest were variations on "Who's piloting the ship?"

Beneath all the questions Rachael heard Aziza say, "Rachael, honey, I'm so sorry." The condolence felt like a cold needle, and she turned her attention back to the mob.

One of the journalists asked, "Can you confirm that he overdosed on the psychoactive neurotransmitter synthesized by the Department of Numinous Cosmology?"

Rachael heard herself repeat Ma'at's assessment. "The serum is safe. Ashley didn't overdose; he was murdered. This whole mission was sabotaged by Samuel Reznick. During the launch sequence countdown, Samuel went into our room, stole some prescription medicine and force-fed the entire bottle to Ashley. The drugs sat inactive in his stomach until we left the dark space dream-state, then they stopped his heart. Samuel used the distraction to gain entrance to the command center, where he tried to turn off the life-support system."

"That's why the masks deployed," one of the passengers realized.

There were many cries for blood or justice, but the only question Rachael would answer was, "Where is Samuel now?"

"The ship has no secure holding cell, but there was a construction suit that only responds to me. After I found out what Samuel had done, I forced him into my suit. Somehow he was able to launch it and escape."

The journalist looked confused. "Where did he imagine he was running to?"

Her answer and all further questions were interrupted by Evermore's voice booming over the shuttle bay intercom. "Everyone please hang on. The construction crew has repositioned the gate farther from the planet, and we're about to exit dark space."

The journalist who had just asked her about Samuel threw his Omni to the floor in frustration. "Damn it! I forgot about the dream-state paradox. None of that got recorded."

Rachael felt that comforting pressure squeezing her as the *Godspeed* crossed the invisible threshold between dimensions, and as suddenly as if she had awakened from a daydream, she was back in the medical bay. Instead of holding Sean, she held the transdermal pacemaker.

She allowed herself to float up and away from Ashley's twisted body. She couldn't bring herself to look away from his skin, darkened with anoxia. All life had left him. Ashley was unmistakably dead, yet that feeling Rachael got when he first entered the trance had returned. She could feel him watching her.

"Ashley, I don't know if you can hear me from where you are. But I'm going to find a way to get you back. I happen to know someone who can build you a new body."

# CHAPTER THIRTY-FIVE

# Planetfall

### Rachael

Evermore's voice from down the corridor shook Rachael from her daydream.

"Ma'at, instruct the construction crew to reinstall the *Godspeed*'s thrusters first and then work on moving the global surveyor and reconnaissance satellites into position." His voice was growing louder. "Asbjorn, I want you and your engineers to inspect the shuttle for signs of tampering. I want the shuttle cleared for departure in two hours. We've come all this way, it would be a shame not to visit the surface." Evermore pulled himself into the med bay with one hand while the other held an Omni in front of his face. "Rachael."

"No! Don't call me that!"

He gave her an exhausted look. "I don't have time for your name games. I'm here to say goodbye to my son. Stay or go, I don't care." He drifted past her without taking his eyes off Ashley.

Evermore hooked his feet into railings on the floor and grasped one of Ashley's cold hands in his own. "My boy," he said, but not in that old-timey, endearing sort of way. Each syllable was given equal emphasis. "My *boy*!" The man started to weep.

"My God, you were so tiny the day you were born," Evermore said. "Until that moment when I held you in my arms, I — God, I'm so ashamed! — I hadn't even thought of you as anything but an experiment." Evermore held Ashley's hand to his face. "I would get so lost in my own reality in those days, and when your tiny body snapped me out of it, I was so ashamed. I didn't want anyone to know what I had done, and I used that as an excuse to stay away, but goddamnit! I missed the moments. I missed all your first moments, and you grew up before I even realized time was passing."

He broke down sobbing again, and Rachael wasn't sure whether she should leave or comfort him. Part of her couldn't conceive of comforting this monster, but another part had enormous sympathy for how much he was forced to suppress.

Evermore kissed the back of Ashley's hand. "There were so many moments when I wanted so badly to show you affection, to tell you how proud I am, and I couldn't. I didn't. I chose the lie I was telling the world over you."

Rachael shook her head until the dust of the past was shaken from between her ears. "Evermore, stop it! Look at yourself, you're a mess!"

Evermore glared at her with red eyes. "You'll have your time to grieve. People will understand and accept your grief. Let me have this."

"I'm sorry, but you're still not thinking straight. We don't *have* to say goodbye."

"No!" Evermore barked. "I know what you're thinking, and absolutely not."

"Don't choose selfishness again. We can build him another body: we know the *exact* ingredients. It's our fault that he's dead. Let's make it right!"

A tear welled up and floated away from Evermore's eye as he turned back to Ashley's body. He reached out and caught it. "We can't. Samuel knew how and when to enter the fetus I grew. Ashley may not even have enough consciousness to remember who and where he is, and we have no way to teach him."

"You don't know that. Maybe he can hear us!" Rachael shouted.

"I'm almost positive he can feel our hearts, but he cannot hear us any more than you can hear your grandmother speaking to you through your bones."

"Well, then, what do we do?"

"We say goodbye so that when he is able to slip free from the crystal armor, he doesn't become a ghost. Now please either shut up or leave." He was silent for a long time.

Evermore's voice was muffled, but she could still hear him say, "I could easily blame my neglectful and cold father for the way I treated you. I had the opportunity to give you everything that I never had. But instead I wanted to shape you into me so you would take up my life's work when I die."

"I'll be in my room if you need me for anything."

Evermore nodded without turning around.

Rachael slipped her legs into the soft elastic sleeve that served as sheet, blanket, and restraint. It gently tightened and held her against the bed. She thought, *It feels like months have passed since we left Mars. It's hard to remember we only left this morning.*

In her dreams, Rachael imagined their descent to the planet. Though her heart was pounding as the landing shuttle plummeted through the atmosphere, it was not thundering out of fear but excitement. As air resistance heated the outer layer of the craft, a million thermo-reactive nano-machines sprouted from the shuttle's hull like as many blades of grass growing in fast-forward. Once the metal sprouts reached optimal length, they each grew a bulb, which in turn sprouted a thousand new metallic filaments, which also grew a bulb sprouting a thousand more until the shuttle was hidden within a nest of hair-thin poly-fibers. Like a white dandelion seed ball, they floated serenely down to the new planet's surface and landed softer than a feather. The shuttle doors opened upon a field of the freshest, greenest-looking grass Rachael had ever seen. Evermore nodded at her. She unbuckled, stood, and walked down the ramp. As she was about to step onto the grass, Evermore softly said, "Rachael?" She turned to face him.

"Rachael?" he said again, without moving his mouth.

Rubbing the sleep from her eyes, she said, "I'm awake."

Evermore was hanging from the handrails outside her bunk. "I'm sorry if I startled you. Were you dreaming?"

She starting pulling away the sheets and nodded. "I dreamed that the landing shuttle was a dandelion seed ball."

"That's beautiful. I'm sorry I spoke so harshly before, my dear. I can only imagine what you're going through." She didn't know what to say. "Anyway, the shuttle's clean, and everything's ready to go. We'll be launching in T minus fifteen."

"Okay, I'll be right there."

After giving Sean an obligatory kiss and handing him back to Aziza, Rachael climbed up the *Godspeed* to the shuttle bay. The seats of the landing shuttle ran along the walls. When they were all seated, the open floor between them flickered to life with a projected image of the outside. The screen gave the illusion that the shuttle had a glass bottom. Slowly the floor of the shuttle bay hinged open, revealing a beautiful view from four hundred kilometers up. They were positioned above a massive sandy-brown continent, surrounded by gorgeous greenish-blue oceans. Puffy white clouds high in the atmosphere drifted slowly through the foreground, casting shadows on the land below and adding a terrifying depth to the image. Edging the tectonic plates were high mountain ranges iced with white, and massive plains of light-brown soil stretched across the expanses between them. The electro-magnets that affixed the shuttle to the *Godspeed* reversed polarity and gave the shuttle a sudden push out the door. They must have been moving closer, but they were so far from the surface the mind didn't have enough perspective to realize they were actually falling at thousands of meters per second.

Rachael realized that she had been hearing a roaring sound for the past few minutes, but her mind had only just noticed. As the shuttle reached its terminal velocity, the roaring increased but never got uncomfortably loud. Rachael had seen the computer simulations, and she knew that sometime during their initial descent, massive kinetic breaks extended to harvest 96 percent of the energy gen-erated by their plummet. When they reached the seven-kilometer mark, five long helicopter blades unfolded and extended. Sometime past six kilometers, they hit the cir-rostratus cloud layer, and their tremendous speed became apparent.

"This part can be rather sickening," Evermore said as he turned off the screen on the floor.

Rachael looked up and around at the eager faces of the other passengers. She was surprised to see what remained of her Lab Seven team staring at her excitedly. She tried to ignore the empty seat beside her, and smiled back at them.

The roaring of air resistance tapered off and was re-placed by the rhythmic, mechanical sound of the rotors eating up air. The rotors arrested their descent, and for a moment Rachael's heart fluttered with excitement as she imagined they had landed, but then the landing shuttle tipped and headed in a new direction. Now that their plummeting descent had slowed to a hover, Evermore turned the screens in the floor back on. They were less than a kilometer above the earth. The ground was miles and miles of dirt and rock.

Evermore walked into the center of the room holding on to overhead handrails. "Eighty percent of the planet is covered by water, and while landing on the supercontinent was my goal, our corkscrew descent took us farther inland than I would have liked. We're heading toward the sea."

The landing shuttle descended gradually as they approached the western coast of the continent, which looked out on a gorgeous turquoise sea. Rachael couldn't see any waves, not even as they got closer. Before they landed, Rachael saw dark green lines in the sand that marked the high tide, and just beyond the reach of the sea, a creep of cool green vegetation laced its way across the ground in spiderweb-like patterns that reminded her of the way the *Lepraria ptilisaccharon* lichen grew among the crystal molecules.

Rachael's body was shaking as the landing gear gently sank into the loose dirt. Evermore smiled at her lovingly, and though her face held its hard, focused resolve, she couldn't stop herself from crying.

The journalists were hurriedly unpacking flying cameras, the planetary geologist recovered his jump kit of scientific instruments, and Evermore moved to the controls for the bay door and paused. "The air is seventy-four degrees with 80 percent humidity, and more oxygen-heavy than you may be used to. It's breathable, and there are no micro-organisms, spores, airborne viruses, or bacteria. However, we have provided oxygen masks for each of you, and I am legally required to recommend you use them." He made a gesture at Rachael to come join him. Once she was standing at his side, he asked, "What do you think of calling her Virginia One?"

Under her breath so that only he could hear, she said, "I think mankind would probably like another virgin planet to fuck over." But she thought for a moment and gave her press-conference answer: "Virginia holds historical significance for us Americans, but let's not forget that we are in the house of Virgo, and perhaps we have found where Astraea has been hiding all these years." The journalists looked at each other questioningly, and Rachael realized that not everyone was up on their Greek mythology. "Astraea is a Greek goddess who abandoned Earth during the Iron Age to become the constellation Virgo. It was said that her return would usher in a new Golden Age for humankind. Maybe, just maybe, if we do things different this time, we can appeal for her to return to Earth."

Evermore winced and said quietly, "That was meant to be rhetorical, but goddamnit if you aren't right." He turned, faced the cameras, said, "Welcome to Astraea," and opened the door.

There was a gasp of air as the shuttle's atmosphere neutralized, and the door opened like a drawbridge. Rachael and Evermore were the first to feel the warm, never-before-breathed air on their faces, to taste its sweetness in their mouths, and to feel it invigorate their lungs.

Rachael walked out onto the ramp even before it touched the ground, unaware of the news cameras rushing out past her. Her feet sank to the uppers in the tender earth. She looked out at the flat landscape. A hundred meters away, the ocean stretched out forever, and, in the opposite direction, far beyond the horizon line, a jagged mountain range rose up into the blue sky.

*God, this place is so fucking empty.*

"Were you lonely, Astraea?" she whispered to the soil. "I know what it's like to be uninhabited."

Evermore walked up beside her. "It's hard to keep it in perspective. We're so far from home, but it all feels so familiar."

The news cameras circled around them. Evermore pointed out to the mountain range and yelled at the journalist holding the controls, "Capture that range; the screens in Nili Terradome will be showing Astraea's mountains by the end of the week."

Rachael looked off at the mountains again, realizing they were the first real mountains she had seen since leaving Earth. Even the view of Olympus Mons from the space plane was translated through wires and screens. Evermore kept walking past her, and, feeling a loneliness in the space between them, she hurried to catch up.

Evermore noticed her proximity but merely said, "Care to join me for a walk?" After a few steps he said, "I liked working with Clyde Kander; he was a good friend, and he always served as my moral compass. It took me a long time to find someone with both those qualities. I don't think I've ever said how much I've enjoyed our mentoring sessions over these months, and I've actually come to value your utter disregard for my prestige."

"Oh, well, that's a holdover from your complete disrespect of me as a human. I simply learned not to take it personally, since you don't give that respect to *anyone*."

True to their recent rapport, Evermore pretended as if he hadn't heard. "I honestly feel you'll be a great CEO of Evermore Industries when the time comes, but there's something more I'd like from you."

She turned to him and growled, "What more could you possibly take from me?"

Evermore seemed taken aback by her anger and held his hands up defensively. "I'm sorry, I had no idea you'd hear it that way." He seemed to close himself off to her. "There's my answer right there."

She rolled her eyes at him. "No. Say it; what do you want from me?"

"I'd like to adopt you as my daughter."

Rachael was stunned.

"I always wanted to adopt Ashley, but I couldn't figure a way to do it without raising suspicion. But the Evermore dynasty has to start somewhere, and my family is as desolate as this planet."

She was silent for a long time. "Doc, all my life has

been driving toward this moment; I just want to take in the scenery while I have the chance."

There was a long silence between them. *Damnit, old man, you've soured my moment!*

Rachael gave an annoyed cough and said, "Why are you even thinking about all that? Look at where were are! Can't you take a moment to experience some sense of accomplishment?" Her eyes filled with tears. "Look at me, I'm so overwhelmed I'm literally weeping. Why can't you feel that?"

He held her out at arm's length and smiled, but there was a tired sadness behind his eyes. "I do, my dear, I do, but this is only the first step in what I hope to accomplish."

As they walked back to the shuttle, following their own trail of footprints, he said, "Rachael, have you thought about what's next? You've achieved your life's goal, but you've got so much life ahead of you."

She shook her head.

"In the past you've been adverse to my attempts at support; if it's okay with you, I'd like to offer some advice." When she didn't resist, he continued, "Before I had any concept of how powerful I was, I dreamed a goal for myself that I thought was high enough to fuel my passion for an entire lifetime, but when I achieved that lifelong dream in a matter of years, I found myself left with nothing. I had used up my dream and had nothing to hold on to. I was depressed for a long time after that. I wanted to solve the world's problems, but they seemed either too trivial or too enormous to inspire me, and I stalled. I have a hunch that this is why the majority of people never achieve their life's work: somewhere inside ourselves we know that the paradise we've dreamed of is this." He gestured at the landscape enveloping them. "A beautiful but ultimately lonely place. For every piece of our achievement that we can share, there are a hundred moments of solitary struggle that no one can understand."

Rachael's gentle weeping gave way to a few racking sobs. She stopped walking to try and gain control over them when Evermore placed a hand on her shoulder. "I know," he assured her. "I understand."

"No you fucking don't!" she screamed. "I never wanted this. I never wanted to be the poster-child for women's rights on Mars. I never wanted to think about whether I was pro-life or pro-choice; I never even wanted to be the next Crellinger. I'm a fucking artist! All I've ever wanted was the freedom to think about things in a way no one ever has." Rachael turned to look at Evermore. "So there's your answer. I have no fucking idea what's next. I don't even really know who I'm supposed to be now. I've completed all my assignments for you, and I don't even have anyone who expects me to be or act a certain way."

Evermore either had no response or had the sense to let her continue.

"The first time I went into dark space, every part of my identity was stripped away, and I experienced true freedom. When I came back and remembered myself, I found out I don't have any idea who I am. I'm still twelve years old trying to figure out where I fit in!"

Evermore shrugged. "You rarely exercise restraint when I've fed you some garbage line; now it's my turn. Rachael, my dear, that's bullshit. You are an amazing scientist, and right here and now you have the power and freedom to do whatever you want. You want to make art? Fine! Do it, but you know where you belong, so stop listening to your defensive ego trying to protect itself. Let go of whatever voice keeps telling you you're not good enough, decide what you want, and take it."

Rachael stared off into the distance for a long time. At some point Evermore left to conduct some obligatory interviews. Lost in her thoughts, she didn't notice him leave and didn't hear Cyrus Ma'at approach.

"It's a lot to take in, huh?"

*He's talking about the scenery.* "Yeah."

"I'm not intruding — do you want to be alone?" he asked.

"No, stay."

Ma'at seemed relieved by her answer. "There is something I have been wanting to talk to you about for some time now. I feel ashamed I haven't brought it up before, but... I wish I'd asked you before taking the director position at the DNC."

"Asked me what?"

"You were our leader at Lab Seven; you turned my meager research on a crystal into transgalactic transportation. I understand that Evermore needed someone to hold the position, and you were still on family leave. He could have made my position temporary, but I bet he never even offered it to you. You deserve to be the director, and I should have talked to you before accepting."

"That's really sweet, Cyrus."

But he was still struggling with something he wanted to say, and it made her nervous. "No. It is not sweet; it is what's right. I will step down if you want me to. Evermore may be a genius, but he has no moral compass, and what he did to you is appalling." Rachael had never seen him so angry, and it made her uncomfortable.

"It's true, he didn't offer me the DNC; just before the Public Health Service raided the E.I. building he offered me vice-CEO."

Cyrus looked confused. "But that was months before we made the gate; in fact, it was right after you exposed the whole city to an — at the time — unknown radiation source. Did he know the PHS was about to shut down E.I.?"

Rachael nodded. "He knew. But you have to remember that Samuel had been manipulating Evermore for a long time. He needed my help swapping the crystal plate build order, so he gave me something I wouldn't refuse."

"But why hasn't he publicly made the announcement yet?"

Rachael looked at him sheepishly. "I haven't fully decided if I want it or not."

"What are your other options?"

"I could teach." But she had dismissed that as an option as soon as UMars contacted her.

"Really? Honestly, Rachael, there is a part of me that is very afraid of what Evermore Industries will become now that it has exclusive access to Astraea. There was a precedent set when Mars was taken over by the first settlers, and if the UN makes the same call for Astraea, I can only imagine what Evermore will do here if he's unregulated and unchecked."

"I don't want that," Rachael grumbled through her newly wept tears. "I don't want to be the one to speak up, or the one to challenge our culture, or the one to do anything! I've felt like the only one for too long, and I'm fucking tired."

"So you were just hoping to tag this victory and fade back into the small life you had before?"

She didn't respond, and after Cyrus had calmed down, he said, "I'm not here to convince you of anything. I just came over to get that guilt off my chest. But for whatever it's worth, if Evermore is offering up some of his unlimited control, I can't think of anyone better suited to handle him."

Rachael found her seat beside Aziza and Sean in the passenger cabin of the *Godspeed*. Sean was staring at something partly concealed in his chubby hand. "Hey, little man, what do you have there?" It was Ashley's silver pilot's wings.

In his attempt to show them to her, Sean fumbled the

wings, and they floated up and away from him. Rachael caught them easily and remembered the way Ashley had looked the first time she'd met him via that video interview so long ago. She squeezed the wings in her left hand until their sharp edges left dents in her palm. Without a word, Aziza reached for her right hand, interlacing her fingers with Rachael's, and they sat in silence as the construction crew manually pushed the ship back into dark space.

# CHAPTER THIRTY-SIX

# Projections

**Rachael**

Deborah had long lines of mascara running down her face. She'd been crying long before Rachael's driver pulled up and parked in front of her condo. The driver got out, opened the door for Rachael, and continued to the trunk. Rachael stepped out and gave her mother a small wave that only made her cry more. Embarrassed for her, Rachael broke eye contact and walked around to the other side of the car, where she unbuckled Sean. Briefly she considered lifting his tiny arm to make him wave at Grandma, but decided against it and set him down in the stroller. She tipped the driver on her Omni and heard his pocket make a *cha-ching* noise. He gave a quick nod of appreciation.

"If you wouldn't mind following me up the walk with the bags..."

"Not at all."

Deborah waited for them on her stoop as if she weren't allowed to leave the condo, and the excitement built in her until Rachael thought her mother would burst. *You are so ridiculous.* She couldn't make eye contact, and so she let Sean occupy her as she pushed him up the concrete walkway that cut a path across the bone-dry lawn, spray-painted green to look fresh and healthy. Finally Deborah's excitement could no longer be restrained, and she leapt off the single step and ran toward them.

"Oh, would you just look at this beautiful, strong boy!" Deborah pulled Sean from his stroller and placed a juicy smooch on his fat cheek. He continued to be as stoic as ever. "You're just a heavy boy, aren't you?"

*Heavy boy, indeed. From the low gravity of Mars to the weightlessness of space, suddenly he feels exactly 63 percent heavier.*

Deborah's exaggerated smile hovered inches from his face. She bounced him. "Hello, my heavy boy! Hello, my heavy boy!" Sean's face muscles twitched. "Oh, is that a smile? Is that a smile?"

Rachael braced for impact.

Sean's eyes grew wide and his cheeks pulled back into the same exaggerated smile his grandma had shown him. This was not the first time Rachael had seen Sean mimic another person's happy-to-see-a-baby face, and most were alarmed the first time they saw it, but Deborah simply exclaimed, "There's the smile. Ooh, look! You've got a tooth coming in!"

The driver followed them and set the bags just inside the door. He nodded appreciation at Rachael again and gave a baby wave to Sean, who gave it right back.

"Oh my goodness, you're waving already? You must be a smarty-pants like your mother." Deborah said, acknowledging Rachael for the first time.

"Hi, Mom,"

"Hi, dear." She gave a quick hug.

*Oh, are we withholding love now? Are you still angry that I left?*

"Can you believe it that he's waving bye-bye already?"

Rachael sat down on the couch in the front room. She felt as if she weighed two hundred pounds. "He is, but he doesn't understand what it means. He's got some kind of echopraxia."

"Oh my God," Deborah whispered. "Is he autistic?"

"No. And you don't need to worry about offending him; he doesn't know what words mean. Also, people with autism usually have a *deficit* in social mimicry." Rachael held out her arms, offering to take Sean back.

"Well, you're the behaviorist, not me." To Rachael's relief, Deborah didn't give him up.

"Mom, I'm not—"

"Oh, you know what I mean. So if he's not autistic, what's—"

"Wrong with him?" Rachael finished her question. "I can't get anyone to diagnose him with anything, so technically he's healthy and fine, but..."

"But mother knows best."

*I can't deny it, and I can't agree without giving her some fuel for some future argument. Well played, Deborah.*

There was a long silence that Rachael didn't know how to fill. She didn't really care about Deborah's current job, or her opinion on the state of the world. Her childhood home had been put on the market the year after she left for Mars, but she didn't want to know how much it had sold for.

"Mom, how are you?"

"I think you should start calling me Grandma so Seanny will learn to call me Grandma too."

Rachael tried to imagine Sean as slightly older. "He's probably going to call *you* Seanny." Deborah smiled, and Rachael repeated the question. "How are you?"

Her mother started to cry again. "Oh, give it up, you don't want to know how I am. I know you came here for an 'I told you so.'"

Rachael couldn't deny that she had overcome her mother's expectations for her and along the way created a means of traveling across the galaxy in an instant, but that wasn't why she had come. She said, "It was hard for me to be the only one who believed in me. Being right only makes me feel more alone. I'm here because I've been flying so high for the past year, and I need to come down. I want to sleep somewhere safe and wake up and be surprised by the weather. So let's just forget it." Rachael closed her eyes and rested her head on the couch.

"I can't forget it. I can never forget that one of my daughters ended her own life, and that if I'd gotten my way I would have kept my other daughter so safe she never would have had one."

That ancient pain tightened its grip around Rachael's throat.

Deborah said, "I read an article that said that planet you discovered—"

"I didn't discover Astraea, I was just the first person on her surface."

"Right. I read that Astraea will allow us to expand out, and people will get some breathing room here."

"It'll be a long time before there's any sort of mass colonization effort."

"That's not the point, Rachael. You've given our doomed race a chance at a future, and that I did anything to stop you makes me just about the worst mother is history."

"Don't you think you're being a little melodramatic?"

Deborah sat down beside her and let baby Sean rest on her chest. "I'm sorry, Rachael. I'm so sorry for being such a terrible mother."

"You aren't a terrible mother." Rachael closed her eyes and thought of the stories Ashley had told her about his mother.

Deborah said nothing.

Rachael wished her mother's vindication or her apology had meant something to her, but she didn't feel any sense of relief, or of deeper connection.

After a long moment of Deborah pretending to fuss over Sean, she eventually said, "Don't you want to say something?"

Rachael opened her eyes and looked at her mother. "Something like what?"

Deborah didn't meet her gaze. "I just thought you might also want to apologize."

Rachael scooted away to the other end of the couch. "Apologize for *what*?"

"Don't yell, you'll upset the baby," Deborah said. "I just thought you might want to get some things off your chest, like how I could count on my hand the number of times you've called in the last four years, or how you worried me practically to death launching yourself into space, or traveling through that Dark Hole you created. Do you know how many times I was sure I'd never see you again? I've basically been living as though you were dead. Anything to protect me from the day I found out it was actually true."

"Well, you know what, Deborah? I've been living that way, too. For all my life there's been this voice inside me telling me that I'm nothing. Worth nothing, and capable of nothing. Now I have all this proof that I'm valuable, but even the admiration of fucking billions can't penetrate this hollow blackness I'll always carry around inside of me."

Deborah held Sean close to her chest and covered his ear with her hand.

"I didn't come here to apologize; I came so that Sean could meet his grandma, and maybe some part of him would remember what you are like so he could one day forgive me."

"Forgive you for what?"

"I'm not done. I don't expect you to understand what I'm talking about, but I discovered a fifth fundamental force, and I'm not going to give up that opportunity to be a single parent. So thank you for being a perfect mirror of the single parent I'd become, you've made it so... so clear that the best place for Sean is with Cyrus and Aziza."

Deborah looked so shocked Rachael would have felt bad for her if she weren't buzzing with elation. She'd been struggling with the decision for months, and Deborah had just set her free.

*No. I set myself free.*

Back on Mars, Rachael's companions in the space elevator were cargo containers destined for the *Godspeed*. This batch of cargo would complete the restock operation in preparation for its second voyage. Evermore Industries was returning to Astraea and bringing two teams of scientists from K&J and UMars, who were interested in learning all they could about the new planet, along with its own team of engineers and contractors, who would begin the design and installation of a space elevator/dry dock complex.

Though she was being lifted away from Mars, it felt as if she were being lowered. With every story she could feel her weight returning, until the doors finally opened on the E.I. Department of Numinous Cosmology's newly acquired dry dock station. Before she'd had the chance to unbuckle herself from the elevator's only seat, one of the workers drove in on a forklift and startled.

"Jesus Chri— er... Chairwoman Dahlia, you scared the—" He stopped himself. "No one told me you'd be visiting us."

Rachael walked toward him and read his E.I. ID badge. "Amanaki, this is an unofficial visit. I just want to make sure everything is in order for our upcoming launch. Please don't tell anyone I'm here."

He nodded understanding and said, "It's an honor to meet you, ma'am. Enjoy your visit."

She made her way to Ma'at's office, trying her best not to be seen by other roving workers. Down a long corridor toward the offices, Ma'at rounded the corner walking briskly toward her. "Rachael, I'm so sorry. I meant to meet you when you arrived, but I lost track of time."

"It's fine. I'm more than comfortable finding my own

way."

They met in the middle and embraced; a short but heartfelt moment passed before Ma'at stepped back and said, "Oh! You have to watch this!" He pulled out his Omni and held it up for her. They stood shoulder to shoulder and watched a short video of Sean taking his first steps.

As Rachael watched, Sean's face scrunched up as he concentrated super hard on keeping his balance, and a feeling of relief settled into her body. *He's normal; he's going to be okay.*

Turning to face Ma'at, she said, "God, he's barely eight months old!"

His pride couldn't be hidden. "Yeah, but he refused to crawl anywhere unless Aziza was doing it with him. This is actually his second first steps. She got him to do it again, by crawling and then standing up. Look at him, you can just see how hard he wants to stand up like her." Ma'at met her gaze. "I know I've said it a hundred times, but we can't thank you enough."

"It's mutual."

Ma'at directed her back the way she had come and shook his head. "He's brought us so much joy I can't believe that's true."

There had been a steady stream of workers loading cargo into the *Godspeed* over the last few days, but Ma'at had scheduled a pressure test to coincide with Rachael's visit. When they arrived, the boarding area was empty, and the hatch had been closed and tagged with a big red sign that read, "AREA OFF LIMITS! Trespassing will result in injury or death."

Without hesitating, Ma'at pulled open the hatch, but it had been closed so recently the two areas were still equalized.

Rachael paused. "I didn't know I'd be interrupting your

tests. Is this safe?"

Ma'at nodded. "We're not really conducting tests. I thought you'd want some privacy, and I needed to give the union a reason for the prolonged break." He waved her in before closing the door behind them.

Once inside they passed through the passenger cabin and climbed up the central corridor toward the aft of the ship. When Ma'at left the corridor to take up his old station in the foreman's control room, Rachael said, "Thank you so much, Cyrus. I know how busy you must be getting ready for launch and—"

"Please, this is the least I can do for you. I wish I had astral projection training so I could do the same thing once in a while."

Now that she was alone, Rachael continued climbing up to the launch bay and allowed herself to try to feel Ashley's presence. She couldn't tell if it was real or imagined, but he seemed far away. *What if he's moved on?* The thought was both hopeful for his sake and heartbreaking for hers.

With the *Godspeed* hanging from the dry dock station, the corridor was aligned so that the nine manhole-size hatches were on the wall. Above each hatch was a green label: "Suit Ready." At the far end was a locker room, where she stripped down and put on her Second Skin electromyographic response suit before returning to the launch bay and positioning herself in front of the ninth hatch. Even though she wouldn't be joining this second mission to Astraea, Ma'at had rebuilt her a construction suit in anticipation of future missions. After the numen scanner read her unique signature, the hatch opened, and Ma'at's voice sounded over the intercom system.

"Everything's all set on my end. I've taped some paper over the monitor in the suit to give you some privacy, but I'll be watching your bio status as a safety measure."

It took her a second to find the camera mounted on

the opposite wall of launch bay corridor; she gave it the thumbs-up, climbed into her construction suit, and lay herself on the vacuum chair, which engaged and held her in place. Rachael took a deep breath and plugged the guide serum IVs into the port on the left arm of her Second Skin suit.

The lights in the construction suit dimmed, and her body tensed into paralysis. All of her muscles locked up in a wave radiating from her heart. Her breath grew short and quick as her diaphragm fought against her tensed abs, and slowly the burning of lactate started to build into crescendos of pain before the relaxant kicked in. It felt as if the heat of tension was melting her, and even though her body wasn't moving, she felt as if she were a liquid dripping through the vacuum chair. Her eyelids drooped closed, and she continued liquefying and leaking into the cracks of the construction suit. The darkness that caught her was oceans deep and perfectly comfortable.

"Ashley?" she said, as if she had tossed a coin down a well and was waiting. It was much deeper than she had expected.

From far away, or near but just very faint, she felt something bush her face, and she was caressed in a memory of him. "Ashley, can you hear me?"

The breath that blew across her was the smell of him, and she was pulled into an out-of-body experience where she was watching Ashley's shaking hands as he held his Omni between them.

*The screen scrolled the message, "Connecting to Dr. Rae Dahlia." He propped the phone against a tall white take-out box with two red dragons woven into the number "88" on the side. It rang and rang, and eventually she answered, saying, "Hello?"*

It seemed like such a mundane moment to her, but with the visuals came a wave of emotion, and she was surprised to feel the giddy sensation of butterflies in her stomach.

As she found herself back in the darkness of the pilot's trance, Rachael remembered stories the construction crew had told her about what it was like to be possessed by the stray revenants that wandered dark space. The experiences the ghosts imparted were automatic and unaware. Ashley's had felt the same way, and she worried that she'd already lost him.

"I'm here, Ashley."

He pulled her into another memory, which she realized had been his last waking moments:

*She was in the piloting chamber slipping into the trance, but Samuel had somehow gotten into the room, and she was forced to feel the horrible choking sensation as her throat struggled to automatically swallow the handful of pills.*

The memory gave Ashley a direction and a shape, and Rachael had the sensation that she was floating inside of him, and that he was enormous.

"I know." She did her best to relive the memory of breaking Samuel's ribs, and trapping him in her old construction suit.

From far away some robotic voice said, "Invalid launch sequence." *Shit, I need to make sure I don't remember my launch code accidentally. Although I'm pretty sure Cyrus can override it if he's paying attention.*

A feeling of confusion overwhelmed her, and it took her a moment to realize that she wasn't confused, Ashley was. "Ashley, you're..." She remembered the difficulty of pulling the transdermal pacemaker from his chest, the long solemn moment when Dr. Shah and his paramedics carried Ashley's lifeless body from the *Godspeed*, the lost, direction-less feeling in her chest as the funeral director handed her his urn.

Rachael had expected anger or panic from him, but all he felt was empty. She pushed herself to the edge of him and pressed her form into his. "We were falling into the planet and you saved us." She remembered the memorials for him, and as best she could what each person had said.

"I can't imagine what it was like for you on the trip out to Virgo, but to us it felt like months had gone by. That eccentric guy you met just before launch, Valenci, recited Moby Dick in its entirety." Then she remembered the trip back and how it only seemed to take minutes.

*Evermore was right,* she thought, and couldn't stop herself from feeling the grief that bubbled up throughout her being. *There's enough of him here to know what he needs to do when we enter dark space, but not enough that he can consciously communicate.*

She remembered every night she'd slept beside him until he responded in kind, wrapping her in an amalgam of memories. She was back in Nili Terradome, yet somewhere in the background was the hum of the centrifuge station on Phobos.

*Rachael slipped between the sheets until she was skin to skin with Ashley's softly sleeping form. She let the warmth of his body, the soft rise and fall of his unconscious breath, and the potpourri of his scent lull her to sleep. In that dream within a dream, her vision extended into the realm beyond. Ashley, glowing with a blueish light, turned to face her, and the two gently kissed through the hole between science and reality.*

# Epilogue

## Marine

I want to tell you about something that happened to me when I was ten years old. Just so you can imagine me at ten, I had dirty-blond hair cut short. I obviously had the same olive-colored eyes, but then, when they weren't hidden beneath my overgrown bangs, they glistened with more of a sense of wonder at the world. On that particular day I was wearing my junking outfit, which was a dirty gray adult-size T-shirt from a local music syndicate tucked into a pair of dark-blue bib overalls. I carried a screwdriver as long as my forearm sheathed into the button-hole at my hip like a sword. To complete the outfit, I wore mismatched knee pads and a pair of old leather gardening gloves with the fingers cut off. The final component was this pair of binoculars, which I would poke between the spaces in this chain link fence that surrounded an enormous strip mine the Seryys had dug searching for titanium. The mine had hit its limit and been abandoned before I was even born, and the old crater was (and still is) home to the largest scrapyard in the United Systems. Everyone called it The Heap, and it was my favorite place in the world.

The mountain of scrap metal in the center of the crater was, and I imagine still is, fed by a conveyor belt wide enough for two landing ships to sit side by side. During regular working hours, The Heap is home to remote-controlled spider-cranes that pick though the metal and haul it to an adjacent area called The Fields, which stretch out for miles in all directions but north, where the water-knife factory takes up acres and acres of land. For those of you who don't know where your dark-space ships go when they're decommissioned, they're sent here, first to the water-knife factory, where the crystal is "cut" off the metal hull with streams of high-pressure water, before their long conveyor belt ride to The Heap.

Each field is owned by a different scrap company and patrolled by surly guards, angry dogs, automated security, and often all three. Either way, The Fields were off limits for a ten-year-old girl. Well... The Heap was off limits, too, but no one ever tried to stop me. Actually, that's not true: Martin tried to stop me all the time.

"Marine," Martin whined, "school is starting in fourteen minutes!"

Without taking my eyes from the binoculars, I said, "Then we'll log on in fourteen minutes. Honestly, Martin, when we're not together do you log into class early and just sit there alone?"

"*No.*" He was indignant. "Marine, we can't log on from here: they track our Vias, and they'll know we're out of bounds."

I must have given him a mischievous smile in reply, because he said, "I hate that look. What did you do?"

"Remember the day we found that telecom satellite?" Martin nodded. "Yeah."

I walked to the heavy-duty four-wheeler that had carried us out this far, and took out a cardboard box wrapped in electrical tape, which was a total hack job. "It was the only thing I could find big enough to fit the circuit board. Get your Via while I start up the network."

Martin raised a questioning eyebrow but said nothing as I paced out 120 meters, the distance from my home to the nearest telecom tower, flipped a switch on the side of the box, and laid it down in the sand. I returned to Martin and explained, "Our location is known by how long it takes our Via signals to bounce off Junkertown tower. I made that box copy our tower's signal. The satellites won't know the difference.

"How'd you know how to do all that?" he asked.

"Dunno," I shrugged, "I just get an idea and know how it's supposed to work."

Dropping our Via goggles over our eyes and aligning the earphones, we found ourselves in a virtual classroom. Mrs. Yabloko stood at the front of the room slightly blocking a whiteboard-size monitor that displayed either pictures or short videos relating to the subject matter. When I looked down I would see that my hand held a pen which I couldn't let go of, and when I flicked my hand a display hovered above my wrist, allowing me to select the color of ink and create tags for each of my notes. The desk also dictated Mrs. Yabloko's lecture into text.

After running an attendance roll call, Mrs. Yabloko said, "Good morning. Which of you can tell me who this woman is and why she is important?"

The picture was from the cover of an RSS magazine, but the caption and title were blurred out. The woman had light-brown hair so short it wouldn't lay flat, and fierce hazel eyes that seemed to challenge anyone looking at the picture. She was wearing a white lab coat with an Evermore Industries patch on the breast pocket. In her hands she held a huge wrench coated in that same light-green crystal the water-knife factory specialized in scrubbing off.

As soon as I saw her, I gasped. This woman had striking confidence, and an intelligence that seemed to radiate from her. The corners of her mouth were turned down ever so slightly, and I could just tell that she thought the photo shoot was a waste of time and she had better things to do.

"Anyone?" Mrs. Yabloko asked.

I didn't know who this woman was, but every part of me wanted to.

"The Mother of Dark Space?" answered one of the faceless classmates from behind me. I thought I recognized the voice as one of the children from Junkertown, but when I looked around the room my classmates were perfect models of obedience and as diverse as the United Systems, though I knew for a fact that there were far more Seryy children in my class than any other nation. I had never even been able to distinguish Martin from among my virtual classmates. He claimed that he also sat at the front of the class, and that whenever he heard me speak, my voice came from an Alba girl a few rows behind him.

"That's what they called her," Mrs. Yabloko said, "but who can tell me her name?"

As I admired this unknown woman's portrait, the blurred-out text beneath the image clarified for just an instant, long enough that I read: "Exclusive Interview with Rachael Dahlia, the Mother of Dark Space."

No one answered, and I wondered if anyone else had seen that.

It felt a little like cheating, but I raised my hand and said, "Rachael Dahlia."

"Correct," Mrs. Yabloko said, and rewarded me with thirty-two kilobytes of bandwidth for my Via and a smiling cat smaylikov to decorate my virtual desk (though only I could see my stickers). "This quarter we'll be learning about Rachael Dahlia. Take notes; there will be a test about her personal history on Friday."

While Mrs. Yabloko lectured about Rachael's place of birth and her early education, I couldn't help but be fascinated. Like me, Rachael didn't do very well in public school. I knew it was because all the things they taught children were boring and the pace was slowed down to give the stupid kids a chance to catch up. With each location the teacher mentioned, the scenery outside the classroom's huge windows shifted, giving some context to how different places on Earth could be. When I had first seen images of Earth, I had marveled at all the different ways the planet could look, but then it only made me angry that I was stuck on Quarry Delta, the fourth planet along a string of dark-space gates known as the Titan's road. Quarry Delta is covered in sand. There are the shifting sand dunes of the deep deserts to the east, the rocky flats encompassing Junkertown and The Heap, the windswept labyrinth of sandstone towers to the west, and the Blackstone badlands to the south.

When Mrs. Yabloko started talking about Yale's synthetic bioengineering department, the scene shifted to huge green lawns surrounded by ancient-looking cathedrals. An hour later we had arrived on Mars in a place called Nili Terradome; then and there I vowed to earn enough bandwidth to be able to train at the Seryy flight school so one day I could pilot my own construction suit or maybe my own dark-space ship, and eventually travel the United Systems.

After we reached the end of the ninety-minute block, the class was dismissed for a half-hour reality break, leaving me hungry to know more about Rachael Dahlia.

As I lifted my Via goggles and squinted against the brightness of the real world, I remembered our original mission. Raising the binoculars I scanned each piece of scrap metal as it drifted down the conveyor belt. With my index finger I hit a long orange button on the lenses and said, "Big Daddy, this is Little Sister. I've got a thirty-minute break."

Through a speaker on the neck strap, a voice said, "I got you, Little Sis. Where have you been? I expected to hear from you hours ago."

"Marine, don't tell him too much," Martin warned.

"Don't worry," I said, then, pressing the button, said,

"Got a test coming up. I can't be caught half-assing it. What are we looking for today?"

"I hear that, Little Sis, we had Ms. Y when I was a kid, I know how she can be. Today we're looking for D.S.S. hull segments. Oh, and in the off chance you see any first-generation construction suits, let me know, okay?"

"You got it." After thinking for a minute, I said, "You had Mrs. Yabloko, too? She must be like eighty years old."

"Hey, kid, I'm not *that* old."

"So you're working the Alexi & Sons spider crane because you like the work? It had nothing to do with blowing out your knees and back at the water-knife factory in the sixties?"

"Cold, Sis, cold. If I didn't know any better, I'd think you were the one helping me out. Hey, you wanna know a secret?"

Martin shook his head no; my eyes lit up, and I nodded, saying, "Yes."

"Mrs. Yabloko isn't real!"

I took a rare moment of consideration before speaking. If anyone stopped to think about it, it was obvious that their teacher was software; I'd figured it out back in third grade when I found out that both my mother and Aunt Diana had had Mrs. Yabloko when they were kids. But Big Daddy was right, he was technically my employer, and making him feel like a dumb old fart was not to my advantage.

"Whaaaat?" I tried to sound as innocent as possible.

"That's right, she's not some nice old lady telling you all she knows about the world, she's a program, she's software!"

"No. That's not true; she's my friend. I'm her best student, and I sit at the front of the class!"

"I'm sorry, kid, but everyone sits at the front of the — goddamnit, you're stringing me along, you little brat."

While I laughed, Martin tapped me on the shoulder

and pointed out to an abnormally large pile of scrap that had been dropped onto the belt. Looking through the lenses I saw a curved piece of hull cradling the junk upon it like a bowl of scrap-metal stew. "Heads-up, Big Daddy," I said. "Got a hull section — maybe a rib? — coming your way."

I hadn't been the only one to see the prized piece; the spider cranes uniformly started to head up toward the peak of The Heap.

"I got you. Where do you think it's gonna land?"

I assessed the top of The Heap and the piles of scrap ahead of it. "Ummm, on the top."

While I laughed at our old joke, Big Daddy grumbled, "Maybe you're confused. I hired you to help me meet my weekly quota, not bust my balls. Where's my good luck charm when I need her? Do your thing."

From the positioning of the other spider cranes it was clear they all had the same strategy: get as close to the drop zone as possible without getting crushed under the tons of falling scrap, then try to out-maneuver the other scrappers in a mad scramble. While most of the time this tactic worked, I noticed a cube of something, maybe one story of an easy-up office building, sticking out of the top of the heap.

"Big Daddy, that rib is going to land on that cube and get deflected west-southwest. If it hits it right, it's going to have some serious speed. Though if it hits it wrong it'll just stay there and that orange spider is going to nab it."

"Make a prediction, Sis."

I turned to Martin. "What do you think?"

He pantomimed what he thought would happen with his hands and said, "I think it's going to rotate and stay on top."

"Head to the southwest corner of The Heap, it's going to come right to you."

"What the heck, Marine, why'd you even ask me?"

I smiled. "Because you're always wrong."

A few minutes before we had to return to class, the hull piece tipped off the end of the conveyor belt and plummeted, rotating one and a half times. But by that time the jagged edges of the cube had been covered in scrap, and the hull landed on top without going anywhere. The orange spider crane ran in and claimed it.

"I told you so," said Martin.

Big Daddy said nothing, but I could hear his disappointment in the radio silence. I had fucked up, and now they were both mad at me.

"Welcome back, class," Mrs. Yabloko said. "We'll continue where we left off, on Mars. Does anyone remember how Rachael Dahlia paid for her three-month shuttle trip to the first colony of Nili Terradome?"

My hand shot up, but Mrs. Yabloko called on someone else and then moved on to talk about the early days of Evermore Industries. For a brief moment, I thought we would get to learn something about numen, the fifth fundamental force that Rachael had discovered, but Mrs. Yabloko moved on with only a brief mention of numen, asking the class to imagine that our bodies were like dim light bulbs, but instead of radiating a few lumens, the energy we cast was visible on the numen spectrum as a swirl of colors that fluctuated with our moods. I raised my hand, and at the end of her sentence Mrs. Yabloko called on me.

"Will you please teach us about the method by which numen particles become quantum entangled?"

Mrs. Yabloko shook her head. "I'm sorry, student, but that's a twelfth-grade science module."

"How do I join the twelfth-grade class early?"

"To be considered for elevated education, your grades must be noticed by the Junkertown board of education."

"And what if that doesn't exist?"

"Then you must appeal to the Seryy Department of Education and Worker Placement."

From outside the classroom walls, I heard a voice calling me. "Hey, kid! Little Sis!"

I looked out the windows across the cityscape of Nili Terradome before realizing that the voice wasn't coming from the classroom but from the binoculars around my neck. I muted the mic on my Via.

"Big Daddy? I'm in class," I whispered.

"Take a break," he shouted. "The mother lode is coming down the belt, and I need you to spot it for me."

I raised my Via goggles and scanned the belt through the binoculars. About halfway to The Heap was a first-generation Evermore Industries construction suit. It had the Greek letter Delta written on the side above a five-by-three grid of ghost decals. Each decal meant the pilot had overcome possession by a spirit in dark space. "What a piece of garbage; why is that a prize?"

"Depending on who stripped them for parts already, it might contain... medical equipment."

I checked back in with the class. Mrs. Yabloko was deep in some lecture about Rachael and Evermore's complicated relationship, and as much as I wanted to stay and hear more about Rachael, I felt like I owed Big Daddy for that bad call I'd made earlier. What was more important? Earning bandwidth and getting into flight school, or earning money and buying parts for the walker? I wanted to do both, but earning money was important right then.

I returned to the classroom and opened a bootleg program on my virtual desk that tricked the AI into thinking I was still wearing my Via and paying very close attention. Setting the Via headset down beside Martin, I started up the electric engine of the heavy-duty four-wheeler and quietly drove away. When I had put some distance between me and Martin, I opened up the throttle and took off toward the conveyor belt.

"Don't leave me on hold, Little Sister, where's it gonna fall?"

"On top?" I giggled.

"Seriously? Every time?"

"It's gonna tumble west, maybe northwest."

On either side of the belt was a high chain-link fence that stretched all the way back to the water-knife factory, but I knew of a weak spot. When I hit it at full speed, the section of fence caved in, creating a temporary ramp up onto the belt. Dodging piles of scrap, I drove down the belt toward the construction suit, hoping to beat it to the end of the ramp. As I approached the suit I heard Big Daddy through my binoculars.

"Holy fff—, Little Sister, is that you up on the ramp? Do you have any idea how dangerous that is? If anyone thinks I sent you up there, I'm going to lose my job!"

"No one will know."

"Says you; the other construction companies have already called the police!"

"Relax, it'll take them ages to get out here. We'll be long gone before then."

Pulling up beside the construction suit, I left the binoculars with the four-wheeler and looked down the belt toward the waterfall of scrap that was slowly approaching. *Plenty of time.* I climbed inside the suit through a round hole in its top. Opening the few compartments, including the one labeled with a red cross, I found nothing that looked medical. Until I saw the needles. Behind a panel in the wall hung two deflated IV bags; a clear tube ran from each one and held the remnants of some lime-green and yellow fluids. On the end of each tube was a thick stainless-steel needle. They were the most medical and valuable looking things in the cockpit, so I grabbed them and scrambled out of the suit. Twenty feet from the end of belt, I ran to the four-wheeler, started it up and backed it into the construction suit, nudging it ever-so-slightly to the west side of the ramp. Then, with less than five feet to spare, I cranked the throttle and took off back toward the collapsed section of fence.

Meanwhile, the fence had been laying on the belt collecting and diverting piles of scrap until enough weight had built up that the belt had grabbed it and begun ripping the fence out of the ground section by section, dragging it toward the heap. While my route down the belt had been blocked by the occasional pile of scrap, my route back was blocked by hundreds of feet of twisting, jerking chain-link fence that wove back and forth, snagging and flipping unpredictably. The floor of The Heap was still hundreds of feet below; exiting the belt was not an option. Hoping the heavy-duty four-wheeler was heavy enough to keep the fencing temporarily still, I carefully navigated through the ever-shifting scrap and fence maze, barely faster than the belt was carrying me back toward the center of The Heap.

"Holy shit, kid, be careful!" the binoculars warned.

As I reached the edge of the chasm, the belt strained against a particularly well-anchored post, and the fence was pulled taught. I gunned the engine and yanked the handlebars toward a ramp of scrap that would launch me toward solid ground and safety. But when I hit the ramp the post gave way, and the fence snapped forward in a wave like a whip weighing over a ton. The four-wheeler was launched into the air and spun with such a force that I was flung off, and that's all I can remember.

No sensation of tumbling through the air. No crash. No pain. Just darkness.

When I awoke they told me about all the bones I had broken: the ribs I had cracked, my fractured collar, my shattered forearm and wrist, my nose, my leg. They would ask me where I found those old needles attached to IV bags. But no one would explain where I had gone and what I had seen.

People say your life plays out in flashes of memory before you die. They told me I had almost died, but the life that flashed before my eyes wasn't mine, it was Rachael's, and it played as completely and as clearly as I have recounted in the previous chapters. They couldn't tell me why. They chalked it up to medication or hallucinations based on the memory of class that morning and didn't ask any more questions. By the way, I aced that test on Friday, without studying. The bandwidth reward offset the punishment for being caught out of bounds.

My mother, Amy, didn't know anything about Rachael beyond the bullet points and didn't like me talking about the dream. The only person who would listen to me — besides you — was Martin, but even he got tired of hearing stories about her.

I guess I'm telling you all this so you wouldn't assume Rachael's story was the opinion of a journalist, or, like, some collection of family myths passed down. When I was ten I experienced Rachael Dahlia's life as though I was her. I experienced being Ashley a few years later. The first time we fired up the walker, one of the pneumatic hoses ruptured and I got a concussion when it came crashing down.

I've experienced being other people as well. Shall I keep going?

*Shall I Keep Going?*

This book took 10 years to get to print. Some of those years I was focused entirely on writing, others I was balancing writing and life.

Having followers helps keep me connected during the writing process and gives me an outside incentive to keep these characters living in my imagination, to keep showing up in front of this noisy keyboard, and to keep writing.

Book Two is outlined. It's coming, but then again so is my first born. So if you want to know more about the future of Rachael's world, let me know by following me on Patreon. The only place where you'll get early drafts, concept art, and a behind-the-scenes look at how the next book is shaping up.

Follow today: www.Patreon.com/Motherofdarkspace

~Tyler McNamara

92914419R00305

Made in the USA
Columbia, SC
03 April 2018